'I would not ... bride.'

'How can I willingly wed a man who despises my station?' Eleanor demanded angrily.

'I'm not talking about that.' Richard smiled, gaining confidence from the bemused look in the lovely azure eyes. 'I'm talking about this.' At last he gave in to the almost unbearable urge to reach out and touch her. Her skin felt like satin under his fingers as he caressed her slender shoulders, ignoring the sharp gasp of surprise which escaped her at his touch.

'Be still,' he murmured huskily as he bent to cover her startled lips with his. He kept his passion under stern control, not wanting to frighten her more than she already was. Gently, seductively, his lips moved over hers. As he felt her body melt towards him he moved his hands to her waist, drawing her closer.

Exultation brought a brilliant smile to his face as he released her. 'Methinks you will not be an unwilling bride, sweet maid,' he murmured.

Since leaving grammar school, Sarah Westleigh has enjoyed a varied life. Working as a local government officer in London, she qualified as a Chartered Quantity Surveyor. Having married a Chartered Accountant, she assisted her husband in his Buckinghamshire practice, at the same time setting up and managing an employment agency. Tired of so hectic a life, they moved to Brixham in Devon, where she at last found the time to indulge her long held ambition to write, publishing short stories and articles for magazines, and a number of modern romances. In writing historical novels, she has discovered a new and enchanting world for her future characters to inhabit. THE INHERITED BRIDE is Sarah's first book for Masquerade.

THE INHERITED BRIDE

Sarah Westleigh

*First published in Great Britain 1991
by Mills & Boon Limited*

© Sarah Westleigh 1991

*Australian copyright 1991
Philippine copyright 1991
This edition 1991*

ISBN 0 263 77321 3

*Masquerade is a trademark published by
Mills & Boon Limited, Eton House,
18–24 Paradise Road, Richmond, Surrey, TW9 1SR.*

*Set in Times Roman 10 on 10 pt.
04-9107-89499 C*

Made and printed in Great Britain

CHAPTER ONE

1347

SINCE leaving the King's highway the track had become even more narrow and rutted. Birds filled the air with their sweet sounds, but budding trees and bushes pressed in hard on either side, hiding dangers only hinted at by the occasional crash in the undergrowth and startled animal cry. Eleanor pressed her knees against the sleek sides of her palfrey, urging Silver forward with a click of her tongue. One part of her was eager to reach safety and the end of a long and tedious week of travel, the other dreading what lay in wait at the journey's end.

Ahead, two men-at-arms, wearing her father's scarlet and green livery, kicked their mounts up a steep incline which was slippery with strange red mud. Eleanor frowned anxiously, hoping that Silver would be able to cope with a track still recovering from the ravages of winter.

'We should see the castle from the top of this rise,' remarked the man riding slightly ahead, reining in and waiting for her to draw alongside. Matching the pace of his large roan to that of her pretty grey, he gestured with his hand. 'I caught a glimpse of the estuary a few moments ago. By Christopher! This journey has taken long enough!'

Eleanor glanced at her short, stocky brother, wishing it had been her father escorting her to her nuptials. He would have been less impatient to have the journey done. Despite his determination to see her wed to the Lord of Wenfrith, he would have understood her nervousness at entering on a new life in a remote western part of the kingdom, cut off from family and friends, wife to an elderly man she had met but once, and that for a mere half-hour.

The jingle of their harnesses was now the only sound coming from the retinue of weary travellers behind her. Her maid, Joan, slumped solidly astride a sway-backed mare, looked as though she might fall asleep in the saddle at any moment. A sympathetic smile touched Eleanor's shapely lips. With her brown wool cloak travel-stained, her hood awry, Joan was barely recognisable as the smart, bustling body who had served her faithfully for so many years.

The pack-horses trudged with lowered heads, moving reluctantly in response to the sharp goad of the servant who was holding their leading rein. Even the guards at their rear were no longer jesting and singing bawdy songs, but were concentrating on the road, eyeing the thickets with suspicious eyes.

Wild boar roamed these parts, so Eleanor had heard, and armed outlaws and footpads were a menace throughout the land. She shot her brother a worried frown. Not even their escort knew that Godfrey carried her dowry in his saddlebags, but its presence made her more than ordinarily nervous. Godfrey, however, appeared unconcerned about the small fortune in his care.

Concentrating on the path ahead, Eleanor's flagging spirits sank ever lower, and she couldn't suppress a little sigh of regret. She would have been content to wed a suitable young knight or burgher's son, but her father could not forget the past. Despite his deep affection, he had been adamant.

'You are a lady born, Eleanor. Why, our line goes back to Earl Godwin himself! Had Harold Godwinsson not lost at Hastings I should have been an atheling, cousin to the royal line of kings! But because we supported Harold, the Conqueror stripped our family of its titles and confiscated all our lands!' Deep-seated resentment at the treatment meted out to his family had made his voice unusually harsh. 'Your forebears became wool merchants, since otherwise they would have become menials on their own land!'

'That happened almost three hundred years ago, and they prospered,' argued Eleanor. 'You've bought land recently, Father. Could you not be satisfied——?'

'I must make provision for Godfrey and your other brothers. I am determined that *your* issue will have lands and titles in their own right. Your marriage to William of Evreux, Lord of Wenfrith, will restore you to your rightful place in society. He is a powerful baron and a kindly man. You will do well as his wife, daughter.'

Eleanor signed again and put Silver to the slippery slope, which the mare mounted with a dainty, sure stride. She herself was proud of her heritage, but not obsessed by it, as her father was. His paradoxical desire to see her wed to a hated Norman noble bewildered and saddened her.

Halfway up the hill the pack-horses behind balked. Their drover used his goad lavishly, cursing loudly, while the men-at-arms in the rear noisily wished all kinds of evil on the poor beasts, beating their flanks with the broad sides of their swords.

Eleanor glanced back, the hood of her circular travelling cloak slipping from her head to reveal a heavy braid of golden hair glinting in the spring sunshine. A sudden movement in the undergrowth caught her eye.

'Beware!' she cried.

Even as she spoke a boar broke cover, charging under the horses' hoofs and creating new chaos. Sounds of hot pursuit, previously masked by distance and their own strenuous efforts to get the pack-horses moving again, now rang out clearly. The beast disappeared into the bushes on the other side of the track and hard on its heels a hunting party, led by a tall knight on a huge black stallion, galloped across in the rear of their train. Eleanor noted the golden castle emblazoned on his black surcoat as he chased his prey into the dimness of the wood.

So intent on their quarry were they that the men barely spared a glance for the stricken party stranded in a quagmire of mud on the track.

'A murrain on the lot of them!' muttered Godfrey, who had no sympathy with knightly pursuits or chivalry.

'Do you think they come from the castle?' asked Eleanor, soothing Silver with reassuring pats on her neck, her own romantic nature responding to the sight of such splendid figures with instinctive admiration.

'The Baron may be entertaining guests. For your nuptials, sister,' said Godfrey acidly.

Eleanor did not reply to this reminder of the purpose of her journey. In any case, Godfrey had turned to help the men restore order. She pressed on with Joan, knowing they could be of little help in sorting out the chaos behind.

As she reached the top of the hill she reined Silver in and sat quite still in the saddle.

The trees ended here. Her heart beat more swiftly as she saw her future home outlined against the westering sun. The castle stood on a promontory of red rock and was larger than she'd anticipated, dominated by an impressive keep which was crowned by the embrasured outlines of its four massive towers. A double curtain wall, sturdy gatehouse and wide moat completed the fortifications, which enclosed a large bailey and numerous outbuildings.

Behind, the silvery waters of the Wen estuary merged into the greys, greens and blues of the sea and was slashed by a river of red and gold springing from the rays of the sun. Where it forged inland a sweep of pasture and cultivation ran down to the water's edge. Many of the sheep grazing the new, lush growth of grass already had tiny lambs gambolling at their sides and a number of calves suckled greedily while their mothers chewed the cud.

The fields where the peasants tended their strips, and where children could be glimpsed slinging stones at greedy seabirds, were of the same red soil as the mud coating Silver's hoofs, and small compared to the vast acreages of the flat lands she knew. The sight of stone walls enclosing isolated cottages, together with a patch of land and a few animals, was unfamiliar.

But the breathtaking view raised Eleanor's spirits considerably. Anticipation brought back sparkle to her eyes. Life in this outlandish region might be tolerable after all!

Their path led along the crest of the hill and on through a cluster of hovels huddled on poor, rocky red soil near the castle walls.

Picking their way through the mud and wattle huts, the stench from the heaps of manure piled at each door became almost overpowering. Eleanor smiled at the gaping children who scattered beneath the hoofs of the horses. Soon they would be her people, and she vowed to do what she could to relieve a poverty which was self-evident.

Between the village and the castle—edging the green where stood a stone cross, the stocks and a pillory—rose a large stone church with a solid square tower reaching proudly to the sky. The priest's abode—hardly larger than the cottages they'd just passed, though it was built of stone and possessed a glazed window—nestled alongside, within the walls of the churchyard.

The drawbridge of the castle was down and the portcullis raised. Their herald sounded a fanfare on his horn, but no gate-ward questioned their crossing of the moat or entry into the bailey. Eleanor wondered at such lack of security and the strange air of suppressed excitement visible on the grave faces of the soldiers and servants trotting to and fro about their business.

'Ho!' called Godfrey. 'Ho there! Attention for the Lord of Wenfrith's affianced bride!'

At his cry an elderly man came hurrying from the keep. By his dress he was no menial, but neither was he richly gowned as would be her future lord. Not that she expected William d'Evreux personally to rush out to greet her.

'Sir Traveller!' cried this personage, hobbling awkwardly down the steps. 'My apologies for the discourteous manner in which you have been received! Maiden, will you not dismount and come inside to rest?'

'Who are you, sir?' demanded Godfrey in his most hectoring voice. Eleanor shuddered inwardly. Godfrey attired himself in rich brocades and velvets, as befitted a wealthy merchant, but had no vestige of courtliness with which to disguise the boorish ways which he had inherited from their mother's sire.

The man bowed. 'My name is Hugh, steward to the Lord of Wenfrith.'

'Then take us to your lord,' ordered Godfrey, swinging to the ground. 'At once! This is the demoiselle Eleanor of Clare, and I am Godfrey, her brother. Surely he is expecting us?'

For an instant an uncomfortable expression of doubt crossed the steward's lined face. Eleanor, stepping down into a mess of accumulated mud, dung and litter, thought only that he was as inefficient in his stewardship as he had been in his welcome!

Stepping fastidiously in her leather riding shoes, the skirt of her gown held high above the noisome mess in the courtyard, Eleanor's heart sank once more as he led the way up the steps to the main door. How could her future lord allow such slackness? She believed him to be a gentle, kindly man, yet surely he was not without authority?

How different was this from the orderly, clean household supervised by her mother! From the large household in which she had lived for five years learning the duties of a lady of the manor! Even from the priory in Ipswich where she had spent the last years of her education. That had been bare of luxury, but spotlessly clean. The Prioress Martha-Mary had seen to that.

She squared her slender shoulders and lifted her chin, her blue eyes snapping determination as she rounded the screen and took in the parlous state of the dimly lit, lofty, graciously proportioned Great Hall. All this would change! Her first wifely duty was to bear her lord the heir he desired. But once wed she would be responsible for the running of his household. If the steward refused to co-operate with her he would go!

'Where is the Lord of Wenfrith?' she demanded, accepting with a nod the mug of small ale produced by a varlet in response to Hugh's order. The liquid was cool and refreshing though a trifle sour, and she sank down on an oak bench with a sigh of relief.

'Demoiselle Clare,' murmured Hugh apologetically, 'I fear the news is not good. Your betrothed husband, William of Evreux, is dead.'

The colour fled from Eleanor's face, leaving it white and pinched. To journey all this way for nothing! No wonder Godfrey was using some colourful oaths! Yet even as she reeled with shock a small voice inside her was rejoicing. A reprieve!

'When did he die?' she demanded flatly.

Hugh did not reply. A clatter from the courtyard and the blast of a horn proclaimed the return of the hunting party. The steward turned his rheumy eyes to peer expectantly towards the screens hiding the great door.

Eleanor stood up, smoothing down her travel-stained gown and adjusting the grey cloak around her shoulders. 'If you will show us to our chambers, sir steward, we will rest tonight and begin our journey home tomorrow.'

But still the steward did not answer. Behind her, the ring of spurs echoed through the hall and an authoritative voice demanded, 'Visitors, Hugh? Who calls?'

Eleanor turned, as did Godfrey, and despite her sorry circumstances recognition brought a gleam of curiosity to her eyes. The tall, imposing figure of the knight with the castle emblem had rounded the screens and stood outlined in the slanting light from a high window embrasure, a hunting bow still slung across his broad shoulders and a bloodied spear in his hand. Even without armour he exuded an aura of knightly valour.

Grey eyes in a shadowy, hawkish face met hers with sharp interest. His dark brows lifted. 'A maid, by all the Saints! What brings this honour to our humble castle?'

'Lord,' gasped Hugh. 'I have not yet had time to acquaint you with everything you should know! This is the demoiselle Eleanor de Clare—daughter of Godwin de Clare, a Saxon wool merchant of Colchester—the affianced bride of William d'Evreux. Her party has arrived earlier than I anticipated.'

'My father's bride? God's teeth!' exclaimed the man, an expression of such astonishment crossing his face that Eleanor was tempted to laugh, except that she, too, was fighting down a sense of unreality.

'Your father, lord?' she murmured. 'I understood the Baron d'Evreux to have no heir!'

'You were mistaken,' said the knight abruptly, striding forward with a pronounced limp, his golden spurs ringing in the silence which greeted his words. He came to a halt before her while the hounds at his heels began rooting among the sparse, stale rushes strewn about the floor, searching for bones and other morsels of food festering there. 'I am Richard d'Evreux.'

He doffed his cap and inclined his dark head in a courtly bow, but his narrowed eyes, no longer friendly, flashed steel. Noting his drawn, thin, weathered face, the new scar cutting the smoothness of one eyebrow, a feeling she could not define sent a slight shudder shivering down Eleanor's spine.

She drew a deep breath. 'You did not die at Crécy?' she asked. 'Your father believed you slain. That is why he desired me to wife—to bear him new heirs.'

'The reports reaching him were wrong.' He shrugged. 'I was sorely wounded, but Prince Edward himself asked the King's physician to minister to me. As soon as I was sufficiently recovered, I returned to visit my father.'

'Prince Edward!' exclaimed Eleanor. 'You fought with the Prince of Wales? We have heard such glorious tales of him! Of his black armour, his skill and bravery, and he so young——'

'Aye, he earned his spurs on that battlefield! King Edward granted me the honour of Wenstaple for my services to his son on that day.'

'You saved his life?' wondered Eleanor in some awe.

'Maybe. Who knows? But I fought beside him, and proudly, too. No quarter was offered, and we gave none.' His jaw tightened and he spoke through his teeth. 'I killed the knight who gave me this!' He slapped his thigh with an angry hand and swung away.

Eleanor swallowed. 'But what of your father?' she demanded, suddenly remembering her mission. 'When did he die? Why was no messenger sent to deter me from my journey?'

'He died but yestereve, demoiselle.'

His anger had been replaced by a brooding intensity which Eleanor barely registered. She could scarce believe her ears!

Incredulous scorn filled her voice. 'And yet you hunt this noon? What reverence is this for the dead!' she cried, blue eyes flashing. 'Take me at once to where the Lord of Wenfrith lies! I wish to pay my last respects.'

Richard swung back to face her. 'I am now Lord of Wenfrith,' he reminded her coolly.

'And Earl of Wenstaple! Maiden, you must show more respect!'

The speaker strode from the shadows where he had remained since entering with Richard d'Evreux. Eleanor had forgotten the other men. Now she saw a comely knight, shorter than Richard, fair of face, his white surcoat charged with a crimson shield slashed with silver.

'I give respect where it is earned!' she rejoined with spirit. 'Do not forget that had his sire lived, I would have become the new Earl's stepmother!'

A sound exploded from Richard's throat which Eleanor could not interpret.

'Enough!' he commanded, nostrils flaring, shapely lips curled in disdain. 'No doubt my father had his own reasons for contracting to wed with a Saxon merchant's daughter!'

The contempt in his voice brought a hard knot of anger to Eleanor's stomach and a spot of colour to each cheek. For perhaps the first time she began to sympathise with her father's attitudes. No wonder he was resentful if he'd had to face this kind of arrogance all his life! Shock took her voice, and though Godfrey began a protest the Earl gave neither time to speak.

'May I introduce Sir Gilbert de Rede, who nursed me through the fever and saw me safely home? He is jealous of the respect due to the life he saved,' he rasped, an edge of bitterness creeping into his voice to overlay the contempt. He turned towards the two very young men standing behind Sir Gilbert, handing one of them his bow and spear. By the time he spoke again he had curbed his emotion. His tone was neutral. 'These are our squires, William of Asche and John of Renaker.'

All three young men bowed in acknowledgment of the introduction, and Eleanor saw a wry smile fade from Sir Gilbert's lips as his light blue eyes met hers.

'His temper is still doubtful, he is not yet fully recovered,' he murmured low, so that only she could hear.

Godfrey finally managed to burst into angry speech. 'Lord, we have travelled long and wearily. It is no fault of ours that our journey is wasted! By the bones of Saint Christopher! We need rest and refreshment for ourselves and our servants!'

Richard regarded the other man from beneath heavy lids, his hackles rising. Short, stocky, bull-headed yet

softly formed, this boorish upstart bore no family resemblance to his delicate, graceful sibling. Whatever else
the maid might be, she was undeniably beautiful, and
probably didn't warrant the contempt he'd lavished on
her in his consternation at discovering her purpose. He
was not normally so rude, even to social inferiors, and
felt shame begin to creep up his neck in a red tide as he
realised his lack of gallantry.

'Supper will be served in half an hour,' he told Godfrey
with a frosty courtesy designed to hide his discomfort.
'Hugh, see to it!'

'Lord.' With a deep bow, the steward scuttled off.

Eleanor drew herself up. 'I still wish to pay my last
respects to William of Evreux and intercede for his soul,'
she informed him coldly. 'Please take me to him. We
shall, of course, wish to remain until after his burial.'

'Naturally.' Was there irony in that forceful voice? A
gleam of ironical humour in the grey eyes? Did he guess
her relief at escaping marriage with his father?

As Eleanor followed him from the Hall and up a
winding staircase to the chapel in the north-west tower
simmering fury kept the colour burning in her cheeks.
The man limping ahead up the uneven steps had no right
to criticise his father's choice of bride! He was the one
deserving of criticism! He should have been keeping vigil
beside his father's body, not amusing himself hunting
boar! The man had not an ounce of genuine feeling in
his whiplash-thin, broad-shouldered frame!

He halted before a curtained archway. 'I'll await you
here,' he murmured abruptly.

Eleanor stepped inside the chapel as he moved the arras
aside. The low murmurings of a priest kneeling at a prie-
dieu beside the open coffin were the only sounds to break
the silence. She walked slowly forward, aware of the tall
figure of Richard of Wenfrith leaning against the stone
jamb, arms folded across his chest, a hooded, brooding
expression on his sombre face.

Then she forgot him as she crossed herself and knelt
in the rushes beside the trestle upon which the dead man
rested. The white coif on his head hid the sparse grey
hair, and death had smoothed many of the wrinkles from
his toughened skin. Eleanor felt a surge of pity and, her

eyes fixed on a crucifix standing on the altar between two flaring candles, knelt quietly for a full five minutes while she prayed to the Blessed Virgin to intercede for her late betrothed's soul.

When she rose to her feet, so did the priest. She met the gentle gaze of the old man and felt comforted.

'What ailed him, Sir Priest?' she whispered.

'An apoplexy,' he murmured. He glanced over her shoulder to the silent figure in the doorway. 'The excitement of seeing his son alive was too much for him, I believe.'

'His death was sudden?' asked Eleanor. Fear caught at her voice. 'He did not die unshriven?'

'Sadly, maiden, he did. I arrived too late to administer the Last Rites. For this reason I keep vigil now.' He crossed himself, his eyes on the crucifix. 'Perhaps the Blessed Lord will heed my prayers, for truly the lord was a good man...'

Silently, Eleanor turned and left, passing the dead man's son without a glance. She began to descend the stairs, but his voice, seeming loud after the hushed atmosphere of the chapel, called her back.

'Your chamber is above, demoiselle. I will lead you to it.'

He mounted another flight of stairs and showed her into a room above the chapel. Joan was there, opening travelling coffers already removed from the pack-horses and carried up, a fact which explained the shuffling on the stair which had threatened to disrupt her devotions.

'I will expect you in the Hall shortly,' murmured Richard of Evreux. He bowed slightly, and left.

'What a disaster, mistress!' cried Joan once they were alone. She had served as Eleanor's nurse and body-servant since the girl had been weaned and she herself a mere twelve years old, and a strong bond of affection bound the two women. 'By the Holy Virgin, what will your honoured father say?'

'He will be disappointed, for certain. He had hoped for much from this marriage. But no doubt he will find another such lord for me to wed.'

Her voice held a sadness she barely knew she felt. She glanced quickly around the large circular chamber, bare

of all ornament and furnished only with a bed, an oak
dresser and a stool. A shaft of sunlight slanting through
a deep embrasure lit the bed, showing the dusty hangings.
The fireplace was empty. Although the day had been
warm for the time of year, a fire would have been
welcome to cheer her spirits.

Throwing aside her cloak, Eleanor wandered over to
the unglazed window. Its oiled-skin shutter was propped
wide, and she drank in the fresh salty air, saw the sen-
tinel cliff on the opposite shore and, peering downwards, the foaming waves crashing against the foot of
the cliff on which the castle stood. A strange stab, almost
of disappointment, pierced her heart at the thought of
leaving this wild, lovely estuary to return to the tamed
countryside of her birth.

As Joan brought forward a bowl of cold water with
which to sponge her mistress's face and hands, Eleanor
slipped out of her travelling surcoat and tunic.

'I have no mourning clothes with me,' she lamented,
examining the contents of her chests.

'You brought clothes suited to the Lady of Wenfrith,'
said Joan flatly. 'This silver-grey kirtle was meant to be
worn under the sapphire surcoat, but you could wear it
with the dark grey instead. 'Twould blend with the silver
threads in the samite. Shall I lay them out, sweeting?'

'They will have to do. Have I a silver girdle?'

'Aye, mistress.' She settled the jewelled belt low on
Eleanor's hips and clucked approval as she slipped the
sideless surcoat over her mistress's head. 'Shall I bind
your hair in the silver caul?'

Eleanor nodded, sitting while the woman unbraided
her long golden hair and brushed it out before confining
it in the fretwork of silversmithery and setting a jewel-
studded silver circlet on her brow.

Joan had barely finished buttoning dainty kid slippers
on her mistress's slender feet when the sound of trumpets
from below announced that the Earl had arrived in the
Great Hall for supper.

Escorted by Joan, who would eat with the castle servants, Eleanor made her way down the difficult, winding
stairs. Nearing the bottom she stopped, so abruptly that
Joan stumbled against her back. Richard d'Evreux's

voice echoed up the stairway, which seemed to be acting as some kind of sound funnel.

'Whatever you say, Gilbert, I still cannot understand my sire!' he was declaring angrily. 'To wed with a Saxon—and a mere merchant's daughter at that!'

A low murmur was all Eleanor could hear of Sir Gilbert's speech, but whatever he said was answered by a derisive snort.

'And what were the Saxons before we came to rule them?' demanded Richard d'Evreux's biting voice. 'A bunch of undisciplined, warring provincials sunk in drunkenness and gluttony! Their so-called King, Harold Godwinsson, was himself nothing but a boorish, usurping traitor! He swore allegiance to Duke William, promised him his support. But what did he do when the chance came?' The question was rhetorical. Richard did not pause for an answer. 'He broke his word and took the crown for himself! He was possessed of not one jot of chivalry or honour! And his warriors fought on foot!' This last, astonishingly, seemed cause for intense scorn.

Eleanor heard Joan's gasp at her shoulder. She herself could not utter a sound. She stood rooted; churning dismay, hatred, contempt—oh! such a confusing mix of emotions—prevented clear thought. Sheer fury brought her first coherent reaction. Arrogant Norman churl! No better than the swine he had killed that day!

He thought all Saxons a bunch of boorish drunks, did he? Did he consider the cold hearts and bloody hands of the tyrannical Norman conquerors preferable? And he despised Harold Godwinsson above all others! So much for her father's vaunted ancestry! It would hold no sway with the likes of Richard d'Evreux!

The voices had faded. The men must have moved. Eleanor lifted her chin, wanting to turn tail and run but knowing she could not. 'Come,' she commanded Joan in a controlled, angry voice.

When she swept into the Great Hall Richard d'Evreux was standing a few paces from the archway waiting for her.

Light from smoking torches and flickering candles lit the gloomy Hall with a soft glow which caught Eleanor's hair, giving her head a gold and silver sheen which

seemed to light up her pale face and add luminosity to
her large blue eyes. Her slender figure and graceful walk
drew the eyes of all the men gathered for the meal.

Richard came forward to escort her to a place of
honour at the high table. She gave him one haughty,
hostile glance before reluctantly placing her cold hand
in his. His strong fingers held hers lightly as he led her
forward, yet they seemed to grip her entire being in their
clasp. He sat her at his right hand, as befitted his father's
betrothed, with Sir Gilbert on her other side. Godfrey
sat on Richard's left beyond several knights, some of
the many fighting men comprising the garrison of the
castle. Had she not known better, she would have believed herself an honoured guest.

Joan and her other retainers had found places at one
of the side trestles and were already laughing and talking
with the castle varlets. The priest, who had been introduced as Sir Piers Ely, said Grace, and the servitors pro-
ceeded in procession from the kitchen bearing the dishes
from which the squires served their masters.

The quality of the cooking was not to Eleanor's
standard, but the salt beef stew was edible and despite
her churning stomach she was hungry. The Earl's squire
served her as well as his master, and she allowed him to
heap a good portion on her wooden trencher, spooning
the food up in a silence broken only by the occasional
remark forced from her by Gilbert de Rede, who appeared eager to make amends for his earlier sharpness
of tongue.

She was acutely aware of the Earl sitting on her other
side. He ate sparingly and in silence, drinking occasionally the red wine which, in one of his few remarks,
he told her came from Burgundy. All around, loud
guffaws, ribald jokes, even hoots and catcalls rang
around the rafters as the wine and ale flowed. Subdued
music floated down from minstrels in the gallery above
the main door but, because the castle was in mourning,
more lively entertainment by juggler or jester had been
banned.

Richard took notice of neither the noise nor the remarks thrown in his direction, apparently sunk deep in
his own thoughts. He wore black—a tight-fitting say

tunic over fine hose, his only ornamentation a jewelled girdle slung low on his hips and bearing his silver-handled knife.

At least in his dress he shows some respect, thought Eleanor, watching him covertly. Again the shudder ran through her body. Was it revulsion? Apprehension? Fear? Perhaps the last, for the Earl was a sombre, almost menacing figure in his black garb. The scar cutting his brow stood out purple, giving him a slightly barbarous appearance emphasised by the thick dark hair curling on his forehead and behind his ears, and the small beard, a shade lighter than his hair, hiding his square chin.

Abruptly, he turned to her and spoke.

'There seems to be no reason to delay the funeral. My father lived in no great state, and would doubtless prefer a simple ceremony. It will take place tomorrow morn, after Tierce.'

'Thank you,' replied Eleanor stiffly. 'We will begin our return journey the following sunrise.'

She wished she did not have to spend a single night under this man's inhospitable roof. The sooner she could leave, the better she would be pleased.

A moment of silence greeted her announcement, then Richard stirred and his piercing grey eyes seemed to challenge her soul. 'Aye,' he murmured. 'To forfeit such a match must be a grave disappointment to you, maiden.'

Eleanor returned his gaze without flinching, though her fingers curled into fists beneath the board and angry dislike flared uncontrollably in her expressive eyes. 'Indeed, lord, I am sorry that your father's plans were so unkindly upset. But for myself I do not care. My father will find another suitor for my hand.'

'But not, perhaps, a Baron seduced by your beauty.'

His words came out flat and calm yet Eleanor sensed an underlying anger in his tone which matched her own. But why? He had no cause now to resent her betrothal to his sire! The contract had been honourably made and fortuitously broken. Fury rose like gall in her throat, but she held her words in check. Let the Earl of Wenstaple, Baron d'Evreux, Lord of Wenfrith, think what he liked! Let him take his frustrations out on her! It made no

difference. She would not demean herself by defending
her birth. 'Twould merely invite more scorn if she did.
He had made that abundantly clear.

'You think me beautiful, lord?' she murmured sweetly
and watched with intense satisfaction as the blood rose
in his cheeks. 'He saw me but once,' she went on quietly,
though her voice trembled slightly. 'I do not think my
looks had aught to do with it. But he knew my father,
Godwin of Clare, well. They met in Westminster Hall,
when both attended Parliament.'

Richard's brows lifted again and a strange, still look
entered those compelling eyes as the dull flush receded;
but he made no further comment, and soon afterwards
Eleanor retired to her bedroom to lie in the big, fusty
bed between mercifully clean linen sheets, while Joan
wrapped her ample body in a blanket and slept on a
straw pallet by the door.

William of Evreux's coffin, shrouded in a cloth bearing
his arms, was borne on the shoulders of six stout men-
at-arms and preceded by heralds bearing his spurs,
gauntlets and heaume. His riderless horse followed
behind. From some almost-forgotten coffer Hugh the
steward had produced enough black mourning gowns
and hoods to clothe these men as well as Richard, the
chief mourner, whose face it was impossible to see,
buried as it was in the depths of the concealing material.
From the same source had come her own black mantle
and the open hood draped over her head and shoulders.

The cortège, preceded by torch-bearers, walked the
short distance to the church, whose bell tolled dolefully
for the manor's departed lord.

Although Sir Piers was the only priest present, he had
called upon every available acolyte and altar boy to add
as much pomp, dignity and reverence as possible to the
occasion. The entire village and all the castle servants
attended, filling the church. To the accompaniment of
their sobbing and wailing the Office of the Dead and a
Requiem Mass were said in an atmosphere thick with
the acrid aromas of tallow, sweat and incense. The body
was carried down to the family vault beneath, where it

was laid to rest until it could be finally interred in a marble tomb.

Richard returned from the church taut and silent. Eleanor had felt saddened for a life so suddenly terminated, but her sorrow was in truth not for a man she had barely known, but for what she herself had lost. Her father had been right, she would have done well enough as William's bride. Her wifely duty would have been a small price to pay for the joy of being châtelaine of Wenfrith, of restoring it to order and pride, of enjoying the heady sea air and the freedom to roam the entrancing shores nearby.

Dinner proved to be a sombre affair with none of the feasting usual upon such an occasion. On the previous evening Eleanor had noticed the lack of spices and herbs with which to flavour the food, and again the little dishes and boxes to which she was accustomed failed to appear. Spices were expensive, and guarded in the most lavish of households, but there could be no excuse for the lack of herbs, many of which could be gathered in the fields and hedgerows if the manor lacked a special garden.

'Tonight,' said Richard suddenly, thrusting a portion of tough salt beef aside and casting her a glittering look, 'we will sup more royally. The boar is already on the spit. I am wearied of this cursed food!'

Reminded of his unwelcome presence at her side and of her forthright criticism of his hunting expedition, Eleanor lowered her eyes, saying merely, 'It will be appreciated, lord.'

'It's why I went, you know,' he said abruptly. 'I meant no disrespect. And I lacked exercise.'

Eleanor realised he was excusing himself, even apologising. Surprised, she nodded. 'I was hasty in my condemnation. Sir Gilbert was right to defend your honour.'

Like a ray of sunlight in the sombre Hall, Richard's face broke into a smile. What a difference it made! thought Eleanor, startled by the change in his appearance wrought by the softening of the firm, well-shaped mouth and the deepening of the lines running down from his long, aquiline nose. She caught her breath, realising that he was a handsome man.

'You are generous, maiden.' He jumped to his feet as the distant bell tolled for Sext. 'I have much to do this noon. I will see you at supper. Farewell.'

Eleanor hurried to corner her brother before he could disappear to his small wall-chamber off the Hall.

'Godfrey, have you spoken to the Earl of Wenstaple of our lineage?' she demanded anxiously.

'No, by Peter, I have not, sister! I have barely exchanged two words with that uncivil Norman since we arrived. His hospitality is mean and his manners leave much to be desired!'

'He cannot help the hospitality, brother. He has been at the castle for too short a time. As for his manners— I think perhaps he is under great strain——'

'By my troth, do you defend him, sister? I cannot wait to bid him farewell!'

'I merely seek to be fair. I dislike him as much as you do.' She wondered why she had bothered to defend the man. He certainly deserved no sympathy from her! 'But I wish William had not died,' she went on wistfully. 'I am quite loath to depart such a lovely place.'

'It holds no charm for me! I must in any case return immediately to Colchester, to my family and the business. Miriam will miss me, and since our sire cannot do much for himself these days, he relies on me.'

'Yes.' Eleanor frowned. 'Father's joints pain him so much. Otherwise he would have journeyed here with me and saved you the trouble.'

'And been insulted to his face! He would not have borne the lord's insults as we have done!'

'True!' A picture of her fiery parent facing Richard of Wenfrith rose before her eyes and she chuckled. 'They would have been well matched! But, Godfrey, promise me to say nothing to anyone of our lineage. I, too, am proud of my heritage and would not have it scorned, as I know it would be.'

'Let him pour scorn! It cannot harm us! Every Norman, high or low, insists upon their place in society and exacts their rightful respect and dues!'

'Yes, and it sickens me, for so many are not worthy of their place! So promise me, Godfrey!' she demanded.

He made a gesture of resignation. 'If it pleases you, sister.'

'It does. Thank you.' She gave him a grateful smile. Godfrey might be rude and assertive—no doubt a typical Saxon, in the Normans' eyes—but he was an indulgent brother. She sighed, suddenly weary of everything. 'I must retire, for we have another arduous journey before us.' She mustered a cheerful smile, unwilling to let Godfrey see just how inexplicably reluctant she was to leave Wenfrith Castle. 'I shall be glad to see our parents again.'

The meat at supper was indeed good, although a mite too fresh. The boar had been young, so had suffered less from lack of proper hanging. Eleanor ate her portion with relish.

Richard was sunk in his own thoughts again. He cannot bear to speak with me! thought Eleanor, slightly amused, slicing away the rotting half of an apple.

In truth, Richard was wrestling with emotions strange and deeply disturbing. He had returned to Wenfrith weary, weakened by illness and railing against the fate that had left him disabled, only to see his father die before his eyes. As if that were not enough for one man to bear, the tantalising wench seated so aloofly beside him had arrived, announcing her betrothal to his late sire! The mere thought of all that youth and beauty in his father's bed made his gorge rise.

As far as he knew William d'Evreux had not been an elderly lecher. So what had possessed him to contract himself to someone so unsuitable?

Gilbert was probably right. She must be of worthy stock, or his sire would never have contemplated the match, however lovely the maid's person or large her dower. Her father represented his borough in Parliament. That had surprised him. Godwin of Clare must be a scion of some influential Saxon family with pretensions to high birth. There were a few such about.

Surely what had been good enough for his sire should be good enough for him?

Richard jerked his straying thoughts to an abrupt halt. His mind was running away with him like a bolting stallion! He reached for his mazer and quaffed deeply of the wine therein.

God's bones! Where had his thoughts led him? He set his mind to go carefully over the facts again.

He had returned from France with honours heaped on his head, but with a mind and body desirous of nothing but rest and quiet. Such galling, depressing weakness was foreign to him and he resented it. He had never fancied the life of a courtier, travelling the land in a restless cavalcade from castle to palace to castle again, and now he positively rejected it.

So how was he to go about the wearisome business of securing an acceptable and necessary châtelaine for Wenfrith and a mother for his heirs? In other words, a wife.

He glanced sideways at the ice-cold, hostile wench beside him, who was turning now to converse with Gilbert. Her full lips, soft for his friend, promised a passion quite at odds with the rigid way she held them most of the time. The gentle curves of her body invited a man's touch. Would it spring into heady, passionate response? Quite suddenly he longed to see her lovely eyes filled with languorous desire, her lips parted in sweet invitation, to feel her body yielding...

Why not? She had reacted proudly to his own obvious antagonism. He could not blame her. Mayhap if he changed his stance...wooed her...

He needed a wife. Despite his eligibility—he had no false modesty on that score—the search for an acceptable and suitable maid among the Norman nobility would be long and weary. Here was one—albeit Saxon—thrust under his nose. King Edward was encouraging the healing of old wounds, attempting to weld his peoples into one nation. He could not object—certainly not enough for Richard himself to lose favour...and there would be little need for her to leave the confines of Wenfrith. If and when he travelled, he could travel alone and so risk no scorn over his choice of bride.

With half an ear he listened to her conversation with Gilbert while his mind worked on.

'Why so pensive, sweet maid?' Gilbert was asking Eleanor quietly. 'Methinks something troubles you.'

'No, nothing, sir. I am merely thinking of the journey home. The way is long and tedious.'

'With a train of men and pack-horses, it must be. If I were travelling to Essex I would take but half the time!'

His pale blue eyes laughed warmly into hers, and Eleanor thought how much she liked this knight. Talking earlier, she had discovered that he had a manor in Somerset and owed knight-service to a baron who served the Prince Edward. He would soon be returning to France to join the siege of Calais, leaving a reluctant Richard behind.

'Maiden!'

The voice on her left cut off whatever she might have answered. Excusing herself to Gilbert, she turned to see what Richard wanted.

'Lord?' she enquired coldly.

'You may have no cause to depart on the morrow.'

His tone was abrupt, and she sensed his body strung taut as a bowstring. Her eyes widened as they met his narrowing stare.

'Not need to leave?' she queried, her pulse suddenly beating faster. 'What reason could I have to linger?'

Richard's tone, though still curt, held a note of gentleness she had not heard before. 'My noble father chose you to be châtelaine of Wenfrith. God knows, the household needs a woman's firm hand!'

His eyes glittered in the candle-light, and Eleanor caught a hint of uncertainty in their silvery depths. She stared back, the tension mounting in her as she waited for his next words. He cleared his throat.

'With my new responsibilities I must needs take a wife. Think you Godwin of Clare would consent to a marriage between us?'

CHAPTER TWO

FOR several seconds Eleanor sat bereft of breath. When she finally found her voice she could speak only with difficulty.

'W-what did you say?'

Richard thrust his trencher aside and stuck the blade of his knife in the board with an irritated stab.

'You know very well what I asked, demoiselle! Well, what think you?'

'I . . . I don't know!' Her mind spun. Her father would probably be agreeable to substituting the son for his sire, but what of her own feelings? Schooling her voice with an effort, she forced out the question nearest her heart. 'Why would you offer for the hand of one you thought unworthy to be your father's wife?'

Lids lowered, Richard concentrated on the enchased hilt of his knife, running a long finger over the patterned silver. A dull flush rose under the dark pigment of his skin. With an impatient movement he grasped the hilt, wrenched the blade from the wood, and thrust the knife back into the sheath at his hip. Only then did he turn to meet her questioning eyes.

His were cool, opaque as a winter sky, but the flush gave him away. He was as embarrassed as she.

When he spoke he covered his discomfort with a drawl. 'Why, for your dowry, maiden, which I believe is rich.' His mouth pulled down at one corner in a sardonic smile. 'I have many calls on my resources. Despite the revenues from Wenstaple, I shall be hard pressed to meet all my commitments. The reliefs and heriots I needs must pay on my inheritance here will be heavy. The cost of restoring this castle, which my sire allowed to fall into a state of such sad neglect, will not be small.'

Eleanor could not dispute the last statement. Ever since her arrival she had been wondering at the shameful decay and lack of care evident everywhere. Her father had omitted to mention her future lord's financial straits, but the reason for William of Evreux's agreement to the alliance with her was plain. No doubt her father had impressed on him the nobility of their line, but the riches she brought with her had surely decided the issue.

Like father, like son, she thought grimly. Oh, to be wanted for herself! Yet realistically that was seldom a possibility except among the lower classes. She had known all her growing years that her husband would be chosen for her, however carefully and lovingly. And that

where advantageous alliances were concerned, personal
preferences went out of the window with the slops.

'The idea does not please you?' Richard's dry tone
brought her back from her reverie. She realised she had
been scowling at the silver-rimmed mazer grasped tightly
between her hands.

'Of being desired for my dowry, lord?' She released
the mazer, her eyes snapping fire. 'For what other
purpose does any noble Norman choose a wife? I can
see no reason why my honoured father should not agree
to a new betrothal.'

'But you, gentle maid?' His voice was suddenly deep
and soft, almost seductive, and Eleanor felt a tremor
pass through her body, as though he'd twanged a string
on some hidden lute. 'Have you a liking for my
proposal?'

'Me, lord?' A rush of colour flooded Eleanor's cheeks
and the palms of her hands became unusually damp.
She smoothed them down her skirt and took a deep
breath. 'I have nothing to say to it. I am but a bar-
gaining counter between your noble self and my honoured father.'

Richard's eyes narrowed as they searched her face,
finding proof that her cool composure was no more than
a façade; and Eleanor lowered hers to avoid a gaze which
seemed like to penetrate her soul.

'Yet I would not bed an unwilling bride,' he
murmured.

Astonished at his words, Eleanor glanced up invol-
untarily to see the brooding expression back in his
hooded eyes. At the same moment she became aware of
a silence around them. Although the rest of the Hall
rang with shouts and guffaws, on the lord's dais an unusual stillness surrounded the two people sitting in the
carved, high-backed, ceremonial chairs.

'Lord,' she whispered, deep colour staining her neck
and cheeks, 'we are overheard!'

'God's teeth!' Richard leapt to his feet. 'Supper is
ended!' he announced in a harsh, angry voice. Startled
exclamations of dismay rang around the Hall. Sir Piers
said a hurried Grace as everyone began to grab up the

tastiest morsels before the servitors swept them from the boards.

Richard turned to Eleanor. 'Come,' he commanded, taking her unceremoniously by the arm.

With the herald's parting fanfare ringing in her ears, Eleanor stumbled along beside him, almost tripping over the inert bodies of Pym and Gem, the hounds, who lay gnawing at the bones thrown to them. Catching the amused gaze of Sir Gilbert, she coloured even more hotly. How easy it had been to remain calm, cool and ladylike while no disturbing young men touched her secluded life!

Richard's grip on her arm relaxed once they had left the Great Hall and begun the ascent of a privy stair to his solar in the Lord's Tower. Eleanor went ahead, stopping uncertainly when she reached an arched doorway shielded by a rusty arras. Richard's long arm reached over her to hold the tattered material aside.

'We will be private here,' he told her gruffly.

The sun was still sinking in the west, its rays pouring through two of the unglazed embrasures in the circular wall to eclipse the light from the candle Richard had caught up from the table to illumine their way. He snuffed the flame and set the pricket on a small table beside the enormous purple-curtained bed.

Eleanor quickly averted her eyes, though the bed dominated the chamber and ignoring its presence was not easy. The air in the Great Hall had been thick with smoke from wood and tallow, but here a sea breeze kept the atmosphere fresh. She took a deep, reviving breath and concentrated her attention on the jewelled statue of the Virgin standing in the niche above an oak prie-dieu. It was the richest object she'd seen since entering the castle and somehow the thought that William d'Evreux had held on to this one sacred treasure afforded her a measure of reassurance.

'Well, Demoiselle de Clare? Would you be an unwilling bride?' Richard's voice had gone cold again, and Eleanor shivered slightly.

If only it were Sir Gilbert offering for her hand! She felt at ease with that fair knight—he did not upset her as did the Lord of Wenfrith, with his dark, stern looks, scorn of Saxons and disturbing tempers. She took several more deep breaths, attempting to still the racing of her heart, to quell the panic rising in her breast.

God's blood! thought Richard angrily. Why does she look at me as though I were the devil incarnate? I have done nought to inspire such fear! But he'd demolished her cool indifference with a vengeance! he thought with bitter satisfaction. He thrust his thumbs into the belt at his hips, resentment rising like a tide to swamp his mind: resentment at his father's untimely death, at the poor state of his inheritance, even resentment of the honour which kept him cooling his heels in England while Gilbert remained free to return to France. Not that he could have gone back yet anyway, with his pestilential leg still plaguing him and rendering him so despicably weak.

He scowled at the maid standing fighting for self-possession, and plumbed the depths of his greatest well of resentment.

God, how he wanted to bed the wench! But, Saxon merchant's daughter though she be, she was no tavern trollop to be taken at his pleasure. If he wanted this maid he would have to wed her. Despite his best efforts to subdue it, the unwanted desire which had gripped his loins at sight of her had grown rather than diminished. What was it about her? Some would say the wench had cast a spell on him!

He studied her covertly, revelling in her beauty while wishing her deformed and snag-toothed and no temptation to his pride. Her small chin was lifted high, her cheeks flaming with colour one moment and pale the next. Despite her cursed fear, her eyes sparked defiance, while her full breasts heaved under the tight-fitting bodice of her sombre gown.

How creamy her shoulders were by contrast to the dark grey of her surcoat and the rich colour which kept staining her neck and cheeks! How smooth and tempting her skin to his hands! And her hair! A ray of sunlight lit it, giving it a golden glory richer than any of the gems sparkling in her circlet. It was made for a man's fingers to comb, thought Richard helplessly. And although he could now probably wed a daughter of almost any rich and noble house if he cared to stir himself, he wanted this maid standing before him.

The strange, compelling emotion she evoked in him, her apparent fear, made him swear forcibly under his breath. 'What is it, maiden?' he demanded roughly. 'Am I so repulsive to you? Is it this——' he raised his hand to touch his scar '—that makes you shrink from me?'

'Oh, no, lord!' Eleanor leapt to deny that charge, sensing his vulnerability and unwilling to exploit it, though in truth the sight of the ugly scar did turn her stomach on occasion. She managed a small smile, which the trembling of her lips made unconsciously seductive.

Richard shifted abruptly as a shaft of fire rent his loins, and was thankful for the long tunic which hid his physical response. But the sudden burning of hidden flames had brought a flare of passion to his heavy-lidded eyes. In his anxiety to hide other evidence of his arousal he forgot to mask it.

Grasping at control like someone sinking into a quagmire, Eleanor caught the sudden flare, the distension of his nostrils, the tightening at the corners of his wide-curved, passionate mouth as he, too, fought for command. She gasped, understanding neither the sudden tension in his body nor the lassitude which seemed to have gripped her limbs.

She gazed at him with wide eyes, but the panic had left them. Instead they were filled with a kind of wonder as she battled with this new knowledge and the strange sensations attacking her mind and body.

Richard desired her. She had seen the expression in too many male eyes not to recognise it, but she had never reacted in this peculiar manner before. Richard had a most unsettling effect on her...

He made her furious, she reminded herself. 'How can I willingly wed a man who despises my station?' she demanded angrily.

'I'm not talking about that.' Richard smiled, gaining confidence from that bemused look in the lovely azure eyes. 'I'm talking about this.'

At last he gave in to the almost unbearable urge to reach out and touch her. Her skin felt like satin under his fingers as he caressed her slender shoulders, ignoring the sharp gasp of surprise which escaped her at his touch.

'Be still,' he murmured huskily as he bent to cover her startled lips with his.

He kept his passion under stern control, not wanting to frighten her more than she already was. But on the other hand the kiss was more than a brotherly salutation.

Much more. Gently, seductively, his lips moved over hers. As he felt her body melt towards him he moved his hands to her waist, drawing her closer.

Exultation brought a brilliant smile to his face as he released her. 'Methinks you will not be an unwilling bride, sweet maid,' he murmured.

Eleanor was so confused she could barely stand. Richard led her to a cushioned stool and she sank down, grateful for his unexpected understanding. This Richard she could tolerate, even like. And as for his kiss...

She preferred not to think of that, and what his words implied. Yet if her wifely duty were no worse... Richard wouldn't ask for her if she didn't agree. And if she left the selection of another husband to her father he would probably wed her to some ugly, pot-bellied, elderly or infirm noble who belched and stank of stale wine...

She looked up into the brilliant eyes awaiting her answer, heard the surf surging against the cliffs below, and suddenly she knew what her reply should be.

'If my father agrees, I will wed you willingly, my lord,' she told him firmly.

Forgetting his resentment at finding himself in such a coil, Richard let out a breath, feeling instead ridiculously pleased with himself. 'I will dispatch a messenger to your father tomorrow,' he said briskly.

'I would like to send him a letter. It will ease his mind to know that I agree to the match, and will smooth the negotiation of a new contract.'

'Excellent.' Richard was on his way to the door. 'I'll send for Sir Piers. He will act as scribe.'

'No need, lord. I can write the letter myself. Godfrey can take it. He will not wish to remain here longer; he is impatient to return and be about his business.'

'You can write?' asked Richard, turning back in some surprise. He could pen a few lines himself, but found the task long and laborious and preferred to avoid such drudgery.

'Yes, lord, and read. The nuns' priest taught me well.'

Richard kicked the logs in the fireplace to increase their warmth and sat himself on another stool.

'What else did they teach you at the convent, demoiselle?'

'When I went there I could only spin and sew. I had spent some years learning how to churn butter, bake bread, order the house varlets, stock the pantry, brew simples and beer—all the things necessary to the running of a great household. I do not think I shall disappoint you in that.'

'I don't think you will disappoint me in anything,' murmured Richard softly, with a look that set her heart thudding.

She looked away quickly, and sought to hide her agitation in a spate of words. 'At the convent I was taught to read and write in both English and French, and the priest also taught me to use the abacus. Naturally, I also learned how to tend the sick, to sing plainsong, to recite the catechism and to understand the Holy Offices.'

They had been hard days to bear, she thought now, ruled as they'd all been by the unrelenting bell. From Matins to Compline, every three hours it had called them to chapel. Eleanor had said goodbye to the priory with deep relief, though to some of the nuns with a regret tempered only by the prospect of escape.

A sound on the stair alerted them to the fact that someone was coming. Eleanor suddenly realised her compromising situation, but Richard seemed not to regard it. He motioned her to remain seated, while he went to the door to waylay whoever approached.

'Lord.' She heard his squire William's uncertain voice on the stair. 'It grows dark. Shall I light your tapers?'

'No, Will, I'll see to it. Bring parchment, quill, ink and sand. Demoiselle de Clare wishes to write to her father. If he consents, we are to be wed.'

'Lord?' Will's voice sounded shocked and even more uncertain.

'At once, varlet!'

Richard's quick temper flared again as he realised that his squire was critical of his choice of bride. Will revered his master as a valiant and noble knight and had told him often enough that in his opinion no lady lower than an earl's daughter was worthy to wed his lord. His pride stung once again, Richard turned back into the chamber, a deep scowl on his face.

Yet seeing Eleanor gazing into the leaping flames as though she belonged in his solar his frown cleared. Instead, a smile of satisfaction lit his lean face. 'The sooner 'tis done, the sooner we can arrange the ceremony. Preparations must have been in hand for your marriage to my father. They can continue.'

'Would it not be better to wait, lord?' asked Eleanor, looking up nervously, instinctively trying to stave off the inevitable conclusion to her decision. 'Your father has been dead so short a time——'

'And I am in mourning. We shall therefore have a quiet ceremony with just my retinue and people from the manor present if they so wish. I hope you were not counting on an elaborate affair?'

'No, lord.'

Richard breathed an inward sigh of relief. He loathed too much ceremony—pageantry at a trial of arms was different, of course—and besides, he was reluctant to flaunt his bride before his peers just yet.

A stab of guilt speared him as he saw her bent head, the droop of her shoulders. She *had* wanted to take her place proudly at his side. But he couldn't face the prospect. Not yet.

'If all goes well, we'll be married on the last day of April,' he told her gruffly. 'The May Day revels can become our wedding celebrations. My people will take you to their hearts.'

She looked up, her large eyes luminous in the firelight glow. 'They will be mine, as well as yours,' she said softly. 'There is much we can do to ease their lot.'

A clatter on the stair announced the return of Will. Richard allowed him to enter the solar this time, and the young man stared at Eleanor with awed brown eyes as he laid the writing materials on a nearby table.

'Is there aught else you require, demoiselle?' he asked respectfully.

'Thank you, Will, no.'

He left the chamber at a nod from Richard, who grinned grimly to himself. Whatever Will might privately think of the match, Eleanor's beauty and talents had already created an impression on his youthful squire's susceptible heart!

'Will you write now?' he asked.

'I would rather write in my own chamber, but I confess it is more comfortable here. My hands will be stiff with cold ere long if I return.'

'You have a fire, surely?' frowned Richard.

'No, lord. The chimney-place is empty.'

With another round oath, Richard stormed to the doorway.

'Will!' he bellowed. 'Get that scurvy steward Hugh up here immediately, do you hear me?'

She heard a distant 'Aye, lord,' as Richard returned to her side.

'By Peter, he shall pay for this neglect!' he vowed angrily. 'But a fire shall be lighted immediately. You should have asked——'

'Lord, there are many things lacking here.' She hesitated. 'I think perhaps the lord your father did not trouble himself over the state of his household.'

'He trusted Hugh, no doubt. And the scurvy knave has let things slip! I've been meaning to order him to smarten things up, but time has been short. I have never lived in such squalor before, even on campaign!'

'Were things better here before you left?' asked Eleanor curiously.

'I hardly remember! My mother was alive then, and my two younger brothers. But, like you, I went to a great household at an early age. That establishment was nothing like this! Grand, with rich furnishings... I became a squire at fourteen and bore arms before I was nineteen,' he told her proudly, and added, 'I won my spurs at sea!'

'At sea!'

'Aye, that surprises you, eh? 'Twas at the battle of Sluys, when we captured part of the French fleet, by the Grace of God.' He chuckled reminiscently. 'I counted myself a doughty fighter, but those huge ships lined up before us would have daunted any man but our valiant

King Edward... 'Twas a fierce, bloody, glorious battle
and we captured rich prizes. Afterwards I bought a
manor, built me a new house.' Suddenly he scowled
again. 'The prizes will be few from the campaign that
ended in my being carried from the field at Crécy!'

'You were created Earl——'

'A liability!' he snorted. 'I anticipate few riches from
that quarter!'

His mood had changed again. Eleanor lapsed into silence, but her mind was working apace. At the sound
of feet on the privy stair, she spoke quickly.

'Lord, I would like to organise many changes here, if
you will permit me. I could work with Hugh, if you will
but give me the authority, even before we are wed...'

Richard had no time to reply, because a nervous
steward poked his head around the arras.

'You called for me, my lord?'

'Aye, Hugh, you scurvy varlet! Why is there no fire
in the demoiselle Clare's chamber? Such inhospitality is
beyond my belief!'

'I'm sorry, lord, but——'

'No excuses! See to it at once! But before you go,
know this. The demoiselle, God willing, will become my
wife ere the month is out. Meanwhile, you will take your
orders from her. She speaks for me in all matters re-
lating to the running of this household. Be not lag-
gardly, or you will be thrown into the dungeon to rot!
Do you hear me?'

'Aye, lord.' The old man's face was a picture of guilt
and fear. 'Demoiselle, I will do my best to serve
you——'

'Be in the Hall when the bell tolls for Prime,' said
Eleanor decisively. 'Together, we will, mayhap, set this
place to rights.'

'Now go,' ordered Richard. 'See to that fire!'

Eleanor rose to her feet, reluctant to leave the comfort
of the fiercely burning logs, but eager to escape Richard's
disturbing company and sort out her emotions.

'I had best go, lord. I must speak with my brother
before I retire to my chamber, so the fire will be lit before
I reach it. I would prefer to write in private.'

A stab of regret, mixed with annoyance at her obvious desire to escape him, brought a frown to Richard's brow. Yet he had made some progress. He couldn't explain, even to himself, why it was so important to him to have her a willing bride. He could take his wedded rights without consideration of her feelings, yet in an obscure way he knew that this course would not be satisfactory.

'Very well, maiden,' he agreed gruffly, picking up the writing materials and handing them to her. 'We will find him. He will probably still be in the Great Hall.'

That was indeed where they found Godfrey, mildly drunk and huddled near the central fire.

'Ah, sister,' he greeted her, waving his goblet in the air. 'I had wondered where you were! We must be away at dawn.'

'*You* must, Godfrey, to carry a letter to our father. I am to remain here.'

Slowly, Godfrey lowered his goblet and sat up straight. 'What do you mean, sister? You cannot have accepted the preposterous proposal put to you at supper?'

Eleanor coloured. Even Godfrey had heard! 'Why not, pray?' she asked haughtily. 'If Lord William was acceptable to both you and my father as my husband, why not his son? I will write a letter for you to take to my father. The only thing that needs to be changed in the marriage contract is the Christian name of the groom!'

'Make all speed,' adjured Richard, choosing to ignore Godfrey's bad manners. 'We wish to arrange the ceremony for the last day of April. I will give you my seal on it. There is time enough for a messenger to return with the new contract.'

Godfrey shrugged. 'If that is what you wish, sister. Let me have the letters early.'

'If I am not about when you are ready to leave, you may send a varlet to collect mine,' she told him coolly, then thought better of her lack of warmth. 'Nay, Godfrey, I'll be up to speed you on your way! But in truth I am tired. I must make haste to write this letter! God's blessings this night, brother. God's blessings, my lord.'

*   *   *

A small house-churl had already lit the kindling when
Eleanor arrived back at her chamber. Joan was fussing
around the child issuing orders, at the same time warming
her icy hands over the flickering flame.

'And about time too,' she was muttering. 'Bring more
logs, scullion. This miserly load will not last the night!'

'Aye, mistress,' muttered the lad, speaking with a thick
local accent. He sidled past Eleanor with averted head.

'What's your name, boy?' she demanded, distressed
to see the thinness of his body and the ragged state of
his clothes.

He paused reluctantly. 'Tamkin, mistress.'

'Thank you for lighting the fire, Tamkin. Are there
logs aplenty downstairs?'

'There be enough, mistress.'

'Then we shall be glad of more, but do not carry too
heavy a load.' She dismissed the lad with a gesture and
turned to Joan, glad to have her solid, familiar presence
near her again. 'Do not be so harsh, Joan,' she scolded
gently. 'The lad is young, and sickly, I believe.'

'A few sharp words will do him no harm,' muttered
Joan defensively. 'What's all that for?'

Eleanor shrugged. 'Nevertheless, be kind.' She hesitated, looking down at the things Joan had noticed in
her hand. 'Joan,' she murmured. 'We are to stay.'

'How so, sweeting?' Joan's broad face creased into a
frown. 'Is aught amiss?'

'No, not amiss. Bring the table and stool over here by
the fire.'

Joan complied, suppressing her curiosity, and Eleanor
spread the writing materials ready. 'I must write to my
father. I am to wed with the Lord of Wenfrith.'

'Mistress!' Joan's gasp of surprise quickly turned into
a grin which spread across the broad face framed by
white linen barbette and fillet. 'Welladay! Who'd have
thought it? And him so proud and all! He disdains the
entire Saxon race, yet he seeks your hand! The Saints
be praised!'

'You approve?' asked Eleanor, startled by her friend's
enthusiastic reception of the news. 'I thought you'd be
upset.'

'With him such an upstanding, gallant knight? And an Earl, to boot? Nay, my lovely, his castle may be sadly run, but that's not his fault, is it? He'll make you a lusty husband. You'll be the envy of many a high-born Norman lady!'

'Oh, Joan.' Eleanor laughed, a trifle unsteadily. 'I must admit, the proposal seemed more acceptable than risking my father's choice again! Even though my future husband is so scornful and surly on occasions.' She paused, blushing. 'Joan, do you know aught of the marriage bed?'

'Me, sweeting? What should I know, apart from kitchen gossip? Didn't your mother prepare you for your wedding night?'

'She spoke of duty, of being submissive, of—of its not being too unpleasant. But—but don't some ladies find pleasure in the getting of an heir? Would that be wrong?'

'Not wrong, my lovely, but rare, when so many are married to men old enough to be their fathers, and who are fat and ugly, to boot!' She smiled at her young mistress with affectionate indulgence. 'But if you can find pleasure in Lord Richard's arms, then God bless you both! It's what I'd wish for you, sweeting. Men find pleasure enough, that's plain, and so do many a lusty wench. There's naught wrong in a bit of carnal love, so long as it's enjoyed in wedlock!'

'But this wouldn't be love!' whispered Eleanor, wondering if she was wrong in dreaming that she might find pleasure in Richard's embrace. That kiss... But how could she think this way when part of her still feared and disliked him for his harsh and arrogant ways? She shivered and pulled her thoughts up abruptly. 'Bring the candle, Joan. I must get this letter written, or it won't be ready for Master Godfrey to take with him tomorrow!'

Joan stirred with the cock-crow, coaxing the fire into new life and warming water for Eleanor's toilet. Wrapped in a warm russet mantle of fine wool, Eleanor descended the winding stair to the Great Hall as the first streaks of dawn lit the eastern sky.

Godfrey was already there, clearly suffering from having drunk too much wine during the previous evening.

'There you are!' he snapped irritably. 'Is that the letter? Come with me!'

Wondering what ailed him now, Eleanor followed her sibling into the tiny, chilly chamber where he'd slept.

Fumbling under his pallet, Godfrey dragged out the heavy saddle-bags. 'Here, you'd better take charge of these. Put them under your mantle. We can't entrust this fortune to a messenger, and I'm not travelling back here again to bring it!'

Taking the weighty bags from him, Eleanor wondered how she could have forgotten the gold. She would have to hide it in her chamber until the contract was sealed.

Unless she trusted Richard with it. But once he laid hands on the money, would he keep to his bargain?

Was she doubting the honour of a chivalrous knight? She frowned, knowing that not all knights were so chivalrous these days, although the King's Grace was attempting to restore knighthood to some of its former glory. And—the blush rose to her face again as she remembered the look in Richard's eyes the previous evening. Her romantic notions had in part been answered, even though the reality of Richard's desire inspired in her apprehension rather than joy. And it was almost certainly rather less than his desire for the bounty she brought with her.

Had he loved her... She pushed the thought aside. That really was the stuff of romantic ballads, of minstrels' tales!

'Ho, there! I bring my seal.'

Richard's voice from the door took the decision out of her hands. The saddle-bags were still in full view.

'Lord! Have you a place of safe-keeping where I can store these until the due date? My brother leaves my dowry in my care, but I have nowhere to lodge it.'

Godfrey's choked cry of 'Eleanor!' was lost in Richard's loud chuckle.

'By my troth! The dower, eh? Yes, I have a strong-box in my wardrobe.'

'You will not touch it before you are wed!' growled Godfrey belligerently.

Richard's face closed into a stony mask. 'You doubt my honour, Sir Merchant?' he grated. 'God's blood, but I'd as soon run you through for that slur! Be on your way, sirrah! 'Tis fortunate you are the demoiselle Eleanor's brother and we need your services as messenger, or I'd have you thrown into the dungeon for your impertinence!'

Godfrey quailed before the cold contempt in Richard's voice, but couldn't resist a final insult, knowing that Richard's hands were tied by necessity.

'Be careful, sister,' he sneered. 'Methinks you are about to wed a raging Norman ram!'

Richard drew in a rasping breath and a low growl broke from his throat. Eleanor thanked the Blessed Virgin that although he wore his hauberk, he hadn't yet attached his sword to his belt, for such was the fearsome expression on his face she feared he might have drawn it. Biting her lip fiercely to stop the cry which trembled there, she stepped swiftly between the two men, thrusting the saddle-bags at Richard with shaking hands.

'Take them, lord. I must speed my brother on his way.'

He looked down into her blanched, desperate face and the deadly mask dissolved. 'Aye, maid,' he murmured grittily. 'I have no wish to come to blows.'

He turned on his heel and limped into the Hall and on towards his privy stair. The words 'with a merchant' hung unspoken in the air and Eleanor knew that, had Godfrey been a knight, honour would have demanded battle.

'Really, Godfrey! Did you have to make such a fuss?' Her voice trembled, but was strong with condemnation. 'The Earl is an honourable knight, whatever his temper! Go quickly,' she added more gently, 'and take my love to our parents.' A sadness settled on her features as she realised that no member of her family would be present at her nuptials. 'I will see you all again one day, do not doubt it. Farewell!'

A servitor handed her a stirrup-cup as she shepherded Godfrey out into the bailey, where his armed guard, pack-horses and own mount waited. Two of the retinue were to remain with her—her own personal guard. They were taking ribald leave of their comrades as Godfrey climbed on to a mounting block and swung into his saddle.

'I hope you do not come to regret your decision, sister. There is time still to change your mind.'

'Nay, Godfrey, I shall not do that. My lord can be gentle and courteous. You upset him.'

'Then, farewell, sister.' He took a deep draught from the steaming cup which she offered. 'God keep you.'

'And you, brother. May Saint Christopher go with you.'

Godfrey made a signal, and the entourage clattered noisily out of the courtyard and over the drawbridge.

Watching the familiar figure of her brother disappear from sight, Eleanor doubted if she had ever felt so forsaken in her life. Then her spirits lifted as she remembered Joan, her dear companion through previous banishments from home. The sun was staining the sky with rosy tints as she turned her back on her brother and returned to the Great Hall which was destined, it seemed, to be the centre of her future life.

CHAPTER THREE

ELEANOR re-entered the Hall to hear Richard calling for food. Her stomach lurched at the thought of facing him again, but she walked steadily to his side.

'Lord,' she murmured tightly, 'I must apologise for my brother. He does not understand the vows of chivalry.'

Richard's lip curled slightly, but he spoke in a neutral voice. 'One cannot expect such finer feelings from a Saxon merchant.'

Eleanor's fists clenched as she bent her head to hide the anger in her eyes. 'No, lord.'

The touch of his finger under her chin startled her. She tried to jerk her head away, but he would not be denied. He grasped her jaw and turned her face to his, noting her heightened colour and veiling lids with an impatient sigh.

'Yet you are different, demoiselle.' He gripped her chin more firmly while his eyes searched her features, ran down the length of her body, and returned to her face. 'With your dignity and grace, you could be a Norman lady born.'

Eleanor's eyes flew open in surprise, new colour flooded her cheeks and then retreated, leaving her skin parchment white. 'Your lordship is most kind,' she retorted stiffly, conscious of her nails digging painfully into the palms of her hands.

For a long moment his eyes held her antagonistic gaze with almost mesmeric force.

'Nay, Eleanor,' he teased gently, the intent expression in his grey eyes turning to amusement as he released her chin and sat down, 'do not be so affronted. I meant no criticism. I merely wonder how it can be...'

Easing the pressure on her palms, Eleanor sank into the chair beside him. 'While I was learning gentle ways in the house of a lord, my brother was travelling with our father, learning the ways of commerce,' she told him quietly. Then, with sudden vehemence, she added, 'And I had thought we were no longer Norman and Saxon, but English!'

'Aye, so we are,' he agreed sardonically.

He drew his knife and avoided her gaze by attacking a haunch of cold boar-flesh set before him by Will. The trestles and boards of the other tables being stacked in one corner of the Hall, Gilbert and his squire, together with all the other attendant knights, squires and men-at-arms, were either sitting on the benches or eating and drinking round the smouldering fire, leaving the couple on the dais isolated.

Richard swallowed a mouthful of meat and shot her a quick sideways glance. 'Are all your brothers like Godfrey?'

Eleanor sat crumbling a piece of hard wheaten bread to occupy her hands. She couldn't eat, the food would choke her. At Richard's words, her fingers stilled. A soft smile curved her lips. 'Cedric is not.'

'How old is he?'

'Two years older than I. He was twenty between the end of Trinity and Advent.'

'Last November? And when is your birthday, demoiselle?'

'I was eighteen at the end of August.'

'You have not been betrothed before? Most maids are wed before they reach sixteen!'

'Nay, lord. My father——'

'Was anxious to wed you to a noble Norman. Well, he is like to succeed!'

'You do him an injustice, lord!' cried Eleanor indignantly. 'He wanted to see me happily wed!'

'But to a noble Norman!' he reiterated cynically.

She couldn't deny it. She lowered her eyes to watch her fingers knead the bread into small rolls of damp dough.

Richard saw her agitation and relented of his goading, though he wasn't entirely sure why. Except that she was very beautiful.

'Your brother Cedric.' He returned smoothly to his previous inquisition. 'Tell me, what is he like?'

'Tall and broad, fair, carefree and——' she hesitated to use the word in describing her favourite brother, but it was the truth '——and chivalrous,' she finished defiantly, her eyes filled with tender affection for the brother so far away, whose circumstances made his ambition to become a knight seem an unattainable dream.

'You have other siblings?'

For some reason Richard's voice had lost the warmth it had begun to hold. Eleanor glanced at him questioningly, but his aquiline nose was deeply buried in his mug of ale.

'Two younger brothers, lord, Adam, who is fifteen, and Henry, a year younger. They are at school.'

Richard grunted and returned his mug to the board with a bang. 'I have to visit Wenstaple today,' he told her abruptly.

So that was why he was wearing mail. 'You have business there?' she asked politely, wondering how her unpredictable future husband would react to her questioning of his movements.

He didn't seem offended. He gave a slight shrug. 'I have to inspect the castle and garrison. I've not seen it yet, I've scarce had time.'

Encouraged, Eleanor dipped a fresh piece of bread in a dish of milk to soften it for eating, since her appetite was slowly returning, and risked an attempt to satisfy her natural curiosity about her new surroundings.

'How far is it? Is the town large?'

'It is distant four leagues or five and a fair size, I believe, enough to warrant the building of a new cathedral. It has grown since I was last there as a boy. I am told the issues and profits should be considerable but, as I said last night, it wouldn't surprise me to find them all swallowed up in the cost of maintaining the defences.'

Eleanor crumbled more bread into the bowl and stirred it round. 'The French do not normally raid so far west as this, do they?' she asked.

'No, the south coast is nearer, its shores more easily breached. Sussex suffers most.' He sighed heavily. 'But the King fears more ambitious excursions, and wants to limit the deprivations. So the Wen estuary must be defended, not only against the French, but against pirates, too. Fish and metals, as well as rich cargoes of wool, leave Wenstaple by ship. A tempting prize to many a brigand captain.'

'And he has entrusted this defence to you! He must think highly of your skills, lord.'

'Maybe.' He sighed again. 'But he has provided few funds, and I have little stomach for the task,' he admitted, wondering why he should be discussing his inmost frustrations with this maid.

'You would rather be in France,' observed Eleanor softly.

That hit too near the bone. Richard frowned, scraped his chair back, and pushed himself forcefully to his feet. 'My horse is waiting,' he said curtly, shattering the momentary rapport between them.

He stood tall and splendid as his squire buckled plate armour to his legs and arms and gilded spurs to his feet. With his mighty sword attached to his belt, he settled his conical helmet into place, arranged the dependant cape of mail around his neck and shoulders and drew on his steel gauntlets.

'Think you there will be cloth for sale there? And spices, perhaps?' Eleanor asked, hoping he would respond kindly to such a domestic topic.

A slight frown crossed his brow and he pursed his lips, but her fear that he was annoyed evaporated when he answered.

'I'll enquire of the constable's lady. Will you have need of much?'

'I shall know better when I've spoken with Hugh. Perhaps next time you go——'

'Make a list,' he instructed, taking his shield from Will and striding to the door, ignoring the limp he could not hide. 'I'll see you at supper. Farewell, demoiselle.'

Gilbert was riding with him, and he, too, wore full armour for this military expedition, but somehow did not look quite as striking as Richard—perhaps owing to his lack of height. He smiled and lifted Eleanor's hand to his lips.

'Congratulations, demoiselle,' he murmured. 'The Earl of Wenstaple is a great prize for a maiden such as you to win. I trust you will give him no cause to regret his choice.'

'I trust so, too, sir,' responded Eleanor stiffly. She had believed Sir Gilbert her friend. Yet even he thought her unworthy of the match!

The injustice of it all made her so angry! What did her birth matter, as long as she could fill the place at Richard's side with dignity and pride? Would she suffer from such censure all her life? And it would make no difference if she proclaimed her heritage from the ramparts! Her father made much of her royal descent, but he was still regarded as a Saxon merchant—a respected burgher, yes, a true noble, no!

Seething, she followed the men to the door, straightening her shoulders, lifting her braided head proudly. She did not descend into the mire of the yard, but stood at the top of the steps to watch both men, despite the weight of their armour and Richard's incapacity, spring lightly into their high, ornamented saddles. Richard's chestnut Great Horse, richly caparisoned, the golden castle emblem shining across its rump in the first rays of the morning sun, harness jingling and glinting, crest tossing, pranced eagerly as a colt until brought under swift control. Both knights turned to salute her as the herald sounded a fanfare and the company moved off; but it was on Richard's back, straight as the lance from which his banner streamed, that Eleanor's eyes lingered. As he passed the village church, the bell rang out for Prime.

Hugh the steward was waiting in the Hall to show her her new domain.

On her way to the kitchen, she quickly inspected the pantry and buttery as she passed along the passage leading from the Great Hall. Here, too, lay the main wardrobe, where clothes were stored and cleaned and precious spices locked away. Hugh ceremoniously handed her the key to the spice chest, which was, as she had suspected, almost empty.

Two large fires flanked the archway through which she entered the huge kitchen, with another, heating the baking ovens, blazing at the far end. The place was already a hive of activity. Scullions, varlets, cooks and, it seemed, almost every churl in the castle were gathered there, some busy, some gossiping, some eating their ration of food. Joan, who had been chattering with one of the cooks, stepped forward as her mistress arrived.

Despite its size and height and the opening in the roof for the steam and cooking smells to escape, the kitchen was the warmest, most comforting place Eleanor had thus far found in the castle—not excepting the lord's solar, the state of which definitely left much room for improvement.

But first things first. Hugh introduced the chief cook, the butler, and the grooms of the hall, the fire-tenders and the chambermaids and sundry other minor officials. An ill-disciplined, surly lot, she thought privately, schooling her face to show nothing of her dismay.

She spoke slowly, watching the assembled faces—ruddy, sallow, wrinkled, plump, youthful, old, sickly or healthy—for any reaction to her words.

'I am sure you'll all want to please the new Lord of Wenfrith, especially as he is also Earl of Wenstaple and as such is deserving of even greater honour. No doubt

you are as aware as he is that things here have become
slack and must be improved.'

A shuffling of feet, the sour looks, confirmed her suspicion that every man, woman, boy and girl had been
taking advantage of a sick and careless lord.

'That is in the past,' she told them severely, 'and will
not be punished now. But know that such laxness will
not be tolerated in the future. Hugh the steward will be
transmitting my orders, and I speak with the full authority of the Earl of Wenstaple. They will be obeyed
instantly!'

Muttered sounds of grudging assent greeted her words.
Joan stood apart, pride and approval on her round, rosy
face with its frame of fresh, clean linen.

How different her tiring-woman was from these ill-
clad, surly churls William of Evreux had gathered about
him! The women mostly still wore a wimple and veil of
coarse greying linen and the men, chaperons of un-
washed wool. Their short tunics revealed mainly bare,
dirty feet and legs. A few of the men, the grooms and
pages, wore faded, rather grimy tunics and hose in
William of Wenfrith's livery colours of yellow and grey,
but she supposed most were serfs giving the house service
due under the terms of their tenancies.

She had spotted Tamkin crouched in a warm corner
by a huge cauldron of bubbling stew, listening open-
mouthed to what she had to say. The bones stuck out
of his skinny arms and legs, he had an open sore on his
shoulder where some load had rubbed it raw. Something
in his thin little face, in the huge grey eyes, tugged at
her heart, as it had done on the previous evening.

'Tamkin,' she said quietly. 'Come here.'

The boy straightened up and sidled forward, looking
scared out of his wits. Eleanor put out a hand to draw
him nearer, but he shrank from her touch.

'Don't be afraid, Tamkin,' she soothed gently. 'I mean
you no harm. Let me look at your shoulder.'

'As I thought,' she murmured as Tamkin reluctantly
allowed her to inspect the wound. 'This needs a cleansing
poultice. Mistress Joan will see to it. Go with her. And
afterwards wait for me in my chamber.'

The lad blinked up at her, a new awe and dawning adoration in his eyes. Eleanor nodded at him, smiled at Joan. 'I'll leave him to you.' She turned to Hugh. 'Let us retire to your chamber.'

Hugh led her to a room in one of the towers flanking the entrance door. Its window embrasures looked out over the bailey, which, despite the absence of the lord and a large retinue, was still alive with men. Some were mounted and tilting at the quintain, while others honed their fighting skills with sword or bow. And among them all ran chickens, ducks, geese, the odd pig and a couple of goats.

'Will you not sit, mistress?'

'Thank you.' Eleanor accepted his invitation quietly, seating herself on one of the two roughly hewn stools at their disposal, careful to avoid catching her gown on a splinter. 'What ails this place, Hugh? Why is it so sadly neglected?'

Hugh shuffled his feet in the stale rushes and plucked at the rough wool of his robe with knotted fingers. 'For many years the Baron's revenues have been falling. There has been little to spare for luxuries——'

'Cleanliness costs nothing,' interrupted Eleanor sharply. She waved towards the window. 'Look at the parlous state of the bailey! One needs must wear thick pattens to walk there in safety! The marsh in the Hall is disgusting! The rushes have not been changed this six months, that I'll warrant! And although it was disguised by the odours of baking, the fetid stink from the pile of rubbish in the corner of the kitchen still had the power to make me retch! No wonder the rats breed so profusely! It is your duty to see to these things! Why did William of Evreux not take you to task?'

'Mistress, he was ill, he had lost interest in the things around him.'

'Ill? I saw him but six months past, at our betrothal. He had survived the journey to London. He appeared well enough then, and eager to replace his heir!'

Hugh shrugged helplessly. 'After his return his health deteriorated. Of late weeks even the prospect of his wedding could not arouse him from his apathy.'

'And you allowed the castle to fester around him! You, who should have seen to his comfort!'

'I, too, am old and suffer sorely from the stomach gripes at times, mistress.' Hugh's voice was shaking, the fear of dreadful punishment draining all the blood from his already sallow face. 'Perhaps I indulged myself over-much. I spent most of my time with my lord. He seemed to need my company, particularly since his squire died of the fever shortly after their return from London.'

He did appear old and frail. Eleanor resolved to have him replaced, but tactfully. She spoke more kindly.

'See first to the things I have mentioned, Hugh. You have clean rushes stored?'

'A few, mistress. We have straw——'

'See that the grooms use what is to hand. Have them sweep out every chamber, and especially the Hall. The trestle boards there need a thorough scrub. Is there no linen with which to cover them?'

'No, mistress. Lord William preferred the wood uncovered.'

'Very well. But I want them scraped clean! See to the cleansing of the bailey, and make sure that ordure is not allowed to collect there in future. And the stables must be kept sweet and clean.' She had visited Silver briefly the day before and been appalled by the condition of her stall. 'If labour is short, see to it that all serfs who owe service are made to work their time. Do what is necessary, Hugh, but do not allow this state of affairs to endure!'

'Mistress.' Hugh inclined his head in submission to her wishes, then raised it again to hold her gaze with rheumy eyes. 'Many of the tenants in these parts are freemen, paying their rents in silver rather than service. There are scarce more than thirty serfs, man, woman and child, on this manor.'

Eleanor nodded. 'Then offer payment for their services.'

'Aye, mistress. They'll likely be glad of something extra.' He hesitated, then seemed to make up his mind. 'Do you wish to inspect the records? They are here, if you want to see them.'

Something in his watery old eyes gave her pause for thought. Was Hugh trying to imply that something was amiss?

'Thank you, Hugh. Yes, I will inspect them. Perhaps you will have them taken to my chamber. For the moment, I am returning to the kitchen. The Earl is not best pleased with the food that has so far been served.' She rose to her feet, then paused on her way to the door. 'By the way, enquire as to which women are skilled with their needles. The entire household needs new livery, and the solar, new hangings.'

Eleanor had forgotten all about Tamkin. She returned to her bedroom to prepare herself for dinner to find him crouched there rubbing tallow into the shoes she used for riding and wet weather.

'Tamkin!' she exclaimed. 'I had quite forgot! I see Mistress Joan has put you to good work.'

'Aye, mistress.' Joan's voice floated ahead of her as she appeared from the small closet and latrine attached to the bedroom. 'His wound is clean. I've treated it as you instructed, and given him a scrub all over.'

'Good. Tamkin, how would you like to be my page? To help Mistress Joan look after me?'

'Oh, lady!'

The admiration had turned into something near worship in his eyes, and Eleanor felt humbled. Her simple act of kindness did not warrant such devotion. 'How old are you, Tamkin?'

'Don't rightly know, lady. Me brother says I were born in the year of the battle of Sluys.'

'That makes you seven. Are your parents alive?'

'My mother be dead, some years since. We don't have a father. Stephen says we be bastards, and not to listen to what anyone says, it mayn't be true, and we be who we be.'

Eleanor's heart twisted with pity for the boy. 'Stephen?' she asked gently.

'My brother. He's the reeve,' Tamkin informed her proudly.

She lifted her finely arched brows in surprise. 'He represents the tenants? He must be much older than you, Tamkin.'

'Aye, lady, he be more'n twenty, I think. He sent me to live in the castle because he couldn't tend me hisself.'

'He's not wed?'

'Nay, lady. He talks of naught but sheep and cattle and raising crops. Next year I be going to help him.'

While she had been talking Eleanor had tidied her hair and freshened her face and hands. 'Not if you are to be my page! Shall we go down to the Hall for dinner? Joan, look after Tamkin.'

Hours later, standing by the fire on fresh, sweet-smelling rushes awaiting Richard's return for supper, Eleanor wondered if he would notice the improvements wrought in just one day.

She still wore the dark grey sleeveless surcoat out of deference to William's memory, but had livened up her appearance by donning underneath a kirtle of rich azure sarcenet. She held her hands to the warmth, admiring the shimmering silk of the tight fitting sleeves, the tiny buttons which Joan fastened so dexterously. Would he approve?

Even as she wondered, the sound of trumpets and the clatter of many hoofs announced the return of Richard and his retinue. She glanced around quickly, making a final inspection to see that all was as she had ordered.

The ring of spurs in the entry warned of his imminent arrival, and a smile of greeting curved her lips. He rounded the screen. The expression froze on her face.

Exhaustion and pain had accentuated the lines of harsh experience already etched deeply on his features. As he walked, his wounded leg dragged. Eleanor gave a little gasp and made to run forward, but one look from hostile grey eyes kept her pinned where she was.

'We are late,' he barked abruptly. 'Is supper not yet served?'

'It awaits your coming, lord.' Eleanor kept the concern from her voice by an effort of will, recognising his determination to deny his weakness. 'If you would care to change your attire, it can wait a while longer.'

'Half an hour,' he threw at her. 'Will! Help me off with this armour!'

Will darted forward, relieving his master first of his helmet, which he placed on a special perch jutting from the wall, then of the remainder of his armour. When Richard was stripped to the thickly padded woollen gambeson which protected his body from the chain mail, he limped towards the privy stair.

Eleanor hardly noticed the stir in the Hall as the other knights shed their armour. Her whole attention was focused on the man limping towards his solar.

His leg *must* recover! Richard would lose his self-respect if it did not! Perhaps, once they were wed, he would allow her to use her knowledge of herbs—but the wound could not still be open! She had caught no whiff of putrefaction...

At last the herald sounded the fanfare announcing Richard's return. Looking rested and limping less obviously, he entered the Hall and, following his lead, everyone took their places at the tables. Eleanor watched as the food was brought in, surreptitiously eyeing Richard's face to see if he approved of the dishes presented to him.

'Ham!' he exclaimed, slicing off a large portion and turning to smile at the silent maid at his side. 'Your idea? Would you like me to serve you?'

'Thank you, lord. Yes, I inspected the pantry this morning and ordered the ham boiled in cider, then roasted in honey. There was not enough for all the tables, but the stew being served elsewhere is well cooked and flavoursome. I ordered a couple of hens who had stopped laying to be slain. We can increase the stocks of poultry by eating fewer eggs for a while!'

'It smells delicious!'

'You may try some if you wish, but first taste the pease pudding. It goes well with the ham.'

Will had passed the platter of ham to John, Gilbert's squire, and now offered his master the enormous round pudding of cooked dried peas flavoured with the cider stock, butter and herbs.

'By the holy rood, you've been busy this day, demoiselle! Food fit for a king!' exclaimed Richard, consuming his meal with evident relish.

Eleanor smiled. 'Wait until you taste the fish, lord! We sent to Lower Wenfrith, the fishing village. It is fresh from the sea and has been baked in butter with herbs Joan found nearby. Lemon balm, parsley, sage and sweet thyme grow freely in a walled patch by the stream which turns the mill's wheel and feeds the moat. I think this was once a kitchen garden, and I would like to have it restored, if you agree.'

'Demoiselle, you have already wrought a miracle in the kitchen! Of course I agree! What else have you done?'

'Have you not noticed the clean rushes, lord? And the lack of ordure in the bailey? Hugh recruited people from the village to cleanse the place.'

'I was too tired to notice the improvement outside,' admitted Richard ruefully. 'But I could hardly miss the clean, fresh smell within. You have been busy, my betrothed. I thank you.'

'No need, lord. It is but a beginning. How did your day fare?'

'Naught so badly. I have set certain improvements in motion. The constable of Wenstaple Castle, Henry of Bagwell, is a conscientious man, but has lacked direction. The collection of the revenues has been sadly neglected. On Sir Henry's recommendation, I have appointed a new receiver, and the income should improve. In fact——' the weary lines on his face gave way to a smile of quiet satisfaction which made him look years younger '—the yield from Wenstaple may well be much richer than I'd thought.'

'I'm glad, lord. I believe the same could be said of Wenfrith, too.' She lowered her eyes, plucking nervously at the silk of her surcoat. 'In fact, you may have no need of my dower.'

Richard's brows shot up, the injured one distorting the shape of the questioning eye beneath. 'How so?'

Eleanor met his gaze reluctantly. 'Hugh gave me the records to study. The tithes and dues here have been laxly enforced. And I find that the bailiff is a drunken fool, incapable of managing your lands. This manor has no need to be so poor! The Baron d'Evreux is overlord of many manors, and has only to exact his dues! They should be a source of much wealth!'

Shrewd eyes sought hers from under heavy lids. 'And so, my betrothed, would you be released from our bond?'

'Nay, lord. I am content with our agreement.' She shielded her eyes with sweeping golden lashes. 'But you, lord, no longer need to wed against your principles in order to acquire my dowry.'

Richard's lids lowered further, masking the grey eyes as he sliced off a piece of bread with which to wipe his trencher. 'Money brings power, maiden, and your gold is to hand.' He smiled mirthlessly. 'No man can own too much.' His lids lifted, taking her by surprise. His gaze met hers with sudden intensity. 'I have no great desire to escape my bond.'

Eleanor let out a deep, silent breath, only then conscious that she'd been holding it. A strange relief flooded through her, bringing with it a new sense of security. She had offered Richard a chance to withdraw, which he had refused. His aversion to her Saxon heritage could not run so very deep after all! Or was it that just his desire for her was greater than she'd imagined? Strangely, even that supposition was more comforting than alarming. To be wanted and useful was surely halfway to being accepted?

But he was speaking again, and she brought her attention back to what he was saying. 'A manor court is due to be held tomorrow. I myself shall preside, and accept oaths of allegiance from the people here.'

'Perhaps I could watch, lord? I remember that at times the moot where I served my apprenticeship could be quite amusing!'

'I wish you could sit by my side, but that would be a breach of etiquette. By all means watch. I shall have Hugh, the old reprobate, to guide me in the customs of this particular manor. He has done the job often enough in the past, though probably badly!'

'He is old and unwell, lord. Do not deal with him too harshly, I beg. Perhaps some younger man could be found to act as his assistant. In time, Hugh can be honourably retired. I believe he served your father faithfully in the ways he needed most.'

Richard's eyes twinkled. 'You show the tender heart of a true woman, my betrothed! It shall be as you say. And it seems I must find another bailiff.' He sighed wearily. 'Such matters fall heavily on my shoulders. I am a fighting knight, not a soft scribbling clerk! Or at least I would be, were it not for my pestilential leg!'

'It still pains you, lord.' Eleanor made her observation a statement rather than a question. 'No doubt it will improve in time. Meanwhile, you are no less a chivalrous knight! Your vows are not all related to fighting. Your people and your King need you here. Be content.'

'Easy words, maiden, for one who knows not the joy and satisfaction of pitting one's strength and skill against a worthy enemy!' he said impatiently, then looked askance at a concoction placed before him by Will. 'What's this?'

'A tartlet, lord, made of apples and honey. The cooks are quite able, given direction. Will you try a slice?'

'Jesu!' said Richard with a sigh of deep appreciation as he tasted the dish. ''Tis well you have taken over the running of this household!'

'Thank you, lord!' Eleanor dimpled him a smile which brought the gleam of desire leaping to his eyes. She looked down quickly, the colour rising hotly up her neck. 'If I am to make further improvement, it will cost a lot of money,' she rushed on nervously. 'Have I your permission to order rushes, certain foods and spices, cloth for new liveries, and clothes for those who work in the house?' Her blush grew deeper, but she pressed on valiantly. 'I would also like to renew the hangings in the solar. Mayhap buy materials to work a tapestry to hang on the wall.'

'Aye, order what you must. The men-at-arms need new livery, too. God forfend that we should live in such primitive misery as this for long!'

Richard had quickly hidden that surge of desire, and now placidly finished his slice of apple tart. Will refilled his maple-wood mazer and he quaffed some of the Burgundy with a satisfied grunt before handing the dish to Eleanor.

'Share my wine, my betrothed. My father kept a good cellar, at least.'

'Aye, lord.' She took a mouthful and handed back the mazer. 'Though the stocks of wine are low, there is plenty of mead, small ale and cider.'

'I prefer wine with supper. There is a vintner in Wenstaple, as well as a cloth merchant and victualler. Get Hugh to choose a trustworthy servant to journey to Wenstaple for the things we need. I shall not be visiting the castle again until after our wedding.'

'Your livery colours, lord. Are they to be as your father's?'

'Nay! I shall have new colours, scarlet and azure. I suggest tunics halved in the two colours, and one leg of the hose azure, the other scarlet.'

'And your badge, lord?'

'The golden castle of Wenfrith. But my blazon must be changed.' He picked up his knife and began to scratch lines on the surface of his empty wooden trencher. 'The castle d'or on a field of gules strewn with lilies d'argent— arms used by the d'Evreux family ever since they received the honour of Wenfrith—shall be in the first and fourth quarters, with the gauntlet d'argent of Wenstaple in the second and my Oxford manor of Acklane's oak d'or in the third, these on fields of azure. Red, blue, gold and silver. It should look well, I think.'

The design had taken swift shape under his skilled use of the knife. Eleanor leaned across to look more closely, aware of the odour of clean male skin faintly spiced with bay. It mingled with the fragrance of the lemon balm Joan had rubbed into her own body before supper to produce a heady mixture. As her head swam and her limbs dissolved to pottage, that same unaccustomed sensation of melting weakness she'd known the previous evening in Richard's arms caused her to draw back sharply. Richard seemed not to notice, though his hand had stilled on the table.

'I'll draw it out and instruct my herald tomorrow.' He thrust the platter aside and turned to speak to the knight on his other side.

The consequent lull in their conversation gave Sir Gilbert the chance to claim her attention. Under cover of the sound of lute, pipe and tabor, he spoke low.

'You have wrought a change in the kitchen, demoiselle, and in the lord Richard, I believe. He seems more content tonight than at any time since he was struck down.'

'We have reached an agreement, sir.' Eleanor's voice was husky as she battled with her wayward senses. 'I do not think you need fear for the Earl's happiness or his honour. When must you depart?'

'So anxious to see me go? I wonder why?'

'No, Sir Gilbert, I am not anxious for your departure,' protested Eleanor in acute embarrassment, well aware that he had sensed her admiration of his fair looks and courteous manner—though her regard had suffered cruelly from his censure earlier that day. 'But you have said that you must leave soon. I merely wondered——'

'I leave at first light tomorrow,' he told her quietly. 'I apologise for my words this morning. I believe I leave my friend in kind and gentle hands.'

Eleanor blushed again, confused by the unexpected compliment. Supper being ended, the remains of the food had been removed and Grace said. The company was lounging around drinking, telling tales and enjoying bawdy jokes.

She sat quietly while Richard laughed at something said to him by a knight further down the table. Although she had not heard the words she could guess their import by the knowing looks pointed in her direction. Such outspoken humour was only to be expected, but the turn of the jests made her uncomfortable nevertheless. When she felt a small tug on her gown she was glad of the excuse to glance down. Tamkin was crouched by her chair, having worked his way through the legs of the attendant squires.

'Is there aught you require, lady?' he whispered.

'Nay, Tamkin, but stay where you are. You may escort me to my chamber in a few moments.'

Richard turned back at the sound of her voice, and saw the boy squatting by her side.

'Is that scullion troubling you?' he demanded. 'Will! Send the churl back to the kitchen!'

'Nay, lord.' Eleanor swallowed. She had forgotten that she would have to answer to Richard for her elevation of Tamkin. 'I would crave my lord's indulgence. I have told Tamkin I would like him to serve me as page. He is here to do my bidding.'

Richard's frown turned into a scowl. 'If you require a page, you can have your pick of the sons of my knights. You do not need to employ a scurvy churl from the kitchen——'

'I would prefer to have Tamkin, lord. I believe he will suit me well.'

'And I would prefer you to have a gentleman born!' thundered Richard imperiously.

For an instant, so deep was his scowl of disapproval, he looked threatening. Tamkin sprang like a small lion cub to his mistress's defence. Before Will could stop him, he thrust his slight frame between the two chairs. Although his whole body quivered with fear, he glared up at Richard, a scowl as fierce as his lord's on his childish face.

'Don't you touch my lady!' he shrilled. 'I'll not let you kill her as you did our lord!'

Absolute astonishment took her breath and brought Eleanor's eyes to Richard's face. With a gasp of horror she grasped Tamkin's arm, pulling him against her.

Richard's stricken face had become carved in chalk. His lips, drawn tight against his teeth, were a thin, colourless line. He sat immobile, only the whitened knuckles of the hand clenched on the board revealing the magnitude of the strain he was under, the tight hold he was keeping on himself.

A dead silence had fallen on the company. Those who hadn't actually heard the boy's words listened to discover what was amiss, those who had were shocked into speechlessness. The minstrels, sensing drama, had faltered to a stop.

At last Richard stirred. His gaze swept over her, piercing her like shards of splintered ice. A trembling began deep in Eleanor's being as she awaited the inevitable retribution. Richard would blame her, would punish them both! Yet Tamkin was simply repeating gossip he must have picked up in the kitchen! Hiding her fear, she gazed steadfastly back into Richard's frozen face as, slowly, he rose to his feet.

'Lord,' she protested, stilling her voice with an effort, her words falling loudly into the surrounding silence. 'The child is not to blame for repeating what others say.'

A quiver passed over Richard's drawn features and Eleanor realised that although his frosty glare had rested on her, he had been unaware of its impact. He had seen nothing of the Hall and people about him. He'd been lost in some frozen world of his own.

'Nay.' Richard's hoarse voice was deadly quiet. 'Tell me, what is it they say of me, scullion?'

By this time Tamkin had realised the enormity of what he had done. But he answered dauntlessly in a clear, if quavering, treble.

'That you did poison our lord to gain your inheritance.'

Richard turned slowly to face the assembled household. 'And you believe this scurrilous lie?' he demanded quietly.

Eleanor had expected a tempest to erupt over their heads, and braced herself to meet it. Instead, this still, dignified, towering figure had turned shock and a dawning suspicion into something like shame.

'Never!' The cry rose in a great shout from his knights and retinue, making the rafters tremble.

A thrill ran through Eleanor's nerves, bringing tears to her eyes. They had been his father's men only a few days since. How swiftly he had gained their loyalty!

'Nay, lord!' Hugh the steward hastened to add his voice to the denial. 'An I discover the cursed churl who began this slanderous rumour, I'll——'

'Peace, Hugh.' Richard's hoarse voice interrupted the man's protestations. 'My father died at sight of me. Mayhap I did kill him.' He turned unseeing eyes on Eleanor and the boy. 'Keep your page, demoiselle.' He sighed wearily. 'He shows devotion, and the heart of a lion in your defence.'

Without another word, he turned and left the Hall, with Will following silently at his heels. Eleanor rose unsteadily to her feet and swept to her own bedchamber, her thoughts in a jumbled whirl.

Tamkin's shaft had struck Richard to the core of his soul. Did he feel guilt for his father's death? Had he perhaps struck him?

Quick-tempered he might be, but Richard was not without control. She doubted he had struck his father. Not, at least, in sudden anger.

But deliberately? She shivered, not wanting to believe him so ruthless or wanting in filial duty, however badly provoked. No, he would not. No more than he would have poisoned him.

'Go to bed, Tamkin,' she ordered the boy wearily. 'I'll not need you again tonight.'

'I'll sleep across your door, lady.'

'Nay, Tamkin, there's no need. Join the others in the warmth of the Hall. But no more gossiping, do you mind me? I am to wed the Earl. I'll have no more accusations of perfidy spread against him. He is a good, honourable and valiant knight, held in high regard by the King himself. See that you speak of him so.'

'Aye, lady. I did but say——'

'Say it no more! And do not listen again to such lies!'

As she slipped into the chamber-gown Joan held for her, Eleanor wondered if her protestations to Tamkin had not been made to convince herself as much as the child. Who else could reassure her that she was not marrying a man with some dark secret hidden in his soul?

CHAPTER FOUR

'DON'T you be fretting yourself, sweeting,' muttered Joan, brushing out the rippling, pale golden hair hanging around Eleanor's hips as she sat on the stool. 'Your future lord is no murderer.'

'I know it, Joan.' Eleanor twisted her fingers together in her lap and sighed. 'All the same, I wish he were of more even temper.'

'Aye, he's fiery, but none the worse for that! You've the spirit to tame him, my lovely. You'll make a fine pair.' She stopped her brushing for a moment to stare dreamily into space. 'The Earl and Countess of

Wenstaple,' she enunciated importantly, rolling the titles
around on her tongue with pride.

Eleanor chuckled, reassured by Joan's forthright
defence of her future husband. Joan must have heard
the kitchen tattle, but had chosen to disregard it. Perhaps
she knew . . .

'Joan,' she asked abruptly. 'Do you know who started
this spiteful tale?'

'Nay, mistress. The story was old when I first heard
it. It came out of the air, and will die in the cesspit.
Forget it, and help your lord to do the same.'

Determined to follow Joan's advice, the next day Eleanor
settled herself on a bench in a dark corner of the Hall
to await the Lord of Wenfrith's arrival to conduct his
manor court.

Strain was clear on his taut features as he took his
place in the ceremonial chair on the dais. For this occasion he wore a long gown of crimson velvet over black
tunic and hose. An ermine collar lay around his throat,
while a gold chaplet, exquisitely wrought and studded
with cabochons of emerald, ruby, agate and jade, sat
regally among the dark waves of his hair.

That in itself must be worth a fortune, thought
Eleanor, unable to tear her eyes away from the sombre
face beneath.

A hush had fallen over those assembled in the Hall.
Old Hugh, who had entered just behind Richard,
carrying the Court Rolls and the Customal, had taken
his place on the dais, together with the beadle who called,
'Oyez,' and who ordered all those who had business and
owed service to the Lord of Wenfrith to draw near. Sir
Piers sat near by, ready with parchment and quill to make
a record of the proceedings.

A man stepped forward. Dressed in a short tunic of
brown frieze and wearing both hose and shoes, he appeared cleaner and better clad than the majority of those
present.

'Yon's my brother, lady,' whispered Tamkin excitedly
from his place, out of sight, on a stool at Eleanor's feet.

Eleanor studied the reeve with new interest. He looked
rather more than twenty, almost of an age with Richard,

perhaps a year or two younger, though Richard tended
to look older than his twenty-seven years. The fellow
was as tall as his lord, with an equally straight carriage.

He executed a respectful bow and spoke in a firm,
clear voice, easily understood despite a strong local burr.
'Lord, the people of your manor have come to offer
homage. We would swear our fealty to the Lord of
Wenfrith.'

He walked towards the dais, his palms pressed together before him. Richard took the folded hands in his
and Stephen intoned the ancient words required of him.

'So help me God and all His Saints, I do swear to be
true and faithful to the Lord of Wenfrith, and to owe
fealty to him for the land I hold of him in villeinage; I
will be justified by him in body and goods and will not
take myself off the Lord's manor.'

One by one, the people extended their grimy, callused
hands to be held in their feudal lord's. Some repeated
Stephen's words, others vowed fealty for land held of
him in free tenure and promised only to execute such
small services as were required of them under their
tenancies.

Richard visibly relaxed during the long but moving
ceremony, and Eleanor's heart swelled, all her doubts
about the union submerged in a surge of pride.

The usual crop of complaints followed: arguments over
work days, over trespass by animals, over the use of the
plough. Many were fined for minor offences against the
manorial laws as set out in the Customal: for not keeping
the path outside their cottages clean, for taking the
Lord's wood without leave. One man was fined for
beating a woman, and two women for fighting with each
other. The day ended with a vitriolic exchange over an
alleged slander.

'He called me bastard!' roared the aggrieved serf, his
small, bloodshot eyes swinging round the Hall like those
of a restless bull. 'I be no such thing, me lord! I can
prove me true birth, unlike some as I could name——'

'Oh, aye?' sneered the accused man calmly, wiping
his running nose on his greasy sleeve in a gesture of contempt. 'At least the reeve bears his base birth without

complaint. You're a liar, as well as a bastard, Seth Pockface. Or maybe 'twas your mother who lied——'

'Enough!' Richard's voice cut short the tirade.

While he sought the opinions of Hugh and those acting as assessors, Eleanor laid a pacifying hand on Tamkin's head and watched the reeve's face for signs of shame or discontent. To be base-born was a disgrace indeed, and cut a child off from all its rights of inheritance. Yet Stephen's demeanour showed no trace of discomfort. If he resented his birthright he had learnt to hide the fact.

When the last case had been dealt with Richard dismissed the court. The ceremony of homage had pleased him, despite the necessity of touching so many filthy and scabious hands. He'd noticed no hint of resentment in their manner, such as he had sensed at Acklane, but rather an air of quiet expectancy. At Acklane, of course, he'd gained his fief by buying the tenure of the manor from a penniless knight; here he was the rightful heir.

Even so, the slanderous accusation of last night could not be widely believed, he realised with relief. Perhaps that was why it had been left to a mere child to throw the scurrilous gossip in his face. No one else thought it worth more than a moment's mischievous amusement.

He shifted uneasily, regretting his show of weakness the previous evening. But although there was no truth in the malicious story, the weight of guilt lay heavy on his soul. He had thought to surprise his father, but the expected rejoicing and feasting on his safe return after so many years of training and campaigning, of founding his own fortune, of possessing himself of a manor and an earldom, had turned into sorrow and self-recrimination. He knew in his mind that he was not to blame for his father's fatal attack, yet his heart would not allow him peace. His hands clenched on the arms of his chair.

Relaxing again, he eased his tired shoulders. Sitting in judgement was satisfying, if wearying, and there was still one more matter he must deal with. He dismissed Hugh, Sir Piers and the beadle with a peremptory wave of his hand.

'Stephen the reeve. I would speak with you!' he called. 'You acquitted yourself well,' Richard congratulated, his thoughtful eyes studying the man who had returned to stand before the dais. Something about the fellow intrigued him. He had not denied the charge of bastardy, yet had pride, and looked to have good blood running through his veins.

As Richard stared into the calm grey eyes gazing steadily into his, a mirror image of his own face seemed to rise mockingly before him. His stomach clenched with a sudden, sickening suspicion.

'Whose son are you?' he demanded roughly.

He heard the little cry and a 'Hush, Tamkin' coming from the dark corner behind, but ignored it. His attention was fixed on the man before him.

Stephen spoke calmly. 'Lord, I think you have already guessed.' His lips curved slightly. 'We share the same sire.'

Richard swore and leaped to his feet. 'How dare you speak thus, serf?' he gritted through clenched teeth. He wanted to knock the fellow senseless, to deny that his father could have been so careless of his marriage vows!

But his innate sense of justice quickly surfaced. 'Nay, 'tis no fault of yours that my father cast his seed so carelessly,' he admitted wearily. 'How many years have you?'

'Twenty-five, come Michaelmas.'

'I was but two when you were born. My mother was yet alive.'

The bitterness in his voice carried to Eleanor. She closed her teeth on the soft flesh inside her bottom lip, trying to stop the tears of relief from reaching her eyes. Did Richard, then, hold adultery a sin, as she did? She had often wondered how she would bear such infidelity on the part of her husband, while realistically expecting to have to accept it. Whatever they protested, most men, and particularly nobles, were far from chaste, relying on confession and the purchase of indulgences to absolve them from their carnal sins. And knightly honour was not prejudiced by such deviations from the path of Christian virtue! Only a show of cowardice could bring that into disrepute!

'Aye, lord.' Stephen's steady voice broke through her thoughts. 'My mother was young and comely, though but a villein's daughter. She was proud that he chose her, though she never wed, for lack of virtue in a woman is shame indeed, and her worth was nil despite the nobility of her despoiler.' He paused, and for the first time lowered his eyes to the ground. 'I had thought the affair ended, but some eighteen years later she bore him another bastard. By then, the lord our father had become a morose and lonely man. She could not refuse to comfort him, but in the end it cost her her life. She never fully recovered her strength after her second child was born.'

'Aye. My father should have taken another wife ten years since!' growled Richard. But then he himself would never have been able to wed Eleanor... A thrust of sudden longing, quickly denied, made his voice harsh as he demanded, 'Where is the other child?'

'His name is Thomas, lord, but he has always been called Tamkin. He lives in the castle, working as a scullion. I have no wife and could not tend him in my cot. I thought he would be warmer and better fed here under his father's protection, though the boy does not yet know what man to call his sire.'

'Tamkin?' Richard's brows drew together. The name sounded familiar... Then memory returned. God's teeth! The insolent young cub who had defended Eleanor, who had accused him...

He spun on his heel, peering into the dark recess from whence the cry had come.

'Tamkin!' he thundered. 'Come here!'

Most people had left the Hall by then. The few who remained looked round at the sound of his call. But Richard had his voice under control by the time Eleanor and a frightened Tamkin reached his side.

'So,' he said softly, his eyes holding hers in a level regard. 'You heard?'

'Aye, lord.'

Richard sank down into his chair, his fingers gripping the carved arms like iron bands.

'It seems your judgement was good in this as in other matters. You chose a page of partly noble birth.'

'Aye, lord. Almost as you wished.'

How could she explain that Tamkin's eyes had influenced her decision? Had she, without realising it, recognised a likeness to him in the child? The notion was absurd! Stephen bore some resemblance, though his hair was of a lighter hue, his face ruddy and less finely cast than that of his half-brother, his eyes smaller, his nose shorter, his mouth less firmly formed. But in Tamkin's urchin face there was no similarity at all, except in the beautiful grey eyes with their long, curling lashes...

Richard's brooding stare left the boy at last. He turned frowning eyes on the reeve.

'Did my father do nothing for you?'

'He made some provision. He gave my mother food and clothing for our keep, though he never openly acknowledged his responsibility for our birth. When she died he granted me tenure of the strips she had inherited from her father, waiving his right to a heriot.'

'Ah!' Richard's eyes narrowed as he eyed the other man keenly. 'My demesne is badly run—the tenants, serfs and freemen alike avoid their dues, yet do not seem to prosper themselves. How long have you been overseeing the way the tenants farm?'

'Only one full season, lord. I have plans to improve their yield.'

'Something needs to be done. My bailiff is a drunkard. The steward is old, and past running the household by himself.' He pursed his lips thoughtfully. 'An you can prove William d'Evreux was your sire—and there seems little doubt of that—then you can claim manumission. If your father was free, so are you.'

'Aye, lord. I had thought to claim my freedom when the time seemed right.'

'I grant it now. Papers shall be drawn up. Think you you could oversee my estates? I shall appoint you seneschal with authority over steward, bailiff and reeve.' He paused, eyeing Stephen keenly again before making his final decision. 'You will have complete control of the day-to-day running of the manor; stand in my stead when I am away, unless my wife remains, when you will answer to her. Well, brother?'

The colour had risen high in Stephen's face. He pulled himself up another inch. 'Aye, lord. I have no wish to leave the manor. In some way I feel tied to this land—

that it is my inheritance, too, though not as lord. I would never challenge its rightful heir.'

'But you might have sought to seize the barony had our father died without legal issue?'

'Aye, lord.'

Richard nodded. 'That's honest, at least. My return must have been a sore disappointment to you! And my father's proposed marriage—that would have been bad news indeed!'

'Perhaps, lord. But my anticipation of success was not high, and my heart is in the land, not in a title. Give me the right to oversee that, and I shall be content.'

'While I shall have a representative who knows and understands my manor, and whose loyalty cannot be questioned! Methinks the arrangement should suit us both, brother.'

Stephen bowed. 'I will serve you as well as I am able, lord.'

'You will move into the castle,' ordered Richard hospitably. 'In a few weeks Tamkin will become page to the Countess of Wenstaple and later, if he wishes, my squire.' He looked down at the boy. 'I forgive you your words of last evening. How does the idea appeal, whelp?'

Tamkin was momentarily speechless, and Richard in any case waited for no reply, but turned to Stephen. 'Do you know the charge he made? That I had poisoned the Lord William upon my return in order to gain my inheritance! What think you of that?'

For a moment Stephen looked startled as Richard's last words rapped out. Then a wry smile touched his mouth.

'Of that scurvy gossip, lord? I have told Tamkin often enough to ignore the tittle-tattle he hears. The manor is always rife with rumours of one sort or another, and the people vent their frustrations in false accusations against their lord. You should not have believed their words, Tamkin!'

'They spoke the truth when they said we were the lord's bastards!' muttered Tamkin defensively.

'Aye. I might have guessed they'd gibe you with that charge once I let you from my side,' admitted Stephen sadly. He reached out to tousle Tamkin's already untidy hair. 'But believe nothing without proof, Tamkin. That way you'll not be led astray.'

'Wisely spoken. You've received some education?'

'From the priest, Sir Piers,' acknowledged Stephen briefly.

'Excellent. We must see that Tamkin learns to read and write. Eh, little brother?'

Tamkin swallowed speechlessly, but Eleanor managed to find her voice despite the lump which seemed to have lodged in her throat.

'Lord, he will bless you all his days!'

Richard snorted. 'No need of such sentimental nonsense!' He raised his voice. 'Varlet! Bring a flagon of wine!'

Once over the first shock, thought Eleanor, he appeared to be finding joy in the discovery of kin, however base born. She knew already that Richard was naturally reserved, holding himself aloof from his more bawdy, rumbustious knights and their boisterous, easy camaraderie. So he would welcome the company of a brother who posed no threat to his own position.

If only he could have accepted *her* into his life with equal pleasure! But Stephen would always remain his vassal, while she, on their marriage, would equal him in rank. This was doubtless the root of his problem.

Richard could be charming, passionate, endearing, loyal... And harsh, domineering, terrifying! she reminded herself ruefully. Wait until Stephen displeased him and caught the rough edge of his tongue! He might look less pleased at the new turn his life was taking! Yet because of Richard's generosity to a man most people would despise, he would be in a position of great responsibility and honour. And he was free to leave the manor whenever he wished.

Whereas she... Once wed, if she wanted to escape her lord, there would be only one honourable way. Retirement into a convent.

She sipped her wine, willing it to warm the sudden chill in her heart.

Much was achieved on the manor in a remarkably short space of time. The supplies arrived, by pack-horse and cart, from Wenstaple and further afield. New uniforms were being sewn for the retainers, some by a tailor in the town, others by the manor women. Tamkin proudly wore the Earl of Wenfrith's new colours with the castle badge embroidered across the front of his tunic, and had managed to put on a little flesh since his diet had improved. Daily, the cooks tempted the appetites of those chosen to grace the high table with dishes prepared from rich and costly ingredients, while the whole household ate better than for many a month. Richard seemed prepared to spend money lavishly, probably in anticipation of her dowry, thought Eleanor with a wry smile.

The incompetent bailiff was banished, to waste his time away in the stews of the town, while Stephen appointed a new one, Gideon, a seemingly jovial man with cold eyes which made Eleanor uncomfortable.

She had herself sewn new crimson hangings and a covering for the big bed in Richard's solar, embroidering his new arms on each one, though she hadn't had the courage to ask him if she could hang them yet. Glass had been ordered for some of the windows, but that was unlikely to be fitted before the wedding.

Everyone in the castle and the vill looked happier, though their cheerfulness owed much to hope for the future rather than to any actual gain to date. But with the return of their new lord, and under the guidance of Stephen as seneschal, the prosperity of the manor was assured—or so the people promised themselves; for after all, hadn't Stephen been an excellent, clever reeve? Hadn't they known all along that their old lord's bastard son would one day bring God's blessing to them all? This was the feeling Joan picked up in her contacts with the other servants.

As the days passed, Eleanor began to explore her new surroundings. Sometimes she rode out on Silver, but when the weather was good, she and Joan allowed Tamkin to show them all the hidden places he had discovered on the shore. Dressed in short kirtles, with kerchiefs covering their heads, they scrambled down cliff paths to tiny coves where the two women sat on rocks and dipped bare feet in the pools, while the boy splashed in the sea. Gulls circled and cried overhead, the sun shone warmly between the April showers, and Eleanor, feeling a child again, basked in the freedom and fresh air, so different from the stink of the town from which she'd come.

She began to expect the messenger to arrive with her marriage contract. Godfrey had been gone for a full two weeks. Meanwhile, Richard was treating her with courteous respect, though she saw little of him. He spent his days with Stephen or his knights, inspecting, planning, training with arms, and hunting. After supper she retired early to her chamber. Once married, she would lose much of her freedom. And would have to come to new terms with her lord.

The messenger had still not arrived when Saint George's day dawned, a mere seven days before that appointed for her nuptials. Richard had ordered a tournament in honour of the Patron Saint of England, and an air of excitement pervaded the entire manor. After confession and Mass at dawn, the preparations moved into full swing. The bailey hummed with life as the Great Horses champed at their bits. The sun glinted on steel and shimmered on brilliant colour as the knights and their destriers were invested with full armour and ceremonial trappings.

A stretch of turf on the cliff-top had been marked out as the tourney field. Huge baulks of timber set on upright poles stretched the length of the lists to divide the opponents. A bevy of bright pavilions had been set up by the knights, with others provided by Richard for the serving of victuals and for the use of the leech, there to attend the wounded. Eleanor was to watch from a platform set halfway along the tourney field, hastily erected and shielded from the weather by cloth striped in Richard's red and azure.

Wending her way through the pavilions, the skirts of her applebloom gown and mantle of Lincoln green—for mourning dress was banished from that day—held clear of the damp grass, her short veil billowing in the fresh sea breeze, she wished again that Richard would be content to sit with her and watch. His leg was not strong enough to bear the strain of the joust, but his pride would not allow him to admit it. Consequently he was one of the six knights ready to accept a challenge from all-comers.

The castle was overflowing with Richard's vassals—those tenants of other manors in his fiefdom not engaged in the siege of Calais—who had come to pay homage to their new liege lord and to enter the lists. Many had brought their ladies.

With the other ladies, Eleanor settled down to watch the spectacle, not sure whether she was more excited or apprehensive. Anything could happen. Men had been killed at such events, or had died later of septic wounds.

Lady Radcliffe, wife of Sir Ralph, whose manor lay on the other side of the estuary, plumped on the bench near Eleanor with a breathless sigh of relief, pushing her young daughter down on a cushion at her feet.

'Just sit still and be proud, Anne,' she scolded. 'Your father will not be hurt. No one will be hurt, or at any rate, not badly. This is merely sport.' She turned to Eleanor with a sad shake of her head. 'I can't understand the child. She seems to dislike anything to do with chivalry. You'd never think she was the daughter of a knight who has fought in the Holy Land!'

'I don't dislike chivalry,' muttered Anne, a child still, though of marriageable age. 'It's the killing, the plundering and burning, the rapine I abhor!'

Eleanor looked down at the dark-haired maiden and met the challenge of rebellious brown eyes with sympathy in her own. 'War is ever cruel and brutal, especially for the vanquished. Glory comes only to those who fight and win. Praise our merciful God that your father was a victor, and returned safely.'

'I want to wed a man who is content at home, who does not find his pleasure in killing!' protested the child vehemently.

'Anne! Hold your tongue! You'll marry the man your father chooses! You have a goodly dower of land, and should win a noble husband!'

The blare of trumpets precluded any further discussion. Every point of ceremony and honour would be observed, although the tournament was a small one. The heralds, with their colourful tabards, shining trumpets and fluttering banners, cantered towards each other,

meeting in the centre of the field, where they made the
necessary announcements. Two knights waited, ready
mounted, at either end of the lists. A marshal proclaimed, 'In the name of God and Saint George! Come
forth and do battle!'

The day was a holiday on the manor, and almost
everyone had come along to see the spectacle. They had
not known such pageantry this fifteen years, and they
raised their voices in loud appreciation. Cheered on by
the enthusiastic crowd, the two destriers charged towards
each other, one on either side of the wooden bar. The
pounding of hoofs, the clash of wood and steel as the
lances hit, the sparks from shield and armour, brought
Eleanor's heart into her throat. She'd never witnessed a
tournament before, and the sight was both magnificent
and terrifying.

One of the knights broke his lance on the other's
shield, thus winning a point, but both knights were still
in their saddles. Armed with new weapons, they were
soon thundering towards each other again.

This time the same combatant managed to insert his
lance under the other's armpit and prise him out of his
saddle. This was certain victory! To assorted cheers and
groans, the knight on the ground raised the visor of his
huge tourney helm to show that he was not hurt,
struggled to his feet, and walked from the field.

'Sir Walter of Chumleigh challenges Sir Ralph of
Radcliffe!'

'Your father jousts!' exclaimed Lady Radcliffe excitedly. 'Sir Walter will be no match for him!'

Caught up in the excitement, the glamour of the
moment, Eleanor watched entranced as Sir Ralph unseated his opponent with an ease born of long practice.
But Anne had hidden her face in her hands, refusing to
watch as her father fought.

'Silly child!' muttered the lady Radcliffe, cuffing her
daughter round the ear.

'Mother, I cannot stay! I shall be sick!'

With a choked sob Anne thrust her way from the
platform.

'Tamkin, see she's all right!' whispered Eleanor urgently. Tamkin knew his way around; Anne would be safe with him.

As the boy slipped away, Eleanor smiled reassuringly at Anne's irate parent. 'Do not fret, lady. Anne will grow out of her fears.'

All the quicker if you don't push her, she thought silently. Poor child. She was probably deadly afeared of being wed to a knight like the one now preening himself at the end of the lists. Portly, bullish, with no finesse, he'd already broken several lances and unseated three knights by sheer brute strength. Now—oh, dear Mother of God!—he was challenging Richard!

Most Holy Virgin, prayed Eleanor silently, don't let him be hurt! Richard had survived one bout, winning easily. But that had been against a young lightweight trying his arms against his mentor. Young Will. Squires were allowed to try their skills and perhaps win their spurs. But Will still had a long way to go before he achieved that ambition!

Sir Thomas of Inneshall was a totally different proposition. Eleanor watched with mounting anxiety as the two men prepared to charge. Richard looked splendid in a surcoat charged with his new arms. He wore her favour, a green veil, tied securely to the golden eagle crest of his elaborate bronze heaume. With her clenched fists pressed tightly against her cheeks, she watched the flimsy material stream out behind his head as his destrier Noble's huge hoofs thundered on, sending clods of earth high into the air. But just before the crash came she closed her eyes, opening them only when a wild, if ragged, cheer rose from the crowd.

'D'Evreux! Wenfrith!' they roared. 'Wenstaple!'

'What happened?' gasped Eleanor dazedly. The huge Sir Thomas lay like a mountain of armour, quite unable to regain his feet.

'Didn't you see?' Lady Radcliffe cried exuberantly. 'Wenfrith tipped him out of his saddle as though he were thistledown! 'Twas all done by skill, the tip of his lance in just the right place——'

'Thank God,' whispered Eleanor, and watched with rather less apprehension as Richard beat off several other challenges by dextrously tipping the knights out of their saddles or removing their heaumes with subtle flicks of his lance. As a display of elegant horsemanship and leashed power his performance was supreme.

When every challenge had been met, Richard remained the only knight not to lose a joust.

'Wenfrith!' crowed the villagers. 'Wenfrith wins!'

Richard acknowledged the shouts before removing his heavy heaume and riding slowly over to the platform where Eleanor sat. Once there, he reined Noble to a halt in front of her and inclined his head in a courtly bow.

'Your favour brought me victory,' he smiled, well pleased with himself and his performance, and strangely proud of the maid who sat like a queen amid the other ladies. Not one of them could compare with her golden beauty and poise! The circlet on her head should surely have been a crown! He caught the soft admiration in her blue eyes, and tipped her a boyish smile. 'Your betrothed is yet able to acquit himself honourably on the tourney field. You need not have feared for my safety.'

Eleanor blushed, unaware that he had noticed her concern. 'Lord, I had no doubt of your honour, but I did not want to see you injured before our wedding day.'

'You are, then, looking forward to our union?'

The words fell softly into the air and, although their conversation was the object of much interest, Eleanor doubted if many had heard what he said. Yet some had, and her embarrassment was all the greater for the knowledge.

She lowered her eyes. 'No doubt as much as you are, lord!' she threw defensively.

Richard's smile faded. What did she mean? Surely she knew how much he longed for her! Was she eager, too? She wasn't indifferent to him, on that he'd take his oath! Or had she met his deep disinclination to unite her stock with his proud heritage with an unwillingness of her own?

His frown deepened. Many a Norman had wed a Saxon or the widow or daughter of a merchant for their gold, or beauty, or both, and without a qualm; so why was he so reluctant? Because of a prejudice instilled from birth! A prejudice which brought with it an attitude

cursedly difficult to change! Yet his father had managed
to overcome *his* qualms.

Will was at Noble's head, and Richard swung from
the saddle, only aware as his foot touched the ground
of just how much the hours of contest had weakened his
leg. Hiding a grimace of agony, he handed his lance and
helm to his squire. Even *he* was not foolhardy enough
to risk the hand-to-hand fighting of the mêlée. Without
strength in his leg he would be on the ground before he
had struck a blow.

He climbed up to the platform, where space was immediately made at Eleanor's side. Still uncertain of what
she had meant, Richard gave her a brief smile as he sank
down beside her.

He had purposely been avoiding close contact of late
because her near presence, her particular essence of clean
femininity spiced with herbs, was too unsettling. She
probably thought him a reluctant bridegroom, despite
that kiss which he couldn't forget. Confound it, so he
was! But he was committed now! And, by God, as a
lover he would be far from reluctant!

When Richard slid into the seat beside her, Eleanor's
whole body tensed. He smelt of sweat, damp wool, horse
and hot metal. Moisture beaded his brow. She had never
been so aware of his sheer physical magnetism as in that
moment of hard-won victory. She knew that his leg was
paining him, yet only the fine lines around his eyes and
the whitening around his mouth gave sign of his
suffering.

She watched the remainder of the tournament without
much interest, cheering when Richard cheered. The for-
tunes of the other knights were no longer of concern,
though the splendid pageantry at the end, as Richard,
as host, acknowledged the bows of both victors and vanquished, brought tears to her eyes.

It was as the last of the knights left the lists that
Eleanor felt a touch on her hand and, looking down,
found Tamkin anxious to speak to her.

'Where is Demoiselle Radcliffe, Tamkin?' she asked
anxiously, since there was no sign of Anne.

'She returned to her dorter with Mistress Joan.'

Lady Radcliffe clucked with annoyance. 'I suppose I'll have to go and see that she's all right,' she grumbled. 'Excuse me, my lord, Demoiselle Clare.' With a quick curtsey, she bustled her way through the throng.

'Mistress!' Tamkin tugged at her hand again, and Eleanor thought with regret that all his childish impulsiveness would disappear once the boy began his training as a courtly page. 'There's a man wishes to speak with you.'

'A man? What man?' frowned Eleanor.

'I don't know, mistress. He be come from afar——'

'The messenger!' exclaimed Eleanor. 'Where is he?'

She turned eagerly and gave a cry of incredulous joy. 'Cedric, is it really you?'

The crowd on the platform had almost dispersed, and she was able to climb down and run to where a young man stood smiling. 'Cedric!' she cried again, and threw herself into his ready arms.

Richard followed more slowly, aware that this must be the brother of whom Eleanor was so fond. He saw his future wife crushed against the broad chest of a brawny youngster with hair the colour of ripe wheat and handsome features split by a roguish grin. A stylish brown felt hat sat upon his head, he wore a cote-hardie fashioned from plain purple worsted, long green hose, and riding boots of finest cordwain. The cape of his yellow chaperon was slit into a fashionable fringe, while the hood, with its long liripipe, hung elegantly down his straight back.

Eleanor released herself from her brother's embrace and turned to introduce him, her eyes brilliant with happiness, her face shining with tender affection.

Richard felt a sharp pang of jealousy twist his gut. Why? he asked himself viciously. Because she looked at the boy in a way she'd never looked at him? What mire was he sinking into now? He gritted his teeth and prepared to be nice to the fellow.

'Lord,' gasped Eleanor, so excited that her breath was coming short and uneven. 'May I present my brother, Cedric? Cedric, this is the Earl of Wenstaple, Lord of Wenfrith! And, God and my father willing, my betrothed!'

Richard was leaning on his sword to ease the pain in his leg. He acknowledged Cedric's bow, and extended a civil welcome. At least the fellow was elegantly dressed, without the ostentation of his older sibling.

'You bring the betrothal contract?' he asked.

'Aye, lord. My father sends his greetings and consents gladly to your marriage with Eleanor, since she also wishes it.' He fumbled in the pouch suspended from his tooled leather belt and produced a roll of parchment. 'Here is the document, lord.'

'I thank you.' Richard took it from him, but didn't peruse the writing. It was signed and sealed and he knew the terms. 'We must find lodging for you within the castle. We are over-full at present, I fear.'

Cedric grinned, a cheerful smile which reflected his sunny nature. 'I shall be honoured to sleep in any corner, lord. I watched much of the tournament today, and envy you your skill with arms. How I longed to enter a challenge myself!'

'You aspire to knighthood?' asked Richard, trying to keep the haughty note from creeping into his voice.

'He has always longed for it, lord! Before he could ride he was tilting at the quintain from a wooden horse!'

'Aye, and I could beat all the others at it, too!'

'Then you'll have to try your skill here. I imagine you will stay to see your sister wed?'

'Oh, yes! You must stay, Cedric! Father would allow it, surely?'

'Aye, I have his blessing, sister. I am to stand in his stead at the ceremony.'

'I am so thankful! I had thought that no member of my family would be here to see me wed! I cannot tell you how glad I am to see you!'

As they walked back to the castle, Richard watched Eleanor's animated face with a queer pain in his heart, realising for the first time that she had not been truly happy, waiting alone at Wenfrith for her nuptials. And he desired an unhappy wife no more than he wanted a reluctant bride.

CHAPTER FIVE

'GODFREY brought back scathing tales of your/lord and his castle, sister, but it seems to me they were much exaggerated!'

Eleanor chuckled. 'You know Godfrey! His manners are never gracious! And it's true the Earl was not disposed to be pleasant when first we arrived. He had just lost his father——' murdered him? No! An unworthy, unwary thought! '—and suffers much from the wound in his leg.'

'I find him pleasant enough,' smiled Cedric, his blue eyes, so like her own, full of an admiration tinged with envy. 'How I would love to joust with his skill and panache!'

'It has always been your dream to become a knight, hasn't it, Cedric? I should hate to lose you to the wars in France, but such an ambition should not be beyond your reach when I am become Countess of Wenstaple. If father would agree, mayhap you could attach yourself to some knight as squire, and so win your spurs in due time.'

'Your husband's patronage would be useful,' murmured Cedric thoughtfully. 'Maybe he would sponsor me?'

'Godfrey warned you not to speak of our lineage?' questioned Eleanor anxiously. Cedric might be tempted to use it as an inducement...

'He told me of your unaccountable distaste for becoming a braggart!'

'Nay, Cedric, 'tis not that! But such a claim would make no impression, it would only earn his scorn. He despises the entire Saxon race.'

'But why, sister?'

'To him, Harold Godwinsson is no more than a treacherous upstart, little better than a peasant. 'Tis better to avoid the issue. I have too much pride in our heritage to offer it up to ridicule. If we ever gain his respect and acceptance 'twill not be through our birthright, but by what we ourselves are.' What a daunting prospect that seemed. Yet had she not often longed to be appreciated for herself alone?

'Never fear, sister, I take your point. Meanwhile,' he added gaily, helping himself to a large portion of venison, 'let us enjoy this feast!'

That night, with the pennons, banners, arms and colours of every knight present suspended from the rafters or pinned to the walls, the Great Hall was as gay as the tourney field. The flaming torches and candles shone on ladies' robes of velvet and silk in ruby and emerald, sapphire and topaz, white, silver and gold. The men wore tunics and surcoats to rival them in brilliance and cost. Glittering and bejewelled, the company sat at tables laden with food. Eleanor had ordered oxen, sheep, capons and geese either killed or purchased, and for days the men had been hunting boar and deer. Fresh fish had been caught especially for the occasion and the cooks had excelled themselves in creating tasty delicacies.

This was more the way it had been at the manor where she had trained, thought Eleanor with satisfaction. And with Cedric sitting on her right hand, her splendid lord in full regalia on her left, what more could she ask?

Hearing of the tournament, a group of travelling entertainers had arrived that day, and they kept the company amused with juggling, magic and ballads of stirring deeds. A jester raised guffaws of ribald laughter with his daring jokes and capers. The heralds were kept busy sounding fanfares as courses were presented, toasts drunk, and prizes distributed—prizes of armour and gold which Richard had provided from somewhere, and much of which he'd won back! As the entertainment grew boisterous and rowdy, Eleanor leaned towards him and spoke quietly.

'Lord, if you and your guests will excuse me, I would like to take my brother to my chamber. I long to hear news of home, and we've not yet had much time to speak.'

Richard frowned, reluctant to let her go from his side, yet unable to think of any reason to detain her.

'Aye,' he murmured gruffly. 'You will find it quieter there. But first, I must mark our official betrothal.'

At his signal, the herald sounded a fanfare. Taking her hand in his, Richard rose, lifting her to her feet. Bowing with courtly elegance, he placed a large ring on her finger. Looking down, Eleanor saw lilies and a castle engraved in the shape of the Wenfrith arms. A balas ruby glowed within its depths like a drop of blood.

She curled her fingers to stop the huge ring from dropping off. 'Thank you, lord.'

'It was forged for Jean d'Evreux, the first Lord of Wenfrith,' he told her gravely. 'It is a fitting sign of our betrothal.'

How apt was that ruby, thought Eleanor with a shiver, when the acquisition of honours like Wenfrith and so many of life's other gains had been—and still were—achieved by the spilling of blood.

'Lord,' she murmured, 'I am honoured.'

'In seven nights,' he reminded her softly, 'you and I will leave the revels together.'

He turned to the waiting company, a knot of anxiety in his gut. Everyone anticipated a wedding, but what reaction would there be to the confirmation of this forthcoming alliance? Would his vassals accept his choice, or look askance at the maid who would become his countess?

'Today, the betrothal between myself and the demoiselle Eleanor de Clare has been confirmed,' he announced in ringing tones. 'I ask you to drink to the health of your future liege lady!'

A cheer rose as the toast was drunk, and others followed: to him, to them both and to their future felicity. Eleanor stood at his side, smiling serenely despite the trembling he could detect in the hand still firmly clasped in his own. The enthusiastic reception of his news brought him both a sense of relief and renewed confidence. He motioned for silence.

'If you are able to stay, or to return later, you will be welcome to attend the ceremony here on the last day of April. We thank you for your good wishes.'

So there would be extra guests for the wedding after all! Eleanor's elation was tinged with anxiety at the thought of housing and feeding all these people for an entire week.

The Earl of Wenstaple should have married in the new cathedral in the heart of his earldom, but, with his father so recently dead, no one would question his decision to wed quietly on his manor.

Richard raised her hand to his lips. 'Go now with Cedric, in peace.'

Eleanor lifted her eyes, but her breath caught and she looked away quickly, aware of a brooding passion in the depths of his eyes which deeply disturbed her. Her hand moved spasmodically, and Richard released it at once.

He addressed Cedric. 'Your sister would have words with you now. I will speak with you tomorrow.'

Several days of cloud and drizzle had followed the tourney, but the thirtieth of April dawned fair. Joan and Tamkin were up before cock-crow, scouring the fields for primroses and bluebells for Eleanor's bridal wreath.

The day before the church had been decked with boughs of apple, plum and cherry, the rushes renewed, the coloured windows with their pictures of the blessed saints cleaned, the crucifix and candlesticks polished until they threatened the sun itself with their brilliance.

The castle had received another cleansing despite the number of guests. Eleanor had found the courage to ask Richard if she could hang the new bed-curtains, but he had shaken his head.

'Give them to me. I'll see to the solar,' he had informed her briskly. 'Stephen will oversee the work in the castle. He knows what has to be done. You rest while you may, my betrothed, and enjoy the company of your brother.'

Eleanor hadn't argued. Arguing with Richard was an exercise she preferred to avoid unless the issue was important. Things had been running smoothly indoors, and having precious time to spend with Cedric made up for not knowing exactly what was going on in her domain.

They laughed and rode together, defying the weather, whenever Cedric could tear himself away from the company of the soldiers or the hunt. His presence kept her nervous worries at bay. Richard was a stern taskmaster and suffered from dark moods, but after his first antagonism he had treated her with kindness and respect.

So why was she so nervous? She didn't know. Perhaps a mixture of a maiden's natural anxiety at her coming initiation into the ways of men, perhaps a lingering fear of his scorn and anger, perhaps even a barely acknowledged doubt that Tamkin's accusation held some element of truth.

'Demoiselle Eleanor,' whispered Anne, who had been helping Joan to deck the bride. 'You look so beautiful!'

'Aye, a sight for sore eyes,' agreed Joan with satisfaction, putting a last finishing touch to the wreath of primroses and bluebells where it nestled among Eleanor's hair, which hung unbound around her hips as a sign of her maidenhood.

She wore a creamy-white kirtle of finest sarcenet, covered by a surcoat of costly cream brocade richly woven with threads of gold, the bodice of which was encrusted with exquisite embroidery liberally set with seed pearls and tiny sapphires. Underneath, a matching girdle spanned her slender hips. From her shoulders hung a mantle of finest silk velvet of a colour to match her eyes. Its edges were bound with the brocade of her surcoat and its hem dragged the rushes in a small train. Her father had supervised the ordering of this gown, intended to demonstrate his wealth and enhance his daughter's beauty.

It did both. Eleanor smiled rather grimly. Richard should have no reason to feel ashamed of his bride. The gown would have graced the chancel of the new cathedral in Wenstaple splendidly, but would very likely look ostentatious in the small church dedicated to Saint Mary the Virgin in Wenfrith!

Escorted by Cedric, surrounded by chattering ladies who held her train out of the lingering mud, Eleanor walked the short distance to the church. As she drew near she saw Richard waiting, with Will and a group of knights standing near by.

He, too, was dressed in cream and gold beneath his crimson ceremonial gown, his knightly girdle and chaplet flashing fire as the sun caught the precious stones studding the gold.

If she was overdressed, so was he; but he had chosen to honour the occasion with costly raiment. His vassals would have no cause to criticise the manner of their lord's union with Eleanor of Clare.

Richard greeted her with a brief smile which dazzled her with its brilliance. She returned it with quivering lips. Richard took her hand and led her into the porch, where Sir Piers waited by the great oak doors.

Sir Piers spoke, asking Richard if he willed to have her to his wedded wife.

'Aye, sir,' he replied, his voice quiet, but firm.

'Will you do your best to love her and hold ye to her and to no other to your lives' end?'

'Aye, sir.'

'Then take her by your hand and say after me: ''I, Richard, take thee, Eleanor, in form of Holy Church, to my wedded wife, forsaking all other, holding me wholly to thee, in sickness and in health, in riches and in poverty, in well and in woe, till death us depart, and thereto I plight ye my troth.'''

Richard's voice did not falter as he repeated the words of the vow. Then it was Eleanor's turn, and although her voice shook, she said the required words with quiet conviction.

An enchased gold ring was pushed on to her finger in place of the great betrothal ring, which she had left in her chamber. Richard's fingers were cool as they touched hers.

Then the great doors of the church swung open and she walked with her new husband down the nave, past the rood screen to the altar rail.

A few of the more honoured guests found seats in the chancel and as many as possible crowded in to stand in the nave, which soon smelled not only of mutton fat from the votive candles at the Virgin's shrine, but also of human sweat and odours from the byre and sty carried in on the villagers' clothes. It was just like William of Evreux's funeral, except that more nobility were present. An acolyte with thick mud on his shoes scurried out of the vestry to join the altar boy, and Sir Piers began the celebration of the Nuptial Mass.

Soon the heavy fragrance of incense smothered out all other odours. Eleanor communicated, and knew that this acceptance of the Host was special. It sealed the

marriage vows she had just made. She glanced furtively
at Richard, and saw his face bent in grave reverence. His
knightly vows had been sealed in similiar fashion, and
he held them in deep respect. She need fear no light
acceptance of his duty to his wife.

The priest said the Benediction, and it was all over.
Richard lifted her to her feet and for a moment looked
deeply into her eyes. Then, swiftly, he pulled her to him
and covered her mouth with his.

In that instant Eleanor knew the same melting draining
of her strength which had come to her before, together
with an aching sweetness which brought a gasp of surprise from her throat. Richard's arms tightened to
support her and his lips firmed on her mouth. Then,
with a short, husky laugh, he thrust her from him.

'Now is not the moment for such sport, my lady
countess,' he murmured. 'Come and meet your vassals.'

Countess! Yes, she was, Countess of Wenstaple! But
it was not the possession of a title which brought the
colour to her cheeks, the wary pride to her eyes, but the
knowledge that she was wife to Richard d'Evreux, Lord
of Wenfrith.

And that he desired her.

Even the feast after the tournament had not been as fine
as the banquet which followed the wedding ceremony.
Richard—or more likely Stephen—must have scoured
the area to secure the bounteous food and the splendid
wine which flowed with such freedom and hospitality.

Eleanor ate sparingly of the rich dishes set before her.
Excitement and apprehension had robbed her of her appetite but made her mouth dry, so she sipped gladly at
the smooth, sweet wine in the mazer she shared with
Richard.

Every now and again, when their eyes met, he seemed
to be trying to convey some secret message of reassurance and promise. She had never felt so close to him
as she did that evening, yet when some of the ladies came
to lead her off to the solar to prepare her for the bedding
ceremony, all the careful rapport he had been building
crumpled in an instant.

This was reality! There could be no escape from the consequences of her decision to wed the Lord of Wenfrith now!

She was barely aware of the laughter, the chattering, the fussing, as she was made ready to receive her husband. Sat at last in the big bed—washed, scented, combed, dressed in her finest, most elaborately embroidered smock—she did notice that her curtains and coverings were in place, that sweet-smelling herbs had been strewn on the floor with the new rushes, and that a huge fire of aromatic logs roared up the chimney.

She hardly dared to look as Richard was brought in from his wardrobe by a bevy of knights to take his place beside her. Sir Piers spoke the customary prayers and blessing over them.

Anne was there, charged with the duty of laying posies of spring flowers on the foot of the bed. Will and other squires brought in cups of hot, spiced wine which were passed around. Sir Ralph Radcliffe, the senior knight present, lifted his on high and cried, "A health to bride and groom! I wish them a merry night ahead, with God's blessing and the gift of fertility!'

A great deal of laughter accompanied the drinking of the toast, some of it too ribald for Lady Radcliffe, who was all too conscious of Anne's tender ears. 'Hush!' she commanded with a frown, but no one, least of all her sturdy, grizzled husband, took the slightest notice.

Although it was quite a large room, with windows open to the sky, the solar seemed overcrowded and airless. The perfume of the violets in the posies combined with the aroma of crushed herbs to fill the atmosphere with a drugging heaviness. Eleanor clenched her cold fists under the covers and took several deep breaths, willing herself not to faint in the stuffy heat.

Sir Ralph leaned forward and kissed her forehead, tickling her with his long greying beard and bushy moustache. Then Cedric wrapped his arms around his sister's rigid form.

'Don't fret, sweet sister,' he whispered in her ear, 'for bed-sport is the most enjoyable of pastimes, and your lord looks at you with passion in his eyes.'

'Cedric!' she gasped, but her tension broke, the faintness receded, and she responded to her brother's broad smile and wink with a wavering curl of her own lips. The muscles knotted in her stomach began to relax.

The moment the last of the laughing party had departed, Richard slid from the bed, leaving Eleanor sitting shivering, wondering why she'd thought it so warm only moments before.

A wooden door had been fitted to the entrance to the solar in place of the tattered arras. Richard walked over and fastened it behind the departed guests, then snuffed all but one of the candles lighting the room. After that he moved to the fire and held out his hand.

'Come, wife,' he murmured. 'We are private now. You are cold. Warm yourself.'

He had retained his shirt, but the fine, loose garment hid little of his outline as he stood before the blazing logs. Blood rushed to Eleanor's cheeks as she climbed obediently from the high bed and reached for her chamber-gown.

'Nay!' Richard's amused chuckle broke through her confused thoughts. 'Come to me as you are, wife. We must learn to be comfortable together, and no one else will intrude.'

Slowly, she walked across the room and placed her fingers in his. Warm, comforting, the glow of his touch raced up her arm to reach her frozen heart, which began to pound as he sat her on the stool and threw himself on the rushes at her feet, leaning his head back against her knees.

Her whole body began to tremble. She kept her limbs still by a supreme effort of will. Nevertheless, Richard sensed her inner turmoil. He twisted around to lean his arm across her lap and looked into her face with a puzzled frown.

'Are you afraid of me, wife?'

'No, lord,' she lied. Or did she? Why was she so confused? Wanting to be held in his arms, yet dreading it, knowing that he was chivalrous and honourable, yet sensing in him also a certain ruthlessness and the ability to be cruel in battle. Yet what knight wasn't a mixture of these things? How else could he fight?

'Then relax!'

His arm across her thighs was making that quite impossible! However, Richard turned back to the fire, clasping his knees in his arms as he contemplated the flames, and her tension did diminish.

'Your brother is a pleasant young man, wife.'

He had chosen an impersonal subject to settle her down. He didn't understand why she was so nervous, but he'd never been with a sheltered virgin before. All his women had been experienced, far from shy. Yet not one of them had stirred him as much as did the maid who now was his wife.

'He admires you greatly, lord.'

'Because of my achievements in the lists, I believe! He's uncommonly well skilled with the lance and sword himself, for a merchant's son.'

Eleanor stiffened, moving her feet instinctively to throw off Richard's touch. He sprang up with an oath. 'Wife, I meant no criticism!' He hadn't, but he cursed his careless choice of words. 'I meant for one not brought up to knighthood!'

'Aye, lord. He cannot help being born son of a merchant, any more than Stephen can help being born a bastard! Knighthood is something Cedric has always longed to achieve,' she choked, as the tears gathered, tightening her throat.

'And so he shall!' Richard felt expansive, and wanted nothing to spoil their union that night. 'He can go to Sir Ralph as squire. His is soon to receive his spurs; he will need a replacement.'

Eleanor looked up, and the glow in her eyes, the smile on her lips, were reward enough. Yet they were not for him, but for what he could do for her cursed brother! The familiar pang of jealousy brought new determination to his approach, yet still he held himself in check, fearful of seeing rejection in those beautiful eyes.

He reached down and took her hands in his. 'Come here, wife,' he whispered softly.

Eleanor rose reluctantly, bemused by the look on Richard's face. 'Lord!' she protested as he drew her close.

'Husband!' he chided. 'Or Richard, if you prefer.'

'Husband!' repeated Eleanor obediently as fire shot along her limbs at the feel of his hands on her body, warm through the thin lawn of her smock. Stirrings, of which before she'd been only vaguely aware, began to grow as Richard's touch moved surely from waist to hip, from hip to shoulder. When he bent his head to cover her mouth with his, a sigh of expectancy escaped her parted lips.

His were warm, moist, demanding, yet tender. Again that tide of sweet helplessness swept over her, and with a small moan she lifted her arms to hold on to his body, a rock in a swirling world of wonder and delight.

Feeling her surrender, Richard uttered a grunt of satisfaction as his tongue tasted the delightful, honeyed cavern of her mouth. New shafts of fire, fierce as the forked lightning which rent the sky, took the last of Eleanor's strength. As she clung, boneless, uncomprehending, Richard swept her into his arms and carried her to the bed.

Before he laid her down he deftly removed her one remaining garment. When he joined her, after drawing the curtains tightly round their snug nest, he, too, was naked. This was no new thing, for it was usual to sleep so in a warm bed, and normal to share a bed, too—but with other women, not a man!

Such confused thoughts raced through Eleanor's mind as she felt the firm, sinewy hardness of Richard's body pressed close against her own rounded softness. She was breathing shallowly, quickly, but so was he, his heart thudding so loudly under her ear that she thought it must burst. Then his hands began to move again and she forgot everything in the wonder of his touch, in the piercing sweetness as his thumb roused her flaccid nipples to taut, erect life.

He kissed her, too. First her eyes, then the corners of her mouth. His lips travelled along her jaw, and the shock as his tongue thrust into her ear brought a gasp of surprise. Then he shifted, and his mouth was pressed to the throbbing pulse at the base of her throat. But it didn't stop there. Slowly, caressingly, it moved downwards until it found the softly swelling curves of her breasts. Lingering moistness remained in the valley between as his mouth at last found its target, the peak so expertly roused by his strong, sensitive fingers.

His teeth nipped gently, his tongue teased; then, as he began to suckle, Eleanor moaned in ecstasy. Her hips rose of their own volition to meet the invasion of his hand of the soft flesh between her thighs. His fingers probed, and Eleanor's breathing became harsh, short gasps of need. Writhing, panting, she clasped Richard's dark head to her breast with a moan of entreaty, though she had no real idea for what she was asking. Just for something, anything, to release the unbearable tension building in her exquisitely tortured body.

Richard moved again, parting her willing legs as he came over her, burrowing his face into the pillow beside her head as he answered her unspoken plea and thrust into the depths of her being.

Her pain was slight, swallowed up in a triumphant release and the knowledge that her husband's loving would be no duty, but an infinite joy. His cry of exultation was muffled, but to Eleanor it was a signal that for him, too, the begetting of an heir would be no unpleasant task. For a long moment he lay quite still, steadying his breath, and then began the long, exquisite journey to fulfilment.

As he moved inside her, Eleanor's arms closed tightly around his shoulders, her hips moving instinctively in rhythm with his. The tension built again, steadily, unbelievably exciting. Wave after wave of sensation washed over her, seeming to drain her strength, to reduce her nerves to quivering, shimmering inactivity, her brain to mindless acceptance of sheer sensuous pleasure. She lay supine, helpless under Richard's passionate assault.

The shudders began deep inside her. She felt him respond, quickening his pace, breathing harshly, and suddenly she was meeting his fierce thrust with a new ferocity of her own until the world seemed to be hit by a bolt from the sky and she was tossed high into the air before spiralling down, down, to find herself lying panting, with Richard's inert body slumped over her, his breathing harsh and ragged.

A deep tenderness swept through her. Was this the fearsome warrior knight, the stern Lord of Wenfrith?

She clasped his heaving shoulders and pressed a soft kiss in the hollow where his collarbone met his throat. She couldn't explain why, but she just had to keep on dotting hot, wet kisses on his damp skin, all over his shoulder, back to the sturdy column of his neck...

'Eleanor!' Her name was almost a groan as Richard at last stirred.

The sound of his voice brought reality swooping back to Eleanor, and, with it, panic. What had she been doing? What must he think of her abandoned behaviour? Ladies were not supposed... 'Lord,' she gasped. 'Forgive me——'

'Forgive!' He shot up on one elbow, a soft curse on his lips. 'Forgive? What must I forgive? You were a virgin. This proves that!'

He swept the curtain back and thrust aside the covers. In the dying glow from the fire the red patch on the linen sheet covering the goose-feather mattress stood out in vivid witness. 'Wife, what have I to forgive?' he demanded more gently.

Colour flamed in Eleanor's cheeks. Her whole body burned with shame. 'Lord, I... Oh, my dear husband, I was so immodest——'

Richard gave a great shout of laughter, closed the curtain, and plumped down to lie half on top of her.

'Wife, what have the old wives been telling you?' he demanded as he gathered her into his arms. 'That it is wrong to enjoy the marriage-bed? Because they found little joy in it, they would deny the pleasure to you, mayhap?'

'I—I thought it was only tavern-wenches, camp followers who...'

'I'll not deny they enjoy their trade, and give much pleasure in the process! But wife, who would choose to lie with a tavern-wench if he had such a wife as you?'

He kissed her gently on the forehead, and Eleanor felt a great surge of relief. 'Then you will not mind——'

He chuckled, deep in his throat. 'Sweet wife, I shall expect it!'

*   *   *

A chink in the bed-curtains told Eleanor that day had already dawned when she stirred the next morning. Richard had gone.

Stabbed by a surprising disappointment, Eleanor wondered where Joan was. She was usually bustling about the room when Eleanor awoke, and although now she would sleep in the chamber above the solar, which had been refurbished as Eleanor's own bower and from which her wardrobe and latrine led, Joan should surely be attending to her mistress by now. She had left a few necessities laid out for her use, but of Joan herself there was no sign.

Eleanor had a need to visit the latrine. Unless she wanted to mount the stairs, she would have to use Richard's, which meant passing through his wardrobe. Slinging her chamber-gown around her shoulders, Eleanor crept to the connecting doorway and peeped through, fearing to find Will tending his master, or at least his clothes or armour. The wardrobe had a door to the stair, through which he could have entered. But it was empty, so she hurried across to her destination.

She was almost back to the solar when Richard strolled in from the stairway. He wore a loose tunic of grey cendryn, and appeared to have shaved, since all signs of overnight stubble had disappeared from his cheeks and upper lip.

He grinned. 'My lady wife! God's greetings!'

His eyes were bright, he looked years younger. Eleanor's heart leapt and blood flooded her cheeks.

'My lord husband! I—I thought you were gone——'

'Only to bring victuals, wife. We will break our fast privately. Are you hungry?'

Eleanor suddenly realised that she was ravenous. She'd eaten almost nothing the previous day.

'Aye, lord! Is that meat?'

'Beef, and freshly baked bread, butter, cheese, a little pie and some sweetmeats. Come, let us go through to the solar and eat!'

The fire had been fed and stirred into new life. Richard must have done it. He seemed happy to fend for himself, and Eleanor supposed it came from years of camping out on campaign with only a squire to see to his needs.

She would certainly not complain if by serving themselves their privacy could be preserved!

'Joan and Will?' she queried. 'You have sent them away?'

'Last night,' he chuckled. 'They will appear here this morn on peril of death!'

Eleanor laughed, accepting a hunk of bread spread with butter and a thick slice of meat. For several minutes they ate in companionable silence, until Richard moved on his stool to pick up his mug of ale.

Eleanor's gasp made him swing back to see what was amiss. His eyes followed her horrified gaze and he shifted again, abruptly, wrenching his tunic together where the side slit had exposed his thigh.

'It sickens you?' he demanded harshly.

'No, husband.'

She had already ceased to notice the ugly scar which marred his brow, but the sight of the damage to his leg had taken her by surprise. The sheer size of the wound was frightening. A long slashing cut had sliced deeply through the muscle. The two edges had knitted together in a ragged join, leaving the muscle distorted by a thick line of drawn, tender skin, edged with proud, discoloured flesh.

Eleanor saw the taut, angry, frustrated expression on Richard's scowling face, the shadow in the eyes which only moments earlier had been sparkling with life and humour, and knew that if their relationship were to prosper she had to make him believe her.

Ruthlessly casting aside all her inhibitions, she slid to her knees beside her husband. Gently, she moved the edge of his tunic and placed her fingers on the wound. Stroking softly, 'You were lucky not to lose this leg, dear husband,' she whispered. 'This was a grievous wound.'

'Aye.' His voice was a low, angry growl. 'My stars were propitious, and with the help of a poultice derived from watercress the physician saved it. But——' He sprang to his feet. 'Damnation take it, Eleanor, I cannot use it as I did!'

He hadn't moved away, and as he stood the wound was right before her eyes. Acting instinctively, Eleanor slid the cendryn aside with both hands and pressed her lips to the raw-looking scar. 'Praise the Holy Mother,' she murmured, 'that you are alive and your leg so much recovered.' Then she laid a cheek wet with tears against his warm, damaged skin.

Richard stood rigid. Shock, sheer amazement and a kind of awe mixed with anger kept him standing stiffly while this lovely young woman wept for his wounds. His whole body jerked. God's blood! But did she pity him?

At his sudden movement, Eleanor stood. Reaching up, she pulled his head down and kissed the spot where the enemy's sword had cut through his eyebrow, and it was not pity that she saw in her clear blue eyes, but a shining faith, tenderness and admiration.

'Be thankful, husband, that you are alive.'

With a muffled groan Richard gathered her into his arms. His kiss seared her lips.

'I thank God, wife, that that Frenchman's sword did not make a woman of me!' he declared in ringing tones, and once more she found herself swept up in strong arms and carried to the bed.

CHAPTER SIX

THE sun was high when Eleanor stirred. Sleepily, she rubbed her fingers over the mat of dark hair on Richard's chest.

'The May Day revels will be over before we arrive, husband! We cannot disappoint the villagers!'

Richard captured her hand and took her fingers to his lips. 'You are right, wife. We should stir ourselves, though I confess I could lie abed all day with you to keep it warm!'

Eleanor chuckled, the new-found knowledge of her power over this autocratic lord giving her a confidence which she had lacked before. 'Call Joan,' she instructed her knight with a gentle push. 'We shall have plenty of time to be private again later!'

'Aye. We'll have our bridal days, never fear.'

He released her hand, sprang lightly from the high bed and strode naked to the door. Eleanor watched the

lithe figure, the broad shoulders, the lean hips, with a
shy pride which the sight of his dreadful scar only in-
tensified. She thanked God fervently for William's death,
then guiltily crossed herself and muttered a prayer for
his soul.

Richard unbarred the door to call for Will and Joan,
then disappeared into his wardrobe, where Will would
attend him. Eleanor slid from the bed as Joan appeared,
a kirtle of soft green kersey and surcoat of apple-red
worsted in her arms.

'The day is bright but the wind chilly, my lady,' she
explained, answering Eleanor's enquiring lift of the
brows.

'I had not noticed. But—"my lady"! That address
sounds strangely on your tongue, Joan!'

'You will have to get used to it, my lady, for that is
what you are! As for the chill, no doubt you've not had
the inclination to mind such matters! You found your
husband to your liking, sweeting?' she murmured archly,
with an impudence only long service and deep affection
could excuse.

Sweet memories and lingering embarrassment at her
own abandoned response brought the blood coursing
again to Eleanor's cheeks.

'Aye.' She let her loose hair fall forwards to hide her
flaming face. 'The marriage-bed is no unpleasant place.'

'And your wifely duty a pleasure, I'll be bound! Well,
there's no sin in that!'

Eleanor lapsed into silent reverie as she allowed Joan
to sponge her down with warm water and rub fresh herbs
into her glowing skin. With kirtle and surcoat over her
body smock, she sat quietly while Joan plaited her hair
and hid it under a thin veil kept in place by a circlet of
green velvet.

'The young men and maids were out before dawn,'
Joan told her as she put the finishing touches to her
work.

'Collecting wild flowers and boughs?'

'Aye. Since then they've been horsing around between
weaving the garlands and setting up the maypole. And
no one has been tormenting the young maids and stealing
kisses more enthusiastically than Master Cedric!'

'Oh, Joan, he always was a tease! He means no harm!'

'We know that, but does Demoiselle Radcliffe? It seemed to me he was causing her no little embarrassment!'

'I'll have a word with him,' sighed Eleanor. Much as she loved her brother, he could be a sore trial at times!

At that moment Richard strolled through from his wardrobe, resplendent in blue hose, a white tunic woven from wool and silk, and a warm, high-collared surcoat of russet frieze.

'Are you ready, wife?' he asked cheerfully, and Joan, taking one look at his relaxed, contented face, bent to whisper into Eleanor's ear.

'Methinks the enjoyment was mutual!'

All that day the village green was a scene of rejoicing. Playing any instrument they could lay hands on, singing, dancing, the villagers made the most of their holiday, celebrating not only the nuptials of their lord, but also the start of another summer when crops would grow, animals breed, and food be plentiful again.

Huge cauldrons of soup were brought down from the castle, together with fine white bread, pies and pasties. An ox roasted slowly over a wood fire, its tempting aroma wafting on the breeze over to dancers and spectators alike.

To the people of the village, after the sparse commons of the lean winter months, the prospect of a good meal brought added zest to the occasion, and the stewards had difficulty in preventing a stampede when the food was served from trestles set up under the maypole. Eleanor watched the villagers snatching up loaves of good white bread, various meats and tasty pies, drinking down the warming soup and quaffing the generous rations of ale and cider. For this one day, at least, they would have full bellies.

A performing monkey had been brought by a travelling showman, and the children and many of the women gathered round him while the men divided their attentions between a wrestling match and a cock-fight.

Eleanor had kept an eye on Cedric during the day and had seen how he paid court to the shy young daughter of the knight Richard had suggested he serve. Watching closely, Eleanor thought Anne not averse to his attentions—he was, after all, the most comely young man present, and his interest must be flattering. But she also noticed Lady Radcliffe watching with a frown on her usually cheerful countenance, and was not surprised when she called her daughter from the dance to sit beside her.

Richard had left his place on the bench at her side to cheer on a wrestling match between two of his retainers. Eleanor beckoned to her brother.

'You are being unusually attentive to Demoiselle Radcliffe,' she observed drily. 'Have a care, brother. She may take you seriously.'

'And what makes you think I am not serious, sister? Anne is a sweet maid. She would make me a fine wife.'

'Cedric! Don't joke! You know Sir Ralph would never countenance such a union! And what of your ambition to become a knight? Anne dislikes fighting men. She would turn from you in a moment if she knew!'

'You think so?' Cedric grinned cheekily. 'I think not, sister.'

'But you must desist! For your own sake, Cedric! Richard is to suggest to Sir Ralph that he take you as his squire. You will ruin your chances of that if you insist on pursuing his daughter.'

'Sir Ralph?' Cedric's eyebrows rose, and Eleanor saw the sudden interest light his irreverent blue gaze. 'Your lord would be my patron?'

'He said last night——'

'What bargain did you make last night, eh, sister?' Cedric's teasing eyes narrowed as he regarded his sister impudently. 'Did he have to pay for your favours?'

'No! Really, Cedric, you are insulting! We were just talking, and he mentioned that he thought you exceptionally skilled——'

'You talked of me on your wedding night? I *am* flattered! I'd have thought you would have been better occupied, sister!'

'Perhaps we were, later.' Eleanor tried to hide her blushes, but Cedric's twinkling eyes missed nothing.

'Richard is chivalrous, a man of honour and courtesy! You would do well to emulate him, brother!'

'Such a spirited defence after but one night! Methinks, sister, that you found my words true, and bed-sport to your liking! Beware, sweet sister, or you will fall in love with your noble husband!'

'Don't talk such nonsense, Cedric! Richard married me for my dowry, and I married him for his title! Had I not, I would have been at the mercy of my father's choice again! And Richard is at least no brutish drunkard! But, Cedric, heed my advice! Leave Anne alone, especially if you join Sir Ralph's household.'

'Aye, sister. Perhaps you are right. When do you think Wenstaple will speak?'

'Before the Radcliffes leave, without doubt. Will our father agree?'

'I believe so. He has spoken of buying me a knighthood, but I didn't want that. 'Twould be worthless. I must earn my spurs, sister!'

'I agree. Cedric, I thank God on your behalf! But have a care, brother. Bide your time. If you still desire Anne——'

'An she is not already wed or promised!'

Cedric sighed, and Eleanor realised that he had indeed been taken by the charms of Anne Radcliffe. But he would soon recover! His was but a young man's fancy, born of springtime and the romantic ballads sung by the minstrels in honour of her own nuptials.

If only marriage could truly be the subject of romance! thought Eleanor rebelliously. But romance, chaste romance, had to be found outside the ties of the unsentimental contract of marriage and the carnal desires of the marriage-bed. Her mind flew unbidden to the image of Sir Gilbert de Rede's fair, gentle countenance and her last sight of him as he had ridden away to join his King in France. A slight sigh escaped her lips.

'You are sad, wife?'

Sir Gilbert's features faded swiftly as Eleanor looked up to find Richard's dark face looming over her, a slight frown furrowing his brow.

'Not sad, husband,' she denied, smiling reassuringly. 'Just annoyed with my wayward brother! He is like to

damn his chances with Sir Ralph before you have spoken!
Have you not noticed how he sighs over Anne?'

Richard's features lightened immediately, and a mischievous smile curved his lips. 'Squires were always thus!
Languishing over some maid or other! He's just anticipating his future role!'

'I have warned him, lord——'

'Just as well. Do not distress yourself over the foolish
young swain, Eleanor. I'll speak to Sir Ralph tomorrow,
before they leave.'

'Thank you, my lord husband. I have been wondering... Think you Sir Ralph would agree to Anne
staying on here? I should enjoy her company, and she
could assist with the needlework...'

And be no temptation to Cedric...

'Aye, you need more ladies to be with you. I'll suggest
it. Do you wish to remain here longer?'

'Let us wait until the bonfire is lit, lord. Then we can
return to the castle and leave the villagers to enjoy their
revels without our presence to inhibit them!'

The following day most of the guests departed. Cedric
rode jauntily off to Colchester to arrange his affairs,
taking his father's remaining men-at-arms with him.
Eleanor's security was now her husband's concern.

Cedric would return within the month to serve as Sir
Ralph's squire at Radcliffe Manor, a fortified house
nestling in a sheltered spot behind a high cliff some three
leagues beyond the Wen.

Sir Ralph, his lady and his retinue, horses and all,
crossed the estuary by boat, ferried by the obliging
fishermen of Lower Wenfrith, who eagerly filled their
purses with his gold.

For the next three days Richard devoted almost all his
time to Eleanor, never straying far from her side. They
explored the cliffs and tiny sheltered coves and rode deep
into the forest. She soon learned that its shadowy depths
were not to be feared, as they followed delightful paths
and glades inhabited by fallow deer and all manner of
wild animals, not to mention the tenants' pigs and fowl.

'Isn't this where you caught the wild boar?' she asked
nervously the first time he took her there.

'Aye, they roam here. But there aren't many; we count ourselves lucky to find one when we hunt.'

'But outlaws and thieves? Aren't they a danger?'

'They inhabit the forests near much-used highways where the pickings are good! They'd not survive long on what they could steal from the few travellers passing here!'

'Yet there is plenty of food——'

'Aye, I'm not saying there aren't a few rogues about and it's as well to be careful, so don't venture here alone without a guard. But they're not the menace they might be.'

'That is good news indeed! This is such a beautiful forest! Just look at the sun shining through the tracery of the branches above! It reminds me of the nave of one of the great cathedrals!'

It was on the fourth day of their marriage that they came across a clearing which brought a cry of delight from Eleanor.

'Richard, it's beautiful! Let us rest awhile!'

Richard chuckled indulgently and dismounted. As she slid from her saddle into his arms, her breath caught. She felt the thudding of his heart under his surcoat and rested against his chest for a moment before moving from his embrace.

Richard slipped the reins of both horses forwards over their heads, knowing that they would not stray. They began to graze contentedly on the new grass springing up in the sun's warmth, while the hounds sniffed and foraged in the surrounding thickets. He turned to find Eleanor gathering wild flowers.

'See!' she cried. 'Primroses and violets that no one found on May Day! Come, help me to make them into garlands!'

Humouring her still, Richard obediently sat on a fallen trunk and began to weave a circlet of the delicate blooms. Eleanor finished hers slightly ahead, waiting for him to finish before leaning over to remove his cap and set her floral tribute on his head. He in turn laid his offering over the ribbon circlet already on her brow.

For a moment they stared into each other's eyes. Richard's were unfathomable, his expression unusually

stern and remote. He looked every inch the noble lord,
and although she knew she had nothing to fear from
him, Eleanor felt a strange, unaccountable, quite un-
reasonable return of her earlier panic. Her eyes widened
as she whispered, 'My liege lord!'

Richard muttered something inarticulate and, in what
seemed like one sweeping movement, flung his cloak on
the ground and tumbled them both down on it. Before
Eleanor had time to do more than gasp in bewildered
surprise he had taken her, quickly, angrily, almost bru-
tally. Mere moments later he lay heaving beside her, his
sudden passion spent.

A confused, churning mixture of conflicting emotions
prevented Eleanor from thinking clearly, but two things
stood out from the jumble in her mind. Her body had
been shamefully willing, had accepted him gladly, had
responded with an urgency to match his. Yet at the same
time her mind had rebelled at such a brutal, punishing
assault.

She rolled away, pulled her skirts straight and sat stiffly
on the bough, clasping her hands tightly together in her
lap to hide their shaking.

'Husband,' she said coldly, controlling her voice with
an effort. 'I had come to expect better treatment from
you!'

Richard, still breathing heavily, pulled himself to his
feet, planted them wide, and glowered down at her.

'How dare you criticise my treatment of you, wife? I
am quite within my wedded rights! I may take you how
and when I please!'

Eleanor felt as though he had slapped her in the face.
A sick sense of failure made her voice shake. 'I will not
be treated like a common tavern-wench!' she gasped.

Richard gave a bark of derisive laughter. 'Is that how
you think I'd treat a whore? An it was, how would you
prevent it?'

His temper had risen alarmingly, but Eleanor felt no
fear. The panic she'd known earlier had had nothing to
do with physical threat.

'I shall rely on your chivalry, lord!' she returned
sharply, and stood to face him, her body stiff with anger

and hurt pride, her eyes challenging him to dare to treat her with anything but courtesy.

'Aye,' he sneered, 'no doubt! I've been behaving like some lovesick squire! But what result has my care and consideration brought? Your eyes tell me that you are afraid of me! So why should I not give you something to fear?'

'Because such brutish behaviour is not worthy of a knight who has fought alongside the Prince of Wales!' she retorted icily.

That shaft hit home. She watched anger give way to cynicism. 'What do you know of war?' he demanded tiredly.

Despite her best efforts her voice began to shake. 'Only that it must be dreadful indeed if it can turn a man into a beast!'

Richard swore. 'Other things can turn a man wild, wife! If you would keep my regard, look at me as you do now, not with fear in your eyes!'

Eleanor's stomach churned anew. What had made her show such panic? There had been no cause! But Richard had calmed down. Now was her chance to mend matters.

'Richard!' she implored softly. 'My dear lord! You mistake me! I do not fear you! I have found much joy in your embrace. You must know that!'

He sighed. 'I had thought so.' The distant sound of the church bell penetrated the glade, announcing the hour of Nones. 'Come,' he said abruptly. 'Let us return. I have to ride to Wenstaple tomorrow. I can spare no more time for fruitless dalliance, but must return to my duties.'

So their bridal days were over. And in such a manner! Eleanor upbraided herself for that momentary lapse. She must keep her inner feelings, so deep, so little understood, well hidden in future; must guard her eyes and her words.

For she had no wish to spend the remainder of her life at odds with her husband, when mutual respect and tenderness were so clearly within their grasp.

She lay in the big bed that night awaiting her husband, but he did not come. He remained in his wardrobe where Will had been attending him.

Should she seek him out? No! She had apologised, tried to make him understand, only to have Richard spurn her overture. He'd caught the horses, called the dogs, and ridden home in brooding silence.

Over supper she had attempted to bridge the divide which had so suddenly yawned between them, but his replies to her remarks had been no more than polite. Further pleading on her part would only hurt her pride and do nothing to soften his.

She burrowed her face into the soft swansdown of her pillow to stifle the sound of her sobs, and soaked it with hopeless tears until she fell into an exhausted sleep.

Richard must have slept on a pallet in his wardrobe. When Eleanor stirred before dawn his side of the bed had not been used. She could hear the murmur of his voice and Will's as they prepared to set out for Wenstaple. Joan would come at a call, as she usually did, but Eleanor wanted to waste no time. Slipping on her chamber-robe and wrapping herself in a white miniver-fur mantle, she ran up the draughty stair to her bower.

'My clothes, quickly,' she cried.

Joan took one look at her mistress's reddened eyes and distressed face, signalled Anne into the wardrobe which lay over Richard's below, and pulled Eleanor against her ample bosom. 'What is it, sweeting?' she murmured, stroking the bright hair with a gentle hand. 'A lovers' quarrel?'

'Nay, Joan, more than that! But I must be ready to hand him the stirrup-cup! I cannot allow him to depart without wishing him God's speed!'

'There's warm water on the fire,' said Joan practically. 'Sit down while I bathe your face. Anne,' she called, 'find my lady's sapphire kirtle! And a clean smock!'

Eleanor dressed quickly. Leaving her hair loose, wrapping herself in the miniver mantle again, she sped down to the Hall to see that the mulled wine for the stirrup-cup was spiced to Richard's liking.

He appeared moments later, arrayed in full armour.

'Have you eaten, lord?' enquired Eleanor in a quiet, steady voice.

'Will brought me something. I did not expect to see you, wife.'

'I have the stirrup-cup. I wished to speed you on your way with God's blessing.'

'Then come.'

His men had eaten and were assembling in the bailey, adjusting girths and preparing to mount. The morning was dark, chilly and drizzling with rain. Nevertheless, Eleanor followed her husband down the steps to the yard and waited while he sprang into Noble's saddle. The huge chestnut pranced as usual, and Richard, with his normal skill, brought the charger under control. Then he reached down for the cup.

The rain had dewed her hair with droplets like diamonds. Joan had been unable to disguise the heaviness about her eyes, but they shone with quiet purpose. A new vulnerability touched the sweet curve of her mouth. Having spent a wretched night himself, Richard recognised the pain hidden behind her calm exterior.

A dull flush rose to his cheeks. 'God remain with you, wife,' he muttered gruffly.

'I shall look for your return, husband. When may I expect you?'

'I do not know. I must remain awhile on this visit; I've lingered here too long and have a deal of business to transact. I'll send a messenger ahead to warn of our return.'

'Then God and all his Saints be with you, my lord. Farewell!'

He held out the empty cup but, instead of giving it to her, clasped the hand which she extended to take it. Leaning down, he pressed the chilly fingers to his warm lips. A pulse leaped in Eleanor's neck, and he could feel the trembling in her hand. Tears glistened on her lashes, mingling with the raindrops, and she caught her bottom lip between her small, white teeth.

'Farewell, wife,' murmured Richard abruptly, thrusting the cup into her hand.

He raised his arm, the herald sounded a fanfare, and Eleanor watched what was fast becoming the familiar sight of Richard and his retinue heading off into the

sunrise. Only that morning the sun was tardy and
Richard disappeared into a damp, grey drizzle.

He was away for over two weeks. During that time
Eleanor busied herself about the castle, renewing her
attack upon the dirt and dinginess of the place.

Everything she did seemed to be achieved through a
curtain of pain. She could not banish Richard from her
mind. After the bright promise of those first few days
the crushing disappointment of his sudden change from
lover to harsh husband had come as a stupefying blow.

She tortured herself with the guilty suspicion that
perhaps her uninhibited response to his lovemaking had
lessened his respect for her, had made it possible for him
to treat her in so rough and careless a manner. She resolved to restrain herself in the future, to be less
responsive, less eager for his touch.

Yet she knew in her heart that the moment he came
near her again her bones would melt, her blood turn to
fire in her veins... He had never given her any reason
to doubt that he was happy with her response. And if
she denied him the pleasure he required might he not
seek it elsewhere?

Her thoughts ran around helplessly, like a mouse on
a wheel. Perhaps the separation was a blessing, she
thought despondently. Perhaps it would give time for
his mood to change. Perhaps he would miss her!

To her own surprise she found that she did miss him.
At night, alone in the big bed, her body ached for the
pleasure he had given her. But she also missed talking
to him, planning with him, asking his advice. He had
created his own niche in her life, and his going left an
unexpected void. In a castle teeming with people, she
was lonely.

The glass for the widows arrived, plain and coloured,
and the glazier's blows, as he fashioned the lead to fasten
it into the embrasures, rang around the Hall. While he
worked in the solar Eleanor slept in her bower, in the
bed which Anne normally used, while Anne and Joan
slept on pallets. The room was small for the three of
them, but Anne was reluctant to be banished to a
chamber on the far side of the castle. So they managed,

and the close contact enabled her to get to know Anne better.

The child was pleasant company, though to Eleanor's mind she was a little too squeamish, shrieking every time she glimpsed a rat or mouse. Eleanor disliked rats, especially in the profusion they enjoyed in the castle, but they were something one had to get used to, like cockroaches and biting insects. The struggle to keep such pests under control was a vain one.

However, there were so many rats running around the castle that even the fiercest of the cats was intimidated. Something had to be done. Having considered all kinds of possibilities, she eventually announced a bounty for every rat's tail brought to Hugh, who would keep a tally and arrange the payments in silver or in kind.

The promise of reward set men's minds to work. Many were the ingenious and amusing ways devised to trap and kill the rodents. A spirit of fierce competition arose among the garrison, though the castle varlets and the villagers were simply keen to lay their hands on some of the reward.

The captain of the guard, Sir Peter Barraclough, an elderly knight trusted implicitly by Richard to defend the castle in his absence, encouraged the sport when his men began applying their fighting skills to the problem.

'Good practice, my lady,' he chuckled at supper one evening. 'A moving target is just what the bowmen need! They've struck down above twenty of the devils today!'

'And still there are more! I wish they did not breed so fast!' Eleanor responded.

'Welladay! They'll not be running so freely around the castle and stables now!'

'Nor around the village. The fishermen say black ones leap ashore from the ships which pass up the estuary if they lie in too close. But those we've caught have been grey, haven't they?'

'Aye,' Sir Peter confirmed. 'But whatever their colour, we're well rid of the vermin if they offend the sensibilities of the ladies! In any case, they eat food needed by both man and beast, and leave no scraps for the dogs!'

'Are the men happy now the barracks have been scoured?'

'Aye, lady. The dorters in the gatehouse have never smelled so sweet! 'Twill not last long, especially when that other horde return to add their dirt! Leave men together without a woman's influence and they become as filthy as pigs!'

Eleanor laughed and turned to Stephen, who was sitting on her other side engaged in earnest conversation with Anne. She waited for a pause in their chat before she spoke.

'How goes the work in the fields, Stephen?'

'Well, lady. The new reeve is well able to supervise the work under my direction. If this warm weather holds we shall have an early harvest.'

'Good. And I see the revenues have improved under the new bailiff.'

'Aye, lady. My brother will be well pleased when he returns. You've had no word?'

A shadow crossed Eleanor's face. 'Not yet.'

'I am surprised he neglects so new and lovely a bride.'

Eleanor's eyes flew to his face. His expression was bland, but there had undoubtedly been condemnation in his words. 'Guard your tongue, sir!' she snapped. 'What your lord does is of no concern to you!'

Stephen bowed his head, acknowledging her rebuke. 'Except when it directly affects me. I spoke out of sympathy, sister. I know how much his prolonged absence hurts you.'

Eleanor writhed at his familiarity, yet could not openly pick a quarrel. She had been impressed with Stephen's bearing at the manor court, but since his elevation he was inclined to presume on his position.

'His duty to King Edward must come before every other consideration,' she retorted coldly.

'Naturally, sister,' he returned with a dismissive shrug.

He despises me! realised Eleanor with sudden anger. He who, although he resembled his half-brother, could not hold a candle to Richard in dignity or strength of character!

Was this why, although they were alike, Richard could awake in her those strange reactions which had culminated in the ecstasy of the marriage-bed, while proximity to Stephen left her with a feeling of distaste? Was this why, although she suffered those sudden fits of panic in Richard's presence, she sometimes felt real fear when Stephen was near?

Thinking about it dispassionately, his abandonment of Tamkin to the mercies of the castle churls had not been the action of a caring brother. And although the news of improved output and revenues was cheering, Joan reported a rising resentment among the villagers which was being reflected in the kitchen gossip. The promise of better things under the new regime had quickly turned sour. Stephen had changed from defender of their rights to a ruthless driver of steward, bailiff and reeve to exact the utmost in work and levies from the tenants.

Perhaps it was necessary. Perhaps he was just showing loyalty to his brother. She didn't know, and although she had ultimate authority, she was not sure enough of the rights and wrongs of the affair to intervene. So she kept an uneasy silence and waited for Richard to return, wondering how he would react when he found out.

His messenger arrived at noon one day soon after. The kitchen immediately swung into new life, preparing supper for the increased numbers, and concocting something special to tempt the lord's appetite.

The long wait was over. Eleanor dressed with great care, her mind in a new whirl now that the dreaded yet anxiously awaited moment had come. Her heart twisted painfully at the sight of her husband striding into the Great Hall some hour before supper, a familiar stranger.

Searching his face for some sign of his temper, Eleanor saw new tight lines around his mouth and eyes. Eyes which refused to meet hers as he took her hand and lifted it to his lips.

'I trust I find you well, wife. Give me time to discard my armour and I will join you in the solar.'

He turned away and Will began to unstrap his greaves.

'Tamkin.' Eleanor spoke low to the page, who followed at her heels like a faithful puppy. 'Bring wine and goblets to the solar. The Lord of Wenfrith will doubtless require refreshment.'

CHAPTER SEVEN

WHEN Richard appeared at the door Eleanor was waiting alone with the wine already poured. She held out a brimming horn goblet.

'You must be in need of this, lord.'

Serving him with refreshment gave her something to do, something to say to bridge the awkward gap of reunion. Her heart beat fast as he took the cup from her hand.

'Aye, travelling is thirsty work.'

He quaffed the beverage with a grunt of appreciation, while Eleanor retreated to sit on a coffer under a newly glazed window embrasure. The lines of strain apart, his face showed little sign of exhaustion; the ride had taxed his leg less than previously and he had put a little more flesh on his bones over the past month.

'Come here, wife!'

Lost in critical contemplation of her husband as she was, his sudden command made her start. She quickly covered her slip, afraid that he would misinterpret a natural reaction. She smiled a warm smile of welcome, rose, and crossed to where he stood.

For the first time since his return he met her eyes. His were bleak, but with an inner bleakness she knew had nothing to do with her present behaviour. How she longed to see his eyes warm and tender again!

Remembering his passionate yet sensitive lovemaking, she refused to believe that the joy they had shared could have incited such brutal treatment! No, it had been her show of panic, nothing else. Like so many fearless men, he despised the emotion in others. And unlike those to whom cruelty and domination gave pleasure, he could not bear for those close to him to wilt beneath his tempers. Whatever the cost to pride or modesty, she must make the first move towards reconciliation. Without a word, she lifted her arms and wound them around his neck.

His breath caught as, unwillingly it seemed, his limbs moved to encircle her yielding body. He held her loosely as he scrutinised her face.

'You are glad to see me, wife?'

'Aye, lord. I have missed you these past weeks. You are looking well.'

'And you.' His thumb found the dark shadows under her eyes. 'Though it seems you have not slept too well while I've been absent,' he observed gruffly.

'And you have grown new lines, my dear lord.' She touched the signs of strain with a gentle finger. 'Why have we punished each other so? We seemed like to become a happy couple until——'

He pushed her from him abruptly. 'Until I lost control!' he threw at her forcefully. 'But, wife, you tried me too far!'

'I know, Richard. And it was for no reason that I can discover! You must forgive a woman's frailties! I do not even understand myself!'

'And yet it seems that deep in some dark recess of your mind you do fear me! I did not want an unwilling bride and I cannot tolerate a shrinking wife!'

She had been right! She picked her words carefully, knowing that their future together might depend on them. 'Husband, I do not fear you! My sudden panic I cannot explain, but it had nothing to do with fear of you! You can be fierce, you can be arrogant and you can fall into dark tempers, but these things do not give me fright! I know you would not willingly harm me!'

'Nay, wife, that I would not.' He drew her to him again and this time bent his head to kiss her. So gentle was the touch of his lips, so brief, that she was left feeling cheated.

But Richard was opening his pouch and fumbling inside. He brought out a golden ornament, which lay in the palm of his hand, sparkling with precious gems, a huge sapphire at its centre. A sapphire for constancy! Did he realise that?

Upon her gasp of surprise he moved to open the fastening of the brooch. Her eyes flew to his, but his lids were lowered as he fumbled with the catch. The next moment he had stuck the pin through the soft material of her gown and fastened the brilliant jewels on her breast.

'Richard!' she whispered. She knew that it was a peace offering and that he had come as near as he was able to apologising for his treatment of her in the forest. 'My lord! I do not deserve such a magnificent ornament!'

'You are my wife!' he responded with a slight return of haughtiness. Then his arms tightened around her again. 'Eleanor!' he groaned. 'I have longed for you!'

His strangled tone told her that the words had been torn from him against his will. The thud of her heart quickened as her arms rose again to hold him.

'And I for you, husband,' she admitted quietly, pressing her lips to his smooth cheek. 'Thank you for the brooch. I shall treasure it always.'

He drew her tightly against the hardness of his body and kissed her deeply, bringing back all the breathless anticipation of those first heady days.

'Supper awaits us,' she reminded him when he released her lips. 'But we have the night ahead!'

'Wanton wench!' he growled. But his voice held no censure, just a husky, amused tolerance. His eyes had lost the gleam of desire and they laughed into hers as he released her. 'I'd better change!'

'Don't call Will, I can help you.'

'If that is your wish, my wife,' he returned softly.

'I must stretch Midnight's legs! Will you ride with me, wife?'

Eleanor yawned lazily, happily sated after a night spent with Richard's strong body lying close beside hers. Yet as full awareness returned, a small prick of disappointment pierced her bladder of content.

Richard had been as ardent in his loving as ever, but through it all she had sensed a mental withdrawal. All was not as it had been. He was holding slightly aloof, not allowing himself complete abandonment to the pleasure she could give him. It was slight, but it was there, and it hurt. And he did not wish to linger in bed.

She sat up quickly and slid to the floor. A ride would blow away the doubts, for surely they must be in her imagination!

'Aye, husband,' she rejoined gaily. 'I swear Silver has missed the company on our rides!'

Half an hour later, as the sun rose ahead, they galloped together along the cliffs, Richard holding Midnight in slightly to measure his pace against that of the smaller horse. Silver was a fast little mare, but no match for the huge stallion, who was built for speed just as Noble was built to carry the weight of armour. Battle-trained, the destrier was Richard's war-horse, Midnight his hunter. Richard loved both beasts, Eleanor knew, and so did she. Only her own Silver rated higher in her affections.

A joyous laugh rang out over the land and echoed across the sea as, hoofs thudding, clods flying, the horses raced side by side. She had not bound her hair and the sensation of speed as it streamed out behind in the wind brought an exhilaration she knew could become an addiction.

'We must do this every morning!' she cried.

'So we shall,' laughed Richard. 'Unless we have more pressing or enjoyable calls upon our time!'

She knew what he meant, and new colour tinged cheeks already flushed with fresh air and exercise.

Silver was blowing, and Richard reined in to a gentle walk so that she could do the same. Eleanor cast her eyes along the range of cliffs and coves, out over the sparkling sea, inland towards the gentle slopes and distant hills, and sighed in contentment.

'Richard, don't you love this place? You were born here. It must surely be in your blood!'

'I think it is. I didn't realise how much so until I returned. Look! See the cormorants on that rock? And yonder, over the estuary! A heron!'

'I saw a sparrow-hawk the other day. I notice the mews are empty. Your father did not enjoy hawking?'

'No, and I've no liking for the sport. I was offered a peregrine in Wenstaple, but refused it.' He paused, eyeing her sideways. 'If you would like a merlin I will arrange it.'

'I don't. I've disliked birds of prey ever since a squire at the manor where I served had an eye pecked out.'

'Then we are agreed. The mews remain empty! Can you use a bow?'

'I tried once, but I could not bend it and my shaft bedded itself in the ground and fell two yards in front of my feet!'

Richard chuckled. 'I'll have the bowyer make you a weapon you *can* bend! Then I will teach you to hunt wild game. That is better sport than falconry!'

'Many would disagree with you, but not me!'

'The horses are rested. I'll race you to that tree!'

He waved towards a windswept birch growing on the edge of the cliff. Eleanor laughed, kicked Silver into a gallop, and leaned over the mare's neck. The palfrey struggled gamely, but, although Richard gave them a few yards' start, he and Midnight arrived at the mark well ahead.

The tree's buds were bursting and soon its inland-leaning branches would be blanketed in silvery green. The thicket of gorse behind was ablaze with golden-yellow blooms. Richard sat quietly waiting for Eleanor to arrive. As she reined in beside him their knees touched and he leaned across to lightly claim her lips.

'A forfeit!' he cried. 'I demand a forfeit! What shall it be?'

'You've just claimed one, my lord!'

'A kiss?' he scorned. 'I can have one of those at any time I choose!' He sat grinning for a moment, enjoying her mock indignation, then his hand flashed to his belt and his knife appeared. 'A lock of your hair! That shall be your forfeit!'

'No, Richard, you'll ruin it!'

'Not I! Be still!'

Gravely, carefully, he cut from underneath, where the loss would go unnoticed. Then he wound the strands around his fingers and tucked the curl into his pouch.

Eleanor sat quietly while he took his forfeit, not averse to the idea that he should want to possess a lock of her hair. The lover-like gesture increased her hope that the past was behind them and that henceforth they would settle down into a comfortable relationship spiced with passion and even affection.

They rode back quietly, enjoying the early morning freshness. As they crossed the drawbridge Richard's mood abruptly changed. A scowl descended on his features.

'Where is everyone?' he growled. 'Is the entire guard still abed?'

The bailey was virtually deserted. A few men moved around near the stables, a number of geese waddled in formation towards the gatehouse and the moat. Richard spurred Midnight through the archway and cursed as a bowstring twanged and the angry hiss of an arrow brought him up short.

'What devil's work is this?' he roared. 'Mutiny?'

'Nay, lord!' Eleanor hurried Silver alongside. She pointed across towards the grain store. 'See, they have killed a rat!'

The grey goose-feathers still quivered on the shaft which had impaled the twitching body. A warning voice roared, 'Fast!' and Richard swung round to glower up at Sir Peter Barraclough, who stood on the battlements with most of the men. Like them, he held a bow with arrow knocked.

'May I ask,' snarled Richard, 'what in Hades you think you are doing?'

'Archery practice, lord,' returned Sir Peter imperturbably. 'At moving targets.'

'God's blood! A dangerous sport! How many men have you killed as yet?' he was asked sarcastically.

'None, lord. Herald sounded the warning. But of course, you did not hear it.'

'Neither would anyone else from far outside these walls! Why did the gate-ward not warn us?'

'I don't know, lord. He will be punished.'

'By Lucifer!' Richard was not to be easily placated and his voice took on a heavily derisive tone. 'What put this ludicrous idea into your head, addle-pate?'

'I did, lord.'

Eleanor's strangled voice was barely audible. He swung round to pin her with his glare, just as the rat was pinned by the arrow. She swallowed, meeting the furious ridicule in his eyes with a sinking heart. But she couldn't allow Sir Peter to bear the brunt of his anger, though in truth he appeared quite unconcerned by his lord's wrath.

'Why?' The word rapped out. 'Never mind!' He wheeled his horse to face to Sir Peter again. 'Stop this nonsense at once, fool! Groom! Take our mounts! Come, wife!'

Eleanor picked up her skirts as he grasped her arm in a bruising grip and hustled her inside, across the Great Hall where servants gawped in astonishment, and up to their solar. She ran at his side, her legs trembling, heart thudding, deep indignation burning in her breast.

He had no need to leap to such damning conclusions! Her plan had been a good one!

'Lord,' she gasped when at last he stopped. 'Your temper will not deflect me from my purpose! One way or another I intend to clear this castle of vermin, or as nearly as may be, and I've enlisted the help of every person on the manor! True, I didn't instruct the archers to use their skills in the matter, the suggestion was theirs, but I thought it a good idea!'

'What other means are being used, pray? Are the men-at-arms fighting these monsters with swords?'

'Aye, lord!' admitted Eleanor defiantly. 'An they can slay them inside the castle! The varlets are building traps, and so are the tenants. Mayhap we can clear the village, as well. I am paying a bounty for each tail brought to Hugh,' she added with rather less assurance.

Richard sat down very suddenly. Eleanor watched, fascinated, as his lips twitched. Then a grin split his face. 'You dislike rats so much, my lady?' he drawled.

'They make my flesh crawl! But they really frighten Anne. And there were so many, and they are so bold,' she finished helplessly.

Richard's chuckle came like the promise of a warm fire on a freezing night. 'Target practice on rats!' he crowed. 'Mayhap Sir Peter's idea was not so bad after all! But the sport must be kept within bounds! I'll speak with him!'

He sprang to his feet and charged from the solar, still chuckling.

Eleanor sank down on the coffer and closed her eyes. Her whole body was trembling with reaction, but her heart was singing.

*   *   *

The next morning, after a gallop along the cliffs, Richard drew Midnight to a halt and dismounted, throwing the reins over the stallion's head.

'Come, Eleanor. I'll teach you to shoot rats!'

His teasing tone brought an answering smile to Eleanor's lips. Once he had seen the funny side of the situation he had taken charge of the rat hunt himself, decreeing that the live target practice should only take place once a week, at a time when normal duties would not suffer. Of course, his retainers were still free to use their ingenuity in their own time, and the sight of men stalking their prey throughout the castle had already become familiar.

She slid from her saddle, threw her own reins over Silver's head, and stroked the silky nose lovingly before planting a kiss between the animal's soft brown eyes.

'Be patient,' she commanded, and turned to where her husband was occupied in stringing a bow made of the finest yew.

Shorter and somewhat more slender than those used by the archers, it bent easily under his strong hands. Excited at the prospect of actually being able to send a shaft winging through the air towards its mark, Eleanor watched eagerly. She had always longed to be skilled with the bow.

'Now all we need is a target! This stump will do. If I can teach you to sink an arrow in that from ten paces, I'll be well pleased with my morning's work!'

'You are over-confident, my husband! I shall take longer than an hour or two to aim well enough to hit so small a mark!'

'Nonsense! Come here!' He buckled a leather guard over the tightly buttoned sleeve encasing her left arm. 'A necessary protection,' he remarked drily. 'The string can cause damage if it hits your flesh.'

The feel of his arms around her, as she held the bow while he placed his gloved hands over her kid-encased fingers on wooden bow and silken string, tempted Eleanor to lean back against his strength. But Richard had his mind on serious business. Ignoring the warm breath on her cheek, which sent delicious shivers down her spine, she pulled herself together and concentrated hard on what he was telling her.

'Put your feet so, sideways-on to the target. Now push with your right arm and pull with your left. Use your shoulders! Straighten your elbow! That's better! You'll find the draw easier as you practise. Are your fingers against your cheek?'

'Yes,' said Eleanor breathlessly.

'Then let them relax. Allow the string to go!'

He removed his hands in the instant that she followed his command. The silken threads snapped forwards to smack loudly against the leather shield, the bow wavered and almost flew from her hand.

'Not bad, but you weren't holding the bow upright. Try again.'

His patience astonished her. When at last he thought she was ready, he took a short arrow from the quiver at his belt and knocked it on the string.

'Now,' he instructed. 'Draw the bow, exactly as I've taught you. Keep it upright! Look along the shaft. Keep steady! Is it pointed at the stump?'

'Yes,' breathed Eleanor.

'Then loose!'

A twang, and the arrow hissed away, missing the target by yards, travelling on to bury its steel pile in the ground well beyond the stump.

Richard laughed. 'Methinks your aim was a little wild, my wife! But you'll not take long to learn.'

'It flew further than two yards!' cried Eleanor exultantly.

'We'll be hunting together before the leaves begin to fall!'

'But I can ride with you before then?'

He grinned. 'Wife, could I stop you?'

Thereafter, when he was at Wenfrith, he devoted the first couple of hours of each day to riding with her and giving her archery practice. But for the rest they met only at meals, coming together again at night in their solar.

He was occupied with training, with overseeing justice, with inspections and the thousand and one other things necessary to the smooth running of a defensive force.

Messengers travelled almost daily between Wenfrith and
Wenstaple, taking instructions and bringing back news
of the garrison there. Occasionally Richard himself
undertook the round journey, arriving home more weary
and in more pain than he was prepared to admit. Then
his temper was fragile, so Eleanor took care to see that
his comfort was assured and that problems which could
wait were shelved.

The day-to-day running of the manor he left to
Stephen, and Eleanor kept to herself her reservations
about the way his half-brother was doing the job. Things
seemed to be running smoothly enough, he had taken a
great burden from Richard's shoulders, and she had no
wish to disturb the peace which existed between herself
and her husband.

She, too, was kept busy. Sometimes accompanied by
Anne and Joan, always protected by a couple of men-
at-arms, she visited the villagers most weeks to make
sure that the spare food from the kitchen was reaching
them and that they lacked no essentials, including po-
tions and poultices for their ills. The remainder of her
days were filled with overseeing the household, spinning,
embroidering and working a large tapestry for the solar.

In this last occupation she was helped by Anne and
Joan. The three women spent long hours of daylight in
the bower, stitching the intricate design which Eleanor
had sketched on the canvas. The black horse was almost
complete, the knight on his back, caught in the act of
spearing a boar, taking shape. He, of course, wore a
surcoat emblazoned with Richard's new arms. All
around were scattered the emblems of his rank and
achievements. This was a work extolling her lord, but
he had not seen it yet.

'Farewell, husband!'

Eleanor handed Richard the stirrup-cup with a brave
smile. He was off again, leaving her behind. Surely if
their closeness were as real as she had thought over the
last weeks he would have taken her with him? There was
no reason why she shouldn't stay at Wenstaple Castle,
and she did not want to be parted from him, especially
now.

She was almost sure she was with child, since twice she had missed her courses. Because of this she felt a strong need to remain close to her baby's father until she was certain, when they could rejoice together.

But on this occasion Wenstaple demanded more attention than Richard could give it on a day's swift visit, so he would be staying for longer. Not for as long as previously he had promised, when she had tentatively asked if she could accompany him. She could have told him of her hope, of course, but then he would probably have forbidden the journey in any case. It would have given him the excuse he lacked.

In the absence of a valid reason for his refusal, he had resorted to a dictatorial stance which Eleanor found distressing after their weeks of quiet accord.

'You would delay us,' he had told her curtly. 'Besides, your duties here would be neglected!'

'Am I then never to leave this castle? Am I a prisoner here, lord?'

'Don't be ridiculous! You shall visit Wenstaple one day, but this is not the time. Do not let us quarrel, wife,' he'd added more gently. 'I shall be looking forward to my return, which will be within the week.'

'Then I shall await it with what patience I can!' she'd retorted quietly. The last thing that she wanted was to become estranged from Richard. Besides, she knew his true reason for denying her the chance to travel with him. He was still ashamed of their union. So far her attempts to make him proud of her had failed.

The depressing knowledge hurt deeply, after all they'd shared. But once the child was born . . . especially if it were an heir . . .

'Take care, husband,' she admonished as he handed her back the cup. 'The mist coming in from the sea is obscuring the path!'

'It will disappear once we reach the forest, and will clear here before long. You will doubtless enjoy a blazing summer's day! Do not fear for me, wife. Take care of yourself.'

'God go with you, Richard.'

'And remain with you. Farewell, wife!'

She could hear the sound of hoofs long after the column of horsemen had disappeared into the mist, and stood in the bailey feeling stupidly depressed. But Silver was waiting! A ride would clear her head and restore her spirits.

With a light step she made her way round to the stables.

'Groom!' called Eleanor. 'I see my mare is saddled ready, but where is Roger Lawtie? He must ride with me.'

Richard had detailed two of his men as her body-guards. She preferred Roger to the sullen Walter Hendy. Wat always made her feel that looking after her safety was a burden he resented. Roger, on the other hand, was always cheerfully ready to ride with her wherever she wished to go. Normally both men would accompany her. But for a quiet gallop along the deserted cliffs so early in the morning Roger would be ample protection. There was no danger there.

The groom hurried off to find her escort. Eleanor adjusted the girth herself while she waited for Roger to join her. He had not expected the call, and arrived still gnawing the meat from a bone. Throwing it down for the dogs, he bowed his greeting.

'My apologies, lady! I had scarce expected a call this morning! Are you sure you wish to ride in this mist?'

His rugged, weathered face held nothing but concern for her welfare, and Eleanor's heart warmed to the man. Sturdily built, and expert with sword, mace, knife and bow, he had shown from the first that he admired his lord's new wife and held her in great respect. She smiled warmly at him.

'Quite sure! I need to blow away the cobwebs which seem to have woven themselves in my head! And I am quite used to riding in all weathers with my lord!'

'Aye, lady.' He grinned. 'I hear you are a creditable markswoman now. But you will not be able to see any target this morning, that I'll warrant!'

'Who told you that?' asked Eleanor as he helped her to mount. 'I have not yet tried my skill in front of any but my husband!'

'He boasts of the speed with which you learn, lady.'

Does he? thought Eleanor in some surprise, and kicked Silver into movement.

With Roger at her heels, she eased Silver into a canter, glad that she had thought to wrap herself in a light woollen cape which would keep out the damp without being too warm. She pulled the hood further over her head, not caring that her sight was partially obscured because both she and her little mare knew the cliff ride so well. Silver could find her way without any guidance from her!

Roger's gelding was not as fast as Silver, and she could have left him far behind, but she did not want to ride hard with the possibility of a baby growing in her womb. The muffled thud of his horse's hoofs a few yards behind were a comforting accompaniment to the sound of Silver's dainty strides.

A figure appeared suddenly out of the mist, making both horse and rider jump. A grey, ghostly apparition, shrouded in a flapping cope, who let out a high, nightmarish, wailing shriek, scaring the gulls into raising an alarm which echoed eerily around the cliffs.

Eleanor gasped in sudden shock and at the same instant Silver reared up, almost unseating her. The mare shied frantically, got the bit between her teeth, and Eleanor lost a stirrup. She heard a string of oaths leave Roger's mouth as he attempted to catch up and grab her bridle, but Silver was a speedy little mare when she wanted to be, and his horse's hoof-beats gradually fell further behind. During the wild ride which followed the only thing that Eleanor could do was to cling on to her horse's neck and pray.

For a while she was content to let Silver run herself out, leaning forward and keeping as still as possible in the saddle. But suddenly she remembered! The cliffs were not straight further along! A deep indentation had been worn into the face of the rock and, though normally the mare would have picked her way around the chasm, now she was bolting straight for it!

If they went over the edge they would land on the rocks below and both be killed. If she threw herself off Silver's back she would as likely suffer the same fate.

'Whoa, Silver, stop!' she whispered desperately. 'Oh, Blessed Virgin, help me!'

But even through her panic Silver sensed danger. Suddenly she snorted, stopped in her tracks, reared, wheeled, and, without further pause, set off inland. For Eleanor, the manoeuvre was too swift, too unaccustomed. The mare seemed to gyrate in mid-air and in the struggle to retain her seat Eleanor lost her other stirrup. Desperation lent strength to her arms, but it wasn't enough: she was catapulted from the saddle and knew a peculiar, timeless sensation as she sailed through the air.

As she went down her body twisted. An agonising pain rent through her as her shoulder hit the ground. A scream of agony tore from her throat. Even as the darkness engulfed her, she knew that she was losing her baby.

Dimly, she had heard Roger's frantic cry, and had returned to vague consciousness to find him lifting her tenderly and putting her on his horse, mounting behind her, and setting off for the castle with her cradled in his arms.

'Did you see it?' she whispered faintly.

'See what, my lady?'

'The man! Or was it an apparition? The grey friar who frightened Silver!'

'Nay, lady. It must have been your imagination! A swirl of the mist, perhaps——'

'But the scream! You must have heard him cry——'

'Gulls, my lady,' said Roger flatly. 'I don't know what scared your horse, but I saw nothing.'

Eleanor was in too much pain to argue. She lapsed into silence and semi-consciousness until they reached the bailey.

Back in the castle, through her pain and despair, she heard the cries of concern, the bustle of activity, felt Joan's hands undressing her. She knew that the village midwife had been called in to staunch the flow of blood. But she knew nothing of the messenger setting off, as though all the hounds of hell were after him, to try to catch up with Richard.

Eventually some semblance of peace returned and she sank into a healing sleep. She surfaced again aware of

voices, of gentle hands bathing her face, of a familiar
voice coming from the wardrobe.

'Richard?' whispered Eleanor.

'Hush, sweeting. He'll be here in a moment.'

'I lost my baby.'

'Aye, sweeting. You gave us all a fright, I can tell you!'

'Eleanor!'

Suddenly Joan's round face was replaced by a dark
countenance made stern by frowning lines of concern.

'Oh, Richard!'

'Sweetheart!'

The word pierced sweetly through her miasma of
hopelessness. He hadn't called her that before! A faint
smile curved her bloodless lips as he took her hand and
held it in a firm, warm clasp. 'Thank God you're all
right! Whatever happened?'

'Silver bolted,' was all Eleanor could manage as the
full horror of her experience rose up to flood her mind.

Suddenly Richard's grip tightened. 'Aye. You should
have taken more care! You did not tell me you were
expecting our child! Had I not the right to know?'

His voice sounded angry. Tears welled in Eleanor's
eyes. She needed sympathy, tenderness, not
condemnation!

'I would have told you soon,' she whispered.

'Why did you delay?' he demanded roughly, relief
from desperate anxiety finding an outlet in a wrath he
could not control.

'You might have refused to let me ride with you.' She
sighed, gathering strength for more words as her misery
threatened to overwhelm her. 'But you needed no such
excuse. You are still ashamed to have married me, lord.'

Her heavy lids closed as weak tears slid down her
cheeks. So she did not see the stricken look in the grey
eyes so close to her own.

CHAPTER EIGHT

WHEN Eleanor awoke from her drugged sleep Richard had gone.

'He turned back from Wenstaple without a moment's hesitation, sweeting,' Joan assured her, 'and made quite certain that you were in no danger before he left to rejoin his retinue. But a man is no use in a sick-room, he could do nothing for you, so he left you to our care.'

'It doesn't matter.'

Nothing mattered. She hadn't realised how much she had yearned for a baby to hold in her arms, how high her hopes had been, until they were dashed. The emptiness inside her seemed to expand daily until her skin became a shell, void of all feeling. No longings, no fears, no hope penetrated the hard carapace protecting her emotions.

Richard returned within the week, earlier than he'd promised. By then Eleanor was up, but only just. That very morning, for the first time, she had climbed the stairs on shaky legs.

'You must stir yourself, sweeting! The longer you lie abed, the weaker you will become! Come, see how dutifully Anne has been stitching the tapestry! But she needs your advice on some of the colours...'

Anne's squeamishness had kept her largely out of the sick-room, after a brief visit on the first day. Eleanor did not hold it against the child. She'd had far too many women fussing over her, and Anne had been better occupied in the bower.

'My lady! You are better!' Anne ran forward, her pretty face alight, and impulsively kissed Eleanor on the cheek. 'How glad I am to see you up again! Dear lady, we have all been so concerned for you!'

Eleanor managed a brief smile which just lifted her lips, but did not reach her eyes. Nevertheless, the girl's uninhibited show of affection brought the first touch of warmth she had known since the accident, and it lightened her heart.

She sank down on her stool and inspected the tapestry, but could dredge up no glimmer of interest in it. Her fingers seemed weak and trembly, her arms like lead, so there was no point in even trying to stitch any of it herself. She pushed it aside.

'You have made good progress,' she told Anne tiredly. 'I'm sure you'll do it beautifully.'

Tamkin appeared at that moment, carrying a steaming bowl of oxtail and vegetable broth. He'd been banished entirely from the sick-room, and was beaming with happiness at being near his beloved mistress once more.

'Thank you, Tamkin. You are looking well. Have you been behaving?'

'Aye, lady! I've been running messages, bringing your food and drink. I've been good, haven't I, Mistress Joan?'

He appealed anxiously to the older woman for reassurance. Joan grinned. After her initial harshness towards the lad—which had been entirely for his own good, she had assured them since—she'd grown fond and maternal towards him.

'Aye, you young scamp! Now, give her ladyship the bread and leave her in peace to eat!'

'Sit here, Tamkin,' invited Eleanor, pointing to the rushes at her feet. 'Would you like some of this?'

'I brought it for you!'

She gazed distastefully at the food, certain that she could not stomach any of it. Her mouth felt dry, yet the thought of taking so much as a drop of water filled her with revulsion. She just wanted to be left alone.

She put the bowl aside and Joan promptly picked it up, clucking reproachfully.

'You must eat, my lady. How otherwise will you regain your strength? And your lord will be angry with us if you are wasted away by the time he returns!'

The corners of Eleanor's mouth turned down. 'Little he cares,' she muttered.

Anne shot her a startled glance, while Joan frowned disapproval. 'Of course he cares! Why else would he come riding back here as though pursued by the devil himself, that's what I'd like to know! Poor Noble was in a great lather, so I heard!'

'And who told you that?' asked Eleanor cynically. Joan was a dear, but she would fabricate any tale to lift her mistress's spirits.

'Will, of course. He rode back too, with a couple of the men-at-arms. And you did not see your lord's face when he first saw you lying abed, so pale and wan...'

Eleanor shrugged, but when Joan held a spoonful of the broth to her lips she swallowed obediently. As the warm liquid seeped down to her stomach a little life seemed to return to her frozen mind.

She was young, there was plenty of time for her to conceive another baby. Yet the thought of lying in Richard's arms again brought a faint shiver of revulsion. That prospect held no more appeal than any other form of activity.

Reluctantly, she ate most of the soup and a bite or two of bread. Then she got up and curled herself into the wide embrasure of an open window.

The hot July sun baked the cliffs and gave sparkle to the tiny waves cresting on the waters of the estuary. The fishing boats were out dragging lines, though most of the fish would be caught at low tide, when the nets, which were strung across sand banks flanking the mouth of the estuary, became exposed. Gulls and a myriad other sea birds swooped and called, swarming around the fishing boats, attempting to pillage the catch as it was drawn aboard.

Life went on out there, but for Eleanor life had ceased with that moment of tearing pain on the cliffs.

She rested her chin on her knees and stared sightlessly out over the sea. Unresponsive to all attempts to bring her out of her reverie, she sat motionless until Tamkin's small hand tugged at her gown.

'Lady!' His voice begged for a sign, and Eleanor slowly turned her head to meet the imploring gaze of his wide grey eyes. 'Lady,' he repeated, seeing that he had gained her attention. 'I have brought you some sweetmeats! Try one of these! It is made from honey and almonds and ginger, and tastes very nice!'

Eleanor smiled. 'So you have tried one to see?' How could she disappoint the child? 'Thank you, Tamkin. Mmm. Yes, this is good.'

'Have another, lady!'

'Not now, Tamkin. Leave them on the table. Perhaps later——'

'Will you go down to supper?' demanded Joan abruptly.

'I don't think so. I don't feel up to it.'

'Then your food will be brought here.' Joan shooed Tamkin away with a wave of her hand. Anne was already elsewhere. As Tamkin disappeared down the stairs, she spoke softly to Eleanor. 'Word has reached us that your lord will be back in time for supper, sweeting. Mayhap he will eat here with you.'

Eleanor stirred, a faint indignation bringing a chill to overlay the weariness in her voice. 'And the message was not brought to me? How so, Joan?'

'The messenger met with Master Stephen, who took it upon himself to save you the trouble of receiving the man.'

'I see.' Well, what did it matter? 'I doubt if Richard will eat with me. He will want to speak with Sir Peter and Stephen, to receive their reports. And to be with his men.'

'Huh!' muttered Joan. 'Your sour face would be enough to turn anyone away! Greet him warmly, sweeting! It was not his fault that you chose to ride out in the mist knowing you were pregnant!'

'I did not know—not for sure.'

Joan noted the hint of a flush on her mistress's face and raised a silent prayer of thanks at the first signs of anything but a listless response for almost a week.

'Let me brush your hair!' Joan almost dragged Eleanor from the window embrasure and sat her on the stool. The rhythmic movements of the bristle on her scalp soon soothed Eleanor into a state of mindless calm—not quite the numb coldness which had held her for days—and from somewhere deep inside some vestige of emotion began to stir.

Richard was coming home. Would she be glad to see him? She thought about it, and for a second something akin to anticipation caused her heart to give an extra beat. But then the vision of his angry face bending over her slowed her pulse with a dragging hurt. A nerve lurched in her stomach.

She didn't know. Would he still be angry? Sympathetic? Harsh? Or tender? It hardly mattered. If a storm broke over her head she would barely be aware of it. If he wanted to hold her in his arms, to comfort her, she would submit to that, too. But his support would come too late. She did not need it now.

Her head was bent over hands clasped idly in her lap when Richard entered the bower. For an instant he gazed at the still, silent figure dressed in a white chamber-gown, her glorious hair falling in a riot of pale gold almost to the rushes, and a strange pain twisted his heart. He had been warned by Joan, and although he couldn't begin to understand, he had believed her when she had said that Eleanor's state was natural after the loss of her baby. Now that the tearing anxiety was over and she was up and about again, he must master his own emotions and treat her reasonably, give her the support that he knew she needed.

She was alone. He walked softly across the room and dropped on to one blue-clad knee at her side.

'I'm glad to see you better, wife.' He leaned forward and brushed her forehead with his lips.

Her shrinking was instinctive, slight, but noticeable. Richard frowned, but kept his irritation under control.

'Joan tells me that you have no wish to eat in the Hall tonight. Neither have I. We will eat in the solar.'

'No! I'd rather remain here.'

'Why, sweetheart? It is more comfortable downstairs. Besides, I have brought several coffers back with me. They arrived in Wenstaple yesterday, a consignment from your father. Our pack-horses were not heavily laden, so I saved the carter the journey here. Have you any idea what might be in them?'

Eleanor shook her head.

'Don't you want to know?'

She shrugged. 'I suppose so.'

'Then come, wife. Let me carry you down——'

'No!' She softened the sharpness of her rejection with a brief smile. 'I must use my legs. After almost a week in bed they feel about as strong as reeds!'

'Aye! I know the feeling!' He gazed deeply into her eyes, and she knew that he was offering her his own dreadful experience of illness and frustration as solace for her own. 'Well, then, let us go.'

She *was* grateful, and tried to show it by suffering his steadying hand on her arm without flinching. After the first touch his warm clasp became reassuring, a source of strength that might be able to lift her from the dreadful apathy into which she had fallen.

Although the evening was warm, a small fire burned in the hearth, a jug of mulled wine keeping warm beside it. Will and Tamkin brought in supper, assisted by a couple of varlets, and they ate it without lingering—or at least, Richard did. Eleanor picked at a piece of chicken and a honeyed oatcake, managing to eat more than at any time since her accident.

Often, she glanced across at Richard, seeing him anew. His hair had grown a little longer and curled lovingly on the high neck of his burgundy-coloured tunic. His experience-hardened features were softened, his long mouth curving in appreciation as he consumed the food set before him. He exuded an aura of masculinity which daunted her, but the smile in his grey eyes whenever they met hers was reassuring. It seemed strangely peaceful, wonderfully domestic, to be sharing her meal in comparative privacy with her husband. Noise came echoing up the stairs from time to time, and Eleanor was glad that she had chosen not to go down.

When at last they were alone again, 'You know, Eleanor,' said Richard, as though echoing her thoughts, 'I find this much more pleasant than eating in so great a company! We must do it more often!'

'Aye. It is becoming quite the fashion now, I believe, for the lord and his family and friends to eat apart from everyone else. Though this solar is hardly large enough for entertaining guests!'

This was the longest speech she had made in a week, but Richard wasn't to know that, or the effort it had cost her. He pursed his lips thoughtfully.

'Nor do we need to, here. My solar at Acklane was designed for just such a purpose.' He smiled. 'I think you would approve of the manor house I have built there.

When you are fully recovered we must journey to see it.'

Eleanor smiled in return. She knew that he was trying to arouse her interest, and had no wish to let him know how dismally he was failing. Yes, it was nice to have him back, to know that his wrath was not about to fall on her head. But all that delicate warmth of feeling for him, which had been growing stealthily in her so that she had hardly known it was there, had gone. She sighed suddenly. So much had been lost in that one fearful instant when Silver had thrown her from the saddle.

'Silver came back.'

She spoke abruptly, the words coming starkly from her thoughts. She had not seen the little mare since, and had no great wish to do so yet, though she bore the palfrey no ill will for her disastrous antics. She had been scared beyond all reason.

'So the groom told me. We had better sell her.'

'That won't be necessary. It wasn't her fault. The apparition frightened her out of her wits. I am looking forward to riding her again once I'm recovered.'

Richard shifted uncomfortably, regarding her from under lowered lids as he stroked his beard. 'You mentioned a grey friar to Roger. He did not see him. The mist was very thick. Are you certain?'

'Quite certain!'

'It wasn't a sheep?'

'A sheep?' She laughed, slightly hysterically. 'Do you think I'm so foolish as to mistake a man's form for that of a sheep?'

'Roger neither saw nor heard anything,' he insisted.

'He was some yards behind. As you say, the mist was thick. And the cry scared the gulls into screeching. So it became lost in their noise. Richard, I did see something! So did Silver! Otherwise, why did she bolt?'

Richard regarded her gravely, still stroking his beard, a habit he had when worried, she knew.

'I don't know. But there has been no stranger, let alone a grey friar, wandering around here. Roger enquired.'

'And you would rather believe him.'

The flat weariness was back in her voice. Richard slid to one knee and took her fragile hand in his strong clasp.

'Nay, Eleanor, I would rather believe you! But...you are both so certain! And what would a man be doing out there alone in the mist?'

'He could have been a smuggler,' she suggested flatly.

'Who attempted to scare you off? That is certainly one solution!'

'Or a ghost.'

'Possibly.'

He didn't believe that, she could tell, but he would humour her. She herself didn't know what to believe, only that she had definitely seen something, or someone, and that the cry could have come from the devil himself. She crossed herself hastily.

'I didn't imagine it.'

Her voice was so weary, so inflexibly certain.

'I don't believe you did,' he admitted soothingly. 'We shall probably never know the truth of the matter. But it makes little difference as long as you are all right, wife!'

'But our baby is lost!'

The sudden, acute desolation in her voice cut through his own calm like the thrust of a sword. His grasp on her hand tightened convulsively as he lowered his head to press her cold fingers against his cheek. 'By my oath, Eleanor! If it was a man and I could lay my hands on him I'd slay him for the damage he has done!'

'Retribution would be sweet, but it wouldn't bring back our baby. Richard, I'm sorry! I shouldn't have gone riding that morning! But I was so miserable...'

Or so she had thought. But her misery then had been nothing to the misery consuming her now! Why had she started feeling again? Why hadn't Richard left her alone?

'Aye, I know it was my fault.' He turned her hand and his warm lips imprinted themselves on her palm, sending a fiery pain leaping along her arm. She flinched, withdrawing her hand defensively. She was not ready to respond physically to her husband yet.

Richard rose abruptly to his feet and turned away from her. Patience had never been one of his strong virtues, and he'd had no occasion previously to deal gently with a woman in distress. He felt out of his element and frustratingly inadequate. He had apologised—a difficult enough task for him—what more did she expect? His own pain was unexpectedly and unpleasantly fierce, and her strange new reluctance to have him touch her sharpened it to an almost unbearable degree.

Yet instinct told him that he had to use his strength to cure her weakness. Had it been any other woman in the world he would have shrugged and left her to it. But this was his wife, normally so proud and spirited, who had become insidiously special and necessary to his happiness.

He swung back to find Eleanor on her feet.

'I'll sleep in my bower,' she told him tightly.

Richard caught his breath. Hot words of scorn rose to his lips, but he bit them back. 'Nay, Eleanor,' he said, as calmly as he could. 'There is no need. If necessary I will go elsewhere. But I would rather lie with you by my side.'

He saw the instant tightening of her face and called on all his reserves of patience. 'I will not trouble you,' he went on evenly. 'I know you need time before you are ready to receive me. But that doesn't mean we cannot share the same bed, wife.'

Eleanor's head drooped. Her emotions went back into some frozen place beyond her control. Her husband had spoken.

After Joan had helped her to prepare for bed she lay taut between the cool sheets, awaiting Richard. For a long time after he had joined her he remained on his back, so near that she could not ignore his presence, yet not touching her. She kept as still as a frightened mouse, scarcely breathing, willing him to forget her and fall asleep.

His breathing was quiet and regular and she thought that he had dozed off, but abruptly he moved, gathering her into his arms and holding her tightly against the length of his warm, vibrant body. His strong, virile touch was an affront to her own listlessness. She froze in his embrace, even tried to push him away.

'Hush, wife. Be still. Relax and sleep. I do but hold you to give comfort and strength.'

She felt the tender touch of his mouth on her hair as her head nestled in the hollow of his neck. The rigidity left her body. She sighed, suddenly glad of his closeness, and relaxed trustingly into the warmth of his hold.

Richard smiled a trifle grimly to himself when he heard her even breathing, felt the soft blow of air stirring the hairs on his chest. He was finding it cursedly difficult to relax himself, with her soft, yielding body held so temptingly in his arms, her hair tickling his nostrils. But he knew that he had won the first round in his fight to reclaim his wife from the prison of despair.

A deep contentment settled on him, but even so it was some while before eventually he, too, slept.

Day by day Eleanor grew physically stronger until at length she knew that she was fully recovered.

If only the deadening apathy would go away! It lay over her mind like a dark pall, weighing her down, rendering her quite indifferent to what went on around her.

She could find no enthusiasm for anything. Even the contents of the coffer her father had sent elicited little response when at last it was opened.

Anne and Joan gasped aloud at the sight of the rich tapestries and rugs revealed to their eager eyes. Richard raised a sardonic brow.

'Someone has been regaling your father with tales of our poverty-stricken state,' he remarked caustically.

'That will have been Godfrey,' Eleanor returned sharply, stung by his obvious resentment. 'Wenfrith Castle was most inhospitable when first we arrived, though through no fault of yours, husband. He but reported what he saw.'

'Aye, no doubt, and your father has added significantly to your dower. What plans have you for these things, wife?'

'Some of the tapestries will warm the walls here in the solar and in the bower, though the largest would be better placed behind the high table in the Hall.'

'Aye, a battle-scene is hardly appropriate for our solar!'

'No. As for the rugs——' she fingered the soft pile appreciatively '—methinks they come from Persia. They will drape well over the coffers.'

Richard had not yet seen the tapestry they were working, and if he wondered why a portion of the solar wall was left bare, then he did not question her disposal of the colourful fabrics imported from far-off lands. As for Eleanor, she directed the hanging of the wall coverings with a show of enthusiasm that she did not really feel. Knights in brilliant surcoats; crusaders with large red crosses painted on theirs; women in flowing, colourful robes; horses; dogs; birds; trees; flowers—all were depicted, the humans and beasts engaged in the activities they loved best—fighting, hunting, making music—against a background of pastoral beauty.

Their vibrant colour lent the stone walls a new life and warmth, and once they were up Eleanor wrote gratefully to her father to thank him for his gift, sending the missive by messenger to Wenstaple, whence it would be passed from hand to hand until it reached him. When was in the lap of the gods. But fellow merchants would be glad to do him the service of carrying the letter.

Richard had suggested they resume their morning rides, but Eleanor had declined. She rode Silver around the village and into the fields out of a sense of duty, but could not raise the energy for anything other than the normal daily tasks required of her.

Richard had proved a tower of strength, cosseting her one moment, yet chivvying her the next, appearing at odd hours of the day to make sure that she was occupied and not moping. He had not pressed his attentions on her in bed, and a warm feeling of gratitude was beginning to take the place of the frigid void which had beset her for so long.

She had not expected such care and concern. She knew that he could not understand her state of mind—she did not understand it herself. But she couldn't shake it off.

Towards the end of August, Richard announced that they were to ride to Wenstaple.

Eleanor raised questioning brows.

'You are asking me to go with you?' she enquired, somewhat coldly.

'Aye; wife. I told you that you should visit Wenstaple soon, and this is a good time, since their annual fair is to be held in a few days' time, on the eve of the day of

the blessed Saint Bartholemew, the day itself, and on its
morrow. It is a great event in the area. You will enjoy
it, and can celebrate your birthday at the same time.'

'Perhaps. But I'm not feeling——'

'Eleanor!' His voice was sharp for the first time since
he had returned after her accident. 'Wife, I have been
patient! But this sickness of yours is in the mind! You
are quite well enough to ride with me. And surely the
change of scene will cure your downcast spirits!'

'Aye. Maybe. A fair, you say?' She pursed her lips in
thought. 'There are a few things I need. Anne and Joan
shall come with me. Tamkin, too. He will enjoy the
entertainments!'

'Excellent!' Richard looked pleased at her show of
enthusiasm, she noted. 'Perhaps you will find something special to buy. We must go well provided with gold.'

The ride into Wenstaple proved a rare pleasure, taken
on a mellow day when the sun played hide-and-seek with
billowing white clouds. The castle stood on the edge of
the town overlooking the estuary, well placed to defend
the busy quay which bordered the river. Although outside
its perimeter, the castle shared one stout wall with the
town it was protecting, while the borough's other
defences ran right down the water's edge.

Richard and his train passed through the barbican,
crossed the castle drawbridge, rode under the gatehouse,
and entered the bailey to a blare of trumpets. The guard
stood to attention and the richly costumed constable and
his lady waited at the great entrance-door, ready to greet
them.

'Greetings, my lord.'

'How now, Sir Henry! Meet the Lady d'Evreux,
Countess of Wenstaple.'

'My lady.' Sir Henry, a tall, austere-looking man of
around fifty, with a kindly twinkle in his dark eyes,
bowed. 'May I present my wife, Hilda, Lady Bagwell?'

The dumpy little woman executed a deep curtsy,
dipping her grey, veiled head in deep respect and quite
careless of the way the costly taffeta of her gown trailed
in the dust. 'Your ladyship!'

Eleanor smiled and inclined her head, almost overwhelmed by the ceremony of their greeting.

'Sir Henry. Lady Bagwell. I have heard much of you from his lordship.'

'All good, I hope!' Sir Henry's jovial chuckle showed no hint of uneasiness, and his wife's smile was warm and welcoming. 'You must be wearied after your journey. Allow my wife to take you to your chamber! It has been made ready as you ordered, my lord.'

Eleanor looked quickly at Richard, wondering when he had given the orders and what they had been, but he was giving instructions to Will. 'Thank you.' She inclined her head, smiled at Hilda Bagwell, and prepared to follow.

The castle was more extensive than that at Wenfrith, and more recently constructed. Fortified towers were joined by extensive buildings able to house an army. Sunlight filtered through the leaded windows of the Great Hall, which was twice the size of that at Wenfrith, bringing new life to the old tapestries hanging on the walls. A fire blazed on the hearth in the centre of the vast chamber, fighting the chill of an early autumn evening. Dozens of servants scurried back and forth carrying huge cauldrons, bowls of all shapes and sizes, platters, cutlery, flagons of ale and wine, goblets and mugs. Minstrels tuned lyres, lutes and pipes in the gallery above. A feast was being prepared.

The Earl's suite was not in a tower, but flanked the Great Hall. The solar was large and oblong in shape, the bed impressive, its blue, brocaded hangings new. The floor had been freshly strewn with sweet-smelling rushes, and a bowl of late pink roses spread its heady perfume through the room. A new wall-hanging caught Eleanor's eye: a colourful representation of the new Earl of Wenstaple's arms.

'I trust all is to your liking, my lady. When last he was here the lord Earl ordered these rooms to be completely renovated in readiness for your visit. Both wardrobes lead from the solar, and there is a room for your ladies' use near by.' She coughed and coloured slightly. 'The latrine is on the outer wall, and private.'

'It will do excellently.'

Anne and Joan immediately went to explore, while a train of varlets carried the travelling-coffers through to the wardrobes. Richard strode in after the servants, accompanied by Will.

'The chamber pleases you, my lady?'

'Aye, my lord. I thank you for your thoughtfulness in instructing Lady Bagwell to improve the apartments, and her for executing them so well. We shall be comfortable here.'

Hilda Bagwell smiled happily. 'Supper will be ready in half an hour. It will wait on your convenience, naturally.'

Richard began to unbuckle his belt prior to shedding his armour. 'We shall not keep you long. Come, Will.'

He gave Eleanor a swift smile of reassurance as he strode from the solar. She went through to her own wardrobe, large enough to be used as a dressing-room like that off her bower at home, but with no draughty run up the stairs to be endured before she could reach it.

Wenstaple was altogether more comfortable to live in than Wenfrith, however much she preferred the latter's magnificent position. As she shed her travelling-garments and allowed Joan to sponge the sweat and dust from her face and body, she found a new reason to resent the attitude on Richard's part that had kept her from the place for so long.

But she was here now. She slipped into a new green kirtle and added a surcoat of strawberry-coloured sendal, the pink and gold figures, woven into the green silk of the cloth-imperial of the tunic, blending with the rich colour of the sleeveless over-garment to give a regal touch to her appearance. The full skirts draped beautifully, unlike the stiff taffeta of Hilda Bagwell's gown, which suited her round figure not at all!

Eleanor smiled slightly to herself and decided not to wear a veil that evening, but to follow the fashion of plaiting her hair into coils on either side of her face with only a circlet to cover them.

Joan had just finished fixing the heavy braids in place when Will called her from the room. She returned carrying a new and exquisite gold circlet set with glowing cabochons flashing many colours.

'His lordship asks you to wear this, my lady. It is a new chaplet befitting your rank.'

'It is beautiful! I must thank him——'

'Later! Let me place it on your brow!' Joan settled it carefully in position and stood back to admire the effect, her head cocked on one side, her honest face wreathed in smiles. 'There, sweeting, you look beautiful!'

Eleanor had already pinned Richard's brooch on her shoulder and slipped the too-large signet ring on her middle finger. With the chaplet on a head held proudly high, she stepped through to the solar to join her husband.

CHAPTER NINE

'Oyez! Oyez! Oyez!'

The cry rang across the market square, seeming to sway the masts lining the busy quay beyond, and echoed along the narrow, winding streets of the town. Standing on the steps of the Guildhall, a goblet of spiced wine in her hand, Eleanor watched the scene before her. Merchants' gaily decorated stalls filled one side of the square and the crowded alleys adjoining. Horses, oxen, pigs and sheep, penned in the other half, lifted protesting voices loud enough to almost drown the cries of the motley throng milling among them; the townspeople gaily dressed in their best clothes, and a few serfs from the surrounding countryside, still dressed in their drab borella, mingling almost unnoticed.

Richly clad knights and squires and their families kept to the fringes of the crowd, but once the opening ceremony was over they would be thrusting their way through the throng, scattering the lesser mortals to obtain a special bargain or see a sight they wanted, like that of the dogs baiting a huge brown bear which was chained to a post near the quay.

Early that morning the news had come through that Calais had surrendered to King Edward. The cross of Saint George fluttered from every rooftop, windows were garlanded in red and white, and the church bells had scarcely stopped ringing, even for the celebration Mass, which they had all attended in the vast cathedral. *Te Deums* were being sung throughout the land, as England rejoiced at the victory of its gallant King.

Richard had been beside himself with delight, calling for three rousing cheers from the entire garrison and household of the castle before they had set off through the postern gate in the city wall to walk to the cathedral. Then Eleanor had walked with her husband down the vaulted nave, and thought that he had not been ashamed to have her by his side.

'Hear ye!' The scarlet-gowned town crier was making his announcement as Eleanor's thoughts rambled. She had heard similar orations in her home town of Colchester, so did not pay too much attention.

'Notice is hereby given that from this day until midnight on the morrow of Saint Bartholemew there is a free fair within this borough. All manner of persons may buy and sell within the same, and are charged with keeping the King's peace.'

The strident voice went on to declare that all should deal justly, that weights and measures should be true, and that all tolls and duties should be paid. Anyone breaking the law would be dealt with by the justice and laws of the realm. A Court of Pie Poudre would sit in the Guildhall to hear all complaints and deal with those who broke the law.

The moment he had finished, someone ran forward with a huge stuffed glove mounted on a long, garlanded stick. Eleanor's interest quickened. She had seen nothing like this before!

'What is it?' she asked Sir Henry, who was standing at her side, he, too, being among the guests of the Mayor of Wenstaple, who was a mercer by trade, by name John Pomeroy.

'It represents the hand of welcome,' he told her, 'and will stay hoisted before the Guildhall until the end of the fair. The tradition goes back to the granting of our charter, nigh on a hundred years since.'

At that moment Eleanor became irritatingly aware that Isobel Dent, the widowed daughter of Sir Henry and Lady Bagwell, had inserted herself between Richard and her mother. Isobel was a dark beauty somewhere in her mid-twenties, tall and slender with sultry brown eyes that rested on Richard with undisguised invitation. Eleanor felt her hackles rise again, as they had done on the previous evening, when she'd first noticed the woman's interest in her husband. Terrible suspicions had leapt to her mind. Was Isobel the real reason for Richard's reluctance to bring his wife to Wenstaple? She couldn't really believe that, yet he had shown a great friendliness towards his constable's daughter, had spent a deal of time laughing and talking to her once the trestles had been cleared and the dancing had begun. But he had declined her invitation to partner her.

'Nay, Isobel. The Countess and I will watch others disport themselves this evening.'

He had turned to smile at her, and his hand had covered hers on the carved arm of her chair, but he hadn't asked her if she would like to dance.

Isobel had left him then, to sway enticingly to the sound of an old country air, partnered in the set dance by an elderly knight who had gone puce in the face in his efforts to keep pace with the younger woman. Richard had watched with an indulgent smile on his lips, but his eyes had hardly strayed from the woman's face. Will had danced with Anne, and Eleanor had been glad to see them friendly towards each other. That would be a suitable match, once he had won his spurs, because he was the son of a knight possessed of several rich manors. Will showed little interest in maids as a rule, being far too busy perfecting his fighting skills and serving his master.

Now she watched with jealous eyes as Richard smiled down at Isobel. She had been aware for some time of the tension gradually building in her husband. So far he had kept to his promise and not troubled her with his attentions, but might he not be tempted to seek solace elsewhere? And who would blame him if he did, since she was denying him the physical release so necessary to a man?

Richard touched her arm and together they followed the mayor down the steps and into the market square. Their escort cut a swathe through the throng as they progressed, though the crowd pressed hard against the circle of guards protecting them. The colourful goods on display whirled past Eleanor's distracted eyes until a pungent aroma caught her nostrils. The merchant had on his stall a variety of exotic spices not normally available in Wenstaple. She stopped, and before they moved on again she had bought plentiful supplies of mustard and pepper, cumin and cloves, mace, saffron and nutmeg, galingale, cinnamon and coriander. After a quick consultation with Richard she added small quantities of the expensive zedoary and cubeb berries to her order. In all, enough to stock the spice chests at both Wenfrith and Wenstaple for a year.

'Are spices all you require, lady?'

Richard's crooked brow was raised in amusement. Eleanor fluttered her lashes, suddenly shy of her husband because of the thoughts which had been running through her head earlier. 'I believe they are, lord. I have seen nothing else to tempt me.'

'What of this?' He had moved on to the next stall, and held in his hand a beautifully balanced dagger, its hilt wrought in gold, and jewelled with clusters of tiny balas rubies. She glanced down at the seal ring still on her finger, reminded of her first reaction to the ruby almost buried in its centre.

'It is beautiful, lord. But what use have I for such a weapon?'

'It would look well in your belt, and could be used in defence, should it be needed.'

Eleanor frowned, shivering slightly at the thought of blood staining the blade the same colour as the jewels. 'You think I am in some danger, lord?'

'We are all in danger, Countess. Many people would have us dead. Why else do we travel so well protected?'

'I—well, yes, I know that! But to carry a dagger! I've not been used——'

'A deterrent only, wife, and a birthday gift!' He turned to the expectant merchant and gave him gold from his pouch. 'Here, let me attach the sheath to your belt.'

The weight at her hip felt strange. Did Richard really think her in danger? Was it the incident on the cliffs that had caused his concern? She frowned; he had not mentioned her accident since they'd discussed it on the evening of his return.

She put such uncomfortable thoughts from her as they moved to the other side of the square to where the horses were tethered. Richard immediately showed interest in a bay destrier, while Eleanor's attention was caught by a sturdy brown pony. Its aristocratic head was up, its ears pricked, its soft eyes bright, and, although its thick dark mane and long flowing tail needed grooming, its coat looked in good condition.

'What breed is this?' she asked the dealer.

'Ah don't rightly know, m'lady. They do run wild on the moors,' answered the man with a shrug.

'He looks a sturdy stallion, just right for riding. Is he broken to the bridle?'

'Aye, right enough; he were owned by a young squire, 'oo 'ave grown to a larger beast.'

Tamkin was holding on to her skirt, his eyes fixed on the gentle face of the pony. Eleanor reached out to stroke the soft nose, looking down at the boy.

'You must learn to ride, Tamkin. Do you like this pony?'

'What's this?' Richard had closed his deal, and the war-horse was being led to the castle. He ran a knowledgeable hand along the little stallion's back.

'The stables do not hold a mount small enough for Tamkin, and he needs something to learn on. He cannot forever ride pillion to one of the retinue!'

'So, little brother, you would learn to ride, eh? High time too! I was in the saddle before I could walk!'

'But you were the legitimate son,' murmured Eleanor so softly that no one else could hear.

'Aye, you've no need to remind me.' Richard's tone was abrupt, but he was still examining the pony, running his palms down its fetlocks and looking at its teeth. 'How much?' he demanded of the dealer.

Eleanor listened while her husband bargained for the animal. At last the deal was agreed, gold exchanged hands, and the pony followed the destrier to the castle stables.

Tamkin, torn between the delights of the fair and the thought of his new pony back at the castle, was eventually left in the care of Joan, who had been persuaded to escort Anne and Will. Both young people were eager to see the performing animals and mummers, acrobats and buffoons, knife-dancers and jugglers, but couldn't be allowed to roam together alone. Eleanor doubted whether Anne would let the squire and page near the bear-baiting or the cock-fighting pits, and guessed Will would make his way there alone after the others had returned to the Guildhall.

She and Richard rejoined the mayoral party of burghers and dignitaries for a meal. Eleanor took the opportunity to bargain with Master Pomeroy for linen cloths to cover the tables at Wenfrith, an innovation long overdue. Joan, Anne and Tamkin had returned before they left for the castle, though Will, having been given the day off, was making the most of his freedom.

Tired but stimulated, Eleanor strolled back with Richard and the others. Entering the inner courtyard through the postern, they saw a party dismounting by the main entrance.

'Cedric!' Eleanor's glad cry echoed across the enclosed space, and the young man turned quickly to greet her.

'Eleanor! Sister!'

Eleanor picked up her skirts and ran, while Cedric strode towards her. First he took her hands, holding her at a distance while he eyed her critically, then he lifted her from the ground in a bear-hug.

'What's amiss, sister? You're as skinny as a quarter-staff!'

'I've been a little ill, Cedric, but I'm better now! It is so good to see you!'

Firmly on the ground again, Eleanor looked fondly into her brother's handsome face. 'You look well, brother. The life of a squire suits you!'

'Aye, and I'm neglecting my duties. But I see my master is fully occupied!'

In her own joy at seeing Cedric, Eleanor had scarcely realised that he was accompanying Sir Ralph and Lady Radcliffe. Neither had she noticed Anne's gasp of surprise when she saw her parents. Now she looked to where the three of them were exchanging greetings, Sir Ralph and his lady having already paid their respects to Richard, who stood waiting impatiently for his wife to join him.

Eleanor walked to his side, pulling Cedric by the hand. 'Richard! Is this not a surprise? Here is Cedric come to visit us!'

'Aye, so I see!' Richard's response was dry. When Cedric was about she had no thought for anything or anyone else! And she looked alive again! Cedric had wrought in a moment the change he'd been desperately trying to bring about for weeks. 'We are glad to see you, brother. Now, wife, greet our other guests!'

'I am so sorry.' Eleanor coloured. Etiquette demanded that she greet the master before the servant! What would Sir Ralph think? 'Sir Ralph. Lady Radcliffe. Welcome to Wenstaple Castle!'

They executed bows and curtsies of respect, and Eleanor was happy to note the twinkle in both pairs of eyes.

'Greetings, lady. We came to visit the fair, and hoped to see our daughter here. Is your ladyship pleased with her services?'

'Indeed, Sir Ralph. And is my brother proving a good squire?'

'Splendid, lady. He learns fast, and is already quite fit to gain his spurs!'

'I'm delighted to hear it!' She turned to Cedric. 'Come, brother! Let us go somewhere where you may tell me of your prowess! My lord, you will excuse us?'

From somewhere, Richard dredged up a warm smile, and bowed. 'Of course. I will go and make sure that the new horses have been taken care of. Coming, Tamkin?'

Eleanor was amused that evening to see Anne sitting at a trestle between Will and Cedric, playing one young squire off against the other. She judged the animosity between the two men to be no more than part of the fun. Feelings were not running deep, and Anne, the little minx, was enjoying her power while keeping both swains at arm's length. Joan was at the far end of the Hall, and Eleanor could not make out whom she was with. Tamkin, as usual, was at her feet.

As for Isobel... Eleanor refused to be upset by the languishing looks directed in Richard's direction, but waited impatiently for the moment when she could reasonably retire, hoping Richard would not choose to linger drinking with his guests. The incessant fanfares as each dish was presented on bended knee had given her a headache, and she longed for the peace of their room. Thank goodness the etiquette at Wenfrith was so much less formal! Unless Richard complained, she had no intention of instituting there all the elaborate ceremonial so often demanded by a man of his rank. Here at Wenstaple it was different. This was the seat of his Earldom and, however wearisome, the full protocol had to be observed.

Grace had been said, the dishes and trestles removed. Richard sat back, his eyes hooded, tapping impatiently on the arm of his chair as he watched a game of

hoodman-blind being played by the younger people.
Eleanor covered his restless fingers with her own.

'Lord,' she whispered. 'I would like to seek the peace
of our chamber. Do you come with me?'

Her eyes were wide and unconsciously pleading.
Richard returned her gaze steadily for a moment before
turning his hand to clasp hers in steely fingers. The pain
of his grasp was reassuring, and Eleanor smiled, rising
to her feet.

A fanfare greeted their departure, as it had their entrance. Anne immediately began to follow as they made
their way to their rooms, though Will did not, intent on
making the most of his freedom. Richard stopped.

'It is early yet, and the revels not over. The Countess
will not need you tonight.'

'Tamkin, join the other pages.' Eleanor smiled at the
child, knowing that he would cling to her given half a
chance. 'They are playing games. You will enjoy their
company.'

'Aye, lady.'

He didn't sound convinced, but turned back obediently. Richard's hand still clasped hers, and his steps
quickened as they neared their room.

A chambermaid was sitting quietly in the corner,
mending a torn shirt. Joan emerged from Eleanor's
wardrobe.

'There are tubs in these rooms, my lady. Would you
and your lord like water brought up to fill them?'

'A bath!' Eleanor turned eagerly to Richard. 'I have
not had a bath since leaving home! What say you, my
lord?'

Richard grinned. 'Aye! Tell them to bring the water!
I hope I can fit myself into this contraption!'

'You will, lord. Yours is twice as large as your lady's!'

Before long a procession of varlets arrived carrying
steaming ewers, which they emptied into the round,
wooden tubs. Joan produced the soap she had made
herself, scented with sweet herbs. The feel of the water
lapping around her limbs was delicious, and Eleanor's
headache disappeared with the steam. She could hear

sounds from Richard's wardrobe, and knew he must have retained a servant or two to help him.

The water cooled quickly, and Eleanor emerged to be rubbed down with a coarse linen cloth. Her skin glowing, she slipped into a pale blue chamber-gown while Joan brushed her hair.

'You may go,' she told Joan at last. 'And take that chambermaid with you! The Earl and I would be private.'

'I'll see to it that no one disturbs you, sweeting. I'm so glad you are feeling better,' Joan added softly.

'Aye, much better. My lord was right! The change has done me good. And seeing Cedric so happy is another delight!'

'He's a good lad. You were always close.'

'Aye. Joan, I'm so glad the fighting is over! Neither Richard nor Cedric will have to leave England now!'

'For the moment, at least. But only the good Lord knows when the King will decide to raise another army! And I doubt if the menfolk are glad to see their chance of glory and spoil disappear!'

'They are ever greedy for more!' Eleanor laughed and sighed, then brightened again. 'Meanwhile, Joan, I have them both beside me! I believe my lord awaits.'

Joan departed, shooing the chambermaid before her, and at last Richard and Eleanor were alone.

'You are downcast, husband,' remarked Eleanor softly. 'I thought today's news had gladdened you!'

'It did, but——' He grimaced, shrugging. 'I wish I had been there!'

'I am glad you were not, husband! I would so much rather have you beside me here!'

'You would?' He came towards her, an almost diffident expression on his normally assured features. 'I had begun to think otherwise, wife.'

'Nay, lord.' He had come to a halt before her, and she reached up to link her arms behind his neck. 'I have always been comforted by your presence. But now, Richard, I am recovered from my megrim!' His arms closed around her as she lifted her lips to touch his smooth cheek and whisper in his ear. 'I would like us to be truly man and wife again.'

With a soft exclamation he held her away for a moment while he looked deeply into her candid eyes.

'Eleanor!' he murmured huskily.

He had used a different soap from hers, and the heady, spicy aroma filled her nostrils as he loosened the ties on her gown. Then she was crushed against his chest, the heat and dampness of his skin penetrating the thin chaisel of his shirt to fuse with her own warm, tingling flesh. Their lips met in the first real kiss they'd exchanged since the baby had been torn from her womb.

His feel was so familiar, so comforting. As they lay naked and entwined in the blue ceremonial bed his touch began to reignite some of the fires which had seemed burned out, of late. He groaned as he entered her and lay for a long moment holding her fiercely to him before he began what, for him, was an unusually short rhythmic journey to completion.

But Eleanor knew that she had not been truly ready. His penetration had been more difficult than in the past. And his coming to a swift climax meant that she had not reached hers.

Yet she was satisfied, relaxed and happy, as Richard recovered his senses and his strength. It always amazed her how completely he could let go, allow his passion to overrule his mind and body for those few precious moments when he reached the heights of physical pleasure and release.

She, perhaps, was less ready to abandon all control, although through his touch she had been lifted to realms of delight she had never imagined existed. Perhaps one day she would reach them again. Meanwhile she felt fulfilled, able to give and receive pleasure, even though, those moments of abandonment excepted, Richard still kept a part of his inmost self from her. She nipped lightly at his ear, and felt him stir.

'How I have wanted you, woman!'

'I know. Dear husband, I thank you for your forbearance. But that is in the past! Perhaps, now, we will be able to begin our family again!'

'Aye! Well, you fell quickly enough, my wife. You just wait and see! Before long you will have a quiverfull of youngsters playing at your feet!'

'Next time, at risk of putting Silver's nose out of joint, you shall buy me a roncey! I refuse to travel everywhere in a lurching, uncomfortable litter!'

'A cob would certainly be a safer mount, and you should come to no harm provided you take things steadily. I'll keep a look-out for a suitable nag. Eleanor, my wife, it is so good to have you back to normal again!'

Perhaps he hadn't noticed her lack of readiness. She prayed that next time she would be able to respond fully to his lovemaking.

Over the next few days they enjoyed little privacy. Eleanor spent much time in the Great Hall with the other ladies, particularly enjoying the company of Hilda Bagwell and Brigid Radcliffe. Isobel kept company with the younger women, and spent a lot of time out in the town, to Eleanor's secret relief. Except that Richard was also prone to disappear into the city, and though he told her it was to visit leading burghers and see to business, she wondered if perhaps Isobel found it necessary to deal with the same worthies.

However, she refused to allow such irrational suspicions to mar the regained closeness with her husband. He was hers, and unlikely to succumb to Isobel's blandishments while he could find his pleasure with his wife!

'Anne tells me you have been low in spirits lately, my lady.'

Brigid Radcliffe's tone was brisk, hardly sympathetic. Eleanor looked at the older woman askance. After two days of friendly discussion, her hostile attitude was puzzling.

'I could not forgive myself for losing the baby,' she murmured.

'Sweet Mary, my lady! Many a woman would be grateful for such a loss! Mayhap you will be thanking

Providence for such a mercy ere many years have passed! 'Tis one way to avoid a house full of brawling brats! It's as well every bout of sickness in the mornings doesn't end with a child! We'd be forever giving birth, and for what! So that they can die of a fever before they reach maturity?'

'You speak with bitterness, Lady Radcliffe.'

'Aye. For many years I was constantly pregnant, yet what have I to show for it? One silly daughter who is refusing to marry the knight her father has chosen for her!'

'Anne is to be betrothed?'

'Within the year, to Baron Oliver of Mangate. She was told this morning. It is more than time. We should have made arrangements years ago; then she would have had no voice in the matter! Now the wench thinks to thwart her father's plans!'

That explained Anne's red eyes when she had attended her earlier! 'Oliver of Mangate? I have heard my husband speak of him.' Eleanor quelled the revulsion in her stomach and tried to speak reasonably. 'Have you met him, lady?'

'Nay. But Sir Ralph knows him from the battlefield. He is a fierce fighter, a great man.'

'In girth as well as reputation!' Eleanor drew a deep breath and chose her words carefully. 'Dear lady, I must sympathise with Anne, although I know your husband has her best interests at heart! Oliver of Mangate has grown fat and old since the days of his glory, and turns violent when he has drunk too deeply!'

'Mayhap she will be a wealthy widow ere long! Many a young girl has wed a worse man than Baron Mangate.'

'That is true. Yet I would beg of you to reconsider this union. I know how Anne must feel! She will be torn between loyalty and revulsion. Dear lady, pray that she is not driven to some desperate act by this decree of Sir Ralph's!'

'Aye. She'd better not return to Wenfrith with you, your ladyship. She pleads to be allowed to wed with Stephen, the bastard brother of the Earl.'

'Stephen!' Eleanor's amazement was total. How had she failed to notice an attachment? She'd been too busy wallowing in her own misery to wonder where Anne spent her time when not at her side! And the news did much to explain Brigid Radcliffe's sudden lack of friendliness. 'That match would be entirely unsuitable, I agree! My lady, I apologise if laxness on my part has allowed a fondness to grow——'

'You've not been well,' admitted Lady Radcliffe grudgingly.

'All the same, I have failed in my duty to your daughter. My brother, Cedric, was much taken by her at our wedding. I knew that that match would not be tolerated, though he is a likeable lad. That is partly why I asked her to come to me . . . so that she would not be under the same roof——'

'Perhaps Cedric should find another knight to serve! Thank you for the warning, my lady. Anne will come home with us!'

'And Cedric shall visit Wenfrith while his future is discussed! Sweet Jesu! What a coil!'

Richard would be furious! Would he be pleased to have Cedric stay? What would he stay to Stephen? Stephen must have encouraged Anne, despite knowing that he stood no hope of winning her. It was all too much! Eleanor stood up abruptly.

'I will send Anne to you if she is in my chamber. I pray for Anne's happiness. She is a dear child, I have enjoyed having her company.'

'You think us harsh parents, my lady. But Anne must learn to grow up. She will become a lady of consequence.'

'Aye, and that is important to you, if not to her. I bid you farewell, Lady Radcliffe. We may not meet again before your departure on the morrow.'

The journey back to Wenfrith was accomplished in an unusual mood of gloom.

Richard, as Eleanor had feared, was angry with everybody, herself included. Most of the retainers had bad hangovers and Will sported a huge black eye, the result of a brawl in the town. Tamkin was sulking because he was not allowed to ride his new pony. Even Cedric was rather less than his usual cheery self, feeling no doubt that his career had been blighted through no fault of his own. Add to these miseries a thin, drizzling rain that seemed to penetrate even the thickest cope, and the cause for dejection was complete.

The herald's trumpet had water in it, and his blast as they crossed the drawbridge ended in an off-key, bubbling warble. However, it was enough to alert those remaining at the castle, and grooms ran forward to take the horses. As Eleanor dismounted, Stephen appeared at the top of the steps, an imposing figure now that he was dressed in the garb of a gentleman. Small wonder that Anne had fancied herself in love with him, mused Eleanor. But that he should encourage such a feeling, without first seeking permission to woo the maid, was unforgivable!

Richard had a deep scowl on his face as he greeted his half-brother.

'Stephen! I beg a word with you in private!'

Stephen raised his brows before allowing them to descend in a frown. 'Won't you take some refreshment first, brother?'

'Nay! This will not wait!'

The two men, so alike and yet so different, stared into each other's eyes. Richard could glare most men down, but Stephen refused to be intimidated. A faint smile touched his lips.

'Then let us go to my chamber, lord.'

He turned and led the way up the stairs near to the screen. Eleanor watched them go with a heavy heart. Richard would storm and rage, but the damage was done. Stephen had as good as seduced the maid under his roof. Richard's standing with his most respected tenant had been badly damaged.

And it was all her fault!

CHAPTER TEN

RICHARD was short-tempered for weeks after that melancholy return, and his lovemaking held little tenderness or affection. It seemed to Eleanor that any woman would have done while he fought his demons of disgust, disappointment and frustration.

He kept active all day, tilting endlessly at the quintain, fighting fierce deeds of arms with his broadsword, honing his skills with mace and axe, riding far and wide over his domains. Eleanor realised that he was punishing himself physically in an attempt to forget the failings of others and his own disability. He sat down to supper exhausted, and afterwards dragged his leg up to their solar, his features drawn into lines of weariness. Her attempts to smooth them away were met with an impatient possession, and it was scarcely to be wondered at that her body was never quite ready to receive him.

No one knew exactly what had transpired between the two men, but Stephen had been subdued for several days after the confrontation, and Richard had still not recovered his normal temper.

Stephen had hurt Richard deeply by betraying his trust. And Eleanor had disappointed him. All his sympathy and understanding over the period of her convalescence had merely resulted in a débâcle he did not wish to contemplate! That Anne had not in fact been besmirched seemed a small consolation for the slur cast upon the honour of his household.

'Stephen has become an upstart!' he muttered angrily one night as he paced the solar. 'To enter into some kind of betrothal with the maid! By Peter! It was just as well the clandestine vows they exchanged were not binding because they were made for the future, and not the present! Perhaps we should find him a wife more suited to his station!'

'I doubt if there is anyone on the manor he would accept,' mused Eleanor, glad that Richard was confiding in her at last, 'otherwise he would have been wed by now. He is looking higher. Anne would have brought a goodly dower of land—Sir Ralph's other manor at Cresswell. That would have given him landed status, while still enjoying the power he wields here. Don't forget, in your absence he is overlord of all your manors.'

'Aye.' He gestured impatiently. 'Mayhap I was rash in placing so much trust in him, but the manor is well run and the revenues are increasing. I have no wish to alter the arrangement. Yet——' Richard sighed in exasperation '—had he but asked I would have granted him a manor! I have one under a steward at Dittingsham. But to act behind my back! That I cannot forgive!'

'He has assumed airs. Husband, I—I cannot truly like him!' confessed Eleanor, voicing her misgivings at last. 'Joan reports unrest on the manor, and I am often met with scarcely concealed hostility, though I am trying to ease the lot of the women and children. Stephen's rule is unduly harsh——'

'Nonsense! The tenants just resent fulfilling their obligations! I had anticipated some resistance; they have become used to my father's oversight, which of late was lax in every way.' He sighed again and, seeing no immediate solution to the problem, changed the subject. 'Do you require another lady to replace Anne in your retinue?'

'I do not wish for the responsibility of having another maiden under my care! The wife of one of your knights, perhaps? That would serve a double purpose: give me companionship and her the ability to be near her husband!'

'Then every married knight in my employ would want the same privilege! The castle would not house the wives, let alone the families! A widow might provide the answer. Isobel Dent, for instance.'

Something clutched at Eleanor's heart. Did Richard want that woman here? But he was eyeing her questioningly, showing no hint of any hidden desire to have a paramour on hand.

'Not Isobel,' she told him firmly, keeping waspishness out of her voice with an effort. 'We are not comfortable together. I'll do without. My dear Joan is ample company, and can manage with help from the castle servants.'

Eleanor hesitated, but Richard seemed in a mellow mood, despite his outburst against Stephen, so she decided to broach the subject which lay uppermost in her mind. 'What of Cedric, Richard? He is still here, but his future must be settled soon.'

Loath as she was to lose the company of her brother, he and Joan having been her mainstays during the difficult weeks just past, she knew that something had to be decided. Otherwise he would become impatient and seek to make his own way. Having served with Sir Ralph he might find a knight ready to accept him as squire, but without Richard's backing it would most likely be a man of little substance or influence, and his subsequent knighthood would carry no status.

Richard pursed his lips, and, although a frown still lay heavily on his brow, he spoke decisively enough. 'He can remain. He has settled well here. He is popular among the men, and I can use another squire. I imagine it will not be long before he earns his spurs.' A faint smile touched his wide mouth. 'Will that arrangement please you, wife?'

'Aye, Richard!' Her face lit up, while her blue eyes swam with tears of gratitude. 'He will not let you down, of that I am sure!'

Richard considered her gratitude with that same feeling of discontent that always assailed him when her affection for her brother became so obvious.

'You showed little liking for Godfrey,' he observed acidly, all traces of a smile gone. 'Why is this brother so different?'

Eleanor glanced at him sharply, not liking the bite in his voice. 'Surely that is plain, Richard? Godfrey is a bullish sort of man, not given to courteous behaviour or diplomacy!'

'Aye! I had proof enough of that!'

'Yet even so, I love him, in a way. He takes after our mother's side of the family, and cannot help his nature.' Her voice softened. 'But Cedric is like our sire, as are the two younger boys. He is naturally considerate, and though light-hearted and perhaps careless in some respects, he has a determined streak in his character that I believe will make him a successful soldier—I have already told you he is chivalrous!'

'You two are alike, and of an age. I suppose it is only natural that you find his company so pleasant.' He stopped pacing and lifted one foot to his stool, resting his arm across his knee to look down on her with a thoughtful, watchful expression in his grey eyes. 'We have been married for nigh on five months now, wife. Do you find your bondage arduous?'

'Bondage! Arduous! Husband, what can you mean? I had thought we dealt well enough together, except ... except when I have annoyed you!'

'And I annoy easily! I know my fault, wife; my temper was always uncertain! Perhaps that is what makes me good in combat! But does it make me a good husband?'

'Lord, I have no complaint. When I think of poor little Anne, condemned to wed with that brute Oliver of Mangate, I can only thank the Holy Mother that my lot has fallen with a just, honourable and generous knight, however uncertain his temper!'

She smiled, gently teasing, and Richard's expression lightened. 'Then I am a lucky man, to have such an understanding and beautiful wife!'

He reached down and pulled her to her feet. She went eagerly into his arms, and afterwards knew by his tender lovemaking that Richard had at last cast off his troubled mood.

During October Edward III returned to England to a hero's welcome and the people celebrated two years of outstanding victories, the nation's first sustained successes on the battlefield since the days of his grandfather.

The rejoicing had hardly died away at Wenfrith when Eleanor and Richard were woken abruptly one night by an alarm sounding from the battlements. Eleanor started up while Richard leaped out of bed, drew on his breeches, thrust his feet into shoes and pulled his gambeson over his head. Will and Cedric would be waiting in the Hall with his hauberk, helmet and sword. In an emergency such as this there would be no time to don full armour.

'Stay here!' he threw at her as he hastened from the solar.

Joan had heard the bustle, the shouts from the tower battlements above her head, and appeared as Eleanor was slipping into her chamber-gown.

'What is it?' Eleanor demanded of her maid. 'Have you heard?'

'A ship, I believe, trying to sail up the estuary while the moon is dead.'

'Is it an enemy?'

'I don't know, sweeting. Time will tell. What will you do?'

'First I must dress. Then I'll go up to the battlements. I must know what is afoot!'

By the time they had arrived at their vantage point on the roof of the tower, archers had manned the battlements below, sheltered behind the curtain wall which overlooked the estuary. The ship slid silently through the water towards the river's narrow mouth. The sharp eyes and ears of a sentry had spotted a gleam of white sail and heard the rigging creak as it billowed in a sudden gust of wind.

As the ship glided between the tall cliffs it became more visible. Sir Peter Barraclough roared a challenge, which met with a ragged barrage of abuse in French.

The broad-beamed ship continued undeterred on its course. As the vessel sailed nearer its outlines could be deciphered: the huge sail; the unidentifiable flag fluttering from the mast-head; the fighting castles at bow and stern; the glint of steel from helmet and sword as the soldiers aboard waved their weapons in defiance, certain that there was no ship near by to halt their progress.

'A French warship, by the Holy Rood! They've forgotten the power of the longbow!' grinned one of the guards whom Eleanor and Joan had joined on the tower battlements. 'You'd think they'd have learnt their lesson, at Sluys and Crécy! These foreign dolts are dead men!'

A sharp order floated up from below. 'Loose!'

The men on the tower, leaning through the crenellations, added their arrows to the shower that fell like hail to find marks in the unfortunate mariners below.

The ship shifted course, steering towards the wider waters inside the cliffs, where it would be out of reach of the deadly shafts.

'Loose!'

Another hail of steel-tipped, goose-winged death flew through the darkness, and new screams of agony reached the tower. Judging from the high-pitched sound of frightened neighing, the knights had horses aboard. Great splashings could be heard above the commotion below as the wounded fell overboard and other men jumped rather than face another annihilating volley. Frantic shouts of command echoed over the water.

Gripped by intense excitement, Eleanor peered into the darkness, leaning out as far as she could over the wall, aware that the few answering crossbow bolts had ceased to fly. Flares had appeared, reflecting on the water further up the estuary. In their light she could make out the fishing vessels putting to sea.

'They're cutting them off!' she cried. 'Well done, the fishermen of Lower Wenfrith!'

'The raider has seen them, too!'

'It's turning tail!'

The exultant shout from the sergeant-at-arms in the next embrasure brought a thrill of victory running along Eleanor's tingling nerves. Richard had done it! His organising powers, his generalship, had won the day!

Their eyes were accustomed to the darkness by now, and they could watch the progress of the stricken vessel with comparative ease. As it turned about, to escape to the open sea, it fell foul of a freshening lee-wind. Though fast being driven out of range, arrows still rained spasmodically on the depleted crew trying frantically to steer the ship clear of the cliffs and catch the wind in the sail. But, inexorably, the boat was being swept around the point, driven towards rocks further along the coast.

Richard's cry went up. 'To your horses! To the cliffs!'

The sergeant-at-arms groaned. 'We must remain here, men! My orders are to keep watch! There may be another of the cowardly bastards hiding in the darkness out there! But by Jupiter, I'd like to join in the sport on the shore!'

'But your warning saved Wenfrith!' consoled Eleanor. She caught her breath. 'Look! There they go!'

The grooms had saddled and bridled the horses at the first sounds of alarm. With the drawbridge lowered, a stream of destriers thundered across and headed for the cliffs, followed by a trail of running men-at-arms, some of whom had snatched up flaming torches. They quickly disappeared into the darkness, their progress plotted only by the occasional bobbing flare.

Eleanor's exhilaration had turned to anxiety. Reluctantly, she left her vantage point to go down to the Great Hall.

The whole household was astir. She took refuge in activity, ordering huge cauldrons of water to be heated in the kitchen, spare linen to be brought for the binding of wounds. Joan was sent to fetch all the balms and ointments that she had in her store. Eleanor feared there would be many wounded to treat before dawn. And Richard would be in the thick of any battle.

On the clifftop, Richard reined Noble to a halt and viewed the stricken vessel with pitiless eyes. The rocks on which it had finally foundered were at the entrance to a small inlet, not far out, but the water would be too deep for the men to walk ashore. The ship was breaking up under the merciless pounding of the waves. The French soldiers would have to shed their armour if they hoped to survive.

Will and Cedric had strapped his leg- and arm-guards on while he had stood on the battlements. His other knights were equally well protected. Cedric and all the other squires wore steel helmets and stout hauberks of thick, boiled leather, some wore steel breast-plates, as did the men-at-arms, who were fast catching up with the lumbering destriers.

The men from the ship, knights, men-at-arms and seamen alike, would be unprotected and at their mercy.

'Dismount! We will go down to the shore to greet them!'

Richard's voice rang out over the water. He wanted the stranded men to know what awaited them on the beach. Led by torch-bearers, the whooping knights, followed by those squires old and skilled enough to bear arms, and some of the men-at-arms, made their way swiftly down the narrow, difficult path to the cove. A section of the force, under Sir Peter Barraclough's command, was left at the top to cut off the retreat of any who escaped the swords of those below, while the younger squires guarded the horses.

Richard, slithering down the precipitous path, closely followed by Cedric—Will, to his own chagrin, had been left behind with Noble—was aware of the pain in his thigh, the weakness of his leg. Grimly ignoring his disability, determined to lead his men into battle once again, he reached the narrow strip of sand just as the first wrecked men began to wade ashore.

'Yield!' he cried. 'You are our prisoners! Yield, and your lives will be spared!'

'*Mon Dieu!* Yield without a fight? Do you think we are lily-livered, to be frightened by a few English swords? *Avancez!* Come and take us!'

With ferocious cries, both sides joined battle. Steel rang against steel. The Frenchmen had of necessity shed their armour, but not their weapons or their pride.

Richard made straight for their leader, the man who had answered his challenge—a mere bantling, light on his feet without the weight of armour. As their swords clashed the soft sand gave under his injured leg. Searing pain brought a gasp of agony to his lips, and before he could begin to attack his wasted thigh muscle failed him. He found himself sprawled on the shifting sand, just managing to fend off a mighty blow from his opponent's broadsword.

The grinning, triumphant face peered down at him as the man raised his sword, threatening the *coup de grâce*. Richard lifted his weapon in a desperate attempt to parry the blow which he knew was coming. He was not afraid to die, had never feared honourable death on the battle-field. But as the deadly blade began to fall Eleanor's face flashed across his vision. It was gone as soon as it came, but in that instant he knew he had no wish to die. With a fierce cry he smashed away the sword and was scrambling painfully to his feet when a lithe body inter-posed itself between the combatants and a new blade took the force of the next blow.

The Frenchman turned to meet this other threat. Richard finished struggling to his feet, leaned on his sword, and watched in frustrated anger as Cedric wielded his to victorious effect.

The fight was more or less over. A few horses had swum ashore and their terrified lungings added to the chaos. But all along the beach the French, overwhelmed by numbers and circumstances, were admitting defeat. Richard limped painfully over to where Cedric stood over his conquest, his sword at the man's unguarded throat.

'Do you now yield?' Richard demanded fiercely. 'Tell your men to lay down their arms! You are outnumbered, and cannot win! We desire no further bloodshed!'

'We yield! *Merde!* But the weather was against us!' He rose gracefully to his feet, a small, strong man with merry eyes, a long, drooping moustache and a shaggy beard. He bowed. 'Gaston de Picard, *à votre service, monseigneur.*'

Two of the French party were too severely wounded to walk, and had to be carried up the precipitous cliff-path. The French horses were persuaded up with much noise and confusion and arrived at the top quite unfit to be ridden. The wounded and the French knights were found squires' horses. Surrounded by Richard and most of his victorious garrison, the prisoners were escorted back to the castle.

Eleanor heard the bustle of their arrival and ordered the steaming cauldrons to be brought from the kitchen. She waited anxiously, scarcely breathing, to see who would enter the Great Hall, and in what state.

Richard, entering with the Seigneur Gaston de Picard, did not see her eyes first seek out his tall figure, or the look of infinite relief that washed over her face at the sight of him. By the time he looked her way her eyes were alight with gladness and turned on Cedric.

He limped across and introduced the three Frenchmen, Gaston de Picard and the chevaliers André de Veysie and Henri de Champs. Despite their dishevelled state the French knights bowed with extravagant courtesy and panache. De Picard's luxuriant moustache and beard, his sweeping gestures, brought a suppressed smile to

Eleanor's lips. For such a short man he projected an impressive presence.

A small figure enveloped in a damp, grey cloak followed at the Frenchmen's heels.

'Brother Pierre-Paul was our ship's physician,' explained the Seigneur with another sweep of his arm. 'He can tend the wounded, if you will allow.'

'Of course. I have water and bandages ready, and salves to prevent the wounds from turning putrid——'

'Grand merci, madame.' The grey friar bowed his head in salute. 'As you can see, I saved my own instruments and ointments by wrapping them in my cloak and tying them to my head while I swam ashore.'

'My servants are at your disposal.'

Richard offered the shivering captives a drink of mulled wine, then had Stephen show the French knights to the guest-chamber. They had yielded themselves as prisoners and the chivalric code prevented any attempt at escape on their part. The question of ransoms would be discussed on the morrow.

The two surviving sailors and seven men-at-arms were escorted to the dungeon, where the Franciscan friar chose to join them, since he wished to be on hand to tend the wounded.

Eleanor was just about to persuade Richard back to their solar when new arrivals spurred the Hall into renewed activity. Fishermen from Lower Wenfrith arrived with half-a-dozen prisoners: seamen who, seeing the ship's captain killed and not being impeded by armour, had jumped overboard to save their skins. Since some of them were slightly wounded, the friar was brought up from the dungeon to tend them before they, too, were dispatched below.

A beach party had been left to guard the wreck during the remaining hours of darkness. The fishermen eagerly agreed to attempt to try to reach it by boat. At first light they would put out and try to board what remained of the vessel, not only to see if any of the French wounded had survived, but also to pillage any valuables that might be aboard.

'What a night! A victory to remember!'

Will and Joan had been dismissed. Eleanor could not understand Richard's lack of jubilation at his success, and sought to bring a smile of triumph to his sombre face.

'Indeed! I failed, woman! Were it not for your brother, Cedric, I should be a dead man!'

'Richard!' Eleanor's heart lurched. Had he truly been in such danger? 'Whatever can you mean?'

'My cursed leg will never recover,' he ground out in frustration. 'It let me down on the soft sand, refusing to stand up to anything more taxing than a minor practice deed of arms. I am no longer a man! My fighting days are over.'

It was all Eleanor could do not to weep at the desperation, the anger, the hopelessness in his voice. He sat slumped on his stool, and she longed to hold him to her, to press his dark head to her breast, to rock him as she would a hurt child. But instinct told her he needed reassurance, not comfort.

'Nonsense!' she exclaimed briskly. 'Who organised the defences? Who led the attack? You may be less able to engage in single combat, but you are a soldier bred and born! Did King Edward fight personally at Crécy?'

'Nay. He stationed himself in a windmill, where he could see the battle and direct the action——'

'And did any of his army think him less of a man for that?'

'He was holding himself in reserve. He would have fought—— '

'Aye, and so would you have done if you had stared defeat in the face! But there is nothing cowardly in doing what you can best achieve! You are a strategist, a leader——'

'Aye, one who leads from behind!'

'Richard!' she exclaimed in exasperation. 'Do you not realise that I am *glad* you can no longer put yourself in such danger? I would rather have you here, not campaigning all over France!'

'Maybe, woman, but *I* would rather be with the English army in France, Scotland, Ireland—wherever it has need of me!'

Eleanor felt as though he had slapped her in the face. That awful, inexplicable panic gripped her, as it had done before, and she lowered her lids so that Richard would not glimpse it in her eyes. As she fought the wave down a blinding flash of revelation told her something she must have known subconsciously for some time.

She loved Richard. The feeling had been growing since that first moment of encounter in the depressing Great Hall when he had stood before her, bloodied spear in hand. Panic had gripped her at times ever since, and now she could see the reason as clearly as the guttering torch on the wall.

She had instinctively feared the power that the Lord of Wenfrith could hold over her. If she fell in love with him she would be so very vulnerable, because he did not love her, and never would. She wondered if he were capable of love. Passion, yes. That, she knew, and gloried in the fact. Tenderness and compassion, too. But love?

She had as good as told Richard that she loved him, by admitting that she wished to keep him by her side! And he had scoffed, dismissing her desire as womanly sentiment, and had stated quite clearly where his heart lay.

The panic subsided, and she knew it would not return. Now that she had admitted the truth in her heart, faced the inevitable consequences, she would be free of her unreasoning fear.

She sighed, laying gentle hands on his bowed shoulders.

'I cannot argue with your desire to serve your King in battle, husband. But since you cannot be conquering nations all the time, will your conquest of my body not suffice? Come, dear lord. Let us seek our bed.'

He did not resist her touch, allowing her to knead much of the tension from the muscles bunched under her fingers. When she urged him to his feet he rose and accompanied her to the bed, flinging off his shirt before easing himself in beside her and settling down with a deep sigh.

Eleanor had never taken the initiative in their love-making before. But he was still tense, reluctant to submit

to the pull of his desire. Perhaps he saw it as another
form of weakness. Eleanor edged closer, massaging his
broad chest, loving the feel of the springy dark hair under
her inquisitive fingers. Her lips found his eyes, then tenderly kissed the broken brow before moving down to
claim his mouth.

As her lips lowered, so did her hand. His manhood
jerked to life at her touch, even as his mouth opened
under hers. With a stifled groan he kissed her deeply,
and before many moments had passed they were lost in
each other, mouths seeking, hands exploring, until
Richard rolled her over, parted her thighs and entered
her with a hoarse cry of triumph.

Richard held nothing back, and Eleanor had never
experienced such bliss. Her responses soared like birds,
she was lifted beyond the realms of the sky to reach the
sun, the source of all power and glory, under God.

Afterwards she held Richard close, pillowing his head
on her breasts. Now was the time for comfort and tenderness. Tomorrow he would be strong again.

Cedric was to be knighted! Eleanor glowed with
excitement.

Although Richard bitterly resented his own weakness,
he was able to recognise and admire the prowess which
had saved his life.

'You won your spurs last night, brother. Do you hold
vigil tonight, and you shall be knighted on the morrow.'

'My lord!' Cedric's open face beamed with joy. 'But
are you certain? The Seigneur was without
armour——'

'And confirms your skill with the sword, *mon fils*!'
Gaston de Picard swept one of his extravagant bows.
One of the knights had found him tunic and hose which
fitted tolerably well. On him the unremarkable garments
looked flamboyant. 'Accept your honour,' he advised
cheerfully. 'You have earned it!'

'You have sword, lance, shield and helmet. I shall
provide your mailed hauberk, and, naturally, your
golden spurs. With what arms will you charge your
shield, pennon and surcoat?' asked Richard.

'The dragon of Wessex d'or in a field of azure. In that way I acknowledge my Saxon heritage.'

Eleanor held her breath, wondering if Cedric would enlarge upon this statement. Had the Conqueror not invaded, Cedric would have been an atheling of Wessex. But Cedric held his peace, and Richard accepted his statement without comment.

Only one man had been found still alive on the French ship, but a number of precious articles had been salvaged, which Richard distributed among the garrison and the fishermen. Father Pierre-Paul was tending the man, a knight too severely wounded to shed his armour and swim. The friar feared that Jean d'Artois would not survive.

'Richard?'

'Aye, wife?'

Eleanor was glad they had brought tubs back with them from Wenstaple, because Cedric would be able to have his ritual bath. Now he was in the chapel. Cleansed in body and soul, he would be in a fit state to receive the honour of knighthood on the morrow. She drew her brows together slightly, then pressed on with what she had to say.

'Think you there is any chance that Sir Ralph Radcliffe would accept Cedric as a suitor for Anne's hand, once he is knighted? Our family is not without wealth——'

Richard leaned forward to stand his pewter goblet on the solar hearth. 'But Baron Mangate is rich and powerful! And the negotiations are well advanced.'

'I know, but I doubt if any contract has been signed. And I do so pity Anne! Cedric is still attracted to her. She will lose her childish ways, will learn discretion. They would do well together.'

Was there nothing she would not seek for Cedric's happiness? Was there nothing he would not do to bring that glow of happiness to her lovely face? Richard shifted irritably. Yet it would do him no disservice to aid her brother further. He hunched a shoulder and smiled, if a trifle grimly.

'I will enquire.' He could not voice his misgivings without offending her Saxon pride. The Radcliffes would not be best pleased. Nevertheless, 'A messenger shall be dispatched within the week,' he promised.

'Thank you, husband. Perhaps we could entertain Sir Ralph and Lady Radcliffe here? Though it would be better if Anne remained behind; it would be well if she did not meet Stephen again so soon.'

'I will demand their presence here to discuss the matter. I must send to France, too, to arrange the ransoms of our French guests.' He chuckled. 'I like the Seigneur and his chevaliers. They are men after my own heart.'

'They are good company, and they seem in no rush to return to their own land!'

'There is no fighting at the present. The moment a new campaign begins they will wish to depart with all speed!'

'I think their lack of urgency has more to do with the great pestilence which is sweeping across Europe from the East.' Eleanor shuddered. 'I hope it does not cross the Channel! They say no one is safe, it strikes so swiftly, and stinking bodies pile up with none to bury them! Towns and villages are being wiped out!'

'Aye. Please God it will not touch us. The King has brought the army home just in time. Come, wife.' He grinned, a wicked grin, not attempting to hide the passion smouldering in the depths of his eyes. 'Do not concern yourself. Let us seek our bed.'

CHAPTER ELEVEN

DESPITE a wintry November mistiness, Eleanor joined the hunting party setting out from Wenfrith. She was by now an accomplished markswoman and had already brought down the occasional prey. The exercise was exhilarating whether they made a kill or not, but a feeling of deep satisfaction added to the pleasure when their quarry was carried home in triumph to boost the contents of the store-room.

That morning the party was large, since they were joined at the last moment by Gaston de Picard and his chevaliers—Jean d'Artois miraculously fully recovered from his wounds—as well as Sir Peter Barraclough and his squire, Sir Ralph and Lady Radcliffe, and Cedric, now an accepted suitor for Anne's hand. Will accompanied Richard, while Brigid—Lady Radcliffe—rode beside Eleanor. A couple of men-at-arms accompanied them to deal with the kill.

Luck was with them. They had not been out long before a startled stag leapt from cover and went crashing through the undergrowth. The hounds bayed, the horn blew, and with wild whoops of joy the party streamed after their quarry.

It led them a merry and exhausting chase before an arrow from Cedric's bow brought it down and the hounds closed in. Richard called them off and, while the men-at-arms dealt with the dead stag, the others began a pleasant, leisurely amble back to the castle.

The path was well-worn, winding to the edge of the forest from whence the track led back to Wenfrith. The men were ahead, Eleanor and Brigid riding a short distance behind, Eleanor scanning the undergrowth for some small animal to add to their bag, when, without warning, Silver whinnied and shied and Lady Radcliffe's horse reared. Even as she soothed the highly strung animal and brought her under control, Eleanor saw the reason for Silver's fright.

Men were dropping from the trees ahead! Dropping on the men from the hunting party and dragging them from their mounts! And the men were without armour!

Confusion was absolute as the riderless horses neighed and pranced, their hoofs mercifully missing the men, who were struggling to throw off their attackers and draw their swords.

Watching helplessly, Eleanor saw the horses extricate themselves from the mêlée and canter off down the path. One by one the men managed to escape their assailants and scramble to their feet, and cries and grunts mixed with the clash of steel as sword met sword or knife. Her horrified anxiety lessened and she began to relax as she saw that the knights were beating off their attackers. The

footpads began to turn and run off into the undergrowth, chased by their intended victims. Richard was
engaged by a hefty fellow who, although he wielded his
sword skilfully enough, was being forced steadily backwards. Eleanor urged Silver forward a step or two in her
anxiety to follow the fight.

As she shifted, her attention was caught by a
movement from behind the bole of a nearby tree.

A man stood in its cover, winding up a crossbow.
Eleanor gave a warning shout, but it went unheard over
the din of the fight, and as he raised the weapon Eleanor
realised that he was sighting it straight at Richard's back!

Her reaction was instinctive. Her bow was still in her
hand with an arrow knocked on, ready to let fly at an
unwary coney or hare. In one swift movement she drew,
aimed and loosed. The shaft flew unerringly to its target.
The man screamed and jerked, the crossbow bolt skit-
tered off into the branches overhead, and Richard's
opponent disengaged and fled.

'God's blood!'

'By Christ!'

'Doux Jésu!'

'Who in Satan's name——?'

'Parbleu! But you provide splendid sport here, *mon
ami*!'

'Eleanor! Eleanor, it's all right, my dear! Here,
dismount!'

The confused babble barely impinged on her consciousness. A wave of sickness washed over her and she
almost fell from her horse to be clasped tightly in
Richard's arms, and after that nothing else mattered.
She leaned against him and shook convulsively, the tears
coursing down her cheeks. Then she was lifted and,
pressed against her husband's chest, carried back to
Wenfrith on Midnight's back.

The horses had not strayed far. The dogs had gone
baying after the retreating attackers. Although Gem came
back with a scrap of woollen cloth in her mouth, no
other sign of the outlaw band remained.

As for the man Eleanor had shot, he would tell no
tales. The arrow had pierced his heart.

Richard carried her up to the solar. Brigid Radcliffe bustled importantly behind.

'Sweet Jesus!' came Joan's anxious voice as she panted into the room. 'Whatever ails my dear mistress?'

''Tis nothing! Do not be concerned, she will recover shortly. Brigid, will you explain what happened? I wish to be left alone with my wife. I'll call when you are needed.'

Once they had left, Richard sat on the edge of the bed where Eleanor lay staring sightlessly at the hangings. She had stopped shaking, but he didn't like the blank look in her eyes. He had seen it before, on the battle-field, when a new knight or squire was blooded.

'Sweet wife,' he murmured, stroking the hair from her brow. Her veil and circlet had been lost somewhere along the way, and one of her heavy golden braids had come loose. 'Eleanor, can you understand what I say?'

Slowly, she turned her eyes to meet his. Her quivering lips moved soundlessly and her eyes filled again with tears.

'Eleanor, sweet wife, you did the only possible thing.'

This time sound did come, thin and whispery. 'I killed a man.'

'Aye. In battle. And, according to Brigid Radcliffe, you saved my life. How can I ever repay my debt?'

'You don't have to, lord. I acted without thought——'

'And would you have done differently had you considered the matter?'

She shook her head, and an overwhelming sense of relief swept over her as she clutched at Richard's hand, warm, vital proof that he was alive and unharmed. 'No. I could never have allowed him to kill you. But—oh, Richard!'

The tears came now in earnest—cleansing tears, washing away her sense of guilt. She clung to Richard's solid body, soaking his tunic as he held her head pressed against his shoulder.

'There, dear wife. You must forget this thing. Such scum is not worthy of your tears!'

Eleanor sniffed, wiping her nose and eyes on a handy kerchief. 'I'm sorry, husband! You must think me foolish

indeed, to be upset over such a matter! I watched the
garrison shower arrows on the Seigneur's ship and
cheered, but I never thought how it would feel to kill a
man myself.'

'Nay, and neither should it have been necessary! Such
affairs are for men to settle! But you proved yourself as
brave as any knight today.'

'I did not feel brave! And I shall fear to go into the
forest again——'

'No need. The vagrants and outlaws have doubtless
gone to more fruitful parts. We have not been troubled
by their like before, and I doubt we shall be in the future.'

'Dear lord, I trust you are right!'

'Thank God the French knights rode out with us!
Otherwise we might well have been overwhelmed! But
we shall be more wary from now on. Had we looked up,
we must have seen them——'

'They chose their position well. Although the low,
spreading branches were almost bare of leaves they were
thickly wreathed in ivy. And the crossbowman was
hidden behind a trunk——'

'Aye, that troubles me a little, that they were able to
pick their spot so well...' Richard stroked his beard, a
thoughtful frown on his face. 'Mayhap they had some
local wretch among their number... Men are scouring
the woods, but the vermin will be long gone. Another
mystery, wife.'

He was referring to her grey friar. Eleanor pushed the
memory aside as an icy trickle of fear ran down her spine.
'Richard, was anyone hurt?'

'A few minor cuts and bruises. Nothing serious. Cedric
came through unscathed.'

'Trust Cedric!'

'Aye. And you are recovered now. Shall I call Joan?'

'No.' Eleanor sought the glittering statue of the Virgin
with her eyes. Her conscience was not yet fully free of
guilt. 'Can you send Sir Piers, or Brother Pierre-Paul?
I must make confession...'

He kissed her gently on the forehead. 'You have committed no crime, my Eleanor. But seek absolution if you
must. As for me, I shall raise a prayer of thanksgiving
for our safety, and for the courage of my wife.'

After she had made her confession and been shriven, Eleanor knelt for a long time at the prie-dieu, gazing up into the calm features of the Virgin. In the flickering light of the candles she had lit, the eyes appeared compassionate, the lips to smile.

'Dear Lady,' she whispered, 'make him proud of me. Let him love me as I love him.'

Advent came, and Cedric, attired in splendid knightly regalia, was off to Radcliffe Manor to attend his betrothal ceremony. He had seen Anne but once, when he had returned with Sir Ralph and his wife after their visit to Wenfrith. Anne had by then accepted the impossibility of marrying Stephen and had thankfully, if not enthusiastically, agreed to wed Cedric in preference to Oliver of Mangate. Sir Ralph had perforce had to agree, because a request from his liege lord was as good as a command.

'She will make you a good wife, and will bring you a fine manor. Father will be delighted,' said Eleanor, patting the golden Wessex dragon emblazoned on his broad chest with sisterly pride.

'If Adam and Henry need help, we should be able to afford it, between us. Our vaunted lineage has brought little profit, but your marriage has brought our family many blessings, sister. You are happy?'

'Aye, Cedric. I think Richard still regrets my Saxon birth, but my husband is a just and generous man, and I have no complaint.'

'Methinks his temper has improved, sister. Mayhap 'tis your influence?'

Eleanor laughed, covering a sensitive embarrassment with a dismissive gesture. 'Now the King is home, his frustration at being unable to join the army at Calais has passed. And his health has improved, he has regained his strength.'

'But the strength will never fully return to his leg, will it? I doubt he will be able to take to the field in battle again.'

'He knows that, and it distresses him. I pray that, by the time another campaign begins, he will be content commanding his garrisons here and at Wenstaple.'

'And, perhaps raising a family. He will make a fond father, I imagine, by the way he treats young Tamkin.'

'Aye, and Tamkin trusts and adores him. Cedric, how I wish I had not lost the baby!'

The old pain welled up again, and stupid tears filled her eyes. As she scrubbed angrily at the evidence of her weakness, Cedric put a sturdy arm around her shoulders.

'Don't weep, sister! There will be other children, never fear! Soon, perhaps!'

Eleanor smiled mistily through the remains of her tears, and put her arms around his waist as he stood beside her stool. 'Cedric, what would I do without you?' she murmured.

'Now there's a touching sight!'

Richard's sardonic voice from the doorway made them jump guiltily apart, though there was no cause. But Cedric had already sensed something of his mentor's resentment of his closeness to his sister, and, although he did not understand it, had no wish to strain their relationship.

Eleanor did not want Richard to realise her continued weakness, and sought to hide her watery eyes.

'I was making my farewells. I leave for Radcliffe Manor immediately. I shall return ere the week is out,' Cedric promised.

'I'm glad you are to remain in my service for the time being. I can use a mighty sword-arm like yours, brother! God speed you on your way, and I wish you joy of Demoiselle Anne!'

'My thanks! Farewell, sister. I will give your greetings to Anne.'

'Tell her I hope to see her soon. God go with you, Cedric!'

'And remain with you.'

By the time he had left the solar Eleanor's tears had dried, but not before Richard had noticed them. Damnation! Was the wench so besotted with her brother that she wept when he was to be away for a few days? Yet he could not dislike Cedric! The hidden anger made his voice brusque when he spoke.

'You will miss him, wife.'

'Cedric? Mayhap, a little. But listen! Is that not the gate-ward's horn? Someone comes!'

Together, they went down to the Great Hall, where Cedric was still saying his farewells.

A guard rushed in, shouting excitedly. 'A King's messenger! A King's messenger!'

A man entered the Hall, wearing the King's livery with the Plantagenet broom badge emblazoned on his arm. He bowed low and approached Richard, presenting the scroll of parchment on bended knee.

'A mug of ale for the messenger! Rest awhile, and await my reply. Come, wife. We will return to our solar.'

Eleanor waited expectantly as Richard broke the royal seal and began to peruse the writing that the parchment contained.

'What is it?' she asked impatiently. 'Not bad news?'

Richard's lean features broke into a smile of satisfaction.

'Nay, but good! Wife, I have been singled out for a great honour! Have you heard of the new order of chivalry King Edward has introduced? That of the Garter?'

'With which he hopes to re-introduce the legendary ideals of King Arthur and his knights of the round table?'

'You are well-informed, wife!'

'What has that to do with the message?'

'I am invited—nay, commanded—to join the Order!'

'You? Oh Richard! What an honour! What must you do?'

'Go to Eltham! King Edward has decided to hold a celebration tournament there in January.'

'A tournament!' Eleanor could not keep the anxiety out of her voice. 'Will you be competing?'

Richard glanced down at the parchment again. 'I think not.' His voice was flat, hiding disappointment. 'It says here that nine of the founder members of the Order will joust together, but nothing of others taking part. Mayhap there will be minor feats of arms. I do not know. But there will be an initiation ceremony, and a Garter feast afterwards.'

'I am happy for you, husband. But I shall miss you while you are away.'

Richard glanced at her questioningly, because genuine sadness had tinged her voice.

'More than you will miss Cedric?' He made his tone teasing, but awaited her response with an anxiety which irked him.

'You are my husband! I have already told you that I wish for nothing better than to keep you at my side! Cedric and I grew up together. Of course I shall miss him, but not in the way that I shall miss you!'

Richard relaxed, and a smile quirked the corners of his long mouth as he pulled her towards him.

'Then you will be glad to know that the summons extends to my wife and certain of my retinue!' He kissed her lips lingeringly. 'Shall we take Cedric?'

'Richard! I am to go to Eltham?'

'Indeed.'

His tone was neutral, but his eyes smiled. He showed no sign of wishing to leave her behind. Her happiness bubbled over into laughter. 'We must catch Cedric! He may still be downstairs!'

'Aye.' Richard laughed with her, his fears set to rest, his jubilation making him feel like a schoolboy. 'Let us spread the glad news! Tonight we will break open a new tun of wine!'

As he followed his wife down the stairs, Richard realised that to leave Eleanor behind would take all the joy from the occasion. He needed her with him! And would be proud to have her by his side.

Where was the nobly born Norman wench who could compare with his Eleanor in dignity, courage and goodness? He could present her at Court without shame. Saxon, Norman, what did an accident of birth matter? Bloodlines were important, but could not transcend the superiority of character. Eleanor had taught him this. The King was right. It was indeed time to heal old wounds, for all those who called themselves English to be united in one nation.

The Great Hall had filled in their absence, everyone sensing that the King would not send a messenger unless the tidings were important. Cedric had not yet gone, and received the news with a whoop of joy and a glad acceptance of the chance to travel with them. And the retinue began to wager on who else would be chosen to accompany the Earl and Countess on their journey.

Travelling with an Earl's retinue was rather different from journeying as a merchant, as Eleanor soon discovered. Richard sent outriders ahead to arrange their accommodation, seeking hospitality in castles, manor houses and monasteries along their way. Instead of sharing a dorter and possibly a bed with strangers, Eleanor found herself sleeping in reasonable comfort and privacy, since the guest-chamber was always made available to the Earl and his Countess. Accommodation also had to be found for the thirty or so knights, squires, retainers and servants who travelled with them, but they were not always so lucky in the quarters allocated.

Once the twelve days of Christmas revelry had finished and the new year of 1348 been well and truly seen in, the household began the difficult winter's journey across the southern half of England. Richard decided to start off in good time, since some of the roads might be impassable and delays unavoidable.

Fortunately, the weather was dry and frosty, so that although the roads were hard-ridged and slippery, travelling was not impossible. Their fingers froze around the reins and their feet turned to solid blocks of ice in the stirrups, but progress was good, and they had time to stop off during the day at ordinary inns, taverns and manor houses along the way for rest, food and warmth.

Richard mostly rode at the head of the column, with Eleanor, Joan and Tamkin—happily astride his little stallion—somewhere in the middle, well protected from footpads by the retinue of armed men. The pack-horses straggled along behind, also well guarded.

Silver seemed to be enjoying the outing, and Eleanor rode in high spirits. Much as she loved Wenfrith, it was good to be out in the world again, and to be accepted as Richard's equal. Few had looked askance, most had given ungrudging respect. Watching Richard covertly, Eleanor had noted the pleasure in his eyes whenever she was greeted cordially and with all the courtesy demanded by her rank. As the journey had progressed, he had relaxed. Now, she believed, his anxiety had been set at rest and he was able to present her with pride rather than diffidence. Not that he had ever allowed his diffidence to show: she had sensed it under the surface of his assured, confident, courteous but autocratic manner.

Her pride in him grew daily, along with her love. How she prayed that there would be no covert looks, no sly innuendos to mar what should be, for him, a time for joyful celebration of his achievements. Maybe he hadn't amassed the riches of men like Henry of Derby, now the Earl of Lancaster, who had fought brilliant campaigns to recover Agenais and Périgord, had overrun half of Poitou, and taken the English King's power almost to the gates of Toulouse. But Richard had excelled himself on the field of battle, and his rewards had been substantial. Her dowry had been merely the sugar-coating on a costly marchpane subtilty.

They passed through Salisbury but, to Eleanor's disappointment, their route did not take them far enough north for her to see Windsor Castle.

'I would so love to see it!' she exclaimed as they came to the bank of the Thames, where it wended its way south in a great loop before turning back towards London.

'I'm told the Round Tower grows apace,' remarked Richard, who had dropped back to ride at her side for a while. 'It will be a fitting home for the round table being specially made for our Order.'

'Our hostess of last night had been there,' said Eleanor enviously. 'She said that although the castle is so large, the tower threatens to dwarf it!'

'Perhaps, at some future time, we will be ordered to attend His Majesty there! Then you can explore to your heart's content!'

'Do you know what manner of place Eltham Palace is?'

'I have not seen it, but am told it is a beautiful building, gracious and more comfortable than any of the royal castles, and is the Queen's favourite residence. I am looking forward to seeing if rumour is true!'

A couple of days later they approached their destination. After the spectacular countryside around Wenfrith, the Kentish land appeared soft and flat, though in truth it was by no means without hills. What would Essex look like to her eyes now? Eleanor wondered. There one could see level fields extending without break to a distant horizon.

'An uneventful journey, praise God!' remarked Richard as they mounted up for the last time.

'The road is becoming busy,' smiled Eleanor. 'It seems that all England is converging on Eltham!'

'Aye.' He cast an appraising eye over a rich procession making its way along the track, its fur-wrapped lord riding in splendour at its head. 'The Earl of Eaton, by his blazon! I don't know him. We'll let him pass.'

'His wife rides in a litter!'

'Perhaps she is with child.'

Eleanor's stomach churned and she felt slightly sick at this reminder of the baby she had lost, but she managed another smile. 'Then she must be much younger than her husband! He is grey and shrunken; he looks too old to get an heir!'

'He has one already! See that knight's pennon, with the Earl's arms differenced by a bar?'

'Then perhaps she is not well enough to ride!'

'Wife, the gossip around the Court will answer all your questions! But beware! Believe most of it at your peril!'

'And beware of assignations, flirtations and all temptation! I know, my lord! I have been well instructed in these matters!'

'Then heed what you have heard! The Court is not the place for those who would lead a quiet life, nor for those with no stomach for intrigue!'

'Then I wonder what I am doing here!'

Richard shot her a strange look. 'Do you wish yourself elsewhere, wife?'

'Nay, lord! Where should I be but at your side? But...I hope we will not be expected to spend too much of our time at Court?'

'I doubt it. Edward knows how I dislike the ceremony and protocol, the gossip and intrigue. He will excuse us from long attendance, I'm sure. The Earl's retinue has passed. Shall we proceed?'

Being a Knight Companion of the Order of the Garter gave Richard privileges not extended to most. He was allocated one of the limited number of private chambers, which had small wardrobes and pallet rooms attached where his gentlemen and her ladies could attend them and sleep. Apart from Joan, Will, Cedric and Tamkin, the remainder of their retinue, even the knights, would have to share dorters with the retainers of other nobles. The men-at-arms would find pallets in the barracks.

Richard had worn only breastplate and sword on the journey, but had brought the rest of his armour with him, including his tourney heaume. Eleanor watched Will hang the pieces on perches round the walls, knowing Richard was still hoping to enter the lists. He had even brought Noble, although he had made the journey on Midnight's back. She knew that he would acquit himself bravely, but couldn't help feeling a deep anxiety. His disability could cause him some humiliating defeat. If only his own opinion of himself did not depend so strongly on his ability with arms! He had proved himself over and over again, and no man could be blamed for an honourable wound in combat!

Eleanor dressed carefully for supper, knowing that she would be presented to the royal couple afterwards. She wore the gown made for her wedding, and with it her new jewelled chaplet over hair held in place by cauls of pure gold. Richard's seal ring was on her finger, his brooch on her breast, and the dagger he had bought her at Wenstaple at her hip. She possessed costly jewellery of her own, but chose to wear only a wrought golden bracelet which her father had given her to mark her eighteenth birthday and betrothal to William of Evreux.

The royal family would occupy the high table, but Richard and Eleanor were shown to places at a trestle quite near by, with other new Garter knights, almost all of whom had campaigned together in France and fought at Crécy.

Once the exchange of greetings was over Eleanor had time to take in her surroundings. Sweet herbs had been strewn with fresh rushes on the floor of the Great Hall, quite overwhelming the usual odours of sweat, smoke, tallow and food. Innumerable torches blazed from silver holders fixed to stone wall and column, while hundreds of candles cast their light on the linen-covered boards.

The high table was hung with an ornate frontal which gleamed with all the colours of the rainbow in the brilliant light, while golden plate and cups studded with jewels adorned its top. The royal gerfalcons brooded on perches above their masters' chairs.

Fanfare followed fanfare as the King and Queen led in the royal Princes, Dukes and Earls. The royal couple ceremonially dipped their fingers into a bowl of water held by a kneeling gentleman and had them dried and kissed by another. The gentleman usher showed them to their canopied thrones and then disposed the others at the table. Grace was said and, amid more fanfares and ceremony, the first course was presented.

Duck, herons, capon, pork and venison. Larks in an almond sauce, tarts and a couple of complicated dishes which Eleanor had never tasted before. Richard began with pork, but Eleanor chose to experiment, and quite enjoyed the amazing mixture of meats, herbs and spices which the server had said was sarsed browet.

In fact she was too excited to eat much. The King was quite as splendid as she had expected. Still in his prime at thirty-six, with the Plantagenets' long nose, high cheekbones and deep-set eyes, he exuded the fair charm and authority which made him such a brilliant leader of men. Magnificent in a surcoat emblazoned with the lilies of France quartering the leopards of England, he wore a small golden crown on his distinguished, tawny head.

Despite a glittering costume, Queen Philippa was rather a disappointment, since her thickening figure was great with child and her features were heavy, displaying her Flemish blood. But she had a kind heart. Had she not pleaded successfully with her husband on her knees for the lives of the six burghers of Calais, whom Edward had ordered to bring the keys of the town to him, with ropes around their necks, ready for hanging?

'Is that the Prince of Wales?' Eleanor whispered to Richard, who had finished his pork and was gnawing the flesh from the roast leg of a plump capon.

He glanced to where she had nodded. 'Aye, that's Edward of Woodstock.'

'He is quite small,' observed Eleanor, slightly disappointed.

'He is not yet full-grown, wife. You forget, he is still only seventeen!'

'But he is scarce bigger than his brother! That is Lionel, is it not?'

'Lionel was always large for his years. He has grown into a hulking lad, and no mistake. John now, he's in proportion for his age. Not too big, not too small!'

'But the image of his father!'

Eleanor studied the earnest face of the small boy intent upon his food. He was the same age as Tamkin, she realised with a shock. Both had been born around the time of Sluys. Queen Philippa had gone to Ghent to await her husband's victorious arrival, and the child had been delivered there, thus earning him the title of John of Gaunt. But whereas Tamkin was still very much an unpolished gem, John had been reared with royal privilege, and had acquired all the princely graces.

Between Prince Edward and Prince Lionel sat Princess Isabel, a solid child of around Anne's age, who preened herself as though she were a beauty, but took unattractively after her mother. Her younger sister, the Princess Jean, was already on her way to Spain to marry the heir of Castile.

The King had set Lancaster in the place of honour. The latter was older, too old for campaigning by most men's standards. Yet he was Edward's most brilliant commander, and by seating him there the King acknowledged his debt to him.

The second and third courses were heralded and paraded, many of the dishes similar to those that had preceded them, but the subtilty accompanying the third course brought a gasp of admiration from everyone's lips. Exquisitely fashioned from pastry and marchpane, smothered in costly sugar, it represented the siege of Calais in amazing detail and realistic colour.

How the kitchens had managed to produce all these astonishing dishes Eleanor could only guess. During the days of the tournament they would be catering for around five thousand people for every meal. The mere thought of the organisation involved made her head spin.

Over the meal the knights talked reminiscently of the glorious campaign just ended. From the landing at St

Vaast the army had marched to Caen, which fell in a
single day, then on through France, playing strategic
games with the amassed French army until, having successfully forded the Somme against the odds, Edward
had decided to make a stand at Crécy. Eleanor listened
to tales of privation, of short rations, of exhaustion, of
their eagerness for the battle to commence! How stupid
the French had been, to fling in their mounted armour
in wave after wave until eventually the army had begun
to dissolve! And she formed a gruesome picture of the
dead piled in walls in front of the English knights and
men-at-arms, who had waited on foot for the archers to
shoot the horses from under their enemy and then fought
them hand-to-hand in a solid, unbreakable line.

Richard had never spoken in detail of the battle. As
these men re-lived it and the full horror of what had
taken place registered on her mind—over eleven thousand
Frenchmen and their allies had died—Eleanor eyed the
elated young faces gathered around the table in something like disbelief. When the battle had ended they'd
been supperless, thirsty, but victorious, and had simply
dropped to the ground to sleep the sleep of exhaustion
on the spot where they had fought! Except for Richard,
who had been carried from the field.

'God's wounds! You were a lion that day! But I'd not
thought to see you alive again, d'Evreux!' cried one of
the knights. 'You looked like to end your days on the
battlefield, as we would all prefer!'

'De Rede saved me,' Richard told them, without his
usual bitterness. In the company of these men he had
regained his self-esteem, thought Eleanor, with satisfaction. His had been an honourable wound, and talking
over old glories had restored his pride. None of the others
were entering the lists, so there was no question of his
being left out because of his disability.

'He's here, somewhere,' supplied one of the other
knights. 'He was looking forward to seeing you and your
lady again.'

'Aye, no doubt we'll meet later.'

'You missed nothing at Calais,' went on someone else.
'By my oath, that was a tedious wait, relieved only by
rumours of plague and the arrival of some of our

families! Even the Queen came! You were better engaged bedding your new and lovely wife!'

'All the same, I wish I had been there!' said Richard,
but cheerfully, and with little sign of real regret. 'We
had some sport with a French raider at Wenfrith...' He
went on to detail the action and boast of the valuable
prisoners he had taken.

'With their ransoms and your share of the spoils of
Caen you'll have riches enough to last you a lifetime!'
cried someone enviously.

Richard smiled, a little complacently, Eleanor thought,
and realised that he was no longer envious of his com-
panions. Some subtle change, which she silently ap-
plauded, was taking place in her husband's attitudes.

After the meal the presentations began. Only a few
bore precedence over the Countess of Wenstaple. Richard
took her trembling fingers and led her towards the dais
and the royal thrones. Richard knelt, while she curtsied
low.

'My liege, may I present my wife, Eleanor?'

'Ah, Wenstaple! You are recovered from your wounds,
I hear!'

'Aye, well enough, Sire.'

'And this is your Countess. Very lovely. I congrat-
ulate you. Eleanor of Clare, isn't it?'

Eleanor curtsied again, speechless.

'I have met your father. A worthy burgher.'

He extended his hand and, as Eleanor dropped to her
knees to kiss the great ring holding the royal seal, her
heart landed like a stone in the pit of her stomach at the
disdain she sensed in the King's attitude.

Queen Philippa smiled kindly as Eleanor kissed her
plump hand, and they passed on to the King's eldest
son.

'D'Evreux!' exclaimed Edward, smiling graciously. 'I
am delighted to see you recovered! And your new
Countess! Congratulations, my friend. I wish you both
much happiness!'

Eleanor could detect no hint of censure in his voice,
though the eyes scrutinising her were shrewd and as-
sessing. She allowed Richard to lead her back to her seat

and sat, stiff-backed, waiting for him to ignore her, since
she had brought him contempt from the King.

'Wife!'

There was some kind of emotion in her lord's voice.
As she lifted reluctant eyes, trying to hide the hurt she
felt, she realised that his held nothing but pride. 'You
are more beautiful than the Queen or the Princess,' he
murmured low, though there was little chance of their
being overheard amid the din in the Hall. 'The King liked
you.'

'He did?' she asked incredulously. Had she become
so sensitive that she had imagined the note of disdain?

'Aye. So did the Queen and the Prince. I was proud
of the way you bore yourself, Eleanor.'

Like a lump of salt in water, the stone in her stomach
disintegrated and dissolved. She lowered her lashes in
case Richard should see the blazing love in her eyes and
be embarrassed.

'Then my prayers have been answered, husband,' she
breathed.

In part, at least.

CHAPTER TWELVE

Now that the frost had disappeared, the extensive
gardens of Eltham Palace were pleasant for an after-
noon walk. Wearing wooden pattens over her shoes as
protection from the damp grass, Eleanor led Tamkin
across a huge lawn towards an artificial lake, where she
hoped the boy would enjoy feeding the ducks and swans.

Jousting was over. For three days she had sat with
Richard in the King's loge watching the spectacular feats
of arms. No one had been surprised when the Earl of
Lancaster had proved himself the most worthy knight,
though Prince Edward, mounted on a huge destrier and
wearing his black armour, impressively skilful despite
his youth, had run him so close that the declaration of
a tie had been greeted with resounding cheers by lords
and commoners alike. Both men were worshipped as

popular heroes and to honour one without the other would have been unthinkable.

As she strolled across the grass Eleanor rubbed her behind ruefully. She had enjoyed the tournament, but after a while even the red velvet cushions had not been able to relieve the hardness of the bench.

The feast of spectacle and excitement still held her imagination. Splendid canopied loges had lined the lists, the royal one in the centre, flanked by Prince Edward's on one side and Lancaster's on the other.

As Richard's Countess, Eleanor had been accorded all the deference due her rank. Richard had received many congratulations on his lovely bride. Only occasionally had she caught a glimpse of disdain in anyone's eyes, usually someone with exalted ideas of their own importance.

Those few would be bound to talk spitefully behind her back, but Eleanor had ceased to worry. Richard had said he was proud of her, and other people's opinion mattered not one whit unless it bothered Richard. She smiled contentedly to herself, hugging her body beneath her warm mantle in secret delight. Her lack of birth no longer had the power to dismay him!

The Queen, magnificently decked out in jewels and ermine and a mantle which almost hid the signs of her pregnancy, with Lionel, Isobel and John sitting fidgeting beside her, had sat in the front row with the King, whose spiky golden crown had risen above the heads of all those surrounding him. Eleanor had looked down from her position in the third row behind a distinguished Duke, and thought that she had never before seen such a glittering couple.

The Prince of Wales had not sat in his loge, since he was taking a leading part in the joust, but Sir Gilbert had been allocated a place there. On the first morning he had smiled across with a bow, and Eleanor had acknowledged his greeting with a warm smile.

'See, there is Sir Gilbert!' she'd exclaimed, calling Richard's attention with a touch on his arm.

'So he has appeared! He was missing last evening, although I was told he had arrived. Some assignation, I suspect.'

'Do you think so?' Eleanor was intrigued. She wondered who the lucky lady was, and determined to find out!

'I wouldn't be surprised, although I myself was occupied with the initiation ceremony, as you know. Perhaps I just missed him.'

Eleanor quickly forgot Sir Gilbert. She was anticipating the coming bouts with an eagerness which would have been entirely lacking had Richard been taking part. Since he was safe at her side, she could relax and allow the excitement to grip her.

She had thought Richard's tournament at Wenfrith splendid, but this was, by any standard, magnificent. The knights' pavilions and banners made a sea of bright colour in an adjacent field, the heralds' and marshals' outfits brilliant splashes against the green turf. The sound of trumpets was almost incessant until two of the gorgeously accoutred knights set their equally as splendid destriers to charge down the lists.

The crowd watched in tense silence as hoofs thundered and clods of turf flew high into the air behind the mighty war-horses. At the tremendous crash as lance met shield the audience erupted into sound. Cheers and boos and raucous sounds of mock-derision met the result of the clash.

'What a blessing their lances are blunted!' Eleanor exclaimed, leaning forward in her anxiety to see if the fallen knight would rise safely.

'They are in no danger.' Richard smiled indulgently. 'No one was hurt at Wenfrith, and these men are more expert at the sport! See, the unseated knight is already remounting.'

The King had insisted that everything be done with the requisite ceremony and chivalric observances. She knew that there were some who found the ritual tedious but, caught up in the mood of those around her, Eleanor enjoyed the colourful pageantry.

The Garter knights not jousting, with their ladies, sat behind the King, in full regalia. Brilliant surcoats blazoned their arms beneath costly blue cloaks, lined with fur to keep out the winter chill. Eleanor particularly liked Richard's hat, made of a stylish felt, lavishly decorated

with plumes and hanging drapery. Each knight wore a
special new insignia incorporating the cross of Saint
George on his left breast, and a blue garter embroidered
with the same cross, 'tied about his leg for his renown'.
If rumour were true, the idea for the garter as a supreme
token of chivalry had come to the King as he retrieved
one dropped during a dance by the young Princess Joan
of Kent, wife of the Earl of Salisbury. He had tied it
about his own leg and jokingly cried, 'The shame be his
who thinks evil of it!' The Princess was very beautiful,
thought Eleanor enviously. Even the Prince of Wales
sought her favour.

The ladies, too, wore exquisite garments and jewelled
circlets over their veils. The fur helped to ward off the
January chill but, despite a warm stone at her feet,
Eleanor had felt the cold steadily creeping through her
body, and after a while had longed for the comfort of
a fire.

Fascinated by this new and glittering world into which
she had been drawn, she was nevertheless glad to escape
for a while before supper to get some exercise. Richard
and the other Garter knights had retired to feast privately with the King, leaving everyone else to sup as usual
in the Great Hall.

'Page! Come here!'

The shrill, imperious voice echoed across the lawn.
Eleanor, roused from her reverie, looked round sharply,
not certain who was being addressed.

'You there!' shouted the boy. He was beckoning
Tamkin.

'Prince John!'

Eleanor dipped a deep curtsy, despite the dampness
of the ground, and prodded Tamkin into an obeisance.
'Bow!' she hissed urgently.

'You are wearing a sword, page. Can you use it?'

'Aye, my lord,' answered Tamkin proudly. Richard
had been teaching him sword-play for months. The
weapon was small and blunt, but that made little difference to Tamkin, who was justly proud of his newly
acquired skill.

'Then come and cross swords with me!' instructed
John of Gaunt imperiously.

Eleanor looked round quickly, searching the grounds for the nurse whom she knew must be near by. She was indeed, on the far side of the lawn, but the woman glanced up without undue concern, being more occupied with John's younger siblings. A couple of guards eyed their young master indulgently, seeing no immediate risk to his person.

John had drawn a sword much like Tamkin's, except that the hilt was more expensively wrought and jewelled. He looked eager, boyish, seeking to relieve his boredom with a feat of arms.

'Do as he bids, Tamkin,' she breathed.

Tamkin stepped forward, his face so flushed with pleasure and excitement that Eleanor guessed his hand was slippery with sweat. She had put a kerchief over her veil to keep out the damp. Slipping it off, she handed it to Tamkin.

'Dry your hands!'

'A wise precaution, but however well you grip your sword you'll not beat me!' exclaimed John, with a natural arrogance which made Eleanor smile.

The boys went through the preliminaries with all the ceremony of their elders, and then the steel began to clash.

From the first blow Tamkin must have realised he was outclassed, but he wasn't one to give in easily. He fought boldly, showing all his innate determination and courage. He was an inch shorter than his adversary, but the months of good food had filled out the flesh on his bones and he was no longer the scrawny scullion whom she had rescued from the kitchen. He was as well-built and strong as his princely challenger.

Eleanor watched with tears of pride in her eyes, because John had been born with a sword in his hand, whereas Tamkin had been learning the skill for only a few short months. Yet he gave the young Prince a decent fight, and when he was down, or the sword spun from his hand, he recovered instantly, ready to resume.

Eventually both boys were panting hard and, when Tamkin lost his sword again, Eleanor called a halt.

'Gracious lord, I think you have both had enough, and you are undoubtedly the victor! Will you not stop now?' She looked across to where the guards were at last showing signs of agitation because a small crowd of interested courtiers had collected. The nurse was waving an urgent arm. 'I think your nurse is calling you.'

'She's not *my* nurse,' said John with dignity. 'She tends the babies.'

'But she is in charge of you at the moment, isn't she?'

'Aye,' he admitted reluctantly. He sheathed his sword with a scowl, but turned to Tamkin with instinctive courtesy, a brilliant smile full of Plantagenet charm lighting his small face. 'You did well. What are you called?'

'Thomas d'Evreux, lord, half-brother to the Earl of Wenstaple.'

'Wenstaple, eh? My brother Edward speaks well of him. When you are knighted, come to me. If I am to serve my father's Grace well, I shall have need of doughty fighters.'

He acknowledged Eleanor with a courtly bow, which she returned with an equally elaborate curtsy, then turned and strolled back to the beckoning nurse.

'Well!' exclaimed Eleanor. 'Who could have expected that? I wonder if he will remember!'

'Aye, he will!' replied Tamkin, a satisfied grin on his sweating face. He was becoming very self-assured! 'Didn't you see? I nearly knocked the sword from his hand!'

'There's no need to gloat! You lost yours several times!'

'I knew I would. He was surprised, so he'll remember,' said Tamkin, showing an astuteness Eleanor could only wonder at.

One day, she thought, he'd be able to hold his own in John of Gaunt's company. One day, perhaps, he would even become a trusted friend despite his bastardy, which he'd failed to mention!

Smiling slightly, she lifted the skirts of her gown, already sopping wet, and turned back towards the palace.

'Come along, Tamkin. And don't trust too much in the promises of Princes!'

*   *   *

An evening without Richard's company loomed ahead, and Eleanor took her seat in the Great Hall without much enthusiasm. Fascinating as it was, the glitter had begun to tarnish in her mind as time passed by. Seated among the ladies she felt a deep dislike of all the gossip they indulged in when their lords were absent. The men's incessant talk of battle and deeds of arms was far preferable to the tittle-tattle of bored and spiteful women! She shut her ears to the words flying about her and wished she could have taken a place beside Cedric or even Sir Gilbert, but in this company that was an impossibility.

She was a Countess, wife to a Garter knight. Cedric had been allocated a place among the lesser knights. Sir Gilbert, whose pennon had been cut off at the end, signifying that he had been promoted to banneret and therefore commanded others in the field, sat with more senior knights. Here rank was everything, and each had to sit with his peers.

After the meal, however, she was free to move around. She was loath to force herself upon Cedric, who was at the centre of a merry group of knights, and she was just about to retire to her chamber when Sir Gilbert sought her out.

'You look pensive, lady, in the midst of all this revelry! Cheer up! An you will take a walk with me, we can explore some of the palace's draughty corridors!'

Eleanor laughed. 'If it weren't raining, I'd rather walk outside! But yes, Sir Gilbert, I will accompany you. I shall be glad to escape the heavy atmosphere in here.'

'Too many torches, smoky fires, wine fumes and sweat! Small wonder that we suffer from dry throats and stinging eyes! You have a mantle?'

'Aye.' She lifted the sumptuous, fur-lined garment from a perch on a nearby column. Sir Gilbert took it from her and draped it over her shoulders. His touch seemed to Eleanor to linger slightly longer than was strictly necessary, and she moved away. 'I am glad to find you can spare me time,' she teased with an arch look to hide her uneasiness. 'I have heard that you've been disappearing from the company to keep secret assignations! Who is the lucky lady?'

'No one who could compare with you, sweet lady,' he murmured softly, and Eleanor flushed at the compliment, while an apprehensive shiver ran along her nerves. Surely Sir Gilbert did not intend a flirtation? A titter followed them as they left the Hall, which Eleanor ignored. Anyone could be laughing over anything. She was being far too sensitive.

The cooler, fresher air soon cleared the muzziness from her head. She smiled serenely at Sir Gilbert.

'You have been promoted,' she remarked. 'How did that happen?'

He launched into a long explanation of some action outside Calais to which Eleanor listened with polite interest.

'I am glad that your talents have been recognised,' she told him sincerely.

'Aye, and my share of the spoil will make me tolerably rich. But Richard has come out the winner despite his absence from the field. He has gained not only an earldom and riches, but a chivalric honour and a lovely wife!' commented Gilbert wryly.

'You are not jealous, Sir Gilbert?' Eleanor's lifted brows indicated amusement, but her tone was more anxious than she had intended. She stopped before an impressive tapestry and studied it intently in the flickering light from a nearby torch, evading Gilbert's eyes. Jealousy was a destructive force, bringing with it enmity and intrigue.

'Nay, for I certainly do not envy him his wounds! But he has been lucky. And his father's timely death put the final seal on his change of fortune, bringing him not only the barony, but the Baron's intended wife.'

'Aye.' She kept her voice flat, but clasped her hands together under cover of the mantle. 'I've been wanting to ask you about that, Sir Gilbert. How did his father die?'

'Why, of an apoplexy, how else?'

She hesitated, then plunged. 'You are his friend, are you not?'

'Always. Richard and I have been like brothers since Sluys. We have been through so much together.'

'That's what I thought. And you would do nothing to hurt him, or tarnish his honour?'

'Not knowingly.'

He was deadly serious. So his apparent flirtation was a game, nothing more. She breathed more freely. 'Sir Gilbert. I have been concerned—nay, worried, by certain rumours which have been flying around Wenfrith since Richard inherited.'

'Rumours?'

'Aye.' She hesitated again, reluctant to voice the scurrilous tale, but impelled by some inner need which she could not control. 'It is said that he killed his father to gain his inheritance.'

The shock on his face broke up into laughter as whoops of derision echoed down the corridor. 'And you believed this?'

'No! Of course not!' Eleanor flushed hotly and glared resentfully into Gilbert's amused face. 'But——'

'But you couldn't quite put the accusation from your mind, is that it?'

'Aye, because it keeps cropping up, and I have no proof that it is a lie! And Richard suffers from a guilty feeling that he was indeed responsible for his father's death. The shock of his reappearance did cause the attack——'

'Aye, it did, but William d'Evreux was a sick man before Richard returned, and how could Richard have foreseen that his sudden reappearance would have such an effect? I saw it happen, dear lady, and Richard bears no blame.'

'Oh, Sir Gilbert thank you! How glad I am that I spoke to you, and discovered the truth!'

Tears of relief and happiness gathered in her eyes and spilled over. Gilbert wiped them off her cheeks with a gentle knuckle, and smiled deeply into her shimmering eyes. Then he bent and touched her forehead with his lips.

'Richard is indeed a lucky man, to have such a wife as you in love with him,' he said softly.

'I-in love? M-me?'

'Aye. 'Tis as plain as the nose on your face.' His forefinger touched the shapely feature teasingly.

'You—you'll not tell Richard?' she pleaded anxiously. 'He doesn't know?'

'No! And he mustn't! He has begun to respect me, I think, but he would be embarrassed by protestations of love!'

'Then the man's a fool! But do not worry, sweet lady. I'll keep your confidence.'

He kissed her forehead again, and Eleanor lifted a grateful face to his.

'I think perhaps I'd better retire to my chamber. Richard will no doubt be late tonight!'

'Aye, and most likely he'll have taken too much wine. Be gentle with him, lady. Such excesses are rare enough in his life.'

'I know. I have never yet known him drunk.'

He bent to kiss her forehead again. 'Then perhaps tonight will be a revelation!'

In fact, Richard did not appear at all until dawn had broken. Eleanor spent a wretched night, and suffered for the tension in her stomach muscles by feeling sick when she woke up. Nevertheless she was up and dressed before he put in an appearance, escorted by a yawning Will.

He looked dreadful and, judging by his fluent curses, felt worse. Unused to seeing him in such a state, Eleanor's stomach turned again.

'Husband!' She moved towards him, concern written on her face. 'Here, lie on the bed——'

'Don't fuss, woman! Will, get someone to bring a pitcher of cold water!'

He disappeared into his wardrobe. Eleanor waited on pins for him to reappear, which he did some hour later. Meanwhile, his head had been immersed in the bowl of cold water, he had shaved, and changed his clothes.

'By God, but that was a rough night!' he groaned, pressing his forehead between unsteady hands. 'I vow I have the worst head since I was a young squire!'

Eleanor stilled her nerves and the sickness in her stomach with an effort. 'Come here, husband,' she instructed quietly. 'Let me massage the pain away!'

'Impossible!' he groaned, but sat obediently on a stool and leaned back against her as she began to smooth his aching temples.

'Was it a good feast?' she enquired softly as her finger traced the broken line of his brow.

'Aye, excellent, but the wine flowed too freely! I doubt if there is a whole head among us this morn!'

'Your heads will mend. Is that better, husband?'

'Somewhat. Your fingers are cool and soothing.'

He continued to relax back against her, and Eleanor carried on with her massage. Eventually he stirred.

'Methinks I should go and seek fresh air,' he muttered without enthusiasm. 'A gallop has always cleared my head in the past! Will you accompany me?'

'I think not. You will ride further and faster without me to hinder you!'

It was an excuse. In truth she felt too upset to wish to ride.

'Aye. I'm no fit company for anyone this morning! I trust I shall be recovered by the morrow!'

'Don't tire Midnight excessively!'

'You know me better than that, wife! All the horses need to be fresh for our journey. I am anxious to see Acklane again.'

'And I to see it for the first time! 'Twas a good thought to break our journey there.'

One for which she was feeling more and more grateful. She hoped her stomach would settle quickly after all the rich food and excitements of the last few days, but a restful period at Richard's manor house would be welcome.

'And necessary.' Richard's voice brought her back to attention. 'The King is holding a series of tournaments this spring. I shall have to attend some. 'Twill be good to test my jousting skills again!'

'Dear lord! Do not test your wound too far!'

'Nay, wife, don't fuss! I know my deficiency, and will do nothing to endanger life and limb. As you have reminded me, my King has need of my services!'

He sounded as though he meant it. Here at Eltham he had found a new peace, a new acceptance of his limitations.

While Joan busied herself packing her things, Eleanor
sat adding a few stitches to the tapestry she had brought
with her in anticipation of a quiet stay at Acklane.
Tamkin had deserted her to play with other pages.

Richard erupted into the calm atmosphere like an
avenging angel, dismissing Joan with a jerk of his arm.

'So, my dear, devoted wife! You turn into a whore
behind my back!'

'What?'

Eleanor stared in disbelief into Richard's furious face
while the sickness rose again in her stomach. She clutched
her hands over her abdomen, felt the blood drain from
her face. For a moment the room spun and she thought
that she would be drawn down into a dark, swirling void.
She took a deep breath, swallowed deeply, and the abyss
receded.

There was more than anger in Richard's expression.
Somewhere lurking at the back of his eyes was a deep
hurt. What had she done to bring such thunder to his
face?

She knew that she couldn't stand—she would just
topple over—but she met his angry stare with quiet
dignity.

'Of what am I accused, lord?'

'You have betrayed me with that treacherous Gilbert
de Rede! I thought I could trust you, both of you, but
the moment I am otherwise engaged you indulge your
preference for his company! You were seen leaving the
Hall together!'

Eleanor shook her head in soundless denial. 'We took
a stroll to clear my head! He did but escort me.'

'You were observed in an amorous embrace!'

'An amorous...' Was that what Gilbert's gentle salute
on her brow had become? Eleanor rallied her wits,
digging her nails into her palms so that the pain would
clear her head. 'Who told you this scurrilous tale?' she
demanded hotly. 'Do you listen to the gossip you have
warned me to ignore? You insult us both, husband. Sir
Gilbert is your friend and, I hope, mine! Our exchange
was innocent!'

'Innocent, you say? I know you have always looked
on Gilbert with soft, inviting eyes!'

'Nay, lord!' Honesty was her only possible defence. She took a heaving breath. 'I admit that when first we met I did prefer Sir Gilbert's fair looks to your dark scowls! But I know now that your proud, stern face hides a considerate and warm nature.' She lifted pleading eyes to his and spoke from her heart. 'I would not change my lot.'

Something of her sincerity must have reached Richard, for he groaned and clasped his head in his hands. 'By God, but my head still throbs! How can I know what to believe, when I have seen with my own eyes the way you look at Gilbert?'

'Do I not look at you with more—affection? Do I not give my body with a passion to meet your own?' Her voice shook. 'Richard, I assure you of my loyalty. What more can I do? What more can you ask?'

If only he wanted her love! She could give that with all her heart. But Richard shook his head, a frown still heavy across his brow. 'I know Gilbert. His intrigues and assignations are legend.'

'But not with me! Ask him, Richard!'

'He denied it, of course.'

'You have seen him?'

'Aye. I sought the churl out! If only the King had allowed a secondary trial of arms! I would have thrown down a challenge! Private jousts are forbidden——'

'Richard! Do not be so foolish! Sir Gilbert has behaved with nothing but courtesy towards me, and considers you his best friend! He saved your life...'

Richard stopped his pacing and turned a haggard face to stare resentfully into her anxious eyes. 'Aye,' he said flatly.

Suddenly, he seemed to slump. He limped over to the bed and flung himself down.

'What does it matter?' he demanded tiredly. 'We leave tomorrow. We'll avoid him this evening at the feast. You'll not see him again.'

'Husband, I care not whether I see him again or not! But this foolish quarrel—there is no foundation for it! It pains me so much, since I am the unwitting cause! There is no need to deny yourself his friendship!'

'Perhaps not.' He closed his eyes wearily. 'We shall not go down to dinner.'

Eleanor rose unsteadily and walked to the bed. The floor heaved beneath her feet, but she forced herself on. Once there, she climbed up the step to sit on the edge where she could lay her cold hand on Richard's brow.

'My dear husband,' she pleaded softly, 'please listen! You told me you were proud of me. Do you think I would do aught to dent your pride? Perhaps I was foolish to forget the gossiping tongues and walk alone with Sir Gilbert, but I swear this is my only crime! We kept to public corridors—otherwise how could we have been seen?—and all he did was give me a brotherly kiss on the forehead! For this you would condemn us both?'

'Nay, wife!' Suddenly, Richard reached up an arm and drew her forcefully down to lie sprawled over his body. He looked long and searchingly into her clear azure eyes. A reluctant smile quirked the corners of his mouth. 'Perhaps I was over-hasty. But Gilbert has a reputation——'

'But I have not! And he holds you in too great a regard to attempt to sully mine! 'Twas an innocent exchange grasped upon by those scurrilous gossips!'

He sighed and drew her head down to rest on his shoulder. 'Aye. I believe it was. The sooner we can leave this sink of intrigue the better I shall be pleased! How the King abides it I do not know! Perhaps that is why he prefers to be on campaign!'

Eleanor lay quietly in his arms, allowing her body to recover its normal equilibrium. The gossip had reached Richard at a time when he was feeling low. Yet even so, in the end, he had believed in her innocence.

But, blessed Jesu! How jealous he had been! Of her, or merely of his own honour and pride? If it were indeed of her... She snuggled closer, listening contentedly to Richard's regular breathing. He had fallen asleep.

CHAPTER THIRTEEN

THE journey to Acklane took them through London. Eleanor's last visit had been on the occasion of her betrothal to William d'Evreux.

The city had changed little. From a distance, the tower and soaring spire of the great cathedral of Saint Paul could be seen outlined against the heavens. Near by, the Conqueror's White Tower sent reflections rippling on the turgid waters of the Thames, while along the river to the west, the dignified lines of the gentle Confessor's West Minster could be glimpsed. London Bridge, its crowded thoroughfare lined by shops, was as colourful as she remembered it, but Eleanor was forced to avert her eyes from the sight of several rotting heads raised high on spikes at the gate, grisly warnings to other traitors and malefactors which sickened her already queasy stomach.

In the narrow streets of the city the horses picked their way through all manner of filth, and the open sewers stank despite the coolness of the weather. Rats ran everywhere, unregarded except by some of the horses, who whickered and shied, startled by a scurrying black or grey shadow running under their hoofs. Eleanor was not sorry to leave the crowded streets behind and emerge into the clearer air of Kensington.

That night they lay near Uxbridge. The following day, making good progress, they passed through Beaconsfield and High Wycombe, crossing the River Thame soon after the hour of Nones. The daylight was already beginning to fade, but they were almost at Acklane.

On the last evening at Eltham she had accompanied Richard to the Great Feast of the Royal Tournament, a riotous party with dancing and entertainment which had gone on late into the night. She had stuck grimly to Richard's side, and been rewarded by receiving his undivided, if possessive, attention. It had not been a comfortable occasion.

Gilbert had not intruded on them. The two men had exchanged frosty bows when they had inadvertently come face to face. Gilbert had looked at her with a bitterness in his eyes that she could well understand. She was, after all, the cause of the split between the two friends, however innocent. After that encounter Gilbert had kept well clear.

For Richard's sake, Eleanor was saddened. As for herself, she liked Gilbert, but felt no great dismay at being deprived of his company. To think that, even for a moment, she had once imagined that she preferred him to her husband!

Richard's arrival at her side caused her to straighten in the saddle and summon a weary smile.

'See!' He pointed with a gauntleted hand. 'Beyond that line of wych-elms lies Acklane!'

Heartfelt relief washed over her face. Perhaps now that she was away from the rich food and stifling atmosphere of the court, she would stop feeing sick.

Unless... The queasy feeling kept recurring, especially in the mornings, and was tending to blunt her ardour, which was unfortunate, under the circumstances. She needed to reassure Richard of her regard, not to give him cause to doubt!

But, praise be, he seemed to believe in her innocence, while blaming Sir Gilbert for acting without proper regard for her reputation. Secretly, Eleanor wondered what would have happened had she given Gilbert the slightest encouragement. Had she known of his reputation as a philanderer she would have acted more wisely, instead of accepting him simply as Richard's friend.

But that was in the past! Acklane lay ahead! By the demesne gates stood the ancient oak from which the manor took its name. The cavalcade passed under its spreading branches and progressed along a track lined with leafless wych-elms and flanked by pasture. Glimpses of a building could be seen through the bare branches, but not until Silver trod delicately round a final curve did the track open out into an open space and the building came into full view.

A gasp of pleased surprise escaped Eleanor. 'Richard,' she breathed. 'It's lovely!'

'It pleases you, wife? I have lain here but a couple of
nights since it was completed, so I cannot guarantee its
comfort, though the household is prepared for our
coming.'

Built of a warm, creamy stone, the building had large
arched windows, all fully filled with glass panes set in
lead. The main building and two wings were each covered
by a roof thatched with sedge. The main entrance-door
was on a level with the ground in a two-storey tower
surmounted by a defensive battlement, the only evidence of fear of attack. Pigeons flew in and out of a
dovecote set among the ventilators at the apex of the
roof.

The steward ran to greet them, escorting them inside
with deep bows of reverence.

The pantry, buttery and kitchen were on their left as
they passed beyond the entrance lobby. Stepping eagerly
through an opening in the draught screens to her right,
Eleanor saw that the Great Hall was lit on both sides by
windows reaching from a foot or two above ground to
timbers so cunningly jointed together that no intrusive
columns were needed to support the roof. This was no
gloomy keep, but a pleasant chamber which would be
full of light even on a dull winter's day. Since it was
almost dusk, torches flickered from horn brackets on
the walls.

The contrast with Wenfrith, even after all her recent
improvements, was total. Despite his long absences,
Richard had spared no expense in furbishing his manor
with tapestries. Gold plate adorned several sideboards
set upon the dais. Possibly the tapestries and plate had
been pillaged from some French château. Not so the
table-dormant, constructed in the latest fashion with
huge pedestal supports, and laid with finest linen and
silver ready for supper.

'I wondered about having the hearth to one side, with
a chimney, like that in the solar,' remarked Richard,
pausing briefly by a welcome fire blazing in the centre
of the Hall, its smoke rising in aromatic spirals to the
vents in the roof. 'But I was told it would not have
warmed so large a space efficiently.'

The solar was entered by way of a wooden stair leading from the dais and through the wardrobe, which here consisted of three small rooms with a latrine tacked on to the end. Again the impression was of light and warmth. Eleanor threw back her hood, picked up her skirts, and ran to the arched window over a wooden floor strewn with matting woven from rushes. If the green vista were not as exciting as the grandeur of the view from Wenfrith, it was pleasingly calm and rural.

Richard waited by the fire, watching her reactions with a faint smile on his mobile lips.

She turned excitedly and ran back to clasp her arms around his waist. 'Husband, your manor is beyond imagining! I shall enjoy our stay here!'

Richard regarded her thoughtfully. 'Would you rather live here most of the year?'

A frown knitted Eleanor's fine brows. 'Would you not need to be at Wenfrith or Wenstaple?'

'I could leave you here while I made periodic inspections.'

He, too, was frowning, but only thoughtfully. Eleanor tightened her arms about him. 'Nay, husband, I have no wish to be parted from you! And in truth, I prefer Wenfrith! How could I live without the sea and the cliffs? I fear my heart lies in the hills and wildness of your domains in the west!'

Richard's hands, which had been lightly holding her shoulders, drew her closer so that their mouths met. 'Mine too! What say you, wife? We'll build an even better manor-house at Wenfrith! Why should we live in a keep constructed in the time of the King's great-grandfather? We will build beside it!'

'Richard! Is that possible?'

'I can think of no reason why not. There is no lack of space, and I have the gold!' He glanced meaningfully at a couple of heavy coffers being carried in by servants. They held his share of the spoils of Caen and the *chevauchée* through France. 'We will build a larger manor-house than this one, with several private chambers.'

'With room for a family.'

'Aye. God willing, we shall soon need space for our brood!' He grinned teasingly, then his expression sobered as he noticed the dreamy expression in her eyes. 'Wife, are you trying to tell me something?'

Eleanor's colour heightened and she concentrated her gaze on the jewelled brooch fastening his mantle. Her sickness had been persistent now for several days, and Joan had noticed.

'Too much rich food?' she'd scoffed only that morning. 'Since when was your stomach so tender, sweeting? When did you last see your courses?'

Thinking back, Eleanor had realised it was at least seven weeks since she'd last bled. In the excitement of being summoned to Eltham she'd quite lost track of time.

Richard's finger under her chin brought her eyes to meet his. Her blush deepened. 'I think I may be *enceinte*,' she whispered. 'I have missed my menses, and have felt sick these last days. I had no sickness before, that's why I wasn't certain, but this time... Joan says it's a sure sign...'

'Wife!' For a moment he drew her close. 'This time you will take great care!'

'Aye, husband, but I will not be treated like an invalid! Women work in the fields until they are delivered!'

'The labourers' wives, mayhap, but not the Countess of Wenstaple!' exclaimed Richard arrogantly. 'I will buy that roncey we mentioned earlier! You are not to ride Silver again! She is far too highly strung to be trusted!'

Eleanor smiled, serene in the knowledge that Richard intended to take care of her and his heir. 'Mayhap we could get her with foal,' she suggested innocently. 'A colt or filly by Midnight should grow into a valuable beast.'

Richard threw back his head and laughed, exposing the strong column of his throat to Eleanor's tender gaze. Perhaps it was just as well it was beyond the reach of her lips. If she allowed free rein to her loving impulses, Richard might begin to suspect...

Then her head was pressed against his chest and his chin came to rest on her veil.

'Sometimes, wife, you come up with the most interesting ideas! I'll suggest it to the groom! And I'll send to the mason who built this manor. We will take him back with us when we return to Wenfrith!'

Apart from a couple of short absences to attend nearby tournaments, from which, mercifully, he returned sound in wind and limb and full of high spirits, Richard remained at Acklane, spending his time inspecting the estate, hunting, indulging in knightly pursuits with his retinue and training Tamkin, for whom he had developed a deep affection. He kept in touch with both Wenfrith and Wenstaple by frequent messenger. Cedric had been an early choice of courier, since he had wished to return to duty at Wenfrith to be near Radcliffe Manor and his betrothed.

For Eleanor the three months spent at Acklane were a time of much sewing of tiny garments in serene anticipation, interrupted by occasional moments of near panic. Supposing something went wrong again? Supposing the birth was difficult? Supposing . . .

Down-to-earth Joan jollied her out of her bad moments. Despite her lack of personal experience of either the marriage bed or childbirth, she was a deep well of information on both, her knowledge gained second-hand from long years of listening to gossip. It was she who bullied Eleanor into waiting for three months before tackling the long journey back to Wenfrith.

That Eleanor should return there soon was taken for granted. Richard's heir must be born within his family's historic fiefdom.

The journey was taken in easy stages. Eleanor enjoyed every moment of the leisurely ride, despite the frequent heavy rain which beset the land, giving the country the wettest summer for many a year. By the time they rode across the drawbridge to the joyful sound of trumpet and horn, and clattered across the bailey to dismount before the steps, they had been away for almost five months and the sun rode high in the sky each noon.

Wenfrith seemed to have suffered less from the wet than Acklane and the countryside between. Things had run smoothly enough under Stephen's stewardship, and he welcomed them back warmly. He greeted his half-brother with a cordiality which Richard returned, and exclaimed over Tamkin's progress.

'You'll make a fine knight one day,' he told the boy, with an enthusiasm which Eleanor thought forced.

'I'm going to serve John of Gaunt!'

Then, of course, the whole incident of the sword-fight had to be reiterated. Eleanor, watching somewhat critically, thought that she detected a slight hostility in Stephen's eyes which certainly did not reach his voice when he congratulated his young brother. He was probably jealous of Tamkin's good fortune. Tamkin would receive all the advantages of being brought up as nobility in an Earl's household. Advantages which Stephen had missed.

But not even a lingering uneasiness over Stephen's attitude and her own unaccountable dislike could mar the joy of her return. However much more comfortable Acklane might be, Wenfrith was home! Although over the last months away the ties which bound her to Richard had deepened and strengthened, it was here that she had found him, here that she had fallen in love!

They settled back into their former routines, Eleanor taking gentle exercise each morning on her new mare— a chestnut cob she called Velvet, because her muzzle was so soft and her nature so smooth and biddable. Velvet did not have the spirit of the brilliant little Silver, who was now in foal, but Eleanor had learned to love her just the same. Accompanied by Tamkin and the guards, Roger Lawtie and Walter Hendy, she rode into the village most weeks to ensure that all was well with their people. She was always welcomed with great courtesy, but she thought that she detected a new reserve in the manner of some of the tenants, both men and women alike.

The village midwife was fortunately not one so disaffected. She assured Eleanor that she had delivered countless healthy babies, and would be honoured to attend the birth of the next heir of Wenfrith.

'Don't you be worriting yournself, me lady,' Bertha had grinned, her mouthful of blackened teeth on full display. 'Alice Waps be expecting 'er tenth when 'arvest be due, more's the pity; 'twas fearful bad timin'! But yourn won't appear till Michaelmas, I'll be bound.

Alice'll 'ave plenty o' milk for the babe to suckle, never you mind.'

Having caught a whiff of the woman's putrid breath, Eleanor had her own reservations about the arrangement, but Bertha had an excellent reputation for competence and common sense. As long as her baby survived, Eleanor felt she could put up with any discomfort, and faithful Joan would be there to attend to her more personal needs. Some of the other village women were experienced in these matters and had promised their help with varying degrees of enthusiasm. If anything went badly wrong, Brother Pierre-Paul would be on hand with his medical skills.

Richard wanted to call in a physician from London, but Eleanor managed to dissuade him, more certain as time passed that she would be able to cope with the help at hand. She had never felt fitter or more contented. Giving birth, as Bertha insisted, 'Be as nat'ral as breathin'.'

August was a hot, sticky month, dry enough for a bumper harvest to be gathered and stored before rain set in. Richard, it seemed, quite enjoyed keeping a critical eye on the reaping, binding and carting to the barns, though he had appointed Stephen as harvest lord, directly responsible for organising the workers. On a couple of occasions he had had to dampen down Stephen's enthusiasm for getting more work out of the labourers than their strength allowed.

'I don't understand,' he'd told Eleanor, stroking his beard thoughtfully, a frown on his face. 'I'd have thought he'd be more understanding of those he used to work among!'

'I've been worried about Stephen for some time,' admitted Eleanor. Perhaps now Richard would be receptive if she voiced her long-held distrust. 'Even before he tried to influence Anne. I believe he resents being ill-born, though he hides it well.'

'I trusted him, and gave him great power!' cried Richard, banging one fist into the palm of his other hand. 'If he abuses it I shall have to strip him of his position. He did not like my countermanding his orders today.'

'He forgets his debt, lord. I think you should watch him.'

Richard stopped his pacing. 'Aye.' He sounded dispirited. 'I had thought to be generous. It's strange how an accident of birth can sour a man's nature.'

'Thank God for Tamkin! Perhaps he was too young to become embittered.'

Richard's face brightened. 'That boy has a brilliant future, if he so desires. He'll be a squire at fourteen, a knight at twenty.' He glanced at her sideways, ready to assess her reaction. 'Perhaps we should send him to another household for training?'

'Oh, no, Richard! I could not bear to part with him!'

'Not even when our own child is born?' he asked doubtfully.

'Even then!' Eleanor couldn't explain her devotion to Tamkin, she only knew that he was the first person ever to have given her his total loyalty, childish as it was. 'He can play with the babe!'

A chuckle from Richard finally lightened the rather sombre atmosphere generated by Stephen's disappointing behaviour. 'He'll be his uncle!'

'I know. But in age he'll be more like an older brother, and that's how I'd like them to think of each other.'

'Eleanor, dear one, you're a sentimental woman! They'll likely be at each other's throats in years to come!'

'Not if I can help it!'

'And anyway, we might have a daughter!'

'So we might,' agreed Eleanor equably. 'Would you mind?'

'Another Eleanor? Not a bit!'

'Good. But I'd prefer another Richard!'

'I'd like a male heir, there's no denying. But if this brat turns out to be a female, then we'll just have to try again, won't we?'

He knelt by her stool and put his hand on her distended stomach. As though recognising its father's touch, the baby kicked. He gently massaged the spot where he'd felt the movement. Eleanor laid her hand over his.

'It's so full of life,' she murmured softly. 'Please God it will be born so.'

* * *

The harvest supper had been a merry affair, with the
entire manor crowding into the Hall, filling it to bursting
point. The fishermen from Lower Wenfrith had been
pressed into service for carting and they, too, had joined
in the celebrations.

The people had come into real contact with their lord
during the harvest and, being nothing if not observant
and shrewd, had noticed his intervention on their behalf.
For the first time in many a month Eleanor sensed approval in their attitude. The vague disquiet which she
had felt over the underlying hostility among the villagers
disappeared.

'There should be no starvation this winter,' she observed contentedly as Richard joined her in their bed.

'The beasts are fattening well. And the walls of our
new manor-house are rising apace. Methinks this will be
the last winter we must spend in this draughty castle!'

'It is never draughty here.' Eleanor smiled in the
darkness as she snuggled closer to Richard. The bed-
hangings had been left undrawn during the hot weather,
but a chill had crept into the atmosphere that evening.
Joan had spread a blanket over the bed and drawn the
side curtains, leaving the end open to the air.

Richard soon fell asleep and Eleanor dozed off, but
the baby was heavy in her womb and her back ached.
She shifted to ease the discomfort, dozed off again, but
slept only fitfully.

She first heard a faint rustle from the wardrobe. Will
often slept there, though sometimes he chose to spread
his pallet in the Hall. Richard did not mind, as long as
he remained within call. Tamkin normally slept upstairs
with Joan.

It didn't sound like Will, though. More like the
movement of a rat. There were still a few about, though
her promise of reward for killing the vermin had been
so successful that the organised hunts had long ago been
abandoned. Richard had appointed an official rat-
catcher to keep the remaining pests under control.

She shut her eyes, willing sleep. Again, the rustle.
Sighing, she shifted her head to a more comfortable position on the pillow, but didn't close her eyes. She felt
unaccountably uneasy. It was almost as though there was

another presence in the room. She lay quite still, staring into the darkness, her senses fully alert.

At first she barely noticed the lightening of the dense blackness by Richard's side of the bed. She sensed rather than saw a movement as the hanging was drawn aside. But as her eyes adjusted she glimpsed an upraised arm outlined against the lighter rectangle of a window.

She screamed.

Used to living for so many years with danger, Richard's reactions were instant. He caught the gleam of cold steel poised above his heart and erupted upwards, letting out a fearsome cry as he grasped the invisible wrist by instinct. Somehow he managed to extricate himself from the bedclothes and bear his attacker backwards to the floor.

Although the fellow was strong, his fighting skills were not as honed as Richard's own. As they thrashed about on the floor Richard closed his steely fingers ever tighter around the assassin's wrist until he felt the man's grip on the dagger loosen. At last! With a cry of triumph Richard smashed the man's hand against the floor, and the weapon spun away.

Now he had to ward off the man's wild grappling. Finding a hold which would immobilise him was not easy. Concentrating solely on his opponent, Richard was unaware that Eleanor had slipped from the bed and picked up the dagger, unaware that Will and Cedric and half-a-dozen other retainers, in various states of undress, had spilled into the room from the wardrobe, their only way in since the staircase door to the solar had been barred.

An elbow punch to the throat, and the body beneath him went limp. Richard lay panting for a moment before he heaved himself to his feet and looked down at the unconscious man, whose face was revealed in the light of a torch borne by one of the new arrivals. He drew in a sharp breath of dismay.

Will silently handed him a tunic, which he quickly drew on over his head, wincing as the material scraped over the raw gouges made by the man's nails. Then he turned anxiously to Eleanor.

She sat, wrapped in a blanket, staring in disbelief at the prone figure of Stephen.

'Aye, wife,' he grated, a mixture of anger and sadness making his voice shake. 'A fitting reward for the brotherly regard I have shown him!'

'Stephen!'

Tamkin pushed his way through the knot of men and stared down in bewilderment at the stirring figure. 'What have you done to him?' he demanded accusingly, first staring wide-eyed at Richard, then appealing to Eleanor.

'Tamkin, come here.'

He came, reluctantly.

'See this dagger? Do you recognise it?'

'Aye, it's Stephen's.'

'And he sought to kill Lord Richard with it. Had I not been lying awake, he would have succeeded.'

'May the devil take you!'

The hoarse, choked voice was barely recognisable as belonging to Stephen. Eleanor shuddered at the venom contained in those few words, and crossed herself quickly to ward off his curse. Tamkin ran across and knelt in the rushes by Stephen's side.

'Brother,' he choked, 'you would not have killed the Lord Richard?'

'Aye, and his simpering wife, and the cursed heir she bears!' croaked Stephen, attempting ineffectually to clear his throat of the constriction put there by Richard's iron grip.

'But why?' Tears were streaming down Tamkin's anguished face. 'I love them!'

'Because the woman has been kind to you?' scoffed Stephen, his voice regaining something of its normal timbre. 'They have given us nothing but our due! Think you *they* deserve Wenfrith? I have worked the land here all my life, it belongs to me!'

'But—but you are a bastard!'

'Aye.' Bitterness etched his voice, cutting deeply into its erstwhile veneer of compliance. 'But without a legitimate heir I could have seized the barony! The people here would have backed me!'

'You think so?' Richard's tone held nothing but scorn.

'Aye, brother! They thought Richard d'Evreux an intolerant, hard overlord. I saw to that, until you interfered! When you were absent their week-works and boon-works were slackly enforced, but the moment you returned their yoke became harsh, and the charges for favours were never waived!'

A stifled gasp brought his cold eyes to rest on Eleanor's dishevelled beauty. 'My noble brother was too busy with his lust and his soldiering to notice what went on under his nose! But you suspected, didn't you, little sister? You made Joan deny the rumours I had so assiduously spread!'

'So it was *you*!' Indignation and deep anguish for Richard's unnecessary suffering made Eleanor's voice tremble. 'Such perfidy! To accuse the lord your brother of such a crime!' Her eyes widened in sudden surmise. 'Mayhap 'twas *you* who poisoned your father! Not all at once, but slowly! That would explain his sudden decline in health after I saw him at our betrothal!'

The little blood left in Stephen's face drained away. In the flickering light of the torch his features seemed to contort. 'Aye! His betrothal! He intended to beget an heir! I could not risk that!'

'God's blood! You confess to my father's murder?' Richard towered over the reclining man like an avenging angel. 'By my oath, but you shall die for this!'

Tamkin had shrunk into a corner, whimpering. 'The potion!' he moaned. 'The potion you said would restore his spirits! I put it in his wine, just as you said, when no one was looking——'

'William d'Evreux had grown careless, no saye was ever taken. Even Hugh normally drank from a different flagon, holding inferior wine.' Stephen hunched his shoulders. 'I did but give him meadow saffron for his pains. It also had a strong effect on his bowels and weakened him, but it did not kill him. Mayhap you did indeed do that, brother!'

A sort of gloating spasm crossed Stephen's face. Richard drew in a harsh breath. Eleanor cried, 'No!'

'He was a sick man by the time I returned,' said Richard grimly, his eyes narrowed in thought. 'Had he had his full strength my appearance would not have shocked him so. Because you had weakened him, he died.' His voice strengthened as he made a ringing declaration of new-found certainty. 'For no other reason!'

Eleanor's heart leapt. Even in the midst of all the
horror of the past hour, she knew a sudden lightening
of her spirit. Richard had been freed from his burden
of guilt! She could almost be grateful to Stephen for
releasing him from the torment that she knew he'd suffered in his soul.

But Stephen hadn't finished. A harsh laugh rang
around the chamber as he threw back his head in
derision.

'Don't let your conscience trouble you further, my dear
Richard! You were not responsible for your so fortunate
succession! Hemlock brought that about! He had been
sick for many weeks. No one would have questioned his
death. No one did! 'Twas in the flagon taken to him
just before your untimely arrival, brother. He took a
deep draught at sight of you and——'

'You damned cur!' Richard stirred the recumbent man
with his foot, like the dog he considered him to be. 'Get
him to his feet!' he snarled.

Joan had followed Tamkin down the stairs, and now
she moved across the solar to hand Eleanor her chamber-
gown, before sinking to the rushes to gather the sobbing
Tamkin into motherly arms.

'Come, my lamb,' she crooned softly, 'it wasn't your
fault.'

'I t-t-trusted him!'

'Of course you did,' murmured Joan, ignoring the
scuffling going on behind her. 'We all did. Dry your
tears, Tamkin, our lady needs us!'

'Yes! Please, Tamkin, will you go down and fetch me
a pitcher of cider?'

Eleanor couldn't bring herself to ask for wine, not so
soon after Stephen's revelation, but cider should be a
safe request, giving Tamkin something to do to take his
mind off things and at the same time getting him out of
the way while Richard dealt with Stephen.

Joan opened the solar door and Tamkin disappeared,
flinging his brother a final, anguished look. Stephen did
not even glance in the boy's direction. He was staring
fixedly ahead, held firmly between two of Richard's most
stalwart men.

'Throw him into the dungeon! 'Tis as well we kept only the French knights and the friar for ransom, and returned the worthless prisoners to their native land! He can have the mouldering hole to himself while I work out what to do with the whoreson!'

'Pshaw!' Stephen spat on the ground at his half-brother's feet. 'You think to frighten me? You dare not bring me to trial! What of Tamkin? Do you want him blamed?'

'Then you will rot in the dungeon!' growled Richard through his teeth. 'I, personally, will see you locked inside and then throw away the key! Take him!'

The men trooped out, and Eleanor was left with Joan.

'Are you all right, sweeting?' asked the latter anxiously.

'Aye.' Eleanor pulled the thin gown around her shivering body. 'But I'll not sleep again. Find me something warmer to wear.'

Wrapping herself in a heavy mantle, Eleanor discovered that her hands were shaking. The full impact of what might have been hadn't really hit her yet, but Richard was safe. Stephen wouldn't trouble them again.

She eyed his dagger, lying on the table beside her own. How readily she would have plunged either weapon in his back had Richard's life been threatened! She had once shrunk from the idea of blood on the blade of her dagger. She did so no longer.

'I never thought I'd bless the pain in my back,' she remarked, with a faint laugh. 'But if I'd been able to sleep he'd have killed us both! Oh, Joan!'

'There, there, sweeting! It's all over now! You lie down and rest! Ah, here's Tamkin. A drink will restore your spirits!'

Tamkin was still sniffing. It took Eleanor's and Joan's combined efforts to reassure and quieten the child. Eleanor hoped and prayed that the shocking affair wouldn't leave a permanent scar on the boy's mind.

Richard was away for almost an hour, and when he returned Joan took Tamkin off. Richard barred the door behind them.

Eleanor held out her hands. 'You were a long time, husband. Did Stephen give trouble?'

'None.' Richard smiled grimly, taking her out-stretched hands in a firm hold. 'He gloried in telling me how he'd been planning to kill us both.'

'This wasn't a sudden impulse?'

'Far from it! Your grey friar ghost was him, sweet-heart. He heard you sending for Roger and ran ahead. He is an excellent, swift runner, so he boasts! And he paid the band of outlaws to invade our forest. I was to be killed, preferably by the sword, but, failing that, by crossbow bolt. You would have been killed, too. He didn't want it to look like murder, so all the men in the party were set upon.'

'You were to be killed by a bolt in the back! The next one would have been for me!' Eleanor shuddered and Richard sank down on the side of the bed and put his arm around her. 'Richard, we've been lucky!'

'Aye, and more lucky still that we went along with the old custom of having sayes of all food and drink taken before it was served! To think we only did it to please the carver and the sewer and all the other servants involved!'

'They insisted that if we wanted to eliminate slackness, things had to be done with due ceremony and according to the rules!'

'So, inadvertently, we took away Stephen's preferred method of murder. He had to resort to violence.'

Eleanor pressed the hand she held to her cheek. 'But he wasn't strong enough for you! Whatever made him try something so stupid!'

'Desperation, I imagine, and the hope that the identity of the assassin would never be discovered.' Richard re-moved his hand from her shoulder and stroked back her hair. 'Time was running out. Once our child was born, there would have been another heir. To kill him too would have looked suspicious.'

'Aye.' A spasm crossed Eleanor's face and she let go of Richard's hand to clutch at her stomach and groan in agony.

'Eleanor? Wife, what is it?'

'The baby,' she whispered, her eyes anguished. 'I think the baby is coming! Oh, Richard, I could not bear to lose this one!'

Richard laid his hand over hers, watching her face anxiously, waiting for the spasm to pass. Once her body had relaxed, he leaned forward and kissed her eyes, her nose, and, finally, her lips.

'I'll call Joan.'

Joan came at a trot.

'Don't worry, sweeting,' she hastened to reassure both anxious parents. 'Your due time is nearly here. The baby will be born alive and well, never fear.'

'A month early! It may not live!' Eleanor groaned hopelessly. 'May the Good Lord have mercy on Stephen! He's done this, too!'

'Aye, the upset is no doubt to blame,' agreed Joan grimly. 'But you cannot be certain of the time. The babe looks large and full-grown to me!'

'Have faith, wife! Stephen will not win! Our child is strong! He'll survive!'

'Or she!' Eleanor managed a watery smile. 'Send for the midwife, Richard, but before she comes up here see that she scrubs her hands! When last I saw them they were thick with grime! I could not bear her touching me...'

Richard kissed her forehead. 'Relax, sweetheart. I'll see she's clean, and the other women too. Joan, take care of her!'

'Do you think I'd do aught else?' enquired Joan caustically.

CHAPTER FOURTEEN

RICHARD could not explain the tension holding his body as Midnight galloped headlong along the cliffs.

With the arrival of the midwife and several worthy village women, he'd felt out of place and useless in the solar. So he had left the women to their own affairs and taken refuge in an activity which normally relaxed his body and quietened his mind. Being a man of action, hanging around waiting for something to happen was anathema to him.

But today he found little solace in the feel of Midnight's magnificent muscles bunching under his thighs. Fury at Stephen's treachery still burned fiercely in his mind, but overlaying it and masking its intensity was anxiety.

He couldn't banish the thought of Eleanor's suffering, the fear of her death, and nothing seemed able to soothe his troubled mind.

She was his wife, and he had grown fond of her over the months they'd been together. She had transformed his life, making it easier and more comfortable, was a stimulating companion, and satisfied his physical needs completely. Most of the time. There had been that patch after her miscarriage, and now of course...

Yet for all her virtues she could be so easily replaced! There were dozens of nubile, well-born women who would line up to become Countess of Wenstaple! Without false pride, he knew that he was attractive to women; he would scarcely need the lure of a title. And as for the child, if that died, he had years yet in which to beget another heir.

How many men of his acquaintance had been married several times, and shown little sorrow at their wife's death? After all, a knight did not form a romantic attachment to the woman he married! The object of his affections should be some unattainable beauty over whom he could sigh with frustrated longing!

Not that he had ever indulged in such nonsense—at least, not since his days as a squire! He remembered with a slight smile how he's sighed over his lord's wife, a woman at least ten years older than himself. At the time she had seemed to him to possess all the womanly virtues—kindness, gentleness and obedience to her lord's slightest command. Once he had discovered the pleasures of sex his affairs had been entirely pragmatic, born of slight attraction, necessity and availability.

Eleanor was compassionate and gentle, but hardly the submissive, characterless female he now realised the object of his boyish adoration had been! Would she hurry to take another husband if he were to die?

The very thought brought unexpected pain. His Eleanor with another man! Her apparent dalliance with

Gilbert had sent him almost mad with jealousy! How would she react if he showed interest in another woman? Would she be distressed by the thought of his marrying again?

Oh, yes, he'd marry again eventually; it would be required of him. But he knew with a deep inner certainty that he would never feel the same about any other woman. Hadn't he realised as soon as he'd seen her that Eleanor was the one wench who could satisfy all his desires? And, by Peter, he had enough experience to know what he wanted! And had gone against all his inborn prejudices to get it!

Reaching a high point on the undulating cliff, he reined Midnight in to a walk, patting the lathered neck apologetically.

'Sorry, old boy. Take it easy now.' He laughed in self-derision. 'You won't be troubled and anxious when Silver foals, will you? No doubt 'tis the sleepless night and Stephen's treachery which have upset me!'

Eleanor would be all right. Everyone said so. The baby might not survive, not having reached its full term, but that didn't bother him. He had to face it. What troubled him was the sudden unacceptable knowledge that if his wife died she would take all his happiness with her.

Annoyed with the turn of his thoughts, he urged Midnight into a trot. The corn stubble was already being grazed and dunged by the sheep and cattle. The fallow field was being ploughed, and now was the time to see to the timber, a profitable and necessary crop. In Stephen's absence he must oversee the reeve and bailiff. From now on they would direct the work according to *his* rules!

With a definite objective in mind, his spirits revived. The midwife had told him it was likely to be Vespers on this first day of October before the baby was born. If it was a boy they would have to name him for the Saint whose day it was. His son would be Richard Giles d'Evreux, heir to all he possessed.

There was much to be done about the manor, and overseeing the harvest had given him unexcepted satisfaction. This land must be in his blood after all! He'd been over-ready to slough off his responsibilities.

He kicked Midnight into a slow canter, whistling under his breath as he made towards a group of serfs working in the coppice under the watchful eye of the wand-waving reeve.

Back in the solar Eleanor watched while the women made everything ready. The bed had been stripped of its coverings and an oiled skin spread over the mattress. Huge cauldrons of water simmered on the fire. Because of the heat, the wooden shutters on the unglazed windows were open wide, bringing a cooling sea breeze to her perspiring brow.

The spasms were coming regularly now, several times between one hour and the next. They didn't last long, seconds at most, but as the day wore on they became stronger and more uncomfortable. Joan held her hands while Bertha or one of her helpers bathed her brow with cool water. The church bell rang for Prime, Tierce, Sext and Nones. Still relief did not come.

'Joan,' she groaned as a spasm threatened to tear her apart, 'send for Sir Piers! I would seek absolution and wish to communicate.'

'He's in the Hall, sweeting, waiting for your summons.'

She signalled to one of the women, who left immediately to return within minutes with the old priest. He walked quietly into the solar, a huge crucifix resting on his shrunken chest, the pyx containing the Holy Eucharist raised on high before him.

Eleanor greeted him with a desperate smile. Then she addressed the women. 'Please leave us.'

'I'll call you if there is need.' Sir Piers reassured the anxious Joan and Bertha with a nod. 'The lady has no immediate need of you.'

Left alone with the gentle old man, Eleanor hardly knew where to begin, but poured out her fears for herself and her baby, her resentment against Stephen, her love for her husband.

Sir Piers smiled benignly, gave her the absolution she required, and assured her that God's will would be done. 'Say an *ave* on behalf of Stephen before you receive the

Host,' he instructed sombrely. 'You must cleanse your mind of all evil thoughts.'

'I will try.'

Afterwards, Eleanor gave the priest a gold noble as a token of her gratitude. 'You have comforted me greatly throughout my time here, Sir Piers.'

'My lady! I hope to serve you and Lord Richard for many years yet!'

He left as Eleanor doubled up with another cramp, a spasm which heralded the beginning of a new phase when more frequent and terrifying pains threatened to over-whelm her.

The midwife gave her some corn-poppy syrup to dull the agony, but the spasms seemed to go on forever. Her muscles were just not strong enough to deliver the tiny living creature struggling to emerge into the world! Verging on exhaustion, she made a supreme effort to ignore the pain, brace herself against Joan, and strain as she was told.

Bertha's triumphant cry came at the same instant as the pain eased.

'Its little 'ead is coming! Thank the Good Lord 'tis not its behind! All will be well!'

She felt the baby slip from her body and a surge of deep relief washed over her.

'A boy!' cried Bertha, holding the infant by its feet and slapping its tiny rump with a large bloodstained hand. Eleanor gasped in apprehension as the sound of the smack rang round the room. Then she forgot every-thing but the joy of hearing her baby's cry.

Infinite peace flooded her. The baby lived! She had borne Richard the heir he desired. 'Let me have him!' she pleaded.

'Aye, in just a wink!'

With swift expertise those capable hands with the grimy nails sliced through the cord and tied a knot. Then, at last, the baby was put into her arms.

Slippery, slimy and as red as a boiled shrimp! Eleanor hugged him to her and kissed the wet down on his head. Was it dark, or just fair made dark by the dampness? Did it matter? 'Little Richard!' she murmured. 'Little Dickon!'

'Aye, thanks be to the 'oly Mother! He be small, but strong; see, 'is nails've yet to fully grow!'

Eleanor let the tiny fingers curl around one of hers. Such a wave of euphoria washed over her that she was scarcely aware of passing the afterbirth. Reluctantly, she allowed one of the women to take the baby from her, and propped herself up on one elbow to watch as he was carefully bathed and wrapped tightly in swaddling bands.

'His limbs'll grow straight as an arrow,' promised Bertha smugly. 'You'll be right as rain, now, me lady. Just you rest. Alice will see to the little lord.'

'Thank you, Bertha,' murmured Eleanor humbly. 'Thank you all.'

'We must see to you now, sweeting,' murmured Joan, her round face beaming with happiness. 'Bertha, will you remove the skin? There, now, lie still while I bathe you and put the covers back.'

'He'll be wanting milk shortly. Alice can't give'm new milk, me lady, so you must be feeding 'im yournself for now. After a couple o' days you must bind your breasts.'

'I suppose so.'

She longed to carry on feeding the infant herself, yet knew her position denied her the privilege. Only the lowest classes fed their own babies. The entire manor would be scandalised if she decided to go against tradition. Richard and she had already given them quite enough shocks with William's hasty funeral and their sudden wedding!

When the tiny mouth was put to her breast and Dickon sucked instinctively, she felt the exquisite, piercing sensation right through to her womb, which seemed to contract. His hair was fair. Golden, like hers. And his eyes were blue. But both colours could change. So said Bertha.

'I'll be leaving you, me lady. Alice can take over now.'

'Aye, just you leave the little scrap to young Kate'n me.'

Kate was a maid hired from the village to assist Alice while she was feeding the baby, and later take over as nurse if she proved suitable. Eleanor felt sad for the child, little more than eleven, who had been born with what some said was the devil's mark on her face. Her upper

lip was ugly and broken, just like that of a hare. But
the girl was clean, had kind brown eyes, a gentle manner,
and Eleanor liked her. She watched as the child crooned
tenderly over the cradle, and knew that she'd made the
right choice.

She was dozing, with Joan and Alice and Kate in attendance, when Richard strode in.

He had charged back when he'd heard the church bell
ringing joyously to announce the birth of an heir. He'd
known then that all had gone well, and had been
strangely humbled. He could beget an heir, but only his
wife could bring him safely into the world. He'd spurred
Midnight into a headlong gallop, leapt from the saddle,
and mounted the steps two together—the first time he'd
managed that since returning from Crécy!

He restrained his eagerness to see his wife long enough
to wash in the wardrobe before entering the quiet room.
Supper was ready down in the Hall. He told the servants
to serve it. He would eat when he was ready.

'Supper is served,' he told the women. 'Go and eat.
I will stay here and call you if there is need.'

Alice and Kate sank to the floor in deep obeisance.
'Lord!'

Joan smiled, giving her usual bob of deference. 'They
are both well, lord. See, my mistress is waking now!'

'Aye!' Richard grinned back, his mood mellow. He
and Joan had long ago come to an understanding. Provided Eleanor was content, Joan would tolerate his mas-
culine intrusion into their lives. But let Eleanor be sad
or disturbed through any fault of his, and he found
himself treated with distant courtesy!

He moved to the bed as the others left the solar.

'Well, wife!' His voice throbbed, deep with emotion.
'So you have borne me an heir!'

'Aye, lord!' Despite her weariness her elation could
not be hidden, and her eyes shone up into his. 'A perfect
boy! Have you seen him?'

'Not yet, nor have I seen you properly, wife!' He
leaned forward to brush her lips with his. Searching her
face in light reflected from the glowing sun, he saw a
mixture of exhaustion and content. She had never looked

more beautiful. His voice thickened as he asked anxiously, 'Are you well?'

'Just tired. I thought he would never come! But I have forgotten all my travail now! Go, husband, and bring me our child!'

For a moment she thought that he would refuse. She saw the horrified anxiety leap into his eyes, and laughed tenderly.

'He will not bite!'

'Nay, but I might hurt him! I am not used to handling babies!'

'Nor will he break! Hands which can be as gentle as yours, lord, will not harm your child!'

Richard grinned sheepishly. 'I suppose not. But I confess to a certain nervousness!'

'He is no more fragile than Gem's puppies! You enjoyed playing with them!'

'That was different!'

She supposed it was, in his mind at least. But Richard went obediently and lifted the baby from among the blankets covering him. The bundle looked so tiny in his hands.

He traced the small features with the tip of his finger.

'Were his face covered, he would look like the mummies which the Crusaders describe! Poor little mite, he can't move!'

'New-born babes are always swaddled. You were, I'll be bound! It keeps the limbs straight.'

'No doubt you women know best. But the puppies wriggled about enough, and they are growing strong and straight!'

Eleanor privately sympathised with his ideas but, as in the question of feeding, could not bring herself to go against custom. She took the bundle from him and held it in the crook of her arm. 'He'll be baptised Richard, of course, but we'll call him Dickon. Otherwise there will be nothing but confusion!'

'Dickon he shall be, until he is old enough to rebel! He shall also be baptised Giles, after the Saint whose day this is. Shall it be this evening?'

Eleanor nodded. The baby was sleeping quietly, but it would be cruel to run any risk of his passing into the next world unbaptised. There was no reason to delay the ceremony. Her presence was not required. Joan would stand proxy for her mother as godmother, and Sir Peter for Prince Edward, who had graciously consented to be a godfather. Cedric would represent himself.

'I'll dispatch a messenger to your parents at first light on the morrow. Will you write?'

'Another time. I feel too tired tonight.'

'I'll eat my supper here with you. Do you wish anything?'

'A dish of milk, perhaps. Nothing to eat. You'd better put Dickon back in his cradle.'

He took the baby with careful hands and tucked it back among the coverings. Then he sat on the edge of the bed and took her fingers in his.

'I believe, wife, that this is the happiest day of my life.'

Through eyes swimming with tears, Eleanor studied his serious face: the grey eyes so intense, the mouth so tender, the slight frown on his forehead as he tried to understand why this should be so.

'Dear lord, it must be so for every man who desires an heir! And I shall bear you many more children.'

'If God so disposes. Rest now, wife, while I see Will about bringing us some supper.'

Eleanor had been up for several days when Cedric brought Lady Radcliffe and Anne for a visit.

'Lady Radcliffe thought it safe enough for Anne to come,' explained Cedric when the ladies had gone off to settle themselves into the guest-chamber. 'Anne herself was keen to see Dickon, and she will not meet Stephen.'

'Does she know where he is being kept?' queried Eleanor with a frown.

She felt uneasy at the two of them being in the same vicinity, but quietened her fears with common sense. Stephen was safely locked away while Richard considered what to do with him. Her husband had not, of course, kept to his threat to let the murderer starve to death.

Although appearing more subdued than before that unfortunate episode, Anne appeared content in her betrothal to Cedric.

'We shall soon be sisters,' Eleanor observed when Anne returned alone. 'Have you fixed the date of the wedding yet?'

'Not yet. I would rather wait until the spring. But mother says we must fix a day soon, because of all the preparations to be made.'

'Cedric is eager, though I shall be sorry when he leaves Wenfrith to live with you at Cresswell.'

'You've almost finished the tapestry!'

The subject was turned and, after Anne had admired her efforts, Eleanor took her up to the bower, which had now become a nursery.

Dickon was in the process of being bathed, his sturdy little arms and legs waving and kicking joyfully as he splashed about in the shallow water. Kate leaned over the side of the copper basin, laughing and tickling the baby.

Eleanor felt a pang of envy, and dropped to her knees beside the bath. Of course, the child wasn't old enough to recognise anyone yet, but Eleanor managed to convince herself that he smiled at his mother. She chucked him under the chin and was rewarded with a gurgle which sounded like laughter. His little fist caught at her veil and almost tore it from her head.

'My, but he's strong!' she said proudly.

'Like the lord his father,' whispered Kate, with the peculiar lisp produced by her deformity.

The following day the messenger returned from Colchester, bearing good news of her family and gifts for the new grandson. His other tidings were less agreeable.

'Despite all precautions taken at the ports, the great pestilence has reached these shores, lord,' he reported worriedly. 'They say it started at Melcombe Regis, not far from Corfe Castle, early last month and is spreading like wildfire, just as it did across the continent.'

'You saw no signs of it?' demanded Richard uneasily.

'Nay, lord. I was travelling too far north, through Newbury and Glastonbury, though in that sacred place the people live in dread of its spreading from Bristol, where 'tis rumoured to be turning the streets into a cemetery. Those with castles and manors in the country are retreating there, hoping this plague will pass them by.'

'They are certain it is the same pestilence?'

'So they say. It begins with pallor and violent retching and shivering, then red blotches appear on the skin and huge black swellings in the groin or under the armpits. The breath of those afflicted stinks. Delirium and agony are followed by death, sometimes within the day.'

'Aye, it is as described by the knights besieging Calais, though some say people drop dead without warning.'

'Prayers are being said in every church and abbey for protection from this great pestilence, and people are being urged to repent of their sins. This affliction must be a judgement from God!'

Eleanor crossed herself and glanced fearfully at Richard. Rumours had abounded all summer about the possibility of the plague crossing the Channel but, like most people, they had thought England isolated and safe.

'It cannot reach us here!' she exclaimed.

'Of course not.' Richard sounded much more certain than he felt. Eleanor knew that the Princess Jean had been struck down in Gascony on her way to Spain to marry the heir to Castile, but he had heard rumours in Wenstaple which he had kept from his wife, not wishing to upset her while she was carrying the baby.

Stories had come from the continent of the mass burial of blackened, stinking bodies, the wiping out of whole villages, and the ravages wrought in the towns and cities. Tales of merchant ships drifting in the Mediterranean without a single living person left aboard. Of the stringent measures ordered to ensure that no plague-bearing vessel tied up at the quay.

Presumably the authorities at Melcombe Regis had been equally vigilant, yet the plague had somehow come ashore. The great pestilence seemed unstoppable. The sweat of fear broke out on his palms, making him instantly ashamed. He, who could face a battle like Crécy with eager anticipation, was being rendered coward by the very thought of this unseen, merciless enemy!

'We will welcome no unknown visitors here,' he decreed, addressing Hugh. 'Anyone without a roof can sleep in the old tithe barn outside the vill. Warn the villagers to admit no one to their midst.'

'Aye, lord.'

The old man's hands were shaking with fear, and Eleanor sympathised. Plagues and murrains among men and animals were all too common, but they were mild by comparison to this great pestilence which had swept across Europe from the East, from as far away as China, so it was believed.

'There's naught we can do but try to keep away from the infection,' said Richard sombrely. He glanced around at the anxious faces gathered in the Hall. 'See that you do your part, and pray.'

Sir Piers stood, straightening his frail figure as though facing some great challenge. 'I must go down to Lower Wenfrith and warn the people there. They, too, must cease to welcome strangers. And I will pray ceaselessly that Wenfrith may be spared.'

'Have we victuals enough to withstand a siege, wife?'

'With the harvest newly in and the animals fattened for slaughter, we could survive here for many months.'

'Good. I must visit Wenstaple again and see that they are properly prepared. Meanwhile, life goes on as normal. I believe dinner is about to be served.'

'It seems that we have not escaped the threat of the Death after all.' Gaston de Picard's sorrowful voice brought Eleanor's eyes to his mobile face. He lifted his hands in a helpless gesture. 'Such a calamity to fall upon Christendom! André, Henri, Jean! We will retire to the chapel with Brother Pierre-Paul, fasting. Prayer for our families in France would not be out of place. Perhaps our penitence will help to turn away the wrath of God.'

Eleanor shivered. Was God really so disgusted with Christendom that he would visit such terrible vengeance upon his children? Surely there must be some other explanation! So many innocents were dying! She crossed herself. This plague must surely be the work of the devil!

'My lady! May I enter?'

'Of course, Brigid. But what ails you? Is something amiss?'

Fear clenched at Eleanor's stomach. By the expression on Lady Radcliffe's distressed face as she entered the solar, something dire had occurred. Had the plague already entered Wenfrith?

'Anne is not with you?'

'No.' Relief surged through Eleanor that Brigid's concern was over nothing more dreadful than an errant daughter! She turned enquiringly to her maid, who was clearing away her washing materials. 'Is she upstairs with Dickon, Joan?'

'Nay, lady. I left there only moments ago. Alice and Kate were alone with the babe.'

Lady Radcliffe sank down on a coffer. 'Where can the wretched girl be? I have searched the chapel and the Hall, even looked in the kitchen quarters. She is nowhere to be found!'

'She is mayhap visiting the church. Or the stables. Have you asked there? Perhaps she has taken a ride!'

'Alone?' Brigid looked doubtful. 'Her side of the bed was as cold as a marble slab when I awoke this morning. She must have left our chamber before cock-crow, and that without disturbing our tiring-woman.'

'No doubt she sleeps soundly.'

'As do I,' admitted Brigid grimly.

Eleanor frowned, wondering what could have possessed the girl to wander off in the middle of the night. But she must be somewhere. Richard and Cedric would soon find her.

She called her husband from the wardrobe, where he had just finished dressing. The morning was sharp with autumn chill, and he wore his padded gambeson. He seemed preoccupied as he answered her call, his lean face cast into the brooding expression which had been foreign to him of late.

He greeted Brigid courteously. 'Good morrow, gentle lady.'

'Richard! Anne has disappeared! Have you seen Cedric this morning? Has he seen her?'

'Cedric was in the Hall when I looked. I did not speak to him.' Brigid's voice took on a desperate tone. 'I did not wish him to start an uproar!'

'You've searched all the likely places?'

'Aye, lord, indoors.'

'Then we shall have to look further afield, and more thoroughly. Don't worry, Brigid! She will be found in some part of the castle, perhaps trapped by an ill-fitting door!'

'She may have decided to visit the church!'

'I will ask the gate-ward. Excuse me, ladies. I will go and make enquiries.'

Half an hour later the uproar that Brigid had feared was fact. The castle was in turmoil.

The gate-ward had been abject in his apologies, fearing more punishment than the lashing he received from his lord's tongue. 'My lord! How was I to know it was not the wench's mother, as she said? Was I to insist on peering beneath her hood to look into the Lady Radcliffe's face? I warned the ladies of the dangers of riding alone, but could I order them to take an escort?'

'But it wasn't the Lady Radcliffe, you niddering fool! Could you not see that the form was too tall, too thin to be that of the Lady Radcliffe?'

'I—it was dark, lord! Everything was cast in shadows! Except Mistress Anne's face. That I saw, plain as my hand!'

He held his trembling fingers before his eyes and bowed his head. Richard cursed in impotent rage and stormed back into the Hall.

'The little vixen!' he grated, staring at Cedric with hostile eyes. 'Why you wished to wed that maid I'll never understand!'

Cedric shrugged. Eleanor noted that he didn't seem unduly distressed by the turn events had taken. Just frustrated and furious. 'She was comely, and possessed of a good dower. How was I to know that she was also devious and dishonest? She asked me to show her the dungeon where Stephen was kept, assuring me that she was disgusted by his actions, glad the bolts were firm, and pleased to be betrothed to me! She even graciously allowed me to kiss her last eve!'

'Aye!' Disgust quivered in Richard's voice. 'Well, she used her womanly wiles to good effect. No doubt that was when she stole your key! You have lost your bride, and I my would-be assassin!'

Eleanor could not help but defend the child from the men's wrath. She had always liked Anne, and felt that the girl had shown spirit and loyalty in seeking to save the man whom convention had denied her. Had Stephen not been a murderous traitor, she might almost have cheered! But Anne had shown stubbornness rather than discrimination in freeing him.

'She showed great loyalty and resourcefulness, lord,' she interposed. 'Misplaced loyalty and ill-directed resourcefulness, but the girl has spirit, which refuses to be tamed.'

Brigid was rocking to and fro in an agony of despair.

'And she, so tender-hearted that she could not watch her father joust, yet she could release a murderer!' she moaned. Suddenly she sat up and spoke fiercely. 'I will tame her when she returns! I have been too lax. I should have beaten the child every day until her spirit was subdued!'

'They are well-suited!' growled Richard, giving Eleanor a filthy look for daring to defend the girl. 'Both are quite unscrupulous in their actions when they desire something beyond their reach! I must go after them. They cannot be allowed to escape!'

'I will accompany you, brother, if you will allow. Anne was, after all, my betrothed!'

Brigid burst into renewed weeping. 'You will not wish to wed her now. No man will. She is disgraced. May the Good God forgive her!'

'Aye, I'll not deny that I consider the contract broken. But I do not wish to see her suffer. The Earl and I will bring her back if humanly possible, and if God so wills.'

'And I'll see that traitor Stephen thrown into the dungeons at Wenstaple! He will be safer there until the King's Justice can deal with him!'

'Then go, with our blessings, husband.' While they were gone Eleanor would try to persuade Brigid to tone down her threat of painful retribution. 'You think they will have made for Wenstaple?'

'It seems likely. It is the nearest borough, with plenty of dark alleys in which to hide, and a port from which to escape abroad. But they may have travelled inland. We will question all those we see, but they have many hours' start. I fear our journey may prove fruitless.'

At the sound of the horn Eleanor gathered her skirts and ran to the door of the Hall, anxiety overcoming decorum. She had hardly expected Richard and Cedric back so soon, yet what else could the blast herald? No stranger would be allowed through the village.

The low, setting sun bathed the bailey and the fields beyond in a lowering red glow. Richard and Cedric led the column of some half-dozen men to the foot of the steps. Eleanor had never before seen Richard slump in his saddle, however weary he might be; had never seen such a stricken look on his face. She glanced anxiously at Cedric, only to see the same expression mirrored there. The men behind looked stunned into witlessness.

'Richard!'

He couldn't hear her dismayed cry, because it emerged as a mere whisper. She watched fearfully as he slipped wearily from his saddle and began to drag himself up the steps.

At the top he stopped. The world swayed as she saw his eyes, sightless with some horror that she could not imagine.

'Richard,' she breathed, flinging out her hands. 'Oh, my dear lord! What can have happened? Did you find them?'

Some great calamity must have befallen the fleeing couple. They must be dead. Nothing else could explain the strange, stunned expression on all the men's faces. Yet why should the death of Stephen and Anne cause the entire party to be in a state of shock? Such deaths would be accepted as natural justice. Her stomach churned with new anxiety. Could there be some other reason?

Cedric had followed closely behind. But Eleanor barely glanced at her brother. Her husband and his strange, almost mesmerised stillness held all her attention.

'Come inside,' she pleaded. 'Come in and rest. You look wearied beyond belief!' She attempted a bright smile. 'Stephen and Anne must have led you a merry dance!'

Richard made no response but followed her inside, as did Cedric. The men, too, entered the Hall rather than return to their barracks. They seemed welded together by some extraordinary calamity, reluctant to be separated.

The Frenchmen were gathered in the Hall and they began to shout jovial greetings until they saw the faces of the party.

Brigid took one look at the men and collapsed on a bench. 'Anne!' she moaned. 'What has happened to my child?'

No one replied.

Eleanor handed Richard a mug of ale. He drank thirstily and a spark of life seemed to return to his eyes.

'What is amiss, lord?' whispered Eleanor.

'We have seen the Gates of Hell,' he told her tonelessly.

Eleanor grasped his arms, partly to shake him out of the faraway place to which he'd retreated, partly to steady herself.

'You speak in riddles, lord! What can you mean?'

No one answered. Cedric stood looking down at his mailed shoes. The men shuffled uneasily, jingling their spurs as they waited for their lord to speak.

'Richard?' she whispered fearfully.

He sighed, visibly pulled himself together, released his arms, and flung himself down on a bench, pulling her with him.

'The pestilence is rife in Wenstaple. We saw the pall of yellow smoke lying over the town and smelled the burning sulphur long before we reached the castle. When we did, it was to see a warning cross painted on the closed portcullis.'

'You did not enter the castle?'

Eleanor could not hide the terror she felt. Richard gripped her hands reassuringly, though his words and tone were full of self-scorn.

'Nay, wife. Your valiant husband turned tail and fled.'

'But not before he had spoken with the gate-ward,' interposed Cedric quickly. 'Not that he got much sense out of him. The fool had drunk himself witless. Who could blame him?'

'Not I.' Richard sighed again, heavily. 'Were I in that castle or in that town I believe I should try to drink myself senseless. The pestilence struck with deadly speed. Half the castle guard died within two days. Sir Henry survives for the moment, but his wife and daughter are dead.'

'Isobel is dead?'

Eleanor remembered the dark, vivacious beauty and her own jealousy, and shivered and crossed herself.

'Aye. The gate-ward cackled that the Bishop himself is dead, together with most of his clergy. There's scarce a priest left to administer the Last Rites. Those poor, afflicted people! But there was nothing to be done.'

'We kept well away from infection, sister. None of us ventured nearer than fifty yards, and we saw no passer-by. The town gate was closed, the warning cross painted on it.'

'Think you Stephen and Anne went into the city?' asked Eleanor faintly.

Lady Radcliffe moaned.

'Not unless they were out of their minds,' retorted Cedric. He shrugged. 'But Stephen must have been desperate; he might have decided to risk it. We abandoned the search for them. Sickness lurks everywhere. I doubt they will escape its clutches, wherever they choose to travel. We had no choice but to return here.'

'Poor Anne!'

Cedric looked more pained at her loss now that the enormity of her situation had gripped him. 'Aye. She was a bonny lass. I pray she might yet survive.'

Richard stirred himself again.. 'But not Stephen!' he asserted vehemently. 'If he does not die of the plague he shall not escape the hangman's noose! When this pestilence passes I shall have him hunted throughout the land!' He paused, then went on quietly, 'I have ordered the guard on the road to the village doubled. The men will keep their distance, and no one will be allowed to pass. As for Wenstaple—if any raider wishes to pillage

it, its crew is welcome to try! My apologies, *Seigneur*.'
Remembering their presence, Richard inclined his head
towards Gaston de Picard and his followers. 'I do not
wish such a fate on any man. But the town is unde-
fended, and will remain so until this pestilence has
passed.'

'There will be few of my fellow Frenchmen left to raid,
if rumour is true, *mon ami*. I think of necessity there
must be a truce in our war.'

'And you will perforce remain here until your ransoms
can be paid! You are welcome, my friends.'

Later, in the solar, Eleanor questioned Richard more
closely, but he could not, did not wish to convey the full
horror of what he had glimpsed over the city walls. He
had seen mountains of dead bodies before, but they had
been enemies clad in armour who would have killed him
had he not killed first. This enemy came unseen and left
a legacy of blackened, stinking corpses which one
touched at one's peril. The thought sickened him. Despite
a bath and change of clothes he still felt contaminated.

Eleanor sat quietly, staring at the tapestry which she
was supposed to be working. Richard had seen it long
ago, and had encouraged her to finish it, saying it would
be the most splendid wall-covering they possessed. But
what good would a wall-hanging be if they were all dead?

She shivered, but smiled bravely at her husband.

'The pestilence will pass Wenfrith by, please God. How
long will it rage?'

'There is no way of knowing, nor of knowing where
it will strike next. We must prepare for a long siege, my
dear. That is the only possible way to hope to survive.'

'And we must! For Dickon's sake!'

'Aye. Were it not for you and Dickon I might have
gone into Wenstaple to see if I could render aid. But
domesticity has made a coward of me, wife, which is
shame indeed.'

'I do not think it shame, lord. I think it is your duty
to remain alive for us!'

'Mayhap. And since I am alive, shall we retire, wife?'

'Aye.' Eleanor's pulses began to beat faster. Sir Piers
had churched her only days ago, before he had departed

on his pastoral visit to Lower Wenfrith. How she longed
to lose herself in her husband's loving!

CHAPTER FIFTEEN

THE next morning dawned clear and beautiful. No one
would have dreamt that there was pestilence spreading
throughout the land.

Yesterday poor Brigid had retired, prostrate, to her
bed. She longed to return to Radcliffe Manor and her
husband, but was frightened to travel. It looked as
though she, too, would be forced to remain at Wenfrith
until the danger had passed.

Eleanor sent Joan to see how she did.

'She just wants to be left alone,' reported Joan grimly.
'She will make herself ill if she carries on so!'

'Poor lady! Imagine how you would feel if a daughter
of yours had behaved so badly! The shame of it!'

'Pshaw! She should pull herself together and forget
the worthless girl!'

'I thought you were fond of Anne, Joan. You knew
her well.'

'Aye, she was a fine enough wench until that Stephen
got his claws into her! But no sense! How could she be
so deceived?'

'Weren't we all?'

'You weren't, sweeting. And I had my doubts. But to
run away with him after he had confessed!' She crossed
herself with a shudder. 'It must be witchcraft! He cast
a spell on her!'

'I don't believe he's a warlock, Joan.' Eleanor followed Joan's example and hurriedly crossed herself in
case. The world suddenly seemed full of evil.

She determined to put her fears behind her and enjoy
the last few days of autumn.

'I'll ride into the vill. The people need reassurance.'

Tamkin was with Brother Pierre-Paul, who had
undertaken to oversee the boy's education. Tamkin's
French was already quite fluent. He was a quick learner.

The grey friar also tended to many of the ailments suffered by the people of the manor, helping her and teaching her his skills. She was glad that there could be no question of his leaving in the near future. He was loved by the entire community. Everyone would be sad when the time came for him to leave.

So she was riding alone, save for her guards, Roger and Wat, when she decided to call in and see if Sir Piers had returned from Lower Wenfrith with news from there.

Dismounting at the lych-gate, she went first in to the church. A couple of parishioners stood chattering in the nave, another knelt before the statue of the Virgin, but there was no sign of Sir Piers.

She walked round the church and took the path across the churchyard to the old priest's house. The stout wooden door was shut. She pushed it open as she knocked.

An overwhelming stench such as she had never imagined possible hit her in the face like a blow. She staggered back a step.

Petrified, she stared into the interior of the room, lit dimly by one small glazed window and the half-blocked light from the doorway.

Sir Piers lay sprawled on the pile of skins he used as his bed. His eyes stared sightlessly towards her, his twisted body already blackening, his precious crucifix and rosary clutched in one lifeless hand.

Eleanor let out a high, keening wail. Slamming the door, she twisted round and ran across the churchyard, fleeing the devilish scene. In her panic she stumbled over a grave-marker and fell to her knees, clutching at the weathered, wooden cross for support. Wild-eyed, chest heaving, limbs shaking, she must have looked as though she'd seen a ghost.

'Lady! What ails you?'

Roger was already off his horse and passing through the lych-gate.

'Stay! Remain where you are!'

Her hoarse, desperate cry stopped him in his tracks.

'My lady?' he asked uncertainly.

'Sir Piers is dead of the plague.'

Her voice trembled and she lowered her forehead to the cross supporting her. 'Sweet Jesus!' she prayed, trying to marshal her incoherent thoughts, to erase the panic from her mind. 'Show me what I must do!'

Roger and Wat both muttered an invocation and made the sign of the cross across their broad chests as they stepped back.

'Tell us what to do!'

She barely heard Roger's cry of anguish. Her eyes had focused on a single word roughly carved into the wood of the cross.

'Fire.'

The full inscription read: 'Daniel the Carpenter, Killed by Fire, January 24th 1335, Aged 27. May his Soul Rest in Peace.'

Fire.

Her mind held a strange clarity and she was thinking fast. She straightened up.

'Roger, Wat, listen to me. First go into the church and clear it of anyone there. Then find the means of firing the house. Flaming arrows in the thatch should do it, but I doubt not you've had plenty of experience in such matters.'

'Aye, lady, but we can't burn the body!' cried Roger, crossing himself again. 'Would you deny Sir Piers his hope of the Resurrection?'

'Don't argue!' She was quite calm now, an inner certainty adding strength and authority to her words. 'This thing has to be done to avoid contaminating the people of the vill!'

'I'll do it.' Wat's voice held grudging admiration. 'You see to the church, Roger.'

'Why so?'

Eleanor used the cross for support, her legs still trembled alarmingly. She spoke carefully and distinctly, as though to a child. 'Once you have cleared the church, I shall remain there until I think I am safe from infection. After the priest's house is fired you may fetch a pallet and blankets. And food and drink. Leave it in the porch. No one is to enter the church. Is that quite clear?'

'Aye, lady.' Roger's voice trembled.

'Afterwards, enquire if anyone has had contact with Sir Piers recently. Make them keep themselves apart. Make enquiries at Lower Wenfrith, but do not endanger your own lives.'

She stood like a statue while the men began to do as she ordered. Wat went off towards the castle. He would spread the news there. What would Richard do?

A trembling began deep inside her. At all costs she must keep him away from her. But that was a problem for the future. For the present, Roger was shepherding the villagers from the sacred building, making it ready to receive her.

When she entered the church her eyes went straight to the High Altar, the crucifix in its centre, and the pyx hanging above. She genuflected, touched the holy water, and crossed herself before turning to bar the great wooden door. She had no key, but the baulk of oak was stout and the sockets firmly fixed to the walls. She knew of only one other entrance, through the vestry. She walked slowly down the nave to the chancel-screen, genuflected again to the Host, then turned to pass through the arch to the priest's sanctum.

That door was already locked and barred. No one could get into the building now unless they used a battering-ram or broke a window, and those were so high in the walls that the possibility was remote. But to a determined soldier trained to storm cities...

What made her think that Richard would wish to risk his life to be with her? She would most certainly risk hers to be with him, to die with him. But she loved, and he did not.

She crossed the church to the steps down to the crypt. She had never noticed an entrance from the outside, but she had to make certain. It was pitch dark down there.

She lit a torch from a votive candle, and made her way down the steps. Bare stone walls surrounded her, the floor above supported by strong columns and arches.

A flash of white caught by the flickering flame reminded
her that here lay the tomb of William d'Evreux. She ran
her hand along its smooth alabaster surface. A thought
came unbidden to gladden her heart. She had lived long
enough to leave William's grandchild as heir to her
husband's honours and estates.

Little Dickon! Tears gathered thickly in her eyes as
she climbed back into the church, but at the same time
hope flared. She had not actually been into the priest's
house. Had touched nothing. Had only caught a whiff
of the putrefaction. She dropped to her knees on the
prie-dieu before the statue of the Virgin.

'Dear Mother of God! Have mercy!'

As she knelt, the first trace of smoke penetrated the
cracks around the door. So Wat had done his job. The
priest's abode was burning. She bent her head in renewed prayer.

It was not long before she heard a thundering on the
oak of the door.

'Eleanor! Wife! Open this door!'

Eleanor straightened and walked slowly across the
rush-strewn flags to lean against the stone column nearest
the entrance.

'Richard?' Her voice was surprisingly firm. 'Please
go, Richard. I have to remain here alone until all possibility of infection has passed. You must see that, dear
lord?'

'Eleanor, I cannot allow you to stay there alone! Let
me in!'

'And infect you, too? Nay, lord. That would be
foolishness indeed!'

'You think I am so craven that I would not risk infection myself to keep you company?'

'Of course not. But you forget your duty to our child
and your responsibility to all the people of this manor!
Without you, what will they do?'

'Survive!' He wanted to add that, without her, he
would not wish to survive. But she would not welcome
such a maudlin confession. He had to be strong for her.

'Eleanor, you need someone with you! If you are sick you will need care, comfort. Who would give it but I?'

'Richard, I do not want you here!'

The words tore at her heart, but had to be said. A profound silence greeted them. When he did speak his voice sounded strained.

'Why not, may I ask?'

'Because of the danger!'

'You know I am willing to share that. Why else?'

'Why else? Does there have to be another reason?'

'Aye, else I will break into your stronghold, woman! I would be with you in your hour of peril!'

'Oh, Richard!' Happiness blossomed in her heart. He sounded desperate, as though he meant what he said. He must be truly fond of her to be so anxious to share her danger!

Yet somehow, for his own sake, she must dissuade him from joining her.

'Well?' His imperative voice echoed within the porch, almost making the thick door shake. 'Have you some dark reason why you do not wish me with you now? You would prefer someone else, perhaps?'

'Yes!' His old jealousy had risen up to provide her with an answer. It came to her like a shaft of fire, burning into her brain, killing off the flower of happiness blooming in her heart. She spread her arms backwards around the column, feeling the cold stone slippery beneath her sweating palms. She had to be convincing, had to make him believe her! 'If I wished to die in anyone's arms it would be Gilbert's!'

The silence which greeted this declaration was frightening. It went on and on.

'Richard?' whispered Eleanor, but so low that he could not possibly have heard.

Eventually she heard a harsh bark of laughter. 'So there *was* truth in those tales! And I believed your protestations of innocence! I trusted you, woman!'

His voice cracked. She had done it! He believed her. She thought her heart would break.

'Well,' went on Richard, biting sarcasm failing to hide the pain he felt, 'I cannot bring your lover to comfort you in your hour of need, but I will not concern myself with you further. May God forgive you your treachery! I think it is worse even than Stephen's!'

She heard his spurs ringing as he strode away. Her victory seemed immeasurably hollow.

Sobbing, she threw herself down on the fusty rushes and allowed her misery full rein.

Just when it seemed as if she had gained Richard's respect and even affection, she had had to throw it all back in his face! If she lived, would he believe that she had told him a lie? Would his pride allow him to take her back?

What if he wouldn't? She would have to leave Wenfrith and all she loved, even Dickon. Joan would probably go with her. But where? Home?

No, she could never be happy living in her parents' house again. Would she find happiness anywhere?

If not happiness, she might find peace and contentment in the cloister. She would return to the priory where she had been educated. The Prioress Martha-Mary would receive her gladly.

Wherever she went her future would be bleak and lonely. In her heart she knew that she was not meant for the life of a nun. Her passions ran too deep. The memory of her husband's loving would torment her for the rest of her life, burning and throbbing in her loins as it burned and throbbed now. Perhaps it would be as well if she did die of the plague.

Her agony lasted perhaps an hour. The fierce desire gradually subsided, leaving her spent.

Hearing movement in the porch outside, she stirred. Had Richard returned? Hope flickered, and was immediately extinguished when she heard the person speak.

'My lady? Are you there?'

Brother Pierre-Paul. She answered wearily.

'Aye, Brother.'

'I have come to offer comfort, confession and absolution if you desire it, child.'

'I desire it, Brother.'

'Your maid, Joan, is with me. We have brought your
pallet and other needs. We will replace your supplies each
morn, and check constantly that you are well.'

'Sweeting?' Joan's voice was choked. 'Will you not
let me enter and tend you, mistress? You know I have
no desire to live if you die!'

'But you must, Joan! Who else can I trust to see that
Dickon is properly cared for? Who else is there to love
him as he deserves?'

'The lord his father——'

'Dickon will need a woman's love.'

A murmured conversation began on the other side of
the door. She couldn't hear properly. Then Joan's voice
was raised again.

'Very well, sweeting. You may entrust the babe to me.
But I'll come often and talk to you.' There was a momentary pause before Joan went on hesitantly, 'Your lord
is in such a dark temper that no one dares approach
him. He was distraught when the news reached him, but
not in an evil temper. What passed between you, that
he returned in such a pother?'

Eleanor closed her eyes, trying to shut out the memory.
'It doesn't matter. Joan, leave me with Brother Pierre-
Paul.'

'Aye, if you wish it. But I will return. Until later, my
dearest lady.'

'Farewell, faithful Joan. If——' her voice broke
'——if we do not speak again, remember that I have always
loved you.'

Joan was audibly weeping. 'And I you, sweeting.'

Eleanor was conscious that she had told her maid
something that she had longed to tell her husband, but
had been afraid to.

If her confession shocked Pierre-Paul he made no sign,
but gave her absolution from her sin without hesitation.
'God will surely forgive such a deceit born of love,' he
murmured, with compassion. 'He will understand your
reasons for lying to your husband, and commend them.

But the Earl is much distressed. I believe he is greatly bound to you by affection. May I not tell him...?'

'If I die, Brother, then I release you from your vow of silence. I will go to my rest more easily knowing that my husband will understand that what I did was done from love. But under no other circumstances.'

'Child, I believe your love will be rewarded by a merciful God. But if you fall ill you must let me in to administer the Last Rites. I cannot allow you to die without receiving the sacrament of Extreme Unction.'

'Nay, Brother! *I* cannot allow *you* to risk your life for my hope of salvation! Others need you, are more deserving of your care, than I!'

There was a pause before Pierre-Paul's soft voice came to her again.

'That cannot be true. Nevertheless, I respect your wishes. If you fall ill, I will say the necessary words and you can anoint yourself. I will leave a phial of the Blessed Oil with your things.'

'Thank you, Brother. And you must promise that no one shall touch my body. Burn down the church,' said Eleanor urgently. 'I'm certain the Earl will build another in my memory when he learns the truth.'

'It shall be as you say. And do not worry about the Resurrection, my child. God is a worker of miracles. He will not keep Sir Piers, or you, or anyone else from salvation for lack of a whole human body. Buried, we all return to dust. Dust or ashes, what difference can it make to Him?'

'Brother Pierre-Paul, I believe God sent you to be here in our hour of need. You are so wise. I cannot tell you the comfort your words have brought me.'

'I am but the servant of God. I will leave you now. Your things are here. Take them in when you will.'

Eleanor opened the door cautiously, ready to slam the bar back into place if anyone was near enough to threaten her isolation. But the porch and churchyard were empty.

They had left her a pallet and blankets, cold meats, bread, a little butter, cheese, a flagon of wine and a pot of ale. Tucked in the blanket she found Pierre-Paul's treasured Book of Hours, together with the small phial of precious oil.

Eleanor put the oil carefully aside, praying that she would have no need to use it. Then she leafed through the pages of the book, admiring the colourful illustrations, reading a few words here and there. Her Latin was not fluent.

But once the friar had gone, God seemed very remote, the Saints just childish representations on a piece of parchment. She got up and wandered around her refuge. Or was it a tomb? Even Jesus and Mary were just statues, cold and unresponsive. The only thing with any life to it was the brilliantly depicted Last Judgement painted on the chancel arch, above the rood-screen. The devil presiding over the tortures of the damned looked real enough. His evil black power seemed to lie like a pall over the whole land.

No bell tolled the Hours. She looked at the rope but, even had she been able to see the sundial on the church wall, she wouldn't have found the energy to pull it. Time passed. Night and day merged into a grey purgatory. People came to the church door to speak to her and to leave fresh food and drink. She drank a little, but food choked her. Joan, Brother Pierre-Paul, Cedric and even Tamkin, who seemed to have recovered his own spirits, did their best to talk her out of her lethargy. She tried to respond, to let them know she was still well. But nothing mattered except the wait. The wait for the fever, the sickness, the pustules, death...

Even life did not matter if Richard did not care. How could he care, when she had thrown his concern back in his face?

One day she heard sounds of hymn-singing on the green, and Brother Pierre-Paul's voice lifted in prayer and exhortation. The villagers had been robbed not only of their priest, but also of their holy place. The grey friar had taken over Sir Piers's flock and was preaching in the open air. It must be Sunday. She had been shut in the church for five days.

Sir Piers had been dead within four. A stirring of hope brought a flush to her pale cheeks. If she survived, her future would depend on Richard. Richard might not want her. But the hope persisted.

When Brother Pierre-Paul called her two days later and told her that she could safely open the door, her heart leapt wildly. Dormant hope flared.

'I have been searching my memory for all I know of this dreadful pestilence and asking the opinions of others,' Pierre-Paul told her quietly. 'It seems to strike within five days of infection—often within two. You have been here seven days, child. I think you are quite safe now. Let me in, and we will make an act of thanksgiving together!'

When Joan arrived, bringing fresh linen and clothes, Eleanor was calm. God had been kind. Perhaps Richard would be, too.

'You don't want to be returning to the castle looking like a vagabond!' Joan chided, viewing Eleanor's unkempt state with a reproving eye. 'I've brought water and a comb. You must return looking your best!'

'Is—is my lord there?'

'Where else should he be, sweeting? He has nowhere to go, since all around the plague rages.'

'Is he well?'

Joan gave her a fleeting glance, then concentrated on braiding her mistress's heavy tresses.

'Aye.'

Eleanor realised that her old nurse and friend was holding something back, but knew better than to ask questions when Joan chose to be taciturn. It didn't matter. After all—her heartbeat quickened—she would be seeing him for herself within the hour.

Dressed in one of her favourite gowns of a saffron colour several shades deeper than her hair, Eleanor fastened the clasp of her brown mantle and accompanied Pierre-Paul and Joan from the church. On her way across the yard she paused for a moment to gaze at the burnt-out shell of the clergy-house. 'God rest his soul,' she murmured, crossing herself. 'But he should not have returned here!'

'He crept back to his lair like a wounded animal.' Brother Pierre-Paul's voice held nothing but infinite compassion. 'Sir Piers had no doubt done his duty in Lower Wenfrith. The plague fires burn there day and night.'

'Oh, no! Those poor people!' Tears gathered in Eleanor's eyes. On top of everything else, this was crushing news. 'I knew them all! Has anyone else been stricken here?'

'So far, no, thank God.'

The stir as she entered the bailey took Eleanor by surprise. A ragged cheer, led, she noted wryly, by Wat, rose spontaneously from a dozen throats. In the Hall it was the same. Cedric took her in a bear-hug. Tamkin darted forwards to cling round her thighs. Hugh greeted her with tears in his old eyes. Will's Adam's apple bobbed alarmingly as he tried to restrain his emotion. Only then did Eleanor realise how much she had become part of the fabric of life at Wenfrith. How much her stewardship was appreciated. New tears filled her eyes, but they were tears of gratitude.

Buoyed up with a renewed confidence, she turned to the friar. 'Where is my husband?'

Joan didn't wait for Pierre-Paul to answer. 'In the solar, sweeting. Where he's been this last week, except when he's been roaming around the manor on Midnight like some lost soul. We've scarcely seen sight or sound of him.'

'Then I must go to him there.'

'I will take you to him, child. Perhaps my presence will soften the meeting,' offered the friar.

Eleanor smiled gratefully. 'Thank you. Joan, I will need you later.'

The blaze of joy in Richard's grey eyes, when he looked up to see her enter the solar, was so quickly masked that Eleanor thought she might have imagined it. Only she knew she had not, and her heart began to thud so hard that she believed Richard must see it through the stuff of her gown.

'Here is your gracious wife, come safely home, lord. Pray be gentle with her. She has suffered much agony of mind in the last week.'

'Who has not?'

Richard's voice was raw. Seeing him now as he stood to receive her, shock ran through her at his thinness, at the ravaged face staring imperiously into her own. He looked in a worse state than when first she'd met him, when he'd been wounded, grieving and frustrated.

Brother Pierre-Paul quickly withdrew, leaving them alone. Eleanor stepped forward, praying silently to be given wisdom in her choice of words. So much—their whole future—depended on the next few moments.

The brush of her dress over the rushes was the only sound to break the silence as she moved. Eleanor's eyes, clouded with pain, were yet alive with expectation. Richard must understand!

He turned away abruptly. 'You will wish to go to Sir Gilbert when this pestilence dies. Until then, I will use another chamber.'

'No, husband! I have no wish to join Sir Gilbert. If you will allow me, I would remain here, your faithful and loving wife.'

He spun round, scattering the rushes underfoot. 'Faithful? Loving?' he spat scornfully. 'What fairy-tale is this?'

'No fairy-tale, lord. If you cannot believe me I will retire to the cloister, but I will never join Sir Gilbert. I have no love for him.'

In the face of Richard's utter disbelief she drew a sharp breath. Pride, embarrassment, anguish, mattered nothing now. She only wanted to make Richard believe in her love.

'Husband!' She took another step nearer, holding out pleading hands, her breath coming quickly in her agitation. 'It is you I love! And, loving you so much, how could I allow you to risk your life by joining me? Yet how was I to turn you away? You, who could so easily have breached the church's defences...'

Heavy eyelids masked the expression in his eyes, but deep lines creased his brow. His tight mouth had not relaxed one jot. Eleanor felt her spirits dampen. Wearily, she turned away.

'I see you cannot believe me, lord. I do not blame you. What I did to you was unforgivable, though it was done from love.' She turned back to face him again, and her voice was a cry of despair. 'But you would not go away! You would not listen to me!'

Richard sank down on a stool and motioned her to the other. 'Come, wife, sit down. We should talk.' His eyes gleamed from beneath his lids as he scanned her taut face. 'Methinks you have become skinny over the last week.'

Eleanor's hands gripped each other in her lap. Was this a breach in his defences? His expression told her nothing.

'As you have, lord. I had begun to hope that you cared for me a little. I believed you were proud of me, at least.' She tried a smile, which wavered pathetically. 'I should have told you from the first, but I so wanted you to value me for myself. My line goes back to Earl Godwin, King Harold's sire.'

He threw his head back in disdain. 'You think to win my love now by telling me of your so-called noble birth?'

'Nay, lord. But I want to keep no secret from you. The time for such games is past!' She took a deep breath and summoned all her courage. 'I love you! I want to stay here at Wenfrith!'

'And to remain with Dickon, no doubt,' he threw back bitterly.

'Aye, that too! But I came straight to you. I have not seen my son for a week, yet I would forgo that pleasure for longer yet if you would but believe me true!'

Richard stared at his hands, hanging loosely between his knees. Suddenly, he looked up, his face a still mask. 'Come here, wife!'

Eleanor slipped to her knees at his feet. He grasped her thick braid, which Joan had left hanging, forcing her head back so that he could search her eyes.

She met his bravely. He released the braid as abruptly as he'd grasped it and dug in his pouch to produce the lock of hair he'd claimed as forfeit all those months before.

He held out the shining curl on the palm of his hand.

'Do you know what I've been doing these past days? Sitting looking at this small piece of you. The only thing I had left. Can you imagine how I have suffered? Thinking you false? Thinking you dead?'

He threw the lock down among the rushes and buried his face in his hands, but not before she had caught sight of the anguish in his eyes.

Eleanor's heart bled for him. 'Dearest lord,' she murmured, 'I believe I do, for I have suffered too. I did not want to die!' Her voice broke. 'Husband, we had such joy ahead! Yet my love sustained me, for it gave me hope that if I survived I could win back your regard.'

'My love gave me none.'

She gasped and gripped his wrists fiercely, tearing his hands from his face. 'Your love, lord?'

'Aye!' He laughed harshly, refusing to meet her eyes. 'I offered myself a sacrifice to my love, and you threw it back in my face!'

'Richard!' With a cry of joy Eleanor flung her arms around his waist and buried her face in his lap. 'If you knew how I have longed to hear you say those words!'

'I thought you would mock me for such a sentiment!'

She lifted her head to stare at him. 'Mock you, my dearest? Never! How long have you loved me?'

Tenderly, he smoothed the bright shining tresses. 'I don't know,' he admitted, and then went off at a tangent, 'I heard you were of Godwin's line at Eltham.'

'You did?' She gasped. 'Who told you?'

'The King himself. He knows your father. Who, I gather, is not backward in boasting of his ancestry! But I had suspected something of the kind. My sire would not have betrothed himself to a truly low-born maid. Why did you not tell me of your birthright?'

'Would it have made any difference? You scorn the entire Saxon race!' she accused. 'I overheard your opinion of Harold Godwinsson the first evening I was at Wenfrith! A drunken traitor, little better than a churl—that about expresses your opinion, I believe! I had no wish to invite your scorn, my lord! But why did you not mention the matter?'

'It did not seem important. I had already discovered that your ancestry made not the slightest difference to my regard for you. One Saxon lady, at least, was worthy of a Norman's regard! You were my wife, and I was proud of you. It no longer mattered what others thought. In any case, attitudes are changing. Mine was old-fashioned.'

'Richard, how could you let me go on thinking you despised me?' she cried. 'Did you not realise the pain it caused me? I suffered anger, frustration and despair by turns!'

'My love, I am sorry.' The distress in his eyes made his apology sincere. 'I still had my pride. I found it difficult to admit, even to myself, that my attitude had changed. I thought you would sense it.'

'Perhaps I did, a little. But I wish you had spoken!'

'Forgive my pride, sweeting.'

''Tis forgiven.' She kissed him quickly on the lips. Her eyes had begun to shine. 'And still you did not love me?'

'Perhaps. Perhaps not. I was certainly jealous beyond all reason when I suspected you of infidelity.'

'Aye, lord. You made it very plain!'

He traced the smooth line of her cheek. 'I believe I did. I think I began to suspect I loved you when Dickon was born. Had you died ... But I admitted it to myself only when you were in such mortal danger. I married you, Eleanor, because, against my will, I desired you and you were on the spot, available. I had need of a wife. To seek another would have been a tedious business for one feeling as I did at the time. I did not expect to fall in love, to discover that if you died all my happiness would die with you.'

She lifted her radiant face to see that most of the lines had been smoothed from his, and met eyes glowing with such love that her mouth went dry.

His lips quirked with tender humour. 'I have made my confession. When did you begin to love me, my dearest wife?'

Eleanor swallowed down the lump in her throat and brought moisture back into her mouth.

'When you walked into the Hall safe after the mêlée on the beach,' she told him huskily. 'I knew then that your safety meant more than anything else in the world to me.'

He lifted her chin with his finger and their lips met in a lingering kiss that was a commitment. His strong arms enfolded her and the heat began to course through her body as though liquid fire ran in her veins.

'Richard,' she whispered. 'My dearest love, how I have longed for you this past week!'

He caught his breath. The love in her heart blazed out at him in a way he'd never dared hope to see. Had he really envied the pale shadow of affection he'd seen on her face when she'd looked at Cedric? Yet that jealousy had surely been the beginning of his own love, if only he'd been honest enough to admit it. He lifted her to her feet, holding her close, letting her feel how much he wanted her.

'I doubt if it was any more than I desired you, woman! You promised me more heirs, I believe?'

He held her crushed against his chest, the passion heavy in his eyes, the evidence of his arousal hard against her abdomen.

Eleanor chuckled, secure at last in his love. 'Aye, husband, I did. But you must make your peace with Sir Gilbert! You were such friends, and he saved your life after Crécy. It is unfair to him to treat him so coldly when he did nothing to deserve your censure! In fact, he set my mind at rest over your father's death.'

Richard frowned. 'How so?'

'He was with you at the time. I knew in my heart that you were not to blame, yet the rumour that you were in some way responsible would not die. Since Stephen's confession, no one can any longer believe ill of you. But at that time there was no one to tell me truly what had happened. Even Hugh might have been covering up for his own sake.'

'You wondered if you had wed a murderer?'

'Not at all! Well, hardly at all,' she admitted honestly. 'But I was glad to have Sir Gilbert's assurance of your complete innocence!'

''Twas a harrowing experience. I did blame myself for a while. I cannot censure you for having doubts!'

She smoothed his broken brow with her finger. 'I know. But my doubts were quickly gone. How could I believe that an honourable, prideful Norman knight such as the Earl of Wenstaple could do such a thing? My eyes and my instinct told me that rumour must be false.'

'I will send a messenger to Gilbert as soon as it is safe to travel again. I will apologise most humbly and ask him to honour us with his presence here. Will that satisfy you, wife?'

'Indeed it will! Oh, Richard, I am so happy! Kiss me!'

A long time later she drew back, suddenly remembering. 'I believe the pestilence will pass Wenfrith by. Please God we have many years yet in which to enjoy our love.'

'I pray so.' He grinned boyishly. 'But there can be no time like the present! I think we are both in need of recuperation after our ordeal! What say you we take a long bed rest? There is little else to do!'

'Whatever you command, lord,' agreed Eleanor submissively, the imps of mischief dancing in her eyes at his teasing.

Even Dickon was temporarily forgotten in the heady anticipation of giving herself in full and perfect love of body, mind and spirit. They had risen to dizzy heights of passion together in the past, yet she knew that now, because their love was complete, they would discover new wonders, new delights, new pinnacles of joy.

The church bell rang out for Tierce, its familiar sound like a benediction.

Wenfrith was returning to normal again.

Young Tamkin becomes Sir Thomas d'Evreux, knight to John of Gaunt. Watch for his own story—SET FREE MY HEART—in the coming months.

THE DEVIL'S BARGAIN
Gail Mallin

Delia knew that she must marry well to restore
the Vane family fortune, now that Charles II had
been restored to his throne. Convinced she had
nothing to offer, she was surprised to attract the
honourable attentions of Squire Bolsover, and
astounded to attract the dishonourable attentions
of Lord Kit Malory . . .

Kit's charms were hard to withstand, until her
brother Jamie's gambling debts put Delia into Kit's
power. Kit would excuse the debts if Delia became
his mistress! Delia would bargain with the devil
himself to save Jamie, but must she ruin her own
reputation in the process?

Look out for the two intriguing

MASQUERADE *Historical*

Romances coming next month

THE DENMEAD INHERITANCE
Janet Edmonds

At 23 Miss Libby Barton had resigned herself to being an old maid, and as companion to the Duchess at Copthorne, Libby derived much enjoyment of the crotchety, witty old lady.

So it was a total shock when Marcus, Viscount Charlbury, visiting at Copthorne, suddenly proposed marriage to her. For years Libby had loved Marcus from afar, and she *knew* that he had never truly noticed her, so what had prompted him?

The answer led to doubts and danger, but by that time Libby had already said yes . . .

BATTLEFIELD OF HEARTS
Joanna Makepeace

Coerced into marriage? Never!

Rather than be forced by her widowed stepmother to marry Thomas Stoodley, Aleyne escaped, hoping to find protection of her cousin. But in this year of 1471, Warwick the Kingmaker had fomented trouble, and the armies of Edward IV and Queen Margaret were set to battle at Tewkesbury.

Sir Dominick Allard, Richard of Gloucester's man, found he couldn't abandon Aleyne on the road, but Richard's solution was also marriage! Swept up in the turmoil, Aleyne had little choice but to accept Dominick . . .

Available in August

Experience the thrill of 2 Masquerade Historical Romances Absolutely Free!

Experience the passions of bygone days
in 2 gripping Masquerade Romances - absolutely free!
Enjoy these tales of tempestuous love from
the illustrious past.
Then, if you wish, look forward to a regular supply of
Masquerade, delivered to your door!
Turn the page for details of 2 extra FREE gifts,
and how to apply.

An irresistible offer for you

Here at Reader Service we would love you to become a regular reader of Masquerade. And to welcome you, we'd like you to have two books, a cuddly teddy and a MYSTERY GIFT - ABSOLUTELY FREE and without obligation.

Then, every two months you could look forward to receiving 4 more brand-new Masquerade Romances for just £1.99 each, delivered to your door, postage and packing is free. Plus our free newsletter featuring competitions, author news, special offers offering some great prizes, and lots more!

This invitation comes with no strings attached. You can cancel or suspend your subscription at any time, and still keep your free books and gifts.

Its so easy. Send no money now. Simply fill in the coupon below at once and post it to - Reader Service, FREEPOST, PO Box 236, Croydon, Surrey CR9 9EL.

--- **NO STAMP REQUIRED** --- →

mps
MAILING
PREFERENCE
SERVICE